Y0-CQD-065

CHICAGO PUBLIC LIBRARY
R01642 93268

Runners' Blood

By James J. Fischer

Runners' Blood

By James J. Fischer

Printed in the United States of America

ISBN: 1-891231-21-9

Library of Congress Control Number: 00-132170

Word Association Publishers
205 Fifth Avenue
Tarentum, Pennsylvania 15084

Chapter 1

The Connecticut weather was perfect, cold and raw with a steady drizzle and little wind. The amateurs would run in their rain suits, and the extra weight would cost them minutes, not that it mattered much to Sean Rourke. He wasn't expecting to be seriously challenged, even though he was still feeling the effects of running the Marine Corps Marathon just twelve days earlier in Washington. It had been his first official marathon, and the strong performance, two hours and sixteen minutes, was a clear announcement to the professional track world of his intention to seriously compete at the longer distance. But now the stiffness in his legs reminded him of why even the best marathoners limited themselves to one or two races each year. Still, after a few sessions with the masseuse and some light workouts he felt ready for today's level of competition. And this was a 10K race, 6.2 miles, a distance at which he ranked among the world's best.

The Thanksgiving Day road race in tiny Bradsford would not normally have attracted a runner of Sean's stature, but it had become a tradition for him. After seven straight victories he regarded it almost as an exhibition. Now with his winnings from major races and the endorsements and appearance fees commanded by an Olympic favorite, the small cash prize, $2000, was unimportant, and he planned to donate it to the track program at the local high school. But this had not always been the case.

A promising freshman miler with a track scholarship to St. Vincent's College, Sean had been homesick for Ireland after just two months in Philadelphia and readily accepted the invitation from his cousin, Mary Conners, to spend the holiday with her family in this small New England town. While he was too late for the fall foliage, he did discover, to his delight and profit, the third annual Bradsford race and its cash prize. It had been Sean's first formal 10K competition, and he would never forget it. The field included some good local runners, many of whom would compete against him year after year. He eventually won by more than twenty yards, but not easily and not without some doubts about his ability to last the longer distance. As it turned out, the route had never been properly measured and fortunately was shorter than 10K. Still, it was a difficult course with a long uphill stretch to the finish. Sean loved hills, and his ability to run them was what saved the day.

The money, which by a strange twist in the amateur rules he was allowed to keep, was enough to get him home for the Christmas vacation. His performance, disappointing perhaps to a person with aspirations to be the best in the world, was a perfect step in his development. As he matured, the longer races eventually became his forte. Four years later, at an age when most distance runners were still far from their prime, he finished sixth in the 10K at the Olympic Games in Atlanta and became the early favorite for Sydney 2000, now less than two years away.

Sean left the VIP tent accompanied by an aide and made his way slowly across the town square, attracting a crowd of fans and well wishers who almost blocked his way. He was hard to miss in the emerald green warmup suit of the Irish national team. The high school band, enthusiastic even in their soaked uniforms, finished a medley from *Chariots of Fire* and broke into "When Irish Eyes Are Smiling." *Must be Mary's doing,* he thought. *They're from the school where she teaches.*

As he approached the starting line, marked by a soggy white banner suspended between two lamp posts, Sean greeted old friends and rivals and surveyed this year's new hopefuls. Joe Lightfoot was there, as he had been every year for the nine previous races. A member of the local Indian tribe, he had won the first two years, "before Sean" as he would say. He had been a standout in high school and, to Sean's dismay, turned down a college scholarship to join a group trying to establish gambling on the nearby reservation. Joe was now the senior manager of a casino successful beyond anyone's wildest dreams. But he still loved to run. "Going to get you today," he said, embracing Sean.

A few years and few million dollars erase a lot of resentment, Sean thought. *Well, I've done pretty well over the years too, and I'll leave him behind on the final hill.*

Sean almost didn't recognize Abi Abbad. Now thirty-nine, and nearing the end of his career, Abi no longer ran in the major races. This would be his first try at Bradsford. Despite his usual broad grin, he could not have been pleased to see Sean.

"I did not expect to find you here," Abi said. "You are supposed to be recovering from Washington."

"I always run this one," Sean answered, towering over the much shorter African as they shook hands. "My cousins live here, and they make me do it for my turkey dinner."

Abi was one of the first great Kenyan runners, but he had arrived in the States too soon, before the big money prizes and lucrative endorsements. Otherwise, he would not have been trying to win a small prize in a small town race with no appearance money. Sean knew Abi had enormous pride and would try his best, but now he would have to struggle for the $1000 second prize. Even this amount would mean a good deal to him back home, and he was traveling to many of the less important races trying desperately to build a nest egg before age or an injury forced him to retire. The image of the over-the-hill athlete who had not provided for his future always upset Sean. *Could be any of us,* he thought. *I hope he can get second.*

Sean's presence at the Bradsford race had attracted crowds of runners over the years. The young hotshot collegians, free for the holiday, turned out in large numbers to measure themselves against the established star. It led to a good collegiate sub-race, but for second or third place. This year there were two exceptional candidates: Jeffrey Bates, pride of the Ivy league, and Wally Grouse, son and nephew of two of America's most famous distance runners, now a student at a small college in Maine. Sean, now an assistant coach at St. Vincent's, had met them both at the Penn relays, where they had handily beaten his own students in the college division race. The two would be rivals for years to come and teammates for their country in the Olympics, if not in Sydney in 2000, then surely in 2004. Now they deferentially approached Sean and Abi who were going through their stretching rituals.

"You're going to take it easy on us, right?" Bates asked extending his hand.

"No, he wants to pay us back for Philadelphia," Grouse said.

"Listen, Wally, I wasn't beating pros when I was your age." Sean's big toothy grin didn't disguise the look of determination in his eyes. "Wait until I get too old."

He was sorry he had said it when he saw the look on Abi's face. And then Grouse made the situation worse when he turned to Abi and said, "I have your shoes from Seoul. You probably don't remember. My uncle ran against you, and I made him ask for them. You were my idol."

"He's related to everyone," Bates interjected. "I have to work at this, but with him it's just in the genes."

"You guys be sure to warm up enough," Sean admonished them. "It's going to be cold out there." He could never resist coaching the younger runners, even when they were his rivals. And it seemed a good way to end an awkward situation. Abi didn't need to be reminded of his age.

"Yeah, cold and wet," Grouse complained, while jogging in place.

Sean glanced upwards. The leafless branches seemed to disappear into the gray sky. No signs of a break. He sniffed the moist air. Then the slightest smile crossed his face. "Just like home. Makes it more fun."

At the last possible moment, officials ushered Sean to the head of the assembled pack. *Rank has its privileges*, he thought, handing his warmup suit to an aide. Sean's thick, unruly dark hair was covered by a hat with a wide brim to keep the rain from his eyes. It was his only concession to the conditions. Despite the almost freezing temperature, he would run in only a singlet that hung loosely from his thin shoulders, shorts and no socks. Like many Europeans, he ignored the popular Lycra and Gore-Tex, preferring instead strong liniments, secret formulas to ward off the cold without adding weight or restricting motion. And he hated wet socks.

A large digital clock, suspended above the crowd on the extension cab of the town fire engine, blinked down the remaining seconds. Beside it the mayor raised his right arm, paused, and fired the starter's gun. Sean went off quickly to keep those behind from stepping on his heels. The Bradsford race started downhill, making it likely that some of the novices, in their excitement, would begin too fast. Road runners and bikers are always conscious of hills. Sean loved to run uphill. Psychologically it was like putting money in the bank. You got to spend it later. Flying downhill he always felt like a spendthrift. In this race you went into debt and paid up at the end climbing back to the center of town.

As usual a few rabbits surged to the front. Some liked the publicity, others the feeling of leading a quality pack. Some seriously thought they were helping pace the other runners and producing a better race. In major competitions rabbits were entered deliberately as part of team strategy, sacrificing themselves, usually not even finishing. Sean could not imagine himself in such a role.

At the first mile he was tenth in a lead group of about thirty. The recreational runners had been left behind. Two unrecognized rabbits and Abi were opening a gap. Abi's style was to race near or in the lead from start to finish. Sean preferred to be back slightly where he could watch his competition. "It takes the body and the brain both to be the best," his coach, the legendary Bob Higgum, had often admonished him. "In distance running you must study the others, learn their strides when they're fresh, and later in the race you'll be able to recognize when they are on the edge and almost ready to come apart. Then throw in a short sprint. Competitors can be broken if attacked at precisely the right moment."

Sean lost a few steps to be sure that he took water from Julie, Mary's younger daughter. He really didn't need to drink on a day like this, but would never disappoint the little girl. She stood in her bright yellow slicker near a bend in the road, a squeeze bottle in one hand and a sign in the other. The previous year it had said, "Go, Sean, lucky number seven." Now a red crayon line ran through the seven and a large eight was written below.

The second and third miles of the course ran parallel to the river, past the knitting mill, long-abandoned but once the mainstay of Bradsford's economy. Its six stories made it the tallest building in the town. Out of the corner of his eye, Sean made his annual assessment of the mill's reclamation. This year it held new condominiums with balconies overlooking the water, which was now clean enough for recreational use. *Nice*, he thought, but then quickly refocussed on the task at hand.

Ten-kilometer races can be lost in the early miles. The beginners are too excited, too intense, slightly off their most efficient stride, wasting valuable emotional and physical energy they'll need later. Sean was completely relaxed mentally but still felt sore from the marathon. Bob Higgum had warned him not to run with so little rest, but Sean felt an obligation to Bradsford. And he always enjoyed the holiday with Mary and her husband Bill, one of the town's police officers. Over the years, they had become his adopted American family.

The first uphill, short but steep, occurred at three and a half miles. Sean had lingered behind a taller runner using him as a shield against the rain and as a draft against the apparent headwind created by the running motion. Now he accelerated up the hill, passing Joe Lightfoot, and tucked in behind Abi. Bates and Grouse followed him, and the two rabbits already almost exhausted went by as if in reverse.

Going down the far side, he glanced back to see what effect his move had produced in the lead pack. Joe was still there as were both of the collegians, and he noticed for the first time a tall runner completely covered in a baby blue Bill Rogers Gore-Tex running suit, a hat with a brim, a parka with the hood raised and long pants. It was a moment that Sean was to remember for the rest of his life, but at the time he simply said to himself, "Boy, he must be afraid to get wet." The newcomer, who had approached unnoticed, was now close behind. He ran with an awkward, choppy motion, not the smooth, practiced gait of a well-coached athlete. Still he seemed comfortable.

They reached the second small hill in the middle of the fifth mile, and Sean spotted the first signs of Abi weakening, a slightly shorter stride and more rapid breathing. He had raced against Abi before, indeed, he had once lost to him. But he was older now, better and wiser, and while the changes in Abi would have gone unnoticed by the other runners, they were a galvanizing message to Sean. In an instant his plan for the remainder of the race crystallized. *Take Abi now, and Joe and Blue Man will fade. The kids are too much in awe of me to make their moves so early. They'll wait too long and will never catch up on that last hill.*

Sean went, and the collegians followed. Joe answered. Abi faded. Blue Man passed Joe and went to fourth. For a short stretch, perhaps three-eighths of a mile, the road dropped slightly. *Bank with-*

drawal. Makes the final climb that much greater. Without thinking Sean shortened his stride to avoid slipping in a rivulet crossing the pavement at its lowest point. The cold water splashed on his bare ankles and into his shoes. The long final climb began.

At five miles Sean led the others around the last bend. There ahead was the sight that would so discourage the exhausted recreational runners who followed. The road rose steadily, framed between convergent columns of trees, seeming to stretch on forever into the dim sky. The welcoming finish line banner remained hidden just beyond the summit. Joe was fading. Sean was tiring too, but he welcomed the hill. He knew it well. This was *his* hill. He had owned it for seven straight years.

The four were stretched out across the road. No more drafting. Bates passed Grouse. Blue Man passed Grouse. Bates came at Sean, but by a third of a mile up the hill it was obvious he couldn't do it. Blue Man passed Bates and pulled alongside. For the first time Sean could study him. Gray at the temples, much too old to be there. Pain on his face. Stride even worse than before. But he seemed hardly to be breathing. It made Sean suddenly conscious of his own panting. He was going hard, all out. Blue Man drew ahead. His hands were clenched into fists, and his feet slapped, no *pounded*, the ground.

As he went by, Sean had the flash of an image from the past. Jogging in Dublin's Phoenix Park, a runner had suffered a heart attack and died on the road despite the efforts of Sean and others to save him. Blue Man went up the hill, Sean after him in a flat-out sprint. Now it was Sean who thought he would die. The marathon had taken its toll. Although he gave it his all, he still finished a good ten yards behind the receding blue figure and collapsed into the arms of a finish-line aide. Grouse repassed Bates, who had given his all in the gallant try at the bottom of the hill, and finished third. Joe was fourth and Abi finished out of the money.

Despite his embarrassed protests, Sean was led to the first-aid station in the firehouse. Joe soon appeared limping and was helped to the next cot. "Cramp at the finish. Must be getting old, but still beat one of the young hotshots. He went too soon. But those two guys gonna be damn good. How about you? You lost." He said it with surprise.

While one of the volunteers massaged Joe's left leg, another, rebuffed in her attempts to administer to Sean, was almost pouring water into him.

"Guess that marathon took more out of me than I thought. Didn't have it at the end." Sean felt absolutely exhausted.

"You college boys supposed to know those things. But did you see the time?" Joe gasped between breaths and swallows.

"No."

"No more, honey. Good girl." Joe fended off the aide with his hand. "Pour some of that stuff into him."

Sean agreed to drink. He was so disappointed, ashamed, he couldn't look at anyone.

Joe knew how it felt to lose, but now he was almost joyous. "Beat last year's time," he exalted. "All of us beat last year's time. My best ever. Lots of good training for me this year."

"Last year was hot. This year was perfect. I left more out there this time, but it still didn't work," Sean said between swallows.

"But that guy ran 28.08." Joe named a figure which while not a world record would have been one of the best times of the year anywhere.

He and Sean both knew that the course advertised as 10K was short. It was a convenient route through the town and had never been accurately measured. This kept the amateurs returning year after year to set their own records. Most were quite willing to fool themselves, and no harm was done. Still, the time was exceptional.

"Know who he is?" Sean asked.

"Not from around here."

"Think he pulled a Rosie?" Sean was referring to a runner who had tried in several marathons to sneak in near the end in front of the leading women. It was impossible to do without being discovered, since major races are video taped throughout. But for a few minutes this tragic, comic figure had even succeeded in being proclaimed the winner of the Boston Marathon.

"No, he was there early. I start slowly. I passed him at about two miles when I came up on you. He must have followed you. He went by when you did in the fourth."

"Yeah, I saw," Sean said, staring at his feet as if rebuking them.

"Anyway, you know how fast he ran the last two miles."

Sean nodded. "Something's not right. Too old. He was too old."

"Yeah, he looked old."

A volunteer appeared holding two urine collection bottles.

"What? No, I'm okay," Joe protested. It was a new experience for him. Even Sean was surprised to be tested after a race like this.

"We may try for TAC approval next year, so we're trying to meet all of the regulations," the newcomer explained.

"Never happen! TAC would measure the course," Sean said under his breath, but he went behind a curtain to comply. As he added his bottle to those already in the basket, he noticed that one was distinctly pink. Many distance runners pass small amounts of blood in their urine during a really strenuous workout, but not usually enough to notice.

Hope it was you, Blue, he thought bitterly and then turned to the volunteer. "Are you really going to test this stuff?"

"They're supposed to go to one of the labs, but don't hold your breath."

"What's the matter, Sean? You on something?" Joe teased from behind the curtain.

"Hardly," said Sean, who was tested routinely throughout the year. "Only my cousin's maple syrup."

"Prizes coming."

Tom Foley, the founder and director of the race, appeared at the door. "Boy, I never thought . . . but he was really good." The trace of a superior smile was on his face. Over the years Sean had become more important to the race than Foley, but now perhaps the proper relationship had been restored. "Hope you'll still come back and try to beat him next year."

Sean ignored the sarcasm. "Who is he?"

"Yeah, where'd you get him?" Joe added.

"Don't know," Foley replied. "His name's Root. Didn't want the prize. Said he was an amateur. Didn't want to wait for the urine sample, but Mattie got it. Just dragged him in here."

Mattie, the erstwhile water pourer, an old-fashioned nurse, was not one to be refused.

"Finally took the money, waved to the crowd, drove off in some fancy red sports car."

"What did you write on the check?" Sean asked.

"Now, Sean, you know we give cash prizes, at your request as I recall. Something about the AAU," he said, laughing, "or was it the IRS?"

Chapter 2

Lin Pao sat in front of the computer in his tiny, windowless office. He was almost content. This wasn't what he had expected to be doing with his life, but he was much better off than most of his childhood friends. The isolation of the training center was the worst part, high in the Wuyi Mountains, more than four hundred miles from Shanghai. Unlike the athletes, Lin had every weekend off. But it made little difference, because there was no regular transportation to the nearest town at the base of the mountain. Occasionally he could catch a ride with a supply van that he knew would return. It would have been a serious mistake not to make it back by Monday morning. The Germans who ran the training center did not tolerate such laxness.

Why were these foreigners here, anyway? Hadn't Chairman Mao taught that the influence of such outsiders was unnecessary, even harmful? Of course that period with its hated cultural revolution was over. And everyone had to admit that there were things to be learned from others if China was finally to leap into the modern world. But these Germans weren't here as advisers, they were in charge . . . in charge of sports, which should be a matter of such nationalistic pride. Lin shook his head as he thought of it. But where would he be if the Germans had not come?

The computer ran through the results of the previous week's track and field events, and Lin chose those that he would graph by hand. He had not yet managed to write a program to do it automatically, but he was working on it. The latest American software was not available to him. Would it even run on the German computer? Why couldn't he have an IBM, as if he didn't know? And if his masters learned how easy it would be to use, they might get rid of him. Then what? He could always call on his uncle's political influence for a place in the Ministry of Economics, but there were too many programmers there. He would be like another ant. The one thing he wanted desperately, as did so many of his friends, was to be an individual. Here he had his own niche. By now he felt he knew the athletes worldwide, almost as if they were his friends, even though he had never met any of them.

He went over the week's news in his mind. Dryx, the great Belgian, had been off for five weeks. Rumor had it that he was injured, but his last 10K in Lyon was FTY, fastest time of the year. A tuned track, good competition, sixty degrees at night, perfect conditions. Still he was getting older, probably past his prime. Would he be a factor in Sydney?

Chadwick's race at Leeds had been disappointing. Shouldn't have run. Bad time. End of a long season. Trying to compensate for losing to Rossi at Helsinki. No love lost there. Should be resting. Lin had no way of knowing that one of Chadwick's many girl friends lived in Leeds. There was only so much information in the graphs, and Lin had to supply the personalities of the runners himself. Occasionally he would find an article describing the private life of an athlete in one of the many sports magazines that were his required reading, but usually he just arbitrarily chose characteristics for his runners, creating some heroes and some villains. Interestingly, the Chinese runners had no place in his imagination.

The computer automatically selected "special results." It was his latest programming success. Outstanding performances, corrected for weather conditions, track surface, and competitors, as well as any unusual results, such as upsets of established stars, were flagged. It was late in the morning when he finished the routine graphs and called up the specials. There was Leeds, not really so special. He scrolled forward. There was Bradsford!

Lin had been a good student excelling in mathematics, standing out among the many fine students willing to work fourteen hours a day in a desperate effort to distinguish themselves and to be chosen to go on to university. Had he deserved to be selected, or was it because he had a powerful uncle high in the government? Chinese style communism wasn't a meritocracy, he realized, it was as corrupt as any other government. But Lin had done well enough at the university to be singled out, without his uncle's help he liked to think, for advanced training in computer sciences. This could be a gateway to the military, or more mathematical physics, or into the rapidly growing business bureaucracy.

Upon graduating he had been selected to go to Germany, all expenses paid by the computer manufacturer, for an in-house training program. Was this his uncle's influence again, or the fact that he had studied German while most of his classmates had chosen Russian? All learned English.

The nine months in Hamburg had been the freest, the most exhilarating time of his life. He had briefly considered fleeing, but his family would have paid dearly. When he returned, Lin was summoned by the dean of the College of Computer Sciences and informed that he was to be honored with the offer of a position at the training center. In reality it was an order, not an offer, but despite the isolation, it turned out to be a very desirable job. Certainly it was better than most of the military outposts. He had his own apartment, newly constructed. Imagine being the first occupant of a room! The food in the communal dining hall was excellent and plentiful and available to him for a nominal charge. It was almost too good to pass up, but still it was a pleasant change to shop in the local commissary and cook for himself in his very own kitchen.

The mountains were beautiful, and the air was so pure. "*Thin* and pure," he said to himself, "that's why we're up here." He longed for a car. They were everywhere in Germany. Still he was grateful for what he did have. His position paid well, and he had nothing to spend money on anyway. He was saving to purchase a motor scooter. This was far beyond the dreams of the typical middle-class couple: "two rooms, one son, two bicycles." Now if only there were more women at the training center.

He interrupted his daydreaming, so easy to do sitting in front of the computer in the dim gray room. On the screen: "Bradsford, Root first, Rourke second, Grouse third, 28.08." Lin Pao was suddenly alert. Rourke hadn't lost at 10K to anyone except Dryx for more than a year. And that was before Dryx was hurt. And the time! It would take a time like that to beat Rourke, but nobody ran such a time so late in the season. Lin had no way of knowing that the course was short.

Where was Bradsford? He typed in the command. Oh yes,

Rourke had won it the last two years. But who was Root? He typed again. Nothing. Lin knew Grouse. He was one of the American newcomers, tabbed as a future star but probably too young to worry about for now. But how far back was Rourke? What were the other times? What were the conditions? Why would he lose an insignificant race like that? And the time! And who was Root, some unknown new star? This was just the kind of occurrence the computer system was designed to detect.

He typed in "source." "Boston Globe, Sunday, December 6," appeared on the screen. It would be from Jonathan Chen, a post-doctoral fellow at M.I.T., who covered the New England newspapers. He could be a little careless at times, Lin thought. With that name, he was probably American born and just did it for the money. But it would be hard to make such a mistake. It was his job to cut out all the articles on track and field events and send them to the embassy. The results were coded and once a week sent to Lin on a floppy disk. Could one of the coders have copied the names in the wrong order? The full articles would follow by mail. It was too long to wait; he had to know at once. The Germans would have to be told, but first the information must be checked. They could not stand something being missed, and they hated inaccurate data even more. Sean Rourke was one of Lin's favorites. It was too early to tell whether Root would become one of his favorites as well.

Chapter 3

Andy Grimes ran along the lonely, country road on a Saturday afternoon in mid February. Even here in northern New England there was no snow on the ground and the sun was shining brightly, reminding him that spring was just a few weeks away. Soon he would be able to run outdoors every day. At this time of year the days were too short to fit running into his busy hospital schedule. And he hated to run in the gym. He preferred to be outside in the evening. It was so relaxing, especially after a long session in the clinic. Only the days when he had to write research papers or the endless grant applications were more stressful than seeing cancer patients. Given his choice he would have spent every day in the laboratory, weekends and holidays as well. Doing the research was so much more fun than writing about it. That was especially true for this project, which had moved along so rapidly without all the little setbacks usually encountered in this kind of work. From the very beginning, the original crazy idea, everything had seemed to go just perfectly.

I have to publish it. I can't keep it a secret any longer. It deserves an all-out effort. Of course this meant that the big laboratories and the drug companies would jump in. *I've been selfish, puttering around with it all by myself. But now I'm just holding up progress.* He knew what had to be done; he just wasn't looking forward to doing it. First there would be the "disclosure of invention" forms to be filed with the university. It had first rights to apply for a patent. There was no question that it would choose to patent this one. Only then could he publish. "Disclose publicly" was the expression the lawyers used. In this country you had a year to file the patent application after the disclosure, but for world wide rights the filing must come first. Those rights were too valuable to ignore.

Well, it has to be done. He had brought home with him the lab books and his own notes and would face the task after the run. This would call for an extra good wine with dinner, and he knew just where one was in his cellar.

With less than a mile to go, he was comfortably tired. His route today was six miles, the classic ten kilometers. After so many years he knew the distances of all the roads near his home. At about this spot he always thought of *the* race. What a success it had been, surprising and a little embarrassing but so satisfying. He wondered what Root himself would have thought.

"I should give myself a transplant," he said and laughed, "and I must remember to send back that money."

He heard the car approaching from behind and reflexively moved closer to the edge of the pavement, not even bothering to look back. Like anyone who has run thousands of miles on public roads, he was aware of where the danger lay. This road was straight and wide, and there was very little traffic, usually only neighbors who were used to his being there and would honk and wave. Anyway, he knew, he could be seen for at least a half mile.

The collision threw him to the berm. First he felt the terror, then the numbness that gradually wore off to reveal pain, severe pain. He realized that he was badly hurt. Inappropriate thoughts filled his mind. His broken ankle had been his only other injury. It had seemed to take forever to heal, in reality less than six months. And those first painful steps. He had gone to the shore to begin his running in the soft sand. How long would it take this time? These injuries were certainly much worse. And he was getting older. Everything took a little longer to heal. At least his mind was still working, that was the only thing that really mattered.

He heard the car brake hard. They were stopping. It hurt too much to turn and look. Were they coming back? Thank God, yes. He needed help.

He heard the footsteps, but he never felt the blow that crushed his skull.

Chapter 4

It was three weeks later, and Sean was working in his small office at St. Vincent's, carefully charting by hand the training results of the school's middle distance runners. "I'll bet a computer could do this," he said to himself. Later in the morning he would review each one's progress with Bob Higgum. It wasn't quite what was expected of an athlete of his stature, but Sean had set for himself the goal of becoming a world class coach as well as the holder of several world records. In fact he sometimes wondered which of these activities mattered to him more. One would be temporary at best and could end prematurely by accident or injury or by the arrival of competitors better than he. The other would most likely be his life long work. Of course any of the records he hoped to set during the next two years would be worth more financially than a lifetime of coaching. But the records were still just dreams, while the coaching was a sure thing. At St. Vincent's he had the opportunity to serve his apprenticeship with a preeminent coach, while at the same time continuing his training under the same expert guidance.

Bob Higgum had made his reputation by finding and developing foreign athletes. Sean had been recruited to be the next in a long line of outstanding Irish milers. A school boy sensation, he had never lost an age group race at 1,500 meters or the mile and had finished fourth in the nationals at age seventeen. St. Vincent's offer, a free college education and the chance to be with Higgum, was too good to turn down. Sean had never regretted his decision, although trading life in a tiny Irish village for the problems of urban America had not been easy at first. Mainly he missed his three sisters, all older, they had babied him since birth. He went back to visit at every opportunity.

It had taken Higgum only a few months after Sean's arrival to spot his real potential, the longer distances. A lesser coach or a more selfish one might have insisted that Sean stick with the mile, the glamor event, knowing that, with a few years of the proper training, an NCAA title was a real possibility. But Higgum had a longer view, and unlike many coaches in high-pressure positions, he had his runner's best interest at heart. He had expected some resistance from his prize recruit, but Sean was enthusiastic about the new plan. He had never liked the countless quarter-mile and half-mile repeats done by the milers, and he loved the endurance runs. The 5K and the 10K were his favorites, for they reminded him of the long informal cross-country runs of his childhood. He and Bob settled on the 5K for his freshman year and gradually built up to the longer distances.

Sean was interrupted by the arrival of a student messenger delivering an envelope from the president's office. "They said to be sure to give it to you personally. There might be money in it."

His name and "St. Vincent's University" appeared on the front in a distinctive part print, part script. "College," Sean corrected in his mind. He thanked the student, and when he was alone again tore open the envelope. It did indeed contain money, which spilled out onto his desk as he unfolded the enclosed note. In the same handwriting were the words "I cheated." Nothing else. He began to count. There were twenty $100 bills. Sean stared at them, genuinely amazed.

This must be a mistake, he thought. *Those guys cheat at poker sometimes, but we never play for stakes like this. Besides it wouldn't be in their nature to give the money back, not unless one of them suddenly discovered religion.* He looked again at the envelope, a standard format with the return address of Grenville University, but lacking the name of the sender. This would be an expensive joke. It just made no sense. He shook his head, resolved not to think about it until he had finished his work, and put the money in his jacket pocket.

An hour later, with the money safely stored in his locker, he was on the practice track. It was sprint day, mile repeats timed by Bob himself. Higgum stood in the infield opposite the start-finish line, stopwatch in hand, dressed in an ancient sweatsuit with a Phillies baseball hat pulled so low in front that the visor rested on his wire-rimmed glasses. He was a small, trim man, in his late sixties, with a face weather-beaten from hours spent outdoors. His stern visage was an illusion, but still his rule was unchallenged. He almost never spoke. A slight nod of his head was the reward for a perfectly run interval, and "Good laddie" served for anything from an unusually fast final lap to a world record. Sean hated the mile repeats, but at least now as the weather improved there were more days when they could be done outside. That made it a little better. After his personal session with Bob, he took off to do the 10K with the undergraduates. Now he was the coach as well as their hero. They were a good group, and he pushed them hard.

When he dressed at the end of the day, Sean felt the folded bills in his jacket. *It has to be for someone else. But there aren't a lot of names that sound like mine, certainly no others here at St. Vincent's. And when have I ever been cheated?* He took the envelope from his pocket and stared at it. And what was the connection to Grenville? Sean knew it only by reputation. Like Oxford and Cambridge its name was recognized everywhere, but not for athletics. Had he ever competed against a Grenville student? Not that he could recall. He did remember that the Grenville track coach was one of Higgum's own. Jim McBride had been a miler at St. Vincent's before Sean. Not good enough for a professional career, he was still talked about as one of Bob's smartest students. In fact he and Sean were frequently compared. About ten seconds a mile was the only difference, thought Sean, but that difference should be worth several million dollars.

Sean had always felt that McBride had been such a strange choice for the Grenville coaching position. Grenville belonged to a group of schools that had chosen to de-emphasize athletics. Why wouldn't McBride have wanted to work with the best athletes? What was Grenville's appeal? Anyway, it seemed unlikely that Jim could be connected with the money. They rarely saw each other. *When was the last time?* Sean wondered. *Must have been at Bob's sixty-fifth birthday party.* There were no poker games that he could recall, and no other connections came to mind. *Where is Grenville anyway? Probably somewhere in New England.* He glanced at the envelope again. *Connecticut.* Then he remembered the exit sign on the turnpike, about thirty miles from Bradsford! *The race! The first prize! Blue Man!*

Though it had occurred just four months earlier, Sean rarely thought of the defeat. After all, he had the perfect excuse, the marathon just two weeks before.

Even Higgum had seemed to ignore it. "So, why did you go? And think of how happy you made that guy. It was the run of his life." Bob was never so generous with the serious competitors. "And it was a good lesson. You should be ready for all your races."

But now all the feelings of that day came back, the disappointment, the humiliation, the funereal atmosphere at the holiday dinner. Knowing that the winner had cheated didn't make it easier. In fact it added to his sense of shame. How could he have been outsmarted by some novice in some little race? And then gradually came the feeling of concern. Could it happen again? He had to find this Root person and learn what he had done.

His first stop was the St. Vincent's library, where an aide showed him how easy it was on the Internet to access university directories. But in just a few minutes his hopes were dashed. There was no one named Root at Grenville among the faculty, students or staff. Next he tried the telephone directories for the communities near Grenville and for Bradsford. Still no luck. Only one "Root," a woman.

Maybe I'll drive up there, Sean mused. *Jim should know if there are any mystery runners winning all the local races, and it will be a chance to talk about his decision to coach at a place like Grenville. I'll be facing the same choices one of these days. And then I can go on up to Bill and Mary's and do my long run in the country, get some clean air for a change.*

"A place like Grenville would want a coach of Jim's ability," Higgum had told Sean, "a gentleman, someone who always put the students' interests first. And they liked the fact that he was young. You know, would be kind of a friend, not an old tyrant like me. And Grenville can afford anything it wants. At that point in Jim's career, he couldn't turn it down. He can stay there forever, or use it to jump back to one of the big track powers."

"Nobody can expect him to do much without athletic scholarships for recruiting," Sean noted.

"So there's no pressure, but there's opportunity," Bob answered. "Jim's already started to win more than he should with his regular students. And people are noticing. I've put in his name to be one of the assistant track coaches for Sydney."

Sean arrived at Grenville late in the afternoon on a perfect spring day. He had seen Jim only occasionally, at track meets or reunions of the St.Vincent runners, but he knew he would be greeted as a friend. Higgum's boys were a close group. With some help, he found his way through the lovely old campus to the athletic facilities. Jim had warned Sean on the phone that he probably would be with the soccer team, since he served as a volunteer assistant coach. There was a feeling of excitement in the air, for the teams were outside at last after months of confinement forced by the weather. Jim waved from the opposite side of the practice field. *He looks older*, Sean thought, as they walked toward each other. Maybe it was the hair, cut close, almost military style and already beginning to grey. And the baggy sweatsuit didn't hide the weight he had gained since the end of his competitive running. They greeted each other warmly.

"So you're changing sports," Sean teased.

"The track team works out earlier in the day," Jim explained. "Soccer is having its two weeks of spring practice now, so I try to help out. Secretly, I just like to kick the ball around, but I make myself useful, help with the training, give them speed drills, things like that. And we give each player an exercise program for the summer." The smile on his face and in his bright blue eyes showed just how much he liked what he was doing. It was contagious.

Sean sat and watched while the practice ran its course. He enjoyed everything about an athletic field, the cool spring air, the grass, the distant cries of the players wafting across the field, occasionally interrupted by whistles, the sound of a foot squarely striking the ball. And there was something about a clod of moist earth, maybe the smell, that brought back happy memories. He loved soccer and often regretted that he had not pursued the sport further. But realistically he knew that he would never have been able to earn his living as a player.

Later Sean helped Jim gather the equipment and close his office. He was to spend the night with Jim and his wife, Helen, before going on to Bradsford. The McBrides lived in an isolated area, and Sean was glad to have Jim's car to follow. He waited until after dinner when Helen was busy with the children to tell Jim the whole story.

"That's really strange," Jim said, leading Sean into the den. The walls were covered with photographs of sporting events, many from St. Vincent's, and a few medals and trophies. Sean couldn't miss the contrast. His own apartment contained few photos but so many awards that most were stacked still in their boxes. Somehow at that moment the pictures seemed more important than the medals, and he examined them carefully. There was Sean himself, depicted on a framed cover of *Track Weekly,* when he had set a meet record in the NCAA 10K championship three years earlier. He had looked so young and so thin. He still did. And such a mass of dark hair. Well, at least that had been trimmed somewhat. But the eyes and the mouth were the same. He was a competitor to be feared, then and now.

"Bob told me that you had lost at Bradsford, but I just chalked it up to your having run the marathon two weeks before. I thought maybe you cramped up or something. I never did look at the times, but you said they were good."

"They were darn good. You know that course is a little short."

"Like so many of them." Jim laughed.

"But this guy had to be fifty years old, and I don't lose to anybody of that age."

"I hope not," Jim said. "Boy, he must be a terror in the seniors."

"If he runs them. No one I've spoken to has ever heard of him, but I'm just starting to look. He had a funny way of running. I can't put my finger on it, but it was just strange."

"Let me know if you find it." Jim laughed again. "I'll teach it to my kids. Anyway, I don't know anyone around here named Root. He certainly isn't one of my runners, and, of course, if he's really as old as you think he is, he wouldn't be one of the students. So that leaves the faculty or the employees, and you said you've checked them both."

Sean nodded. "Yes, and the local phone books, they're all on the Internet."

"Somehow I don't think I'm going to be much help, but I'll keep my eyes and ears open and ask around. Maybe it's an alumnus who lives nearby, or maybe someone who used to be associated with the university. There are lots of possibilities. It's not a common name."

"The other thing is that he may turn up next fall, but my curiosity won't let me wait that long to try to find out about him. I really should stop running Bradsford. It doesn't fit into my training schedule anymore. I just do it out of loyalty."

"But it would be fun to go back and kick his ass, if he has the guts to try again," Jim said and smiled.

"That too."

Sean spent Saturday in Bradsford trying to learn anything he could about Root. He spoke to some of the local runners, but none could remember having run against him or having seen him practicing on the nearby roads. He checked Root's address from the registration form, and it turned out to be fictitious.

"There's no reason to suspect he cheated," one of the race officials, the owner of the local hardware store and a good friend of Bill's, told Sean. "Remember, we did urine testing last year. Everyone was clean. We probably won't bother doing it again this year. We decided not to get certified. TAC came down, and there were some things they didn't like. We just thought it was too much trouble." Sean smiled, knowing full well that TAC would have objected to the distance.

Sean left Bradsford with one important finding, a newspaper photo of Blue Man crossing the finish line. "Why didn't I think of this before?" he said to himself. On his way back to Philadelphia he stopped again at Grenville and left a copy with Jim McBride. Jim didn't recognize the runner but promised to show the photo to his associates at the university.

In the car Sean had time to ponder the whole strange affair. How had he been cheated? Joe confirmed that Blue Man had run the full distance. How did an old man—well, a pretty old man—cheat so effectively that he could beat an Olympic quality runner? Drugs? Sure some are hard to detect, but what kind of drug could make *such* a difference? And why send back the money? The more Sean thought about it, the more nervous he became. *Am I missing something big, something that's going to cost me? Did I waste four months ignoring him? But how could I have known? Who is he? Where is he?*

Chapter 5

It was still cool in the mountains in March, but Lin Pao often sat outside in the bright sun drinking his midmorning tea from a thermos. It felt like spring, no matter that he had to wrap both hands around the thin plastic cup for warmth. And the arrival of the pretty doctor, that too made him think of spring. He smiled as he remembered the first time he saw her. Under her white lab coat, she had been wearing a T-shirt with a large picture of a black mouse. Above its smiling face were the words, "Hi, I'm Mickey," and under its yellow feet, "Disney World." Lest anyone think that she had squandered her entire salary on this black market treasure, she appeared on successive days sporting a duck, a smiling orange dog with a thin tail, and a pair of chipmunks. Either she had been to America or, he hated to think, perhaps had a boyfriend there. In his mind he called her Mickey, although he knew her name was Xiaojian, and he tried to think of ways to do more than just say hello.

Well, those were his pleasant daydreams, but one unpleasant matter kept intruding, Root and the Germans. He was determined to face it later that very morning. Lin had created a new file for Root, and it had taken him only two weeks to obtain the full copy of the *Boston Globe* story. Race conditions had been good, and all the times were fast. Root had caught Rourke in the final half mile. But now, almost four months later, he had nothing else. Lin had searched his old files, but the name Root was nowhere to be found. He tried the official record books and even old running magazines, but the result was always the same. The Germans would not be pleased with his news.

In the post-Mao era the People's Republic of China was attempting to show a more friendly face to the outside world. Part of the plan included hosting the Olympic games in Beijing. Its leaders were so confident of the ultimate success of their bid that preparations had begun in the early 90's. New superhighways were being built in and about the city. The airport, primitive by the standards of any modern metropolis, was to be expanded and renovated. New housing for athletes and new athletic facilities were to be constructed. This serious commitment of resources would be worthwhile if it helped to establish a new image of a more humanistic society, and, of course, if it encouraged a lucrative tourist trade.

Equally important was to have the Chinese athletes perform spectacularly on their native soil. With the available raw material, more than 700,000,000 individuals, only expertise and facilities were needed to develop a winning team. These could be purchased. Aware of the athletic success of the East Germans during the cold war, the Chinese turned to this group of coaches and trainers, who had fashioned powerful teams using any means available. Many of them, now the objects of civil and criminal proceedings in their reunited country, were happy to accept sanctuary and highly paid positions in China.

The first bid to host the Games was unsuccessful mainly because of the incident in Tiananmen Square. The world watched in horror while tanks rolled over helpless students and the committee voted to send the Olympics to Atlanta and then to Sydney. With the cynical assumption that moral indignation is short-lived, China looked forward to the year 2004. Meanwhile, an outstanding team performance in Australia would whet their appetites.

The Germans came en mass, at least thirty coaches, trainers and medical personnel. A new training center was built within a few months in the Wuyi mountains and was surrounded by security equal to that of the most important military bases. The Chinese employees were selected with great care.

"It's as if we were prisoners in our own country," one of Lin's friends had complained. There was no question where the authority lay. To disagree or to disobey was to be banished. Discipline was strict and performance standards high. On the other hand, there were ample rewards for those who could take the pressure.

Reinhardt Jurgen was the supreme commandant. Lin had seen him only once, at a distance, pointed out by one of his colleagues. He was being helped into a new Mercedes. It was hard not to notice a car like that in China. Jurgen was tall and thin, in his sixties, maybe even early seventies, and was too warmly dressed for the early spring. Lin remembered a heavy coat with upturned collar and a hat. He could barely see the wire glasses and the thin lips.

Despite the constant tension, Lin Pao enjoyed his new opportunity. The German masters had wanted a computer-based system to monitor the performances of leading athletes. Through the Chinese Secret Service, they had established a system of "eyes" to report on athletic events worldwide. The "eyes" were Chinese living abroad, like Chen who had filed the first report of Root. They were loyal to the PRC or willing to cooperate for money or out of fear of retribution to their families living at home. Lin thought of them as friends, although he had never met one. They were like his runners, living in far-off lands and known to him only through the reports of their activities.

He poured the last of the tea into his cup and thought back. As soon as the *Globe* article had arrived, Lin Pao had dutifully reported the performance of the mysterious Mr. Root to his superior, Manfred Schultz. Lin could remember the meeting perfectly. It was on the day before Christmas, and some of the Germans had decorated a tree. As expected, his information had generated considerable interest.

"And Rourke was sound, not injured? But of course not. The time, it was too good." Schultz answered his own question.

"Herr Schultz, we have no records of this Root. He is entirely new."

"And the newspaper said nothing?"

"It spoke only of Rourke, of his seven victories."

"Pao, you say it is an isolated village, this Brotspferd."

"Yes, but he runs always there."

"And in November, when the race season is complete." Schultz had risen from his desk and was pacing the sparsely furnished room. He was a short muscular man, a man of action. A former athlete, Lin imagined, perhaps a gymnast. Schultz stopped and stared out the window. Lin could see beyond his back a panoramic view of the mountains that were so typically Chinese. He loved them.

Schultz pondered this new information. He barely noticed the mountains, and when he did their softness and the mists were depressing reminders that he was not in the Alps. Sean Rourke was high on the list of major competitors for Sydney. That he should lose to an unknown, presumably an American, in an insignificant race was not right. Was there a new star being kept under wraps, competing only in races that would not be noticed, waiting to be sprung on the unsuspecting athletic world shortly before the Games? It was just the sort of secrecy the computer system had been designed to detect.

"So Jurgen was right with his computers. And I thought they would be a useless waste. Jurgen is always right." He said it just loud enough for Lin Pao to hear and then turned suddenly on his heel and once more faced Lin.

"You will discover everything about this Root. Everything. Do you understand?" There was no chance for Lin to respond. "At once. These Americans think they are so clever. They will learn who is clever. Go."

Initially the pressure had been intense to find out something about this unknown runner. When Lin Pao's attempts met with little success, Schultz was quick to criticize. He had a volatile manner and seemed to fill a room with a sense of violence. Lin was physically afraid of him, although he knew that was unreasonable. Still he faced their weekly meetings with apprehension, knowing that he would be questioned and have nothing to report. Root had become an obsession with Schultz.

But then, after several weeks the questioning had stopped. At first Lin Pao took this as a bad sign. Perhaps they had given up on him, and he was to be replaced. But two more months went by, and nothing seemed to change. Finally Lin had summoned all his courage. This was to be the day when he would finally inform Schultz that the investigation had stalled completely.

He screwed the cup back onto the thermos, placed it in his small knapsack and started to walk slowly toward the low cinder block building that housed the offices of the Germans. This was a regular weekly meeting, and he had made the trip so often that he was able to time his arrival so that he was knocking on Schultz's door at exactly eleven. He waited until the end of the routine business to bring up Root.

"We have found nothing," Lin apologized, "despite all our efforts."

"Ja, Ja."

"But I have tried everything, all the old records, all the American and the . . ."

"Ja, Ja."

"We have tried our best, Herr Schultz and . . ."

"Ja, Ja. Where are the reports from the Tokyo Marathon?"

Back in his office Lin sat at his desk staring straight ahead at an old calender saved because of its magnificent pictures of the Chinese countryside. He had brought it back from Germany, and it was turned now to a view of the very mountains that were on the other side of the wall. *As good as a window,* he thought when he hung it, *and the sun is always shining.* Now he puzzled over the meeting with Schultz. How could it be after all that pressure? Was it just a mistake? Perhaps it had been a test of the monitoring system, of him, and there really was no Root. But it couldn't be. He still had in his file the original newspaper clipping from Chen. There was even a photograph of Root. At his insistence, Chen had managed to obtain a copy of the *Bradsford Weekly News*. It wasn't a good picture, he recalled. Obviously it had been raining, and the print was dark. And somehow it made the runner look old. Suddenly Lin wanted to examine it again. He reached for the file, by now thick with the documentation of his failures, and searched through it, finally dumping the contents onto the desk. Where was that photo? He opened the other drawers and finally in desperation even got down on his hands and knees to look under the desk. But by then, he knew it was hopeless. The photograph was gone. Lin was overcome by a feeling of dread.

Schultz and Jurgen always ate in the private dining room, the one reserved for "honored guests" of the Republic. Both felt more comfortable among their own kind. Jurgen even smiled occasionally and joined in the general conversion. Today, however, they were alone at a table some distance from the others.

"Pao suspects nothing," Schultz said with barely disguised contempt. "He dutifully reported today that no records of Root exist."

Jurgen laughed. "Did I not tell you, Schultz, that it was absolutely necessary for us to have direct access to the Secret Service? But do not be so hard on him, he does his job thoroughly. We need more like him and less of these other lazy incompetents."

"And he speaks German, although that may be his worst feature.

I simply cannot stand to listen to him." He laughed too. "But who would have expected such a bonus from his computer system?"

"Nothing is as important as knowledge, Schultz. Always remember that."

"Ja, and hard work. Our two new technicians have already duplicated the purification procedures. And three new ones from Friedburg will join them before the fifteenth."

"You are sure we will be ready by October?"

"Jawohl, mein Herr."

"So für Stuttgart."

"Für Stuttgart."

A rare grin spread across Jurgen's face. It surprised even Schultz. "And we get the bodies to eat?"

"Of course. So many that you will grow sick of them."

"I grow sick of eating this Chinese food. We should have our own German cook, as in the old days."

"And our own German athletes too," Schultz added, "Aryan athletes."

Chapter 6

Over the next several weeks, Sean showed the photograph to runners, sports writers, and coaches, but no one recognized the mysterious figure, not even Bob Higgum, who seemed to know everyone. Sean heard nothing from Jim McBride until by chance they met at the Empire Games in New York. It was one of the last major events of the indoor season and the most prestigious. After the usual exchange of warm greetings, Jim mentioned the picture.

"I may have a lead, but I didn't think it was enough to call you."

"Anything's better than nothing," Sean answered eagerly.

"At first I passed it around to some people in the athletic department and got nowhere. Then it occurred to me, because it sounded so strange, that perhaps it was some scientist in exercise physiology who had come up with a new gimmick. Finally I spoke to a professor in the medical school who recognized the face, but he couldn't remember the name. He said the guy was well known in the school, been there forever, but he hadn't seen him for a while, and he didn't think his name was Root. I planned to show it to a few others before I bothered you."

Sean was only bothered because he hadn't learned about it sooner. By now, Root's identity had become an obsession with him. "Didn't you show it to anyone else in the medical school?" he asked, but then gathered from the look on his friend's face that perhaps he was pushing a little too hard.

"Not yet," Jim explained. "They're on the other side of town, and I hardly know any of them. This guy's wife was a friend of Helen's, and they came to dinner. I happened to think of it, and I had a copy of the photograph at home."

"Can I come up and talk to him?"

"Boy, you really want this Blue Man bad. He did send back the money with an apology."

"That's not enough. I've got to know how he did it. It's not just out of curiosity, or for revenge. I'm worried. Something isn't right. That phony name and address, and now you tell me he's from the medical school. You and I know people who cheat. What do they gain, a couple of seconds? But this was different. This guy wasn't a serious runner, and he was old. Suppose he discovered something really important, some drug. If some professional runner finds out . . ."

"Well, nobody is going to be using it tonight, so just concentrate on Tambello. When you get a chance, come up and stay with me. I'll introduce you. This professor's a good guy, if he can't help, I'm sure he'll find someone who can."

It had been a long winter. Higgum had chosen a radical training program, which had left Sean with a few doubts and many disappointments. He was competing in the mile and the 5K. Bob wanted him doing really serious speed work eighteen months before his planned assault on the longer distances. Only Higgum would have dared such a strategy, and only he could plan so far ahead. Only he would willingly sacrifice an entire running season for the possibility of greater triumphs in the future.

Sean was sufficiently concerned with the plan to consult Jim. The answer came back as if from Bob's own mouth. "Run long, once a week, ten miles one week, fifteen the next. If you do, you won't lose much endurance, and you'll be able to shift back easily. If you don't, it will take months to train again for the longer distances." Jim McBride had learned everything from Bob, including that one never argued with the master.

Sean was sick of losing. Two 5K victories against good, but not great, competition and one third place finish in the mile, that was not much to show more than halfway through the indoor season. But he was getting faster. Actual racing was so much better than just training. The track fraternity, initially shocked by his entry in a mile race, soon realized what was happening, so at least he suffered no loss of stature while he lost races.

The Stanton Mile at the Empire Games was named after a wealthy sponsor. It's prestige and the size of the prize usually guaranteed one of the finest fields of the winter season. This year, however, the presence of the Ethiopian, Christian Tambello, by consensus the outstanding miler now campaigning and the early favorite for Sydney, had reduced the size of the field. It was bad for morale to be humiliated if you had pretenses of performing at his level. Right now he could not be beaten at this distance. The field included Pachenkov, a Russian, good enough to place and eager for the appearance money and the prize money, and Bill Shoat, an aging American miler, Olympic bronze medalist six years ago and a great crowd favorite. Shoat's reputation translated to appearance money. He was past his prime but could still challenge Pachenkov for second place. Brains and experience versus youth. Shoat would pace himself and hope that Pachenkov would wear out chasing Chris. Sean smiled to himself. It would be a pleasure to watch.

Then there were the perpetual middle-of-the-pack finishers. Some he recognized, others were newcomers. As the Olympics approached, they began appearing in larger and larger numbers. But what was *his* role in this field? Well, you didn't argue with Bob, so when Sean found out that he had been entered he just trained that much harder. More of those dreaded quarter-mile sprints.

As Sean came out onto the track, Bob approached as he always did to give last minute advice. "Go out as fast as you can, run away from them, and then hold on."

Against Tambello? Sean thought, but he nodded in agreement and headed toward the starting line. Funny, he hadn't noticed any black runners. What was it that the public address system was saying that caused such a groan from the audience? Because of an Achilles tendinitis, Tambello was not running.

The gun sounded. Sean sprinted from the starting line and at two hundred yards settled into a pace he could barely maintain. Two of the youngsters started to go with him, then changed their minds, then came on again and found themselves halfway between Sean and the rest of the pack of more experienced runners. *They're done for*, Sean thought. *Rhythm is everything*. You can run fast from wire to wire; you can start fast and hang on; you can start slowly and accelerate; but you can't stop and start. At the longer distances you can use carefully planned spurts to break the will of an opponent, but not in a race this short.

Shoat tucked in behind Pachenkov, and both played the waiting game. Sean could imagine how Shoat must feel. *He wants his third Stanton Medal so badly, and with Chris out he can almost taste it. Oh, let him wait just a little too long.* It was the American Sean feared. He felt sure that Shoat could outsprint the Russian. Several runners passed the pair, nervous, unwilling to hold back so long. Finally Shoat must have realized this was not Pachenkov's day. Too much racing, too much chasing the dollar, too much spending the dollar between races. Shoat set off after the leaders. He reeled them in. Fourth with 400 meters to go. Third with 200. Past Crestwell, last year's NCAA champion, into second.

Damn curves everywhere, there's hardly any straight, thought Sean. The wooden track was narrow and had eleven laps to the mile. The curves were steeply banked and tight. Intimate. No, claustrophobic. Runners from St. Vincent trained on a similar track and traditionally did well in indoor meets. *It's an acquired skill. I guess I've acquired it, but I don't have to like it.* Instead he pictured in his mind the long straight road leading to his village, uphill, the way he ran the loop as a schoolboy. Most casual runners learned to go out in the hardest direction, uphill or into the wind, and saved the easiest way back for when they were exhausted. But Sean always ran home uphill.

His head throbbed, his chest burned, his lungs cried out for oxygen. Out of the corner of his eye he could see, but he would have known anyway, the others were coming. *Why isn't there a hill on this damn indoor track? Try to catch me up a hill sometime, Shoat, you bastard.* It was the wrong race, in the wrong place.

Sean could go no faster. He had reached a level of energy expenditure he could barely sustain. All the great runners, certainly all Higgum-trained runners, learned to come closer and closer to the fine edge between efficient running and collapse. It demanded the concentration to preserve the perfect form even when certain muscle groups cried out in pain. It required the discipline to breathe properly, slowly and deeply and in rhythm with the stride when all the natural reflexes say to pant, and especially to prolong the exhalation phase against the desperate urge to gasp for new air. When a single component of this carefully coordinated effort begins to fail, efficiency drops and it is necessary to slow to avoid total collapse. An experienced rival like Shoat recognizes these subtle changes and goes for the lead.

I will die on this track before I let you pass, Shoat. Sean left the final curve. The straight ahead was lined with trees and it went uphill. He felt Shoat. He heard him. How could he have heard him above the roar of the crowd? For the spectators this was almost as good as if Tambello had run. An American favorite was running down a popular European who had dared to stray into the wrong distance. He felt the footfalls on the tuned track in time with his own. Up, up the hill he went and through the tape with Shoat on his shoulder.

Gasping for air, he doubled over in pain. Two experienced aides straightened him up as others were doing to Shoat on the opposite side of the track. He was surprised at how quickly he recovered. Shoat approached, threw his arms around his shoulders. "You SOB, you stole it," he said but with a smile. "You got real guts. You distance guys love pain."

"Thanks, thanks," was all that Sean could mumble.

"It was my fastest time of the year. Would have given Chris some trouble," Shoat said.

"It was my fastest time ever," Sean answered.

Sean acknowledged the cheers, repeated as he stepped onto the podium to receive the first-place medal. Crestwell was third. He was delighted with himself but clearly in awe of Sean.

"I didn't know you could do that," Crestwell said shaking his head.

"I didn't either," Sean replied. "Good luck. You have a great future."

After the award ceremony, he showered and dressed. Bob Higgum was waiting in the stands watching the high school relays, always scouting, prospecting for new talent.

"You can't imagine what that did for me," Sean said to him.

"Oh yes I can." There was a strange smile on Bob's face.

"It was just what I needed."

"Yes, a run like that will clean the old pipes. It went just like I planned in September, but I can't resist saying that I don't think you believed me."

"But suppose Tambello had run?"

"Now, now, I never said you'd be the world's best miler."

"But you knew before the race."

Higgum just grinned.

"How?" Sean asked.

"Next weekend you have off. You'll be forced to withdraw from the 5K because of a hamstring. It will come upon you suddenly next Friday afternoon."

Sean stared.

"But the crowd in Chicago won't be too disappointed because there will be a last minute entry named Tambello."

"But . . ."

"It's all legal. Chris wants to run a 5K, and he'd like a chance to win. Can you believe he's thinking of moving up? Blarney. He's a miler, born to it. But it'll do him good, just like this did for you."

"How could you arrange such a thing?"

"What are friends for? I'm not training any milers, and Tom Donovan never trains marathoners. I hope his man wins gold. I hope mine does too."

Chapter 7

Higgum's trade had given Sean the time to visit Grenville. He set out on Thursday, being careful not to let anyone know that he was going to skip Chicago. An early cancellation would have brought out the 5K runners for a chance to take on Tambello at their own distance.

Sean stayed with the McBrides. "I've arranged for you to meet with Paul Sorin at the medical school tomorrow morning," Jim said. "Take the picture with you. Paul still couldn't remember the guy's name last week, but he's sure he can find someone who will. Saturday you can do your fifteen miles out here. The weather has been warm and there's no snow. There are great running roads in the suburbs, some dirt, some paved. I have them all measured. The team comes out here to train on weekends. It's a good break for them. Bob says I'm to push you hard."

"Bob is everywhere," Sean protested.

"Some of my guys will run the first half with you, and then you'll meet another group to bring you home." Jim grinned.

"Well, I'll try to keep up with your relay team," Sean replied without much concern.

"Oh, and I'll have a little surprise for you at the end. My best runner will join you at about twelve miles."

"So the stakes have been raised." So much for the relaxed weekend following his satisfying victory in the mile.

The medical school was adjacent to a hospital in the central city about three miles from the main campus. Socioeconomically it was about a million miles away. Like so many of the major urban hospitals, it was surrounded by lower class almost ghetto-like housing. *Such a small city and still it has a slum*, Sean thought, locking the doors of his car as he drove the last few blocks to the designated parking garage.

A spectacular Greek facade marked the formal entrance to one of the world's premier medical schools and research centers. It was hidden among the surrounding additions, that had taken almost every square foot of available land, eventually devouring the old commons, the tennis courts and the fountains. Sean's vision of shiny new buildings of ultramodern design with long wide corridors leading to spotless laboratories was quickly shattered. The facilities were old and the halls were packed with filing cabinets. Elsewhere storage closets had been built along the walls, thus narrowing the passageways.

"How do the fire marshals let them get away with this?" he muttered, remembering the hassle when he had attempted to store athletic equipment in the halls of the gym.

He followed the guard's directions and soon was knocking timidly on an old wooden door with a frosted glass window, no name, and 'B303' in peeling paint. No answer. He could see through the window that the lights were on. Another knock. No answer. Slowly opening the door, he found himself face to face with a bearded young man with unkempt hair in a dirty, once-white lab coat, open shirt, blue jeans, and sandals. The large room extended to include the next two doors from the hallway.

Long rows of benches were jammed with equipment unfamiliar to Sean. There were surprisingly few bottles and little glassware. It looked more like an electronics shop. Sean's knowledge of science was rudimentary at best, gleaned from a few watered-down courses in biology and physical fitness with the college athlete in mind.

"I knocked," Sean explained.

"Never bother, just come in."

"I'm looking for Professor Sorin."

"Paul's in there." He pointed to a door in the left wall near a row of old-fashioned sash windows.

Sean was greeted warmly by a short man with salt and pepper hair, probably about fifty, wearing a long sleeved shirt, a faded tie, and baggy suit pants. He had been seated behind an old wooden desk heaped high with papers and journals in seeming total disarray. They shook hands, and he waved Sean to a tired looking two-seat sofa.

"So, you're Jim McBride's friend, and you have a mystery."

"It's awfully nice of you to see me. I'm sure you must think I'm crazy."

"Not at all, glad to help if I can. Never met Jim before that dinner, but our wives both volunteer at the art gallery. Really enjoyed him. It's a whole different world over there, and we hardly get to see any of them."

Sorin spoke of the main university as if it might have been on an alien planet. "Anyway, during the party he produced this newspaper photo, heard I was in physiology and thought I might know the guy. Apparently scored some incredible athletic feat. Thought he might know some useful training methods."

"Do you work in exercise physiology?" Sean interrupted.

"None of that here," he responded with a sly smile. "Too mundane, too applied, not sexy enough. We leave it for the less prestigious universities. Far be it for us to do anything practical," he added sarcastically. "Hard to find a real physiologist here. They even wanted to change the department's name to something molecular. No Nobel prizes in exercise physiology."

"But you did recognize the picture." Sean took a copy of the photo from his pocket and handed it to Sorin.

"Right away. It's not a good likeness, but I've seen him around here for years." Sorin examined the picture carefully. "I still can't remember his name, but I know it's not Root. I looked up Root in the directory to check. There are no Roots here. It just won't come to me, but I know that I did something with him once, probably served on some committee. He could be one of those clinicians." Sorin said it as if they too were an alien nation. Sean looked disappointed.

"Don't worry. We'll find out. We'll drop down to the faculty dining room for lunch and show it around. Somebody will know." Sorin grabbed his jacket, put the picture in an inside pocket, and they walked out through the lab and down the hall.

The lunchroom was large and plain, with windows that ran from floor to ceiling. A short cafeteria line provided sandwiches and soup. The tables were packed with seeming clones of Sorin and the white-coated laboratory worker. They found seats at a table with six of Sorin's colleagues.

"Friend of a friend," he introduced Sean. "Looking for a mystery man, who's here at the medical school. I recognize him, but I just can't place him," he said, handing the picture around the table.

"That's Andy Grimes," responded an older man in a white lab coat seated at the end of the table. "Haven't seen him for a while. He must be on sabbatical."

"What does he do?" Sean dared to ask.

"Don't know. A clinician type. But he once took a course I taught. Very rare, clinician types don't do that. Too busy earning money."

"What kind of course was it?" Sean asked.

"Oh, genes and things. Don't know what he'd do with that," the man responded.

"Wasn't he the one who was killed?" another asked. He had paused with his sandwich halfway to his mouth, and Sean swiveled to stare at him.

Over his shoulder Sean heard a third person reply, "Yeah, I'm sure. The radiation guy. It was in all the papers. Hit by a car."

"I'm sorry I said that about him," the first one apologized. "Hope he wasn't a friend, but it sounds like you didn't know him well."

"No, no." Sean was too surprised to know what else to say and fell into a stunned silence.

"I'm sorry," Paul Sorin said. "We'll try to find out what happened."

The conversation at the table quickly switched back to science. It was a heated exchange, and meant absolutely nothing to Sean. *These people don't speak English, and they don't speak in sentences*, he thought.

After lunch Sorin deposited Sean with his secretary, Ceily Roberts, and then shook hands with him warmly. "Good luck, got to go write a grant."

The last remark meant nothing to Sean. He turned and smiled at the secretary. "I'm trying to find out something about an Andy Grimes. He's supposed to be a 'clinical type,' or *was*. He was killed in some kind of accident."

"Let's start with the catalogue, Mr. Rourke," Ceily responded. "Here he is. He's in, *was* in radiation oncology. It says his secretary is Beth Markham. Want the number? Want me to ring it? The address is here too."

"What is radiation oncology?" Sean asked.

"It has to do with cancer," Ceily answered. "The address is in the cancer center. I know Beth. She's been here forever. You could talk to her."

"I'm not sure I'd know what to say."

"I'm so sorry." She turned to Sean. "Was he a close friend?"

"What made you think that?"

"Just the way you looked when you mentioned the accident," she replied.

"It was just that I had to see him. It was important, and I never expected anything like this."

"Is it about his research? Did you work with him?"

"No, I ran with him. That is, I used to run with him," he corrected himself. "He was just an acquaintance."

"Take Beth's number just in case you change your mind." He took the slip of paper, thanked her, and left.

That evening Sean invited Jim and Helen McBride to dinner at a popular restaurant near the campus. "My turn," he had insisted over their protests. "You fed me last night." During the meal he described his experiences at the medical school.

"And you think he invented something, something unfair, to make him run faster?" Helen asked. She was short, with dark curly hair, vivacious, with an infectious smile. Everything about her said "warmth." The mother of two, she had also adopted the entire track and soccer teams. She was prepared to adopt Sean as well. Jim had obviously told her the whole story. "Somebody else must know about it," she continued. "They all work together. It can't be a secret. Why don't you go back and find out?"

"Damn, I didn't even think of that," Sean said. "There could be others in on it, and we have no idea who they are."

"I didn't mean it like that," Helen added quickly. "They can't all be involved in cheating. I meant others would know what kind of research he did. In fact it's hard to believe someone as famous as Dr. Grimes would cheat in a race. He was treating a close friend of mine for breast cancer. She thought he was wonderful and was horrified when he died. Now she can't bring herself to go to anyone else, although I keep telling her she mustn't delay. It's been more than two months."

"Two months?" Sean looked surprised.

"Yes, I think so. Sometime in February."

"But then he was killed *before* I got the note and the money. Someone else *must* be involved," Sean said trying to conceal his anxiety. After hearing that Grimes had been killed, Sean thought his search had come to an end. Now, he realized, it might only be starting.

Next morning was sunny and cool. Forty-two degrees. Not perfect running temperature but a luxury, almost tropical, for those who tried to train outside through the winter. Jim's runners arrived on schedule at eight. After the usual ritual, stretching, drinking, nibbling the last Power Bar, the first group of undergraduates set off with Sean.

"Why don't you come with us?" Sean asked Jim. "Looks to me like you're getting a little heavy."

"I'd be happy to show you how it's done, old buddy, but I have to drive the second relay team."

This group of six undergraduates was to accompany Sean for the first seven and a half miles. They set off through the attractive suburb along a rural road with almost no traffic. The students were impressive. They chattered about school. Sean questioned them about their careers and aspirations.

They say you should never run so fast that you can't talk, Sean thought, *and these students talk nonstop.* Two had already been accepted to law school. There was a physics major and a molecular something major, already accepted to medical school, and an economist going to graduate school. No dumb paid athletes here.

"Chip is in labs all day," one of the lawyers-to-be remarked, "and never gets to practice with us during the week. He should be the best. He always is in September, and then we all catch up during the year."

"I try to run in the morning," Chip said, "and Jim often comes out to help. He understands."

At the midway point they met Jim's second group of students who took over for the first. Chip and the economist-to-be stayed on. The other four went back with Jim. The students were good company, and Sean began to see the appeal of coaching at a place like Grenville. They ran for fun and they trained hard, but they didn't have the pressure of using it to earn a living. He wondered, though, how he would feel coaching athletes who really were never going to compete at the highest levels. Would it be frustrating? Would he just get tired of it after a while? Would it seem like a waste of his time and effort? He did volunteer as the coach of a club for underprivileged teenagers in central Philadelphia, but that was different.

As they approached the twelve-mile mark, Sean spotted a slender figure stretching against a tree trunk. The short dark hair fooled him at first, but as they drew near he saw that it was an attractive young woman, who began to jog slowly in place.

So this was Jim's surprise, his best runner, Sean thought. Shouts of "Hi Susie, Hi Suz," came from the undergraduates.

"Now Jim will get you," Chip warned. "She's better than any of us, and he springs this trick on us all the time."

The intense young woman ran beautifully. Her feet seemed hardly to touch the ground. She was one of those natural waif-like runners, whom one could only watch in amazement. *Zola Budd's twin,* thought Sean.

The others dropped back, and Sean and Susie ran side by side to the finish. Jim greeted them. "Isn't she great?" he said, grinning from ear to ear. Breathless, Sean could only nod his agreement. "If only she could train seriously, she'd be the best runner I ever had, NCAA champion, Olympics, anything. She's going to Oxford on a Rhodes. I'm trying to convince her to run for Paul Hopwell. He'll owe me big for that."

Sean added his words of praise before the undergraduates drove back to the college leaving Sean and Jim to ponder how best to approach the mystery of Dr. Grimes, "Root."

Chapter 8

Sean waited anxiously for Monday when he could call Beth Markham. *I just don't do this kind of thing very well,* he thought. *Maybe I should hire a private detective. No, that would be silly. I just have to do it myself.* Finally, he dialed. A pleasant voice, dignified and reserved, answered.

"I tried to find Dr. Grimes last Friday when I was visiting Grenville, and I was shocked to hear the news."

"Oh, are you the person Ceily told me about?"

"I'm a friend of Paul Sorin, and she was kind enough to help."

"She said you knew Dr. Grimes from running or something?" She paused. "You must not see him very much if you hadn't heard."

"No. We raced together once, and he asked me to come and see him if I ever visited Grenville."

A pause. Suspicion?

"I'm so sorry then that we couldn't help you."

"Do you think I might come and talk to you about him sometime? I mean I have a friend in Grenville whom I visit frequently. It's Jim McBride, he's the track coach," he stammered. "I'd just like to find out more about him and what happened."

"I'm not sure that's really appropriate. And it's so difficult to think about the accident, maybe we should just let it alone."

"But it would take just a few minutes."

"Where did you say you were from, Mr.—?"

"Rourke, Sean Rourke, and I teach at St. Vincent's in Philadelphia."

There was a long pause. Then in a much more subdued voice she said, "It seems like such a long way to come for nothing." Was she weakening?

"No, I come up all the time anyway. I'll just give you a call the next time I'm there. Thanks a lot."

"Well, I don't know . . ." But he had hung up.

Sean was kept busy for the next two weeks preparing the track team for the upcoming eastern intercollegiate championships. St. Vincent's had its usual group of promising runners, many recruited from abroad, including for the first time two from Africa. The warm spring had been kind to the runners at the northern colleges. Their training was far ahead of usual for that time of year, and they were ready for the heat of Washington, D.C. Much to the delight of Sean and Bob Higgum, the team was quite successful, winning five medals and garnering three fourth place positions.

Susie Fredricks was the only student from Grenville who had qualified for the championships. Sean watched her work on a term paper between heats and win the 5K final by more than a hundred yards. *If only she had been born really poor and needed a scholarship,* Sean thought.

Bob joined him in the stands. "Now that's a *real* runner." He pretended to have no interest in the women's events but seemed to know all about Susie. Was that because of Jim, who was there coaching her, or had he noticed Sean's attention? "There's gold all over her. Ha, ha. Maybe the wrong kind of gold. She's not hungry enough, or mad enough."

"I'm not hungry or mad," Sean quipped.

"No, but you're driven, and maybe by the best reason of all."

Sean didn't want to ask what that was.

* * * * *

The following week Sean was back at Grenville, determined to meet with Beth Markham.

He and Jim were in the den discussing strategy.

"She obviously tried to discourage me from coming, when I spoke to her on the phone," Sean said.

"She probably doesn't want to talk to anyone about it."

"It was more than that. I'm sure that she recognized my name."

"Maybe she's the one who sent the money. Look. I found a copy of the newspaper article about the accident." Jim shuffled through some papers on his desk and came up with a clipping. "It *was* in February, so it did happen a couple of weeks before you got the money."

Sean leaned over his shoulder, and they read together.

"Not much here. Crazy. Middle of the day. Country road," Jim muttered.

"And no leads on the bastard."

"No, and I don't think they've found anything since," Jim added.

"Pretty famous. Look at that list of honors." Sean whistled.

"No good to him now."

"No. But it makes me that much more anxious to find out what kind of research he did. I think I'm just going to appear in Ms. Markham's office, unannounced, maybe shortly before lunch hour."

Jim's copy of the university directory provided the number of Beth Markham's room in the Department of Radiation Oncology. As Sean approached, he could see through an open door a slim, brown-haired woman sitting and typing at a desk positioned to guard the entrance to an inner office. Four holes in the wall above the doorway and a rectangular patch of unfaded beige paint were all that was left of a nameplate that must have been in place for many years. Miss Markham's name was on her desk. The office was not as neat as Miss Markham. It was strewn with half-filled boxes. Papers and books were heaped everywhere, on top of shelves, filing cabinets and even on the floor.

"Hello. I'm Sean Rourke. I spoke to you on the phone last Monday." She visibly recoiled. "I was up visiting again, you know, Jim McBride, helping him with the runners." He kept searching for something to say. "And I thought I would come to chat, as I said I might. Well, I was right here. I know I should have called, but I was right here. Could we—I mean do you have some time? Are you free? It looks like you're moving." Foot in mouth. "I'm so sorry. Those must be Dr. Grimes's things."

"I'm trying to organize them, but there's only so much time in the day. I'm assigned to two other doctors now. I need a break." She looked crestfallen.

"Then it's time for lunch."

"No, I can't," she said.

"But you said you need a break. Someone else can cover the phone, and it looks like you've filled enough cartons for one morning. Come on, it will make you feel better to talk about it, and I'm a good listener." She nodded and reached for a coat in the closet by the door.

After a pause in the ladies room she seemed more composed, and soon they were out on the street leading away from the hospital. The weather was warmer, and sidewalk vendors were peddling lunch to the medical center employees who had emerged from their labs and operating rooms to sample the first of the spring weather.

"Where to?" he asked.

"There's a nice little restaurant under one of the art galleries," she replied. "You don't need reservations, and the food is good."

Ten minutes later they were seated at a small corner table by a window that opened onto a subterranean courtyard. The other diners were university types, a little better dressed than those he had encountered in the faculty dining room.

"Would you like a drink? Some wine?"

"I never drink at lunch while I'm working."

"I don't drink much, usually just wine with dinner. I'm a professional athlete, a runner." Sean thought he saw the slightest expression of fear cross her face. Was it because of what he had said? "One can't hurt." He turned to the waiter and ordered two glasses of Pinot Grigio. Perhaps it would help her to relax.

They talked around the topic. The weather was warm. The restaurant was nice and so convenient. The wine was good, but they shouldn't drink too much. The area around the hospital was improving. Someday soon you might be able to walk to the central university without wishing you had a gun. Now apparently you went by shuttle bus, Sean had learned. Finally the purpose of the visit could be put off no longer.

"How long did you work for Dr. Grimes?"

"For more than twenty years."

"You must have known him very well." He almost regretted the words before they were out of his mouth. Had they been romantically involved? Sean wondered. Probably not. He had to say something. "I ran against him in a race. He was very good. I never had a chance to know him very well, but he told me that I must come and visit him if I ever got to Grenville. I didn't. I mean I wasn't coming to Grenville very often. But he seemed so nice, and he must have loved running a great deal. I always planned to visit him when I had the chance. But when it came, it was too late."

She said nothing, and the expression on her face kept changing from wonderment to profound sorrow to . . . something else.

"Then since I had been looking forward to it so much, I just had to find out something about him. I really didn't know him well at all."

"That's the only time you ever saw him?" she asked incredulously.

"Yes," Sean admitted. He could hardly tell her about the false name and the picture.

"He ran a lot and biked too. He worked twelve hours a day, but he would either come in late in the morning so that he could run before work, or come in at six so he could run after. But I didn't know he was ever in a race." She paused. "Of course, he ran the New York Marathon once. That's a race. But it wasn't like he ran to win. He just ran to run, to do it, like others in the medical school. Many of them run in New York. He used to joke about getting too old for it."

"Do you know how fast he ran the marathon?" Sean asked eagerly.

"No. It wouldn't mean anything to me anyway. But he had a picture of himself crossing the finish line, two years ago I think, and there's a clock in the picture. I know because I just packed it." The waiter served the pasta.

Beth looked up. "How could he be hit by a car? Who would believe it? He was so careful. He even wrote a letter once to the local newspaper about traffic safety. I typed it myself. They were going to pass a law that you had to run on the left-hand side of the road, and he tried to tell them that sometimes it was better to be on the right-hand side, you know, depending on the curves and things. And he was running near his house, where there never was much traffic."

Sean knew some of the details from the article Jim had found. The thought of a hit-and-run accident made him cringe. He could remember several close calls. Beth was wiping her eyes with her napkin. They had to get away from all this talk of death.

"What does a radiation oncologist do?" he asked.

She tried to compose herself. "He treated cancer patients with radiation. Many of them were cured. There were patients he had treated twenty years before who still came to 'follow ups.' They loved him. He was really good. Everybody in the university who got cancer came to him. But the whole department is good, it's a wonderful department. People come from all over, patients, other doctors. And, then, there's all the research. I know. I type the grant applications, dozens of them. There are millions of dollars of research grants in this department."

She was regaining her composure. Sean sensed that recalling the old days was easier for her than dwelling on the nature of this death.

"What are these research grants?" he asked. It sounded like a safe topic, and he remembered that Paul Sorin had said he had to write one.

"When the scientists have a research idea, they write a proposal describing what they plan to do, and why, and asking for money to do it," she explained.

"They ask the medical school?"

"No, no, the medical school never gives them anything, at least that's what Dr. Grimes used to say. I think it gives them some, but he meant that it doesn't give them enough. The big money comes from outside, from the National Cancer Institute, 'NCI' we say, and the Leukemia Society, and the American Cancer Society and a few others. I know the due-dates by heart. There are just certain times when they accept the applications."

Trying to stick to safe topics, Sean asked, "Did he have any family?"

"His wife is dead. That was the worst thing we ever went through. Well, almost the worst. He has two children. They don't live around here, but one of them, Sally, came to help me with the office. She took some personal things and financial records, but they weren't one tenth of the total. The rest was left for me. But I can't complain, she's doing his house. It must be impossible. He saved everything. I've been working for weeks trying to clean out the office. You saw it this morning. Nobody even wants to be involved. They treat it like a shrine. I guess I'm part of the shrine too."

"Did Dr. Grimes do any research that might have involved his running?"

"What do you mean by that?" Beth asked.

"Well, you know, anything that would be related to exercise or exercise physiology or something like that."

"No, his research was entirely related to cancer."

"Are you sure?"

"Of course, I'm sure. I'm the one who typed all the grant applications and all of his papers. I would know if any of them involved running."

"But it might be in a roundabout way," Sean suggested. "Perhaps something to do with hormones? Don't they use them to treat cancer, and some of the runners use them too?"

"I don't recall that his work involved anything like that, and I can't think of anybody else in his group who was doing it either. Why are you so interested?" She stared directly at him.

"Just curious." Sean looked away. "I think he wanted to talk to me about some research. I told you, I'm a professional runner."

"You do it for a living? You must be good."

"I was in the last Olympics."

Sean could see that Beth was becoming uncomfortable. She glanced at her watch. "Oh, it's way past my lunch hour. I really have to go back."

"But you said you didn't have anything pressing."

"No, but that doesn't mean that I should stay out past my lunch hour. There's plenty for me to do."

"Well, wait. I'll get the check and walk you back."

"No, I can go back by myself. Thank you for the lunch, Mr. Rourke." And with that she turned on her heel and walked out of the restaurant.

Sean was left to sit and wonder. *She seemed to get so upset when I asked about the research, and also when I mentioned the Olympics. She must know more than she's letting on.*

Chapter 9

Beth returned to the office, feeling angry and confused and guilty about the letter. Who was this Rourke, really? Was there such a thing as a professional runner? She guessed there must be. But he obviously wasn't telling her the whole truth, though there had been plenty of opportunity to do so. He was pumping her for information, and she had given him too much.

Why hadn't someone else found that damn money, like Grimes's daughter? Could she get into trouble for having waited two weeks before she sent it? Would someone think that she had meant to keep it? That would never have crossed her mind. However, she had thought of burning it and the note. What had Grimes been doing? She knew enough about his professional budgets to know that he would never cheat. Usually he didn't even bother turning in his expense accounts for trips and meetings, unless she badgered him to do it. And he obviously intended to send the money back to Rourke, but he hadn't done it. Anyway, how could anyone possibly know when she had found it and how long she had waited before she sent it.

Thoughts tumbled through her head as they had often in the last few weeks. When no satisfactory explanations came to mind, she constructed unsatisfactory ones. In her wilder fantasies he was murdered because of unpaid gambling debts. But she knew that was ridiculous. How could he have been killed on the road? It just didn't happen in real life. But it did, of course, she knew. An undergraduate had been killed about two years earlier in a similar accident. Rourke didn't look like a policeman and certainly not like a gangster. No, he actually seemed quite nice. But if he had the money now, why was he here?

Well, there has to be a way to check on him, Beth thought. *There must be some record if he really ran in the Olympics.* She was sitting at her computer thinking instead of typing.

"Everything is in here somewhere," she said out loud. She closed Word Perfect and called up Netscape. "Atlanta and Olympics and Results," she instructed the Alta Vista search program.

There's the one I want, "Track and Field." I wonder which event. Well I'll try them all. There aren't that many. Hmm. There he is, sixth in the 10,000m. That must be meters, they're like yards. That's maybe five miles, same as Dr. Grimes used to do. How can he earn a living if he was only sixth? Maybe it's like horse racing and you don't have to win to get some money. Anyway he must be what he says he is.

Now that Sean seemed less threatening, her curiosity began to take hold. *Maybe he knows the answer. Maybe this is my only chance to find out. He said he was here for just two days. Suppose he never comes back. I wasn't very friendly.* She reached for the university directory. *McBride, McBride, here he is, head coach, men's track and field.* There was no answer at the office. *I can't call his home. Guess I'll just have to wait until tomorrow.*

But by evening her curiosity had won. She dialed McBride's home number. A woman answered.

"Is James McBride at home? This is Beth Markham. I work at Grenville. I want to ask him about someone, a runner." She felt she owed the woman some kind of explanation.

"He's about to eat."

"Please, it's important, and it'll just take a minute."

"This isn't about Sean Rourke?" Helen paused. "Are you Dr. Grimes's secretary or ex-secretary or, I'm sorry, or whatever, whom Sean talked to today?"

"Yes."

"He's right here, himself, I'll get him."

"No, wait. I—I wanted to find out if he's—he's for real."

"Well, he's really eating his real pasta right here, right now." She laughed. "I'm Helen McBride."

"Is he really a famous athlete?"

"He's pretty famous. He plans to be more famous next year. Here he is."

"It's Dr. Grimes's secretary." Helen turned to the room. "Says she wants to know if you're real. I told her you eat like you're real."

Sean rose from the table and took the phone from Helen.

"Hello, how are you. So, you're checking up on me. Satisfied?" A pause. "No, I can't now. I'm at a dinner party," he responded, exaggerating the formality of the evening. There was only one other guest, and that was Susie. "Tomorrow, Saturday. Which guard? That's the second entrance after the one I used today. Great. Nine it is. Goodby and thanks."

"Is that the Dr. Grimes from the medical school?" Susie asked as he returned to the table.

"It was his secretary." He looked into her face. It had taken some maneuvering to arrange this "date." "Hey, don't be a cradle robber," Jim had responded when Sean suggested that Susie might enjoy a home-cooked meal.

"He's not," Helen had said. "She's twenty-two and a senior. Sean's only three years out. He just seems more mature."

To Sean, Susie looked very young indeed, like one of those pre-pubescent Romanian gymnasts, except that they all were short and Susie was perhaps five foot six. She was thin, "painfully thin" his mother would have said, but not "concentration camp survivor" thin. The muscles were all there, anything but wasted. Her beauty was in her face. Audrey Hepburn, an Audrey Hepburn who flew over the ground without touching it, so smoothly and seemingly effortlessly. No breasts, no buttocks, not for Playboy, but maybe for him. The "wondrous Susie" he said to himself. Who had first called her that, one of the undergraduate runners? It clearly meant "unobtainable."

"Wasn't he killed?" Susie looked from one to the other.

"Hit by a car while he was jogging," Sean explained.

"That's a lesson for all of us," Jim admonished.

"I thought so," Susie said. "A person I know, a friend from childhood, named Ted Whitfield, worked in his lab several years ago. He had a great time, and really liked Grimes and one of the post-docs, Ann something, who taught him the lab techniques. He could never stop talking about her. Said she was the most brilliant person he had ever met. I started out in molecular biology my freshman year and thought of working with someone in the medical school myself. Many undergraduates do it. It looks good on the resume for medical school, and some say they learn more in the laboratories than they do in class. But then I switched to environmental studies."

"Did you find it more interesting?" Helen asked.

"Well, it just seemed more important. In the long run it would affect so many more people. And Grenville recently received a major gift, millions of dollars to strengthen the program. It's a very exciting time."

"But can you study that at Oxford?" Sean asked, already thinking of missing someone he hardly knew.

"I'll do some biology and some political science, mainly government," she replied. "I think that combination appealed to the committee."

"Yeah, that and the three-point-nine average and the track and the volunteer work and on and on. She just blew them away," Jim bragged.

For Sean, the meal ended too soon, and Susie left to drive back to school in her own car. Sean was excited about the prospect of meeting again with Beth Markham, but it was Susie who occupied his thoughts.

Chapter 10

The next morning, after an early run, Sean drove back to the medical school. The outside entrance to the Cancer Center was locked for the weekend, and Sean had to enter the main hospital and make his way through a series of tunnels that connected the buildings.

Beth was seated at her desk when Sean found her. She arose and led him into Grimes's adjacent office and closed the door behind them. It was a scene of disarray, even more so than the outer office. Half-filled storage boxes covered most of the floor, and the extensive bookshelves were largely empty. Fade marks on the wall showed where pictures had been removed.

"Just put them on the floor and sit there." Beth motioned toward a stack of brown workbooks on one of the upholstered chairs that, together with a couch, and an old-fashioned desk and a desk chair, made up the furnishings of the room. She sat at the desk. "I was doing pretty well with the cleaning until they told me last week that I had to do the lab offices too. Then they dumped all this stuff here."

Sean's eyes were drawn to several framed pictures on the desk and on adjacent counter tops, obviously ones that Grimes's children had not wanted to save. Most were group photographs from professional meetings. Blue Man was easily recognizable.

Beth watched him without speaking. Finally she rose and searched through a box on the far side of the desk. "This is the picture of the New York Marathon I told you about. It's a good likeness. Sally looked at it and turned it facedown. She said it would always remind her of how her father died." She produced a mounted photograph of Grimes accompanied by several other equally tired looking runners at the moment of crossing the finish line. Above their heads was a banner proclaiming New York City Marathon Finish Line and the official clock at three hours, twelve minutes. *The standard commercial photograph that's sold to participants*, Sean thought. Grimes looked suitably exhausted but jubilant.

"I was very disturbed by our conversation yesterday," Beth continued as Sean stared at the picture. "I think we both know that we were not being completely honest. If we're going to get to the bottom of this, and I want to just as much as you do, we're both going to have to be completely open and straightforward." Sean had not said a word.

"You see, I know that you're here because of the two thousand dollars. So do we have a deal?"

Sean nodded assent. "Were you the one who sent the money?"

"Yes."

"Where did you get it?"

"I found it while I was cleaning out Dr. Grimes's desk. It was in an envelope with your name on the outside and 'St. Vincent University' written underneath. The envelope was open and it contained the money and the note that you received. At first I didn't know what to do with it, give it to his daughter, or maybe take it to the chairman. But the truth of the matter is that the note upset me terribly. I didn't want to believe that he would ever have cheated anyone, so I just kept it for several weeks without telling anyone."

"For several weeks!"

"Oh, I wasn't going to keep the money, although I *was* tempted to just destroy it. I kept trying to think of some reasonable explanation of what he could have done, but none seemed to make any sense. It seemed obvious that he wanted the money sent to St. Vincent's. I didn't know your address but felt sure they would find you, especially once they saw what was inside. I didn't add a note or anything, just assumed that you would know all about it."

Sean laughed. "Well I almost didn't, but that's a long story. I finally decided that it must be from Grimes, and that I had to come up here and talk to him about it." No sense telling her about the phony name and all of the detective work it had taken to find Grimes, even if they *were* going to be more open now.

"When you first called, I didn't want to see you. I was really frightened. I didn't know whether you were coming to collect a debt, or were an investigator of some kind. And even yesterday at lunch I wasn't really sure that I could trust you. I was afraid that I had said too much. And then, of course, I called your friend McBride, and his wife said that you really were who you said you were." Sean reddened. "What did she mean when she said you were going to be more famous next year?" Beth asked.

"She hopes that I'll do well in the next Olympic games," Sean answered. "That's what makes a runner really famous and prosperous."

"What was the money for?" she asked. "Why did you want to come up here to see him? Wasn't it enough? I sent everything that was in the envelope."

"No. It was exactly the right amount," Sean answered. "Thank goodness."

"How did he cheat? What did he do?"

"He beat me in a race, and he couldn't have done it fairly."

"How do you know?"

"Just look at this picture." Sean handed it back to her. "He ran a marathon in three hours and twelve minutes. That's a good time for a fifty-year-old man. He was a good amateur runner, but I would have finished an hour ahead of him, that's ten or twelve miles. There's no way that he could ever beat me fairly."

"But how could he cheat? You mean he didn't run the whole race or something?"

"No, I'm sure he ran the whole race, and I know how fast he ran the last two miles because I saw him. No, he must have taken something."

"But don't they check those things, like those hormones and things that people take. Don't they know that?"

"Well, this wasn't a hormone. Probably it was some kind of stimulant or something."

"Don't they test for them too?"

"Not always, but actually they did test in this race, and they didn't find anything."

"So then he didn't cheat. You don't really know that he cheated."

"I know he cheated. He's a doctor, a famous scientist. He must have discovered something that they didn't detect with the regular screens. That's why I'm so interested in it."

"You mean you want to use it yourself, you mean in the next

Olympics so that you'll do better than sixth."

How did she know that? She's been checking up. "No, I hope to do better without it." He laughed. "But if he developed something that's legal, I'd certainly like to try it. More likely, it's not legal. I don't cheat. I just don't want anybody else to be doing it *against* me."

"But why did he have to give you the money? Did you find him out somehow? Was he paying you off? Were you blackmailing him?"

"No, no, no," Sean shook his head. "I didn't even know who he was, and I certainly didn't know how he did it. I still don't know. The two thousand was the first prize. He was giving me the prize that I should have won."

"But doesn't that show that he wouldn't cheat? He never cheated anyone. And he had tons of money, and he certainly wouldn't cheat for two thousand dollars. He wouldn't cheat for anything."

"You know, now that I'm learning about him I think you're right. One of the officials told me after the race that Grimes didn't want the money. He kept telling them he was an amateur and wasn't going to take it. They finally just shoved it into his hand, and then he got into a little red sports car and drove off. He wouldn't stay around for the ceremonies or anything."

"That would be the Porsche. It was his favorite," Beth interrupted.

"Hmm. Finally it's starting to make sense. This was a little race in the middle of nowhere. He probably never thought that there would be cash prizes, or urine testing, or people like me in the race. And anyway, maybe he didn't even know whether he would win the race. He was just trying something that he discovered, and it worked a lot better than he thought." Sean was thinking out loud. Then he smiled. "He must have loved it. What runner wouldn't? It's like a dream, to find some way to perform like that, and maybe it was even legal. Of course, it wasn't legal in spirit, and it would only be legal until they discovered how he did it and banned it," he added ruefully. "Even so, he must have had a great time."

"But what could he have discovered?" Beth asked. "He didn't do that kind of research."

"I don't know, but I've got to find out. In a way, maybe his sending me that money was an invitation. He must have known that it would just be a matter of time before somebody learned what he had done."

"Well, I'm sure he never meant to cheat you or anybody else, and I don't think we should go around telling people that he did. I like your theory that he didn't know how well it would work and he didn't know that he would win."

"He certainly wasn't trying to cheat me out of the money. Look, all I want to do is find out how he did it so that no one else can use it. If you'll help me do that, I'll never tell anyone the real story." She nodded in agreement. "I'll just tell people that I met him in a race and that he asked me to come and see him because he had developed some new training method or some nutrition aid or something like that, which he thought would be really good. You know, he was really excited about it, and he wanted me to try it. And by the time I finally got up here to see him, he had been killed."

"I like that idea, and he would have liked it too, that somebody knew what he had discovered. But we must never mention the money or that he did something dishonest. Is it a deal?"

"Deal." They shook hands like two business partners, or was it, Sean wondered, like two conspirators?

Beth suggested that they get some breakfast, and they walked toward the hospital coffee shop. From time to time she nodded to acquaintances they passed on the way.

"You seem to know everyone," he remarked.

"I've been here for more than twenty years. Grimes and I, we were real fixtures. It's almost impossible to believe that he's gone. Here, we'll go into the Republican Club," she said, pointing him toward a doorway.

"The Republican Club?" he asked.

"Run by the volunteers. It's nicer but more expensive than the regular cafeteria." He looked puzzled. "You know, the Republicans are richer so they can afford to eat at a better place. It's a joke." If so, it was wasted on Sean, whose own idea of Republicans was more likely to include terrorists than wealthy businessmen. They settled into a booth. She chose a gooey chocolate doughnut and coffee. It had been so long since he had eaten something like that, he wasn't even jealous. He had a banana and a cup of tea.

"How are we going to find out about this discovery or invention or whatever we should call it?" Sean began. "Do you understand the kinds of things he was doing?"

"Well, I typed all of his scientific papers, so I know in general what they're about. I'm no scientist and certainly don't understand everything that's in them, but I'm sure that none of them dealt with exercising."

"Do you have copies of all the papers?" Sean asked.

"Yes, of course. We call them reprints. There are dozens and dozens of them. I could give you the most recent ones. Do you think that you'll be able to understand them?"

"Well, I'm certainly no scientist either," Sean replied. "I majored in English literature but did take some biology courses. I've always thought that I would eventually be a coach, so I've read a lot of books about exercise physiology, health problems, injuries, and things like that. And the runners' magazines are full of tips, articles on diet and vitamins and training plans. They pretend to be scientific, but sometimes I wonder."

"So, *do* you think you'll be able to read the papers?" she asked again.

"Maybe, if they're simple. If I can't, we'll just have to get somebody to explain them to us."

"It just occurred to me, if he had published this thing, then lots of others would know about it. Right? This must be something really new, something that he never had a chance to write about."

"If it comes from his previous work, then maybe we'll get some idea where he was headed," Sean replied.

"The other thing would be the research grants," Beth said. "They describe work that's planned for the future. They'd be more up-to-date, but of course, they wouldn't tell you which of the experiments actually worked."

"Do they publish the research grants?"

"No, they're just proposals, and they're kept more or less secret. They're read by the reviewers, but that's just a small number of people, and they're not supposed to talk about them. Anyway, I have all of the grant applications." Then she paused. "You know, I think it would be all right for you to read the grants, but maybe we should ask the chairman first."

"The chairman?"

"Dr. Kerr is the chairman of the department. I think it would be best if you asked him if you could look at the grants. It would be only right. I'm sure he'd let you do it. We'll just tell him what we agreed on before, that Dr. Grimes wanted to talk to you about something that would help you in your training, and that you never got a chance to do it."

"How will I get to see Kerr?"

"I'll set up an appointment the next time you come up, if he's in town. He's often out of town."

"What kind of person is he?"

"Nice, a real gentleman. I'm sure he'll say it's all right. And he'll be able to tell you whom to go to for help if we can't make any sense out of the papers. I can think of some people, but he would know best."

They had finished eating and walked back to Beth's office where, after some searching through filing cabinets, she produced copies of about twenty research papers.

"Some nice easy bedtime reading," Sean joked. "We'll soon know what kind of scientist I would have made."

Chapter 11

Two weeks had passed before Sean managed to return to Grenville. In the meantime, he had traveled to the Midwest and won a 5-K race against good competition in a good time. He returned some $20,000 richer. As his aged car chugged up the Merritt Parkway, he was eagerly looking forward to his weekend. He had an appointment with Kerr and a real date with Susie for dinner the following evening.

Sean placed considerable importance on the meeting with Kerr. It had become obvious to him that he was going to need help in trying to understand whatever it was that Grimes had discovered. He had worked patiently over the almost two dozen reprints that Beth Markham had supplied, but only his natural stubbornness had made him persevere. Reading scientific papers, was not something he took to naturally. He was discouraged not to find anything directly related to enhancing athletic performance. All Grimes's work seemed in some way related to cancer treatment. If there was a secret hidden in the reprints, it was not obvious at first glance.

The clinical papers were the easiest to read but seemed the least relevant. Usually several different cancer treatments were being evaluated and compared. He quickly learned to recognize the graphs that plotted the percentage of the patients who would be alive for any period of time after a particular treatment. It was kind of like posting betting odds thought Sean, who was amazed by what seemed the coldness of the approach. Still he supposed it must be necessary; even if just a few more percent survived that would be an enormous number of human lives saved. And it gave him a different view of the nature of Andy Grimes. He was not just some mad scientist who had cheated and beaten him in a road race.

The papers describing laboratory research were even more difficult to understand. Many of them involved treating animals that had cancer. It took Sean a while to realize that the rats and mice were raised by the hundreds, all to have identical tumors. This made it possible to fairly evaluate and compare different methods of treatment. Almost all of the treatments had something to do with radiation, which, of course, was Grimes's special interest. Many of the papers were totally confusing, but Sean soldiered on dutifully. He was determined to be able to tell Beth Markham that he had read every one of the reprints.

Sean let his mind wonder back to Susie. He knew so little about her and wondered whether she bore any resemblance to the person he was creating in his imagination. According to Jim she had been allowing her training to slip and devoting her time to the preparation of an honors thesis. The thesis was due in May, and since there were few final examinations for seniors, it was Jim's hope that she would begin serious training after it was completed. His real goal was for her to win the NCAA championships in her final year. These would actually take place after her graduation and could not possibly interfere with her devotion to her academic work. Jim clearly hoped that Sean would inspire her to increase her training. If she did well in this competition, perhaps she would continue to run after graduation, even though she steadfastly denied it.

Back to the papers. Some described chemicals, drugs, administered to the animals along with the radiation to help kill tumor cells. It seemed unlikely to Sean that any of these agents would enhance athletic performance. There was one theme, however, that caught Sean's attention. Several papers addressed the idea of giving more oxygen to the animals, or rather more oxygen to the tumors in the animals. The expression "hypoxic tumor" was used frequently. "Hypo" meant "too little."

I knew learning Greek would be good for something, he thought, recalling his classical secondary school. But what caused the tumors to have so little oxygen? And why would one want to give them more oxygen? Wouldn't this just make them healthier? Apparently the readers were expected to know the answers. Sean was sophisticated enough to recognize the importance of oxygen in exercise, but none of the things that were being tried on the animals seemed to have any relevance to athletes.

Most of the papers had several authors, Grimes himself and usually two or three co-workers. One name that appeared with regularity was Joseph Blackburn. Perhaps he could be useful in explaining some of this work.

Sean's exit finally arrived, and he began the last twenty miles of his trip along rural roads through a New England countryside dotted with small towns. *So pretty, and so different from Pennsylvania*, he thought, *even though they're not very far apart.* He wanted to be running. *Maybe I can convince Susie to join me tomorrow. Those 5K people can always use more distance work.*

After an early morning workout he found his way to the Cancer Center. Bart Kerr's office was larger than Grimes's, and it was guarded by two secretaries. Kerr was late, but Sean was ushered inside and had several minutes to examine the room. One wall was completely covered with diplomas, certificates of society memberships, honors, etc. Quite a show, thought Sean. Elsewhere there were photographs, Kerr lecturing, Kerr attending a banquet, Kerr with a group of scientists, Kerr meeting important individuals, Kerr with his family, Kerr's children, Kerr and his boat, Kerr with his dogs. From the appearance of the office Sean took an instant dislike to the man. It was totally unwarranted, as he was soon to realize

"Sorry, sorry," Kerr said as he rushed into the room. "Let me get you some coffee." Of course, it was the secretary who brought the coffee several minutes later.

Kerr wore a long white clinician's coat with his name embroidered in blue thread above the pocket containing his radiation badge. He was of average height and build, but he seemed to take over a room when he entered. Perhaps it was the red hair, now fading, or the ruddy complexion, or just the vigor of his movements. Several small scars on his face said to Sean, "ex-athlete." Kerr was used to being the center of whatever activity was at hand, probably with good reason.

"Beth Markham told me a little about you," he began, leaning back in his chair and placing one foot on the desk, as if announcing that he would be taking a short break from his busy schedule. "She said you were a friend of Andy's and that you had met him running.

You're a famous runner, an Olympic runner, isn't that right?"

Sean flushed, embarrassed. "I ran in the last Olympics, but I don't have any medals to show for it. I'm hoping to do better next time."

"Still, that means you're very good. Andy Grimes wasn't a serious runner. He just ran for fun. Anyway, Beth said that he told you he had developed some new training method and wanted you to try it, but by the time you got up to see him he had been killed."

"That's right," Sean replied, hoping that Beth had not overdone her job. "I didn't know Andy really well," Sean paused. It was the first time he had ever used his first name. "but he was so enthusiastic about his discovery. He said that it had helped him tremendously, and he was sure that it would help me as well. He wanted to try it out on a really first-class—well you know what I mean—a really serious athlete. He wouldn't even tell me what it was about, just said come and he'd show me. At first I didn't think much of it. People are always trying to give us advice. They have diets, or vitamins, or food additives that they're sure will help a runner to break a world's record the next time out. Most of them don't do anything at all. But then when I found out later that Andy was a famous doctor at a famous medical school I thought there might be something to it."

"So you came up to try to find out?" Kerr asked.

"Yes. At first when I heard about the accident I thought that would just be the end of it. But I have a friend here, Jim McBride, the track coach, who knew of Grimes. And his wife knew Grimes very well. Apparently he cured one of her best friends of cancer. They insisted that I come over here to try to find out what he was doing and to see if anybody else knew about his work. What surprised me was to find out that he was in cancer research. It doesn't seem to have anything to do with exercise physiology or anything like that."

"That's quite true," Kerr agreed. "It's hard to put the two of them together. Maybe this discovery didn't come from his professional work at all. It might be something that he learned while he was running. It might have nothing to do with what he did here."

"I never even considered that possibility. I just assumed it would be something that came out of his medical research."

"You're probably right, although I can't think of anything right now that would directly apply to what interests you."

"Beth Markham gave me some of his papers to read."

"Oh. How did you make out with them?"

"Well, I have to admit I had a little trouble understanding most of it."

"I've had trouble understanding lots of Grimes's work myself." He smiled.

"None of it seemed to be related to exercise except for some oxygen things that I didn't really follow very well."

"Tumor oxygenation was one of Grimes's special interests," Kerr explained. "In our business we try to destroy tumors with radiation, and in order for it to kill cells most efficiently there has to be a certain amount of oxygen around. In that sense the tumor starts with an unfair advantage. All the good tissues have enough oxygen, unless maybe the person is having a heart attack or a stroke, . . ."

Or is in the middle of a race, Sean thought.

". . . and most of the tumor has enough too. But not all of it. There's a small part, called the 'hypoxic' part, that doesn't have enough oxygen and is protected against the radiation. And the effect is very big. If just one in ten thousand of the tumor cells were hypoxic—that's just one hundredth of one percent of the whole tumor—it would be as hard to kill that little bit as all the rest that was well oxygenated. So you can see why there's so much interest in tumor oxygenation."

"Wow!" Sean stared, wide eyed.

"We have several people who work in this area. Some are world famous. Blackburn is one of them. A radiation biologist. You might try talking to him."

"I noticed his name on several of the papers."

"They often worked together. I think he would know everything Grimes was doing."

"Miss Markham pointed out that the papers would all represent work that was done several years ago."

Kerr nodded.

"And perhaps he wouldn't have published this if it's very new."

"Possible." Kerr shrugged.

"She said that there are things called grant applications that describe work that you propose to do, so perhaps the idea would be in there, and that I should ask your permission to look at them."

"I don't have any objections to your looking at his old grant applications, although I'm not sure you'll be able to understand what he wrote. But again maybe Blackburn or someone could help you. Of course, the latest stuff might not be in the grant applications either."

"I don't understand. How could he have done the research work if he didn't have any money for it? Doesn't he have to get the money from these grant applications?"

"There are other sources," Kerr said with obvious pride.

"Where does it come from?"

"Well, this is a clinical department, so some comes from patient fees. Some comes from donations. These can be our most useful sources of funds, because usually there are no strings attached. The money can be used to support innovative research, the real longshot ideas. If a prominent scientist like Grimes wanted to take off on some crazy project, he would have had the money, and he wouldn't really have had to tell anybody what he was doing. I'm not sure how much I'd have liked it if he was spending our money so that he could run faster in these little road races." He laughed. "But knowing him it would have gone for some good purpose. You might want to try the business office. They would have a record of his expenditure of these departmental funds, and perhaps that would provide some clues.

"Anyway, tell Beth that she can let you have the grants. Tell her to delete the budgets; they contain private information about people's salaries. Talk to Joe Blackburn. He's the most likely one to know what Grimes was doing, and if he doesn't know he can help you find somebody who does. Oh, another thing Joe could do is to go through Grimes's lab books with you. That's something you could never do by yourself. It would take him some time, but I think he would want to do it anyway. Maybe he's already done it. Beth should have all the records. Have her sort out those from maybe the last two years, before you meet with him. We could have asked some of the people who actually worked in Grimes's lab, but most of them have left. It's amazing how fast they all disappear when the principal investigator isn't around anymore."

Kerr faltered. It was the first real emotion he'd shown. "It's just hard to imagine that he isn't here. We were together for twenty years. He was the best person in the department. I wish I had ten more like him. Everybody wishes they had ten more like him."

"Were you here when he was killed?" Sean asked.

"God, yes." Kerr put his foot down and leaned forward in his chair. "They called me from the hospital. Someone had finally recognized him. You know he was out on the road with no identification. He was hit by a car that never stopped. I guess he died instantly. Thank God for that. Poor bastard never knew what hit him. Somebody found him and called the ambulance. They brought him here, but he was dead already. One of the surgical residents knew him. Must have seen him at some of the oncology conferences. So they called me, and I came in to identify him. He lived by himself. I called Beth and found out where his daughter lived, and then I had to tell her. Hardest thing I ever did. We often have to tell families that someone has passed away, but usually when they're dying from cancer everyone has expected it for a long time. Often they're even relieved. But that sure wasn't the case here." Kerr had become much more subdued.

"Then after I went home, I remembered that he had a couple of dogs. I knew there wouldn't be anybody to take care of them, so I drove out to his place. On the way I had to go past the spot where he was hit. The police were still there—yellow tape all over the place—looking for tire marks, I guess. They never did find out who did it. Craziest damn thing, it was right in the middle of a straight road out in the country. There's no traffic. Weather was good, no snow, roads weren't slippery. Anybody could have seen him. Broad daylight. It wasn't like they were coming around a curve or something. Maybe they were drunk or on drugs."

He looked off into the distance for a moment and then continued. "Anyway, I went down to his house. The whole thing was wide open. He had just left it that way when he went out to run. He lived in the country, and I guess out there they never lock the doors anyway. Nobody had been there. His wallet and his watch and stuff were all lying there, even his briefcase with the work he'd taken home. Some of it was spread out on a table as if he'd actually started to work before he decided to go out. Too bad he didn't keep working on it and take a day off from the running. Anyway I took care of the dogs. Cute little things. I just put them in the car. They wouldn't have done much to scare off a burglar. I brought them home to stay, until his daughter could get them. Guess it could happen to any of us." Kerr stopped and stared down at his desk. He pushed at the tip of a letter opener so that it spun around like the blade of a compass. "You ever have any close calls with cars? You must if you do a lot of running, or do you train just on tracks?"

"Yeah, I've had my share," Sean said. "The deliberate ones make you wish you had a gun."

"You mean there are people who *try* to hit you?" Kerr picked up the opener and waved it menacingly in the air as if hoping to come upon just such a person.

"They don't try to hit you, they just try to scare you or run you off the road. Kids sometimes. They think they'll have a little fun watching you jump into the bushes."

"Do you think that could have happened to Andy, and maybe somebody just got a little too close?"

Sean shrugged.

"Makes you want to find out who the hell it was. Who knows?" Kerr threw the opener on the desk. "Oh, listen," he was back to business as usual, "there's just one condition. I'll give you all the help I can, and you can tell any of the people that you have my permission to try to figure out what Grimes was up to, but if you find anything, if he really did make a discovery, then I have to know. It's important that it gets handled the right way. He has to get the credit, and if it's worth something—some of these discoveries are worth a lot of money—then there are other rules for how we have to handle it. For example, the university will have to patent it, and if there were earnings they'd go in part to the university and part to his family."

"I understand that," Sean said. "I'm certainly not here to try to steal his invention. I probably wouldn't know how. If it's a training method that really works and is legal, then I'd like first crack at it. If it works and isn't legal, then I want to be sure that nobody uses it. That and satisfying my curiosity are all I want."

Kerr rose to usher him out. "Good luck. Let's hope he discovered something really terrific right before he was killed and that you lead us to it. Without you, we never would have thought to look. It would be a good way for him to go out, something to remember him for." He shook Sean's hand and patted him on the shoulder as if they had been good friends for years.

Sean went back to Beth Markham's office and described the interview to her. "I liked him. At first I didn't think I was going to, but the more we talked the more I did. He's really straightforward. Tells you just what he thinks. He seemed to feel that Blackburn was the most likely of Grimes's collaborators to be of help. What's he like?"

"Blackburn's a real biggie." Beth laughed. "That's a local joke. He's famous, but he's huge. One of his techs told me that Blackburn holding a mouse is the funniest thing she's ever seen. Anyway he's been here for years too and did a lot of work with Dr. Grimes. He's not a doctor, I mean, he doesn't practice. He's a radiation biologist. I think he's away at a conference right now, but I can try to arrange to have you meet him next time. Meanwhile, I'll get you copies of some of the grant applications without the budgets."

"Oh, he also said that you would have the lab records and that we might ask Blackburn to go over them for us. He thought maybe the last two years, I guess that would be the new stuff that might not yet be in the papers."

"I've been trying to organize them, but I haven't managed to finish." Beth seemed apologetic. "It's been harder than I expected. I think that some may be missing."

"Missing?"

"Maybe I just haven't found them yet. I was trying to do this office first and hoping that someone who worked up there, like Ann Grossman, would do the lab. But they all left. And when the new people, who were taking over the space, began to send down boxes of records, it was obvious that I had to take charge. I'd hardly ever been up there. What a mess. The more recent notebooks were scattered around, some in the offices, but others still out on the lab benches. When I started to file them, there were a few gaps. It was easy to recognize, even though I don't know much about the work, because the books are numbered and dated. I assume the missing ones are up there somewhere and I just haven't looked in the right places. They're never supposed to be removed. I hope they aren't the ones Blackburn will want."

"Well if you could just get me the ones you have. It sounds like a long-term project anyway."

Sean left the office with a feeling of dread that he couldn't explain. The interview had gone well, and Kerr's backing would obviously open most doors. What could it be, the fact that Kerr had no easy answers, the missing notebooks, or maybe the size of this next pile of reading material? No, it was hearing the details of Grimes's death. He could see the man running on a lonely country road in the bright midday sun. He pictured him in his Gore-Tex running suit. "Blue Man." And he saw the car approach, and the collision, and the body thrown into the air. And he even saw the dogs waiting for their master to return as they must have done hundreds of times before, but this time in vain. Sean pictured them small and white, like the Westie who ran with him when he was a boy. As she grew older and he faster, she could no longer keep up and was left to wait by the door. She had been gone now almost ten years, but thinking about her still brought tears to his eyes.

Chapter 12

Leaving the hospital Sean had, on sudden inspiration, purchased a dozen roses from a sidewalk vendor for his date with Susie. But as he pulled up in front of her dormitory he felt embarrassed by the flowers on the seat beside him. Perhaps he had overdone it. Susie was standing by the curb wearing a long blue coat, stockings and real shoes. "Civilian clothes," she was to call them. It was such a contrast to the standard college uniform, a bulky sweater, blue jeans, and an Orvis parka, that he spotted her instantly among the other students. He leapt from of the car. She opened the door and would have been in before he reached the other side except for pausing to pick up the flowers from the seat. He pushed in a fold of coat and closed the door behind her. Several students stared as he returned to his seat.

"Oh, I could have managed. Are these for me?" She looked surprised and pleased and a little embarrassed.

"Yes."

"You didn't have to."

"Well, I wanted you to know that this was a real date, and I didn't ask you because of Jim."

"Oh, I knew that. I was just kidding when I said that he must have made you take me to Gino's to fatten me up."

Gino's was an Italian restaurant about a mile from the campus. The best in the town, some said, the best in the state. In the parking lot the valet opened the door and helped her from the car, but she made it to the entrance of the restaurant first and insisted on holding the door for Sean.

"Modern woman," she said with a huge grin and forced him to enter first. The long hallway was already filled with customers overflowing from the cocktail lounge. The walls were covered with autographed pictures of sports figures and entertainers and many photographs of the Grenville soccer team. They pushed their way through to the hostess and were immediately taken to a table that offered privacy but still had a view of almost the entire restaurant. Waiting customers stared after them enviously.

"Normally, it's impossible to book a table here on a weekend," Susie advised him, "but Gino is a fanatic soccer fan, and Jim is the assistant coach. They have team dinners here, and Jim brings the whole track team several times a year. When he calls, there's always a table. Sometimes, he told us once, they have to sneak through the kitchen the line is so long outside the door."

The waitress approached.

"Would you like something to drink?" Sean asked.

"Oh, yes, some wine. Let's have the Nozzole. All the food here goes better with a red, even the fish and chicken. Everything has a ton of garlic on it."

Sean ordered it. The waitress paused. Susie's license appeared in her hand as if this were a practiced ritual.

"I know." She smiled at the waitress. "Last year I looked fourteen, but actually I make it with more than a year to spare."

"I'm sorry," the waitress apologized. "We have to do it."

"Now you should ask him too," Susie teased. "Doesn't he look too young to drink?"

"Well, he looks like he might just pass," the waitress responded as she left to get the wine.

"I think they'll be carding me when I'm fifty, but it's not fair that they always ask the woman."

"With most couples the women are probably a little younger," Sean replied.

"Still it's not fair. They should ask everyone or no one." She laughed. "My father was in Boston Garden to see a Knicks game about a year ago and went for a beer at halftime. Apparently everyone was asked to show an ID. He's in his fifties, and he said the man next to him must have been in his seventies."

The wine arrived and was duly sampled and served.

"It's very good," Sean said.

"It's an above average Chianti," Susie said, "usually quite good."

Sean had discovered wine in the United States. His father and his friends drank ale or stout and could not have afforded good wine. His mother did not drink at all. He was trying to learn, but the Italian wines still baffled him. They didn't seem to be as neatly categorized as those of the orderly French. Susie was obviously well ahead of him on the subject. They ordered mixed hot antipasto, merluzzo oregenato for her and scampi fra diavolo for him.

"Must have pasta under it. Coach's orders. Pasta should be tax deductible, that's a Bob Higgum joke."

"How did you ever get to St. Vincent's? You have so little accent, I keep forgetting you're not American."

"When you're young, it fades pretty fast. I've been here for more than seven years. Funny, it doesn't seem that long. Bob recruited me to be his next great miler. He has scouts everywhere, especially in Ireland, and I had won a few age group races over there."

"What made you go into running?"

"I guess I've done it as long as I can remember, to school every day, rain or sun, on errands for my mother, along the country roads, across the farmers' fields. I loved it. I still do. Sometimes when I'm just walking somewhere I get this urge to run. As a kid I couldn't have told you why. I probably still can't. But you must know the feeling. When I started football, that's soccer to you, in a youth program, we did more formal running as part of the training. I found I liked the running better than the football. I was good enough to keep playing until the last two years in school, and to be on the first squad, but by then I was running so well that the track coach made me stop. He said he would have a heart attack watching people kick at my legs. It was the right thing. My running got much better."

The antipasto arrived, and they began to eat.

"Is your family still in Ireland?"

"Most of them. Various aunts and uncles and cousins have come to this country, most legally, but some just came and never went back. There's much more opportunity here." She was so easy to talk to. He described his village. It originally had existed just to support one of the well-known Irish estates.

"My father works for the manor house, which is now run by the government and open to the public as a tourist attraction. He's a gardener, not the most senior gardener or we could have lived on the grounds. That's his lifelong goal. Even so, I was allowed to run on the property. It had great trails."

Susie pushed the platter across the table toward him, so that he could help himself to more. Her eyes never left his face.

"He's a good man. Very quiet. Very patient. Nothing changes very rapidly in those great gardens. You put in all that work, and the benefits come slowly, but they last."

Susie was more interested in hearing about his mother.

"She's a housewife," he replied. "Here you would say she's 'just' a housewife. At home most wives still don't work. They marry late and set about having children. Most husbands don't want their wives to work. There are good things about that way, always having your mother around when you're small, but it's already started to change."

"So you came to the United States. Did you leave a girl behind?" She was staring at her wine glass.

"No, I haven't had a lot of girls to leave anywhere." He looked at her, and it suddenly occurred to him that he had never seen her wearing lipstick.

"I haven't either." Now she was looking right at him. "I mean, boyfriends. Well, there's no good name for them," she stammered.

"How did you take up running?" he asked. The waitress had cleared their plates and brought the main courses.

"It was in ninth grade, my first year away in boarding school. We were all required to take part in some sport, and after a week of being hit in the shins with field hockey sticks I decided to try something I could do by myself. I went out for the cross-country team. We had a beautiful course in the Massachusetts mountains. In the fall it was really spectacular. I think I like being by myself. When you're running no one can disturb you, and it's the perfect time to think. My best papers were composed on that cross-country course. We had a wonderful track coach, a minister, Rev. Becker. He'd run for Harvard. He loved running. We were all madly in love with him. None of us suspected it at the time but he was, well, he wasn't the kind to be involved with women. But he was a wonderful friend, the first person to try to convince me that I was good, and he converted me to flat running. I liked the 5K right from the beginning, although I've done the mile. I never lost during the last two years." She said it proudly but then added, "But I shouldn't be bragging to someone like you."

"If Jim has his way, there will be lots to brag about," Sean answered.

She looked across the table realizing that she had never seen him run in competition. He had a mass of dark brown hair and blue eyes. A thin face. Everything she could see was thin, neck, arms, wrists, hands. *Probably eats 10,000 calories a day and not an ounce of fat anywhere. He looks like me.* She remembered the time spent as a young teenager staring in the mirror waiting to see curves. Eventually she stopped waiting. *We're running machines.*

He was not really handsome. His expression was usually serious, quizzical, but he was quick to smile. And he seemed happy even when he wasn't smiling. At first glance he looked young and eager, like a schoolboy ready to recite, but a closer examination revealed the lines of a face that was used to expressing determination and strength. And the eyes were those of a competitor, with a direct gaze that seemed to capture everything but reveal nothing, always unruffled.

"I don't think that Rev. Becker ever expected to have a runner good enough to compete on a national level in college," she continued. "For him running was just recreation. 'Real pressure comes from within,' he used to say. 'Put whatever amount of time you want into it and enjoy what you get out of it. It's not the most important thing in life.' He wasn't a competitive person, or maybe he was and just pretended not to be. But he never expected that I would get anything from running except my own enjoyment. Not a scholarship. Well, I certainly didn't need one of those, or fame, or anything."

"But you did pick a college with a really good coach."

"That was totally by accident. My relatives have all gone to Grenville for generations, so the track coach wasn't important. But Rev. Becker knew of Jim and spoke to him about me. That was nice of him. He still follows my running and every now and then writes me a letter. He would never push, but I'm sure he's proud of me." She paused and sipped her wine. "It's funny though, the less pressure he applied, the more I put on myself. Since I didn't know what would satisfy him, I just worked harder and harder. Clever of him. But I'm sure he's always known that some day I'd just give it up."

"Are you going to give it up?" Sean asked.

"Yes, but I haven't had the heart to tell Jim. He's going to be so disappointed. It just makes me feel guilty, but there are too many other things to do that seem more important. I've been finishing my honors thesis and my training has really slipped."

"Jim was hoping that when the thesis was done you'd start serious training for the NCAA's."

"I know he wants that, but now I have a chance to publish my thesis. My adviser thinks it's so good that it would be accepted as a paper. That's going to be a lot of work, and I want to finish it before graduation while he's still here to help me. Of course, I'll run in the big tri-meet against our old arch-rivals. I owe that to the team, but I'm going to train just hard enough to win. Then we'll see about the Nationals."

"Be careful," Sean said, as he emptied the last of the wine into their glasses. "That's the surest way to lose, trying to set a limited goal like that."

"I've always won it in the past," she said with a shrug of her shoulders. "I think I know what time I'll need. I've run against them all before. And if I don't win, well, that's just the way it'll have to be." Susie didn't look happy about it as she said it.

"If you've cut back your practice mileage, you won't be able to finish one of those thousand calorie desserts they have on the menu," Sean said with a mischievous smile.

"Oh you just watch me," she answered and grinned.

When they left the restaurant later, Susie waited for Sean to help her with her coat, and she waited to have the car door opened. On the way back she sat silently holding the flowers. As he said good night in the archway outside of her dormitory, she turned back and pressed herself up against him with her head on his shoulder and the roses squashed between them. He put his arms around her gently. Her hair tickled his nose.

They stayed that way for a moment, then she pulled back. "Thank you for my flowers and for the evening," she said, then turned and quickly ran into the building.

Chapter 13

Sean and Bill Connors sat in a corner booth at Sparky's, a roadhouse a few miles outside of Bradsford. They were early for a long delayed meeting with Lou Gurci, a police colleague of Bill's from the neighboring town in which Andy Grimes had been killed. Two glasses of draft beer stood in front of them. "Cafe" spelled backward in red neon script glared through the window and reflected off the shiny black Formica table top, providing most of the light.

"We should have eaten here, but Mary wouldn't have liked it. It's good, and it's real cheap. They make all the money on the beer and hard stuff. The food's just a come-on," Bill explained.

The roadhouse was about three-quarters filled, and most of the patrons were eating.

"Places like this are as near as we have to your pubs. I'll bet everybody in here knows each other."

Indeed most had nodded to Bill as they entered. A number even called to Sean by name, recognizing him from the races. There was a lot of good-natured joshing. "Can't train for the Olympics on Sparky's food," someone shouted to them. Everyone laughed.

Gurci had called ahead to say that he would be a few minutes late. He was on duty, but it seemed to be the only time that they could all get together.

"I mentioned to Lou your interest in Grimes," Bill said. "He's on the force in Medford, where Grimes lived. It's about twenty-five miles from Grenville, real country. Lots of the faculty live out there. Nice if you want space. Anyway, he perked right up, insisted on meeting with you. The Grimes accident was assigned to him, and he's always thought there was something a little weird about it."

"I don't know what I could tell him except what I've heard secondhand," Sean protested.

"Lou Gurci is a darn good cop. He spent years in New York City. Took a couple of bullets. Finally said to hell with it and decided to get a job out here. He had some old friends who fixed it up for him. These are the best police jobs there are, in these little towns. The only thing that's going to kill you is boredom. I hardly ever have a serious crime to investigate. We break up some domestic stuff, give a lot of speeding tickets and try to keep the kids from drinking too much. Every now and then somebody thinks they'll come in to do some hard stuff, sell some drugs, pull a string of robberies they think the hick cops won't be able to solve, but they usually learn pretty quickly. We have all the latest gadgets, computer hookups to all the big places, everything. But the biggest thing is, we know everybody, and everybody knows us. If anything's going on, we're going to be the first to know about it."

He's so perfect for the part he just described, Sean thought as he looked across the table at his cousin's husband. Bill Conner was a big man with pale hair and ruddy cheeks. He looked like a Teddy bear. *As strong as a bear.* Sean knew it from the time they had struggled to unload the lumber for Mary's new kitchen. *He looks so bland it's disarming, but he's tough and smart, practical, down to earth.*

"This must have been quite a change for Gurci," Sean commented.

"I think he likes it. A lot of cops who get hurt just go on disability and then maybe work as a security guard or something. But Gurci likes being a cop. He just got sick of the big city."

"I can understand that," Sean said.

"Let me tell you, though, that Lou Gurci is really smart. You'll see that when he gets here. If he tells you he smells a rat, you better put away the cheese."

A short, muscular man with thinning black hair approached across the room. He wore an open neck shirt under a tan windbreaker.

"Hi, you got to be Sean." He stuck out his hand. "I'm Lou Gurci." He slid into the booth and waved to the waitress.

"Tonic water with lime." He put his beeper on the table and turned back to Bill. "I'm on third call, but Joe's out on something, so I probably should play it straight."

He inspected Sean, then got right to the point. "Bill must have told you that I'm the officer of record on this Dr. Grimes accident case. I was the first one there. A neighbor driving home found him on the road. Had a phone in the car and called 911 right away. I was only about half a mile away. No hope of doing anything. He had a real bash on his head. It must have killed him right away, but there was no glass or anything."

"Sounds horrible." Sean shuddered. "You know I'm out on the roads a lot. That's not the kind of thing I like to hear about."

"Sorry."

"Like I told you, Sean's been trying to find out what kind of research Grimes was up to, but he keeps hitting stone walls. All of Grimes's assistants have left, and some of the laboratory records are missing," Bill Connors reminded Lou.

Lou turned toward Sean. "Maybe you should just tell me the whole story right from the beginning, how you got involved with this guy."

"Well, I suppose you want the true story." Sean laughed. "I've made up so many stories to cover why I'm looking into it, that I can't even remember them anymore."

"That's how we catch a lot of the bad guys. Just tell me what really happened the first time, that'll make it a lot easier."

"Sounds like I'm the suspect," Sean said and laughed nervously.

"No, no, I didn't mean it that way." Lou waved his hand as if to dismiss that possibility. "It's just if you keep telling me what you told other people wasn't quite true, I'm never going to get it all straight."

Sean described the whole affair to Lou from losing the race to getting the money in the mail and tracing down Grimes. He told him about Grimes's phony name, Root, and about the note that came with the money.

"There's something fishy here, but I don't know how to put it all together." Lou frowned. "This case just doesn't want to be closed."

Sean squirmed to get more comfortable on the hard wooden seat. "When I'm dealing with the people down at the university, I tell them that Grimes and I met at a race and that he invited me to come see him because he'd invented something that would improve athletic performance and wanted to try it on a world-class athlete. That's the story I made up with his secretary, Beth Markham's her name, so we didn't have to go into all the business of the money and the cheating and things. She said she wouldn't help me unless I agreed not to bring up any of that stuff. Everybody seems to believe me. They all liked Grimes and have been really nice about letting me try to find out what he was up to, if anything. The funny thing is that nobody can quite figure out how his research, I mean his regular cancer research, fit in to anything like this. They've sent me around to some of the scientists that he worked with, but nobody's come up with any good clues. But there are some really strange things going on over there."

"How's that?" Lou asked.

"Well, as Bill mentioned, almost everybody who used to work with him has disappeared."

"What do you mean, disappeared?"

"This all comes from Beth. Apparently one went back to China. Another one went out to the West Coast. She was planning to go anyway but left early, and now nobody knows where she is. She's supposed to start her new job out there in September, so I guess we'll find her then. Another, an Aussie, who just worked for Grimes part time on a special project, also left, and nobody knows where he is either. He too was finishing his time, a postdoctoral fellowship in another laboratory, so he was due to leave anyway. But it just seems like too much of a coincidence. And then there's this thing about the lab books."

"What about the lab books?" Lou leaned forward.

"Well, all the research is really well documented in bound notebooks. Whether the experiments work or don't work, the results are kept forever, so no one can go back later and say there was some fraud or faking results or something."

"But what's so strange about that?" Lou asked. "Sounds like that's what they should do."

"No, no. The strange thing is that some of the books, the later ones, aren't there."

"What do you mean, they've been stolen?"

"Well, nobody knows where they are. They're not all gone, just some of them. See, there are separate books for each kind of experiment. Some go almost right up to the present with no breaks. But others have gaps, dates when we know people were working, but there are no records."

"Would the people who left take the records with them?" Lou

asked.

"The original records are supposed to stay in the lab. You know, if it's their work they could take copies or summaries, but the original records should stay there. And all the others are there except these particular ones right near the end."

"This is really fishy." Obviously a favorite expression of Lou's. They ordered another round of drinks.

"How much money is in this running business?" Lou asked. "I mean normally it'd be none of my business, and I wouldn't ask, but do you guys make a lot of money? Is it worth a lot of money to win?"

Sean never knew whether to be embarrassed or proud of how much money he made. "There can be a lot of money in it. There's more if you're from a big country like this one. In the trials for the United States marathon team for Atlanta, first prize was one hundred thousand bucks. That wasn't for winning the Olympics, just for winning a place on the team."

Bill let out a whistle.

"And there weren't even any Americans who were top prospects to win a medal. I don't know what the hell they'd have given them if they ever actually won gold. A million bucks, I suppose."

Lou rubbed the stubble on his chin.

"You know," Sean continued, "when the Olympics were in Seoul, the Korean government supposedly gave every guy who won a gold medal a salary for the rest of his life. They never had to work again. The home country really wants to win medals."

"I think I know what you're getting at," Bill said.

"Why not steal the secret and bump him off for it?" Lou drew his hand across his throat.

"But runners don't do things like that," Sean protested. "We're not angels. There are all kinds of dirty tricks, cutting people off, elbows flying everywhere, tripping, that's a little obvious, and of course you'd never drink out of a water bottle that wasn't your own. But we're not out there killing each other, literally."

"Why the hell not," Lou said. "The druggies are bumping themselves off every day for a few grand. You're talking about a guy making a hundred thousand or more. You've got too much faith in your fellow man. I could easy see somebody getting popped for that amount."

"But they'd probably get caught anyway," Sean answered.

"Maybe, maybe not," Bill added.

"You think Grimes's death wasn't an accident?" Sean asked.

Lou took a long slow drink from his glass, leaned forward to be sure the next booth was empty, and after a pause that seemed to Sean to last for minutes, continued in a low voice. "Look, I'm not going to tell anybody what you told me. Okay? You just keep quiet about what I'm going to tell you now. I think Grimes was murdered. And let me be straight with you right off, nobody at the station goes along with this. I tell them the same things I'm going to tell you, but they don't listen. To them it's open and shut, a hit and run accident. Chief thinks I'm nuts. Open cases don't look good on paper. And nobody wants to hear a whisper about murder in our fancy little town, just when lots of the rich city people are beginning to move out here."

Sean and Bill were both leaning forward and staring at Lou with rapt attention.

"But hear me out. Grimes was running along a straight road with no traffic, February but no snow, plenty of room, in broad daylight. He could have gotten off the side of the road if he needed to. The car swerved and hit him. You could tell by the tire marks. Now sometimes kids do that, they play games with the runners and the bikers, come close and blast the horn or open the door. And maybe that's what happened, and they just got too close. But I'm not buying it. Anyway then they backed up, and I think somebody got out of the car."

"But they could have backed up to see if they could help, and when they found him dead they just took off so they wouldn't get caught," Bill offered.

"Yeah, they could have, but it smells funny. I think they did it on purpose. Only problem is I don't have a motive, that's why nobody listens to me. I did some snooping, talked to the daughter and some of his friends. Got hell from the chief for bothering them, when he found out. I tell you, he and the mayor are mighty pissed at me over this. Anyway the guy's so clean he squeaks, a real saint. Had lots of money and nobody to bump him off for it. Two nice kids, already got lots of money when their mother died, can wait for dad to die to get the rest. No gambling debts, no drug debts, no debts at all, not even a mortgage. Not running around with anybody else's wife. Don't know about politics at the university, but he had the same job for years. So what's it come to?" He shrugged his shoulders.

"Nobody's dumb enough to mug a jogger," Bill added trying to be helpful. "What are you going to get, a ten-buck sport watch?"

"And there's all these other little things too, so I keep the file on my desk, and when I have time and the chief isn't looking, I think about it."

"What kind of things, Lou?" Bill asked.

"Well, I told you I saw the body. Had this whack on the back of his head. But it wasn't right. Nothing out there to hit his head on like that."

"He could have been thrown up on the car, maybe hit the hood or the windshield," Bill suggested.

"Anything's possible, Bill. But it just didn't look right. Like the body was too close to the spot where we figure he was hit."

"How about the postmortem?" Bill persisted.

"Crappy. Body goes to the famous medical center, and they do a worse job than some hick coroner. Probably don't want to cut up their buddy, don't want any pictures of him lying there naked and bloody with his head bashed in. They say he died of a blow to the head. Real big help. Don't tell you nothing you need to know. I was so pissed when I got that report I would've dug him up myself, except he was cremated."

"Boy, that would have caused some trouble," Bill said and laughed.

"Yeah, yeah, it sure would have," Gurci agreed. "Maybe I'm not being fair. They did all right. I'm just mad because they wouldn't say it was homicide, so I could get the chief off my back. I like to give them some shit. They think they're so damn good. But you know, if there is something funny going on down there, maybe this wasn't just being sloppy. Maybe somebody in the med school is covering."

"I can't believe that," Sean said.

"You got to think of everything," Lou said. "Like the tires. There's something fishy about the tires."

Sean was getting sick of the expression.

"We got great tire prints where they stopped fast. Course we got pictures of them and they're real weird looking." Sean hoped he wouldn't say fishy again. "So I sent them off to the Feds. We've got one of these new systems to do that. Comes right back what kind they are, Michelin MXM's."

"A lot of people have Michelins now, Lou," Bill pointed out.

"No, let me finish. This is a very special tire. Couple hundred bucks apiece, and they wear out fast. But real high performance."

"They'd be too expensive for kids," Sean said.

"Some kids have a lot of money to waste," Bill argued.

"Nah, the funny thing was the size of them," Lou said. "They were narrow."

"What do you mean they were narrow?"

"You know what the hot rodders do. They buy real wide tires, wider than stock. You see those Corvettes and Camaros and things. Damn tires must be a foot wide. You can always squeeze a couple of extra inches even without modifying the fenders."

"So?" said Bill.

"So, here's a guy, spends maybe a thousand dollars for new rubber to juice up his car—these sure as hell weren't original tires—and then doesn't buy the big wide ones. First of all they're better, and second they tell all your friends you got a hot rod."

"What are you getting at?" Sean asked.

"I've been thinking about it a lot. This is a guy who wanted a fast car, and he didn't want anybody to know it, didn't want to stand out. What kind of guy does something like that?"

"I don't know, maybe a guy who runs over doctors."

"Nothing's right about this case. Anyway, Sean, you've been real helpful. Couple times I've been ready to give it up, and then something always comes up. What you told me is sure going to keep me going a little while longer. Maybe we can find that motive. If anything else happens, you let me know."

He started to get up. "I better go back and see how the little town's doing." He threw some bills on the table and then turned back. "This thing he invented, it wouldn't have to be just for runners, would it? Suppose it helped the pros." He stopped. "No offense, you're a pro athlete, but like basketball and football. Suppose it made a halfback run faster. That'd really be big money. People would kill for that."

"What if you could give it to the army and make all the soldiers run faster?" Bill thought of basic training, the only running he had ever done in his life. "Maybe some country tried to steal it."

"Come on, you guys are really too much," Sean protested.

"Now wait." Bill defended himself. "Suppose you gave it to someone, like the Green Berets, before a mission, and they could all run six miles just as fast as you can. You don't think they would want that?"

Sean just shook his head.

"Anyway, nice to meet you. Stay in touch." Lou walked toward the door greeting acquaintances as he went.

Sean and Bill decided to have one more beer before returning to Bradsford.

"That's a lot of weird stuff," Sean said when Lou was gone.

"Lou goes off like that sometimes. Everybody thinks he's crazy, and then it turns out that he's right."

"Well, I don't think he's going to be right about this one, but I have to admit I don't understand it. I can still see that guy passing me on the hill. He was really hurting. Whatever he took, it didn't make it easy for him, but he was beating me all the same."

"You know, Sean, I don't like to bring this up, but you might just be in some danger looking into this thing."

"Oh, come on," Sean said. "You can't be serious."

"I am serious. You should listen to what Lou said. And some of the others who are helping track this down, they could be in danger too. Suppose somebody finds out that you're getting close?"

"Well, who's to find out. Who would even know what we're doing? And anyway, we're not getting close."

"If Lou's right, then somebody had to know about it from the inside."

"Well, I wasn't on the inside. I got suspicious because of seeing him race."

"But you wouldn't have been suspicious, and you wouldn't have put it together unless he sent you the money. He sure didn't send everybody two thousand bucks. Nah, I think it was somebody inside. Course they might think they're the only ones who know. They might not have known that he was out showing off with it. Maybe it was one of the people who was developing it with him. It could be someone who's still there, and then they'd know that you were looking."

"God, you guys all have too much imagination. Maybe you don't have enough big crimes out here, and you're dying to find a mystery."

"Well, watch out for this Blackburn fellow and the other lab people. You may be about to meet the guy who did it."

"This is crazy."

"No, it isn't. Look, maybe this has nothing to do with running. Suppose this thing cures cancer. That's what he really worked on. Suppose someone knew and tried to steal it. Boy, that would be worth plenty, not just hundreds of thousands, but anything you wanted, millions, billions."

Sean paused. "No. I'm not going to consider that. If I hang around here any longer, I'll start to think like you two."

Bill shrugged. "Anyway, you be careful."

Chapter 14

The real reason that Sean was in New York's Central Park on this warm May Sunday was to be with Susie. The pretense was lending his name to a co-ed medley relay race being sponsored by the New York Racing Club to support park safety. He had asked Susie to be a member of his team. It was impossible for her to turn down the invitation to run the 5K leg for such a good cause. If she felt trapped, she was too gracious to show it.

The race was in honor of a woman jogger who had been brutally attacked on one of the trails and left for dead but had made a miraculous recovery to run again. Today's event would raise public consciousness of violence against women and raise funds for improved lighting and more frequent patrols in the park. A number of celebrities as well as some of the elite runners based in New York City were entered. The organizers were delighted to have someone of Sean's stature agree to participate and allow his name to be used for publicity. The format consisted in sequence of a one-mile leg for men, a one-mile leg for women, a 5K leg for women and a 10K leg for men. In addition to Susie, Sean had recruited a male miler from St. Vincent's and a woman from the University of Pennsylvania, who trained frequently with his group.

Warm weather had brought out thousands of spectators and hundreds of would-be runners, for a massive 10K fun run was to begin as soon as the last of the twenty elite relay teams had started on the final leg. The park was in its spring finery following a mild winter. Flowers were in bloom, and the leaves on the trees formed a lacy green canopy over the paths, seeming to capture the warmth of the sun. European tourists were everywhere, no doubt attracted by the favorable rate of currency exchange. Many had sought the pleasure of the park for a Sunday morning.

There had been many last-minute changes in entrants. It was meant to be informal, and no strict rules applied. Not until a few hours before the start had a hastily Xeroxed program become available. Sean scanned the list of competitors. Many of the names were unfamiliar. To him that meant there would be no serious challengers. But then he laughed at his smugness. "Maybe there will be another Blue Man," he muttered.

The best of the lot had Marge Winton in the 5K and Henri Bahel at 10K. He did not recognize the names of the team's milers. Winton and Bahel were seasoned professionals, probably members of the same running club. Marge had never quite made the U. S. Olympic team, but she was of that quality. It was unlikely that she would lose to Susie.

Bahel had represented Algeria in the 10K in the last Olympics but had not made it to the final round. Sean had not heard of him since, although he knew that he was now living in the States. "Where has he been training, and what can he do?" he wondered.

The teams assembled. The mayor was introduced by the president of the club, and after a mercifully short speech in which he recalled the bravery of the honoree and reminded the audience of the importance of their cause, he fired the starting gun. The Winton-Bahel team's milers were good, better than Sean's. The male was the third to tag his teammate—batons were not being used because of the longer distances—and she managed to maintain the same placing. Sean was less concerned about the first two teams than he was about the margin enjoyed by Winton-Bahel, almost thirty seconds as Susie set off after Marge Winton. "Don't be distracted by trying to catch her. Just run your own race," he admonished Susie, as Marge left while they were still waiting for their second miler.

The women ran what was called the upper circuit at the north end of the park. The initial mile and a half was the same as the men would run at the beginning of the final leg. Susie started sixth. Runners from the slower teams trailed out behind. Marge, and then Susie, disappeared from his view. They would reappear in about fifteen minutes.

Sean hoped to be able to hear something of their progress by standing near the race officials who were in contact by walkie-talkie with the observers and water stops along the route. At one mile Marge was second and Susie was fourth, but there was no information about the times. He removed his warmup jacket and began to stretch. Near him the other 10K runners carried out the same rituals. At the two-mile mark, standings and times blared out of the loudspeaker. "Winton, 19:31; Turcott, 20:28; Fredricks, 20:42." Marge Winton had clearly come to run. She was opening the gap with every stride, and she was not one to fade at the end. Sean sipped Gatorade and waited.

The crowd noise began. You could follow the progress of the runners by the cheering along the route. Finally Marge Winton came into view. Composed and running well within herself she would wait another hundred yards before beginning her kick. Sean watched with the eye of an expert. Excellence never failed to thrill him. " I hope I never reach the point when I can't get high watching something like this. And I'll be using that high to my advantage soon, real soon, I hope." Marge started to sprint. Two hundred yards. One hundred yards. Bahel began jogging in place. Into the transition box she came at full stride, slapped Bahel's backward stretched palm, and he was off.

Sean punched the countdown button on the first channel of his quartz chronometer and waited. Finally the moving roar began again. Jill Turcott and Susie appeared running side by side. Susie was on the left. He could tell she was in trouble. The classic smooth stride was uneven, and her breathing was labored. Wise old Marge Winton had done in the competition. She stood now beyond the finish line with a smile on her face, ready to welcome her victims.

I never should have asked her to run, Sean thought, feeling guilty. *She knew she wasn't in good condition, but she couldn't say no. But how was I to know that somebody like Marge Winton would be here? Otherwise, she would have been fine. Damn, why did I take the chance?* Neither runner could kick. They were already expending energy as fast as they could generate it. Each refused to give in. *She's really tough.* He beamed with pride. They came on in a dead heat. Sean started to jog in place. He was sky high, too high. He wanted Bahel.

He felt Susie's hand and shot forward. But in the moment they were side by side he heard her gasp. "Your race, your race. Slow."

She was telling him what he had told her.

She's right, he thought. *I am too high.*

It was a Bob Higgum expression, "the perfectly crafted race." He said it over and over again like a mantra. Discipline. Discipline. Craft the perfect race. Sean went up the hill that led away from the start-finish line toward the northeast corner of the park, running comfortably at a pace that would allow him to loosen gradually. He completely ignored Turcott's teammate, who had started alongside and in his excitement had actually forged into the lead. For the first time Sean looked at his watch and compared channel one with channel two, which he had instinctively punched as he started his leg. Two minutes and thirty-two seconds. An enormous gap to make up. *More than half a mile,* he thought, *but Bahel doesn't know that, and he does know me. Let him sweat. He knows I'm back here. Let him run himself into the ground.* There were enough curves on the course to prevent Bahel from seeing him until he was much closer.

Sean had run this course in the past and had ridden it the day before to refresh his memory. He knew there was a steep decline just ahead. Down the hill he went, past the skating rink, now dry, then back up to almost the same elevation on a shorter and even steeper hill, one of the more difficult segments. It was here that Turcott's partner was left behind. South along the west side of the park, up and down a series of minor hills, until finally he passed Tavern on the Green and Fred Lebow's statue and the finish line for the New York Marathon painted permanently across the roadway. "See you in six months," he said to the statue.

Now he was in full flight. Across the southern edge of the park he went. Many in the crowd recognized him. The others could tell even at a glance that this was no ordinary runner and no ordinary effort. Casual visitors to the park stopped to stare. Accustomed to the usual weekend joggers, they were astonished by his speed. Misjudging it, a young couple with a baby stroller began to cross the road ahead of him but pulled back abruptly when they realized how quickly he was approaching.

"It's Rourke."

"Who?"

"The Irishman, Sean Rourke. He's second."

"Look at him go!"

The more sophisticated spectators had counted the gap. "You're gaining on him. He's just ahead. Go. Go." A gray-haired man in a Nike running suit leaned over an inside barrier and shouted through cupped hands, "Thirty-five seconds. You can get him." A nod of thanks. Turning north. A hill. A downhill. Toward the bicycle rental stand. Had he crafted the perfect race? *I should see him at any moment now, somewhere near Cleopatra's Needle. And I want him to see me and to panic on that steep hill leading toward the Met.*

Sean raised his arms to the crowd, which responded with a roar. Bahel heard and turned and saw. Sean started up the hill. From his earliest days he had never lacked the killer instinct. He had the ability to singlemindedly focus on what it took to win. Now he felt like an assassin stalking his prey. Bahel tried to go faster. *You've had it, fellow*, thought Sean. He continued to gain, running comfortably, past the museum and up a second little rise just when you expected it to be flat. Bahel was weakening. Around the curve at the base of the reservoir Sean twenty-five yards behind. Around the S-curve. Bahel was breaking up. Sean followed him around, and there was his secret weapon. A long uphill straight with tall trees on both sides. This time it was real. Amid wild cheering Sean went past him with a hundred yards to go.

This was supposed to be fun, Sean thought. *We were doing this for a good cause. That's what I told Susie to get her to come down here. Sure, Marge Winton ran her down, Marge Winton would have to. But how about Bahel? Was he ready for this race? Did someone almost force him to enter as I did Susie? Was he doing it just to lend his name to something he thought was worthwhile?* He looked across at Bahel and smiled. Slowing he reached out his hand. Bahel took it, and they crossed the finish line together with arms upraised.

Susie handed him a container of water and poured another one over his head. She seemed to like the effect. She threw her arms around his neck and kissed him on the mouth. "I don't like you at all," she said, grinning from ear to ear. "You're a damn lousy runner." Both sets of teammates were hugging and pounding the backs of their anchormen, and then each other, and then all eight of them. Even Marge Winton seemed pleased.

Sean had remained behind, greeting the early finishers in the fun 10K race until he finally was overwhelmed by their sheer numbers.

He signed autographs, chatted with the other runners and race officials and reporters, and posed for countless photographs, often arm in arm with some proud runner whose family held the camera. It had created enormous good will and, he hoped, additional donations.

It was early evening as Sean entered the well-appointed lobby of an apartment house on Central Park South. "This is where she lives?" he said to himself in awe. The doorman announced him by intercom to the penthouse.

"Down in a second," came from the box and was duly repeated to him.

Moments later the elevator door opened to discharge Susie resplendent in a short black dress and a single strand of huge pearls. Sean's heart leapt.

"We'll walk, the restaurant's just a block," she said, taking his arm and steering him down the steps and to the left. A few minutes later they pushed through a revolving door and entered a comfortably furnished restaurant, modern with classical decorative elements. Susie was greeted warmly by the maitre 'D.

"Miss Fredricks, we haven't seen you for so long. How are you? How is your father?" The man was short and elegant, handsome, Sean noticed, and he spoke with a trace of a European accent, but he seemed so friendly and informal.

"We have your favorite table in front or perhaps you would like to sit in the alcove." Susie thought for a moment. "Thank you, Franco. Why don't we sit in the alcove? Then if we have a great row we won't disturb the others." Franco thought this was hilarious.

"Oh, then you are planning to have a great fight, right here. That would be wonderful." He laughed and turned toward Sean.

"Franco, this is Sean Rourke, a very famous runner who is going to win a gold medal in the Olympics."

Sean was embarrassed. "She exaggerates," he protested.

"No, no," Susie continued. "He won the benefit race in Central Park this morning."

"Oh, I saw that it was going on. Well, that's wonderful. We must celebrate."

"It was a relay race, and Susie and I were both on the winning team," Sean clarified.

"Then we will have a double celebration. Champagne for you both." Franco was genuinely pleased. He led them to a table in a small alcove hidden from the view of most of the restaurant. The enthusiastic greeting had caused other diners to turn and stare. Celebrity watching was a favorite hobby in a restaurant like this. Sean wondered how the other guests would characterize Susie and him. Not likely to be movie stars, he thought.

"Father says that this is the finest Italian restaurant in New York City. He calls it 'his local neighborhood restaurant.' Unfortunately it opened just as I was leaving for boarding school, or I would have eaten here even more often. There's nothing my father likes better than good food and wine."

The champagne arrived.

"Were you glad we ran?" Sean asked after the first toast.

"Oh, yes, it was wonderful," Susie replied with enthusiasm. "It was the greatest thing I've ever been part of. I've never won anything like this before."

"I was afraid I talked you into it."

"Sean, I wouldn't let you talk me into it. I wanted to do it, and you were wonderful." Sean blushed. "You know, I've never seen you run before, in competition that is. At first I didn't realize what a big deficit I'd left you until they told me the times. That was really depressing. I thought I'd surely disappointed you. When you were out, we didn't know what was happening. All we heard from the stations was that Bahel was leading and you were second. We expected that, but they never told us by how much. Then we began to hear the roar. I knew that it was too loud to be just polite cheering for the leader. It had to be a real race. When he came around the corner, I started to count and to pray. But then you appeared about six seconds later, and I knew you had him. You just ran right past him. And then taking his hand was unbelievable."

"I've never done anything like that before, but then I thought of you and well, you didn't quite expect to run against Marge Winton, and I thought Bahel probably didn't quite expect to run against me. It was just supposed to be for a good cause."

"The press went crazy. It was on the six o'clock news and then all about how you stayed. You'll be better known here for this than anything you win."

"Maybe when I don't win the New York Marathon next fall they'll think I was just being nice." Sean laughed.

A tall elegant waiter approached. After a round of greetings and introductions he left menus and a wine list the size of a small book.

"I was so worried that you would hate me for this."

"But why, Sean?"

"For throwing you in against Marge Winton. I didn't know she'd be here."

"But you didn't throw me into anything. I came because I wanted to."

"I shouldn't have let her do you in."

"She didn't do us in. She just beat us."

"She's a professional. She did just what she wanted to."

"She didn't do anything wrong. Were you that disappointed in me? If I'd done better, you wouldn't have had so much opportunity to show off," Susie said sharply.

Sean was taken aback.

"But she outsmarted you, hanging back so that all of you would chase her and use yourselves up, and then just running away from you."

"But you don't know she did that. You couldn't even see what she was doing."

"I didn't have to see. I knew what she was doing."

"Maybe because you would have done the same thing."

Sean had to stop to think. "You're right. Under the same circumstances I would have done the same thing."

"But then how can you criticize her for doing it?"

"I can't. 'Strategy' isn't a bad word, and she's a smart veteran. But I should have been able to protect you from her."

"You don't have to protect me. I don't want to be protected."

"But when you're coaching, you know, you want to have your runners prepared."

"This isn't a coach-runner relationship," she said testily. "Anyway, you did tell me what to do. I just didn't do it."

"Well," he said and laughed, "you told me the same thing and I did do it, so I guess you're the better coach." The waiter had returned.

"All right, well I'll do the coaching now." She ordered for both of them.

Sean started to open the overwhelming wine list, but he was interrupted.

"Let him pick," Susie said. "Even father can't make sense of that wine list." She nodded to the waiter, and he left.

"But I was just so worried that you weren't having fun." Sean resumed the conversation. "I certainly wasn't disappointed. In fact, I was really proud of you. You were showing real guts."

"You were surprised that I had real guts?"

This wasn't going the way Sean had intended. What he wanted to say just wasn't coming out right. "No, no, I didn't mean that."

"Well, I did have fun, and I was satisfied with what I did."

"It's always fun to win."

"Grrrr," came from Susie.

They were interrupted by the arrival of the first course, but Susie continued

"Sean, I run just for fun, and after next month it'll be over. So if we're going to have some kind of relationship it's not going to be because I'm another runner."

It doesn't make sense, Sean thought. *She pretends not to care about winning, but she never could have gotten this far without being really competitive. I let Bahel tie, but that was only after I knew I'd really won.*

"Okay, okay," he said. "But let me finish. Running could be useful to you. You probably don't have to earn a living. . . ."

"I intend to earn a living," she interrupted.

"Now Joanie Benoit, the woman who won the . . ."

"I know who she is."

"Okay. She's testifying before Congress about air quality. Apparently they're trying to revoke the Clean Air Act. They're going to listen because of her reputation. From what you say, you may be in the same position some day, with your interest in environmental things. If you had an Olympic gold medal dangling around *your* neck more people would listen, and you could do more good. I hope to have the same kind of influence for my inner-city youth projects."

"Umm," she said noncommittally.

"And even if you stop running, I'll bet in whatever you do you're going to really hate to lose."

The waiter approached with the entrees.

"Have you ever seen Cosi Fan Tutte?" she asked, leaving no doubt that the conversation was to change.

"No," he said. "I've never actually been to an opera."

"Well, see the woman sitting at the second table from the corner in the blue dress. She's my favorite Despina. She's wonderful."

Sean glanced across in the indicated direction. "She doesn't look like a diva."

"What did you expect, three hundred pounds and a helmet with horns?" They both laughed. The woman was quite attractive. "She plays a young girl, the maid, not Brunhilde."

They turned their attention to the food.

"It's the best meal I've ever eaten," Sean proclaimed.

"And," Susie said, "since we did so much exercise today, we can have dessert."

Later as they were leaving, they stopped to say good night to Franco. "That fight was terrible," he said. "Such a scene. All the other patrons were complaining. We thought we would have to give them refunds." They all laughed.

Sean accompanied her to the door of her apartment but was not invited in. They kissed. He looked into her eyes. "I really like being with you," he said.

She smiled. "I like it too. And I liked the day. And I do like winning."

Chapter 15

Schultz and Jurgen were on their morning walk. It had become a ritual. As usual they finished by circling the athletic fields.

"I knew it would go well as soon as we had our own technicians. We now have more than enough for our purposes," Schultz reported.

"His purification procedure has proved satisfactory?" Jurgen asked. "It is safe to use?"

"So it seems. We have administered small amounts to a 'volunteer.' Of course, we did not choose one of the better runners for this first experiment. There were no ill effects, so with your permission we are ready to go forward."

"We should prepare two runners, in case something goes wrong with one of them. Pick young ones."

"Jawohl, Herr Jurgen. I know the ones, from the countryside, unsophisticated. They will do whatever is commanded without question. Otherwise, they go back to their villages in disgrace."

"Precisely. Do not choose Chao Lee. He would be nothing but trouble. Let him learn his new role by losing. It will be a lesson to all the others, who have been on the team in the past, that this is a new regime."

"Sehr gut, sehr gut." Schultz laughed.

"And the woman, she cooperates?"

"Yes, of course. She has no choice. She herself carried out the first administration."

"You trust her?"

"She suspects nothing," Schultz assured him. "To her it was just an unfortunate accident. And she knows nothing of how we took the laboratory notebooks from his house. We have more information about his work than she does, and we really do not need her. Still it is best to keep her here, where we can be sure she can cause no trouble, and to involve her in case someone must take the blame."

"A very wise precaution," Jurgen agreed.

"Might we now try for Stockholm, to begin by winning the world championship?"

"Patience, Manfred. It will take time for them to adjust. We must not fail in public. First they must race here. Perhaps the times can be slightly exaggerated by the friendly press. We will make up some excuse for not submitting the records, too much wind or too few official timers, so no one will examine the results."

"Then they will all have to accept the challenge at Stuttgart." Schultz grinned broadly.

"Some will be so brave, others will hide. The Germans will have no choice. They must run at home."

"It will be our triumph."

"Slowly, Manfred, slowly. We have not yet even seen its effects. The theory is elegant, but the proof is always in the experiment."

"But if it worked for the old man, how much better for a trained athlete. It must work. It *will* work!"

Chapter 16

Joe Blackburn was a huge man, tall and fat, who seemed about to burst from his clothes. From a distance it would be hard to imagine that this jolly man with his round red face and protruding belly could be a world-renowned scientist, but after a few moments of conversation in his office it seemed more plausible. Sean was disappointed but not surprised when Blackburn denied any knowledge of research related to exercise physiology.

"I thought I heard a story about someone showing Grimes's picture around. Was that you?" Blackburn asked.

Sean launched into his tale of how he had met Grimes. He sometimes amazed himself with how easily he had learned to lie.

"And by then he was dead?"

"Yes. At first I thought I'd forget about it, but it just seemed to stick in my mind. Eventually I spoke to Dr. Kerr, and he gave me permission to look into it. He said to try you first, that you'd be the most likely person to know what Grimes had been doing." Sean was learning to drop the chairman's name at every opportunity. It tended to bring cooperation.

"I am very familiar with Grimes's work. But it was all cancer related. There was never anything about exercise or muscle strength or anything like that."

"Do you think that any of this oxygen business could be involved?" Sean asked.

"Did he tell you that?" He leaned forward, and his manner suddenly seemed to change.

"No. But in reading about his research, it's the only thing that seems even remotely related to exercise."

"Oh." Blackburn seemed almost relieved. "Well I could see how you might think so, but I was involved in all that work, and it really wouldn't fit. Do you know much about hypoxia in tumors?"

"Only what Dr. Kerr told me, that it protects the tumor from radiation, and that even though only a small part of the tumor is hypoxic, the effect is very big."

"That's all. You mean you're trying to learn this from scratch?"

"I guess so."

"Well, you're brave, but you may be taking on too much. I'm just afraid it's all going to be a dead end anyway."

Sean looked disappointed.

"You don't even know if this was just some wild idea? Grimes had lots of crazy ideas to go along with his good ones."

It seemed like a question, and Sean answered, "No."

"You don't even know if he ever tried it to see if it would work?"

Sean shook his head. His agreement with Beth kept him from admitting it to Blackburn.

"So there. I'd like to help, but it's hard even to know where to start." He shrugged his shoulders and leaned back in his chair, seeming on the verge of tipping over. Sean instinctively lunged forward, half expecting to have to catch him.

"Could you just tell me a little more about this tumor hypoxia business?" Sean asked after assuring himself that Blackburn was safely balanced.

"You're really fixated on that."

"Well, why are there hypoxic cells in the tumor?"

"Good question. Remember the tumor is a lump that isn't supposed to exist. There simply isn't enough blood supply to get oxygen to all of it. As it grows and takes up space, the tumor will push the existing blood vessels farther apart. Each blood vessel can feed tissue only a certain distance away. You know, the oxygen and other nutrients have to diffuse out, and they can go only so far before they're entirely consumed. It's sort of like watering the lawn with soaking hoses. Each hose covers only a certain width, and then you need another hose running parallel a little distance away. There just aren't enough hoses to cover this new growth. Even worse, sometimes the tumor simply compresses the blood vessels, pinching them so that the blood can't flow through as well. Are you still with me?"

"Yes. And it's beginning to make sense, not that I could have thought of it myself."

"Good. Here's the interesting part, what Kerr was telling you. When you try to cure a tumor, you can think of it as two jobs, killing all of the well-oxygenated cells and killing the hypoxic cells. It's almost like curing two separate tumors, except that you have to cure both to score one victory."

"And it's the tiny hypoxic one that causes the most trouble?"

"Exactly. Now think of how different this is from the athlete's problem. *We're* trying to get a little more oxygen into that last tiny bit of a tumor whose blood vessels are pushed aside and pinched. *You* want to get much more oxygen to an entire muscle that's using it too fast but whose blood vessels are normal. It's just not the same. That's why I don't think that our approaches would work for you."

"But maybe some would be good for both. Grimes's papers mentioned hyperbaric chambers, where you breathe oxygen under high pressure. Shouldn't that work?"

"They wouldn't be of much use to you." Blackburn scoffed. "They weigh about a ton. They don't even work very well for us."

"Why not?" Sean asked.

"Well, ah, how much do you know about the way oxygen is carried through the body?"

"A little. It's on the hemoglobin, right, the red stuff?"

"Right. And you know that hemoglobin is saturable, it holds only so much oxygen, and it only works over a very narrow range of pressure?" Blackburn spoke more slowly and his eyebrows went up as he saw Sean's blank expression. "The sigmoid curve?" Now he was shaking his head from side to side.

"I'm sorry, I. . ."

"No, no. No reason you should. Ah—" He paused to consider how best to explain. "Look. Suppose, just suppose, that there were no red blood cells, no hemoglobin. Then the blood would only carry the oxygen that was dissolved in the plasma, the salt water, like dissolving carbon dioxide in soda. You know, the bubbles. The more pressure, the more gas dissolves."

"Okay," Sean said.

"But it wouldn't work. Oxygen dissolves very poorly in water. To have enough in the blood to survive, you would need a pressure of maybe three atmospheres of pure oxygen."

"Three atmospheres!" Sean let out a soft whistle. "That's fifteen times more than we normally breathe, right, because we're at one atmosphere, but the air is only one-fifth oxygen?"

"That's right. And even in the hyperbaric chamber at three atmospheres of pressure, the plasma is a *lousy* carrier. *If* you could dissolve enough oxygen, it would *be delivered* over a wide range of pressures, from three atmospheres maximum to almost zero when the oxygen is all gone. The body doesn't like that at all, because out in the tissue there are enzymes, little machines, that use up the oxygen to do work and to make things, and they prefer to get their oxygen at a certain constant pressure. It's like having the right fuel pump for your automobile engine. You don't want one that's constantly changing its pressure and squirting in too much gasoline or not enough. The same holds true for the enzymes. They go bonkers when the oxygen pressure is too high, and that makes you act like you're drunk. It's called oxygen intoxication."

"And the hemoglobin doesn't have these problems?"

"It's such a clever design. There are just two important things to know about how the hemoglobin carries oxygen. First of all, it can hold just so much, it's like a bucket. Each molecule of hemoglobin can hold four molecules of oxygen and no more. Then the bucket is full. Second, it's the pressure that makes the oxygen stick onto the hemoglobin. If it's higher than a certain amount, the oxygen will stick. If the pressure is less, it comes off. It has to go on and off easily if this is to be a good transport system. Hemoglobin is designed so that it takes a certain minimum pressure to get the oxygen to stick at all, but then very little more pressure to fill it completely."

Sean was smiling. "And I'll bet that normally there's enough pressure to fill the hemoglobin."

"Just one-tenth of an atmosphere of oxygen is all it takes. So normally when the blood leaves the lungs it's completely full."

"And of course that explains why it doesn't help all those football players to run over to the sidelines between plays to grab an oxygen mask," Sean proclaimed. "Since you have enough oxygen in regular air to fill the hemoglobin, more oxygen pressure doesn't make any difference."

"Right. Unless you have some respiratory disease, you don't need any of those tricks like pure oxygen or hyperbaric oxygen."

Blackburn huffed as he spoke, like someone who might just have such a respiratory condition. "Now when the blood moves away from the lungs to a place where the pressure is a little lower, like the capillaries in the tissue where it's being consumed, the oxygen will come off the hemoglobin. And the pressure doesn't have to drop much to let the hemoglobin give up an enormous amount of oxygen. That's what happens in the tumor or the muscle, just the reverse of the loading in the lungs."

"It's so simple."

"Simple and clever. With the oxygen loading and unloading this way, the oxygen pressure everywhere in the body is regulated to be pretty much the same, that is in a very narrow range. And it can almost never get to be too high."

"Aha."

"And except for you athletes who try to use oxygen too fast, the system has plenty of excess capacity. During normal activity the hemoglobin has to give up only about twenty-five per cent of its oxygen to the tissue to meet its needs. It comes back to the lungs still three quarters full. You may think that's not very efficient, but it was nice to have that big reserve when we had to run away from sabertooth tigers."

"Or from Paulo Rossi in the last 400 meters," added Sean under his breath.

"You can appreciate that nature went to a lot of trouble to evolve hemoglobin and to set the loading-unloading pressure in just the right range to work well in our atmosphere, on our planet."

"But things can go wrong."

"Oh, sure. We talked about a tumor growing between the blood vessels, pushing them further apart, so they just can't feed the space in between. The oxygen pressure falls. More oxygen comes off each hemoglobin molecule. The blood goes through a little faster. But it's a losing battle. The oxygen is diffusing out of the blood vessel, but it never goes far enough because it's being consumed along the way. It's the oxygen pressure that is the driving force for the diffusion."

"So you need more pressure to push the oxygen farther out," Sean interrupted.

"Yes, but here comes the catch. This wonderful carrier system was designed to keep the pressure the same everywhere, so the enzymes will work properly. It just wasn't designed with tumors and radiation therapists in mind."

"That's what the hyperbaric oxygen chambers could do," Sean was quick to suggest.

"But the hemoglobin is already full, remember?"

"Damn. That's right. So then why even have those chambers?" he asked, suddenly feeling dejected.

"Because a little more oxygen dissolves in the plasma at the higher pressure. It helps us, but not very much."

"But that's very frustrating," Sean complained. "It seems there's no way to make things better. So what could it have been that Grimes discovered?"

"Hold on a minute. We don't even know that Grimes discovered anything."

There was a knock at the door, and before Blackburn could even respond, a tall, blond, athletic-looking woman in a white lab coat entered the room and placed a folder on his desk.

"Oh, let me introduce you," Blackburn said. "Cindy Helms has been a post-doc with me for several years. She's worked closely with Grimes's group. Sean Rourke is an Olympic runner from Philadelphia. He's heard that Andy was involved in some kind of research that may make you run faster, but I can't think of what it might be."

They shook hands. She had a firm grip.

"We'll be neighbors. My husband and I are moving to Philadelphia next year."

"Oh, you'll like it, it's a great place," Sean replied.

"I never heard that Grimes did any research on running," Cindy said, turning toward Blackburn. "Although I think he ran as a hobby. Too bad his people have all left, or we could have asked them."

"When Andy died, his group pretty much dissolved," Blackburn explained. "A couple of his people who worked directly on projects with us just joined our group. There were some others, a Chinese woman, and another woman who was going to the West Coast anyway, who must have been gone in a week."

"How did they manage to leave so fast?" Sean asked. "Somebody told me that these research positions were hard to get?"

"You bet they are," Cindy answered. "Tom and I just went

through the process and were very lucky to get assistant professorships at Penn. It's even harder when you're trying to find two spots in the same city."

"She's just being modest." Blackburn interrupted. "They were dying to get her."

"Anyway," Cindy continued, "one of Grimes's post-docs, Ann Grossman, a fantastic scientist, had a job lined up already for the fall semester. The only reason she was with Grimes was that she had to wait a year to get a position in Seattle. Imagine, she would only go there. She joked once about how it was as far away as she could get from New York, where she grew up. I think she got into outdoor stuff, camping and hiking. It takes real nerve to be so choosy, but she was good enough to pull it off. She just left early, probably decided to take an extra long break. Wish I could do the same. How about it, boss?" She grinned at Blackburn. "I never did figure out what she was doing with Grimes. It wasn't our kind of research."

"Didn't she work right here?" Sean asked.

"No. Actually they had a small lab on the next floor, right above us. It's closer to some of the core facilities they wanted to share. They do more molecular biology up there. That was her field."

"And the Chinese woman?"

"Nancy Li? We called her Nancy because no one could pronounce her real first name. I think she just went back. Nobody ever got to know her very well. I could hardly understand what she said."

"But I thought you all worked together so closely that you knew everything Grimes was doing. It sounds like they could have been working on something without anyone knowing."

Blackburn obviously didn't like to hear that. "No, no. Believe me, it would have been impossible. Cindy or someone would have known."

"But, Joe, there were things that didn't involve us. Remember, about three years ago he started a genetics project." She turned to Sean. "He actually went out to San Diego for a week and paid to take a course to learn the laboratory techniques. When he came back, he began to work more in the lab himself. That was really unusual for someone at his level, especially one of the clinicians."

"It's true. I used to go over to his laboratory and pretend to be surprised to see him there. Then he'd chide me with something like 'well I just had to see how really easy it is to do the kinds of things that you do.'" For the first time Blackburn actually seemed to show some sadness at his colleague's death. "We knew each other and worked together for years. I never thought that someday he wouldn't be here."

"I've got to go now," Cindy said, turning toward the door. "But we'll be nearby. I'd be happy to talk to you about this stuff when we're in Philly. It must all seem really strange to you, if you have no background. Anyway it was nice to meet you."

Sean waved to her and turned back to Blackburn. "What happened to all of Grimes's laboratory equipment? Wouldn't that tell us what he was doing?"

"It was cleaned out. I never heard that there was anything special. The business office usually lets it be known when equipment is available, and people from other labs come and take what they need. It's like a giant garage sale, except everything's free."

"So, no one knows where it went?" Sean was amazed.

"Oh sure, records are kept of the bigger things. They have to do it for the granting agencies. The business office would know. But believe me it's not going to tell us what he was doing. Well, I don't know what more I can do to help. With so little to go on, it's hard to even know where to begin. If I were you, I wouldn't get my hopes too high. But keep me posted on your progress and let me know if I can be of further help."

Sean thanked him profusely, but left with a sense of disappointment. "Damn it, why didn't I get here a few weeks ago before all those people left," he said to himself.

Since Sean was staying in Grenville to have dinner with Susie, he decided to train on the university track in the late afternoon. The team had completed practice—they were in final preparations for the three-way meet with their traditional rivals now just several days away—and the track was deserted except for a few recreational runners. He completed a strenuous workout and was covered with sweat as he walked slowly to the water fountain. After drinking and wiping his face on his shirt, he started to jog across the practice field. There was still time to get in a leisurely five miles before meeting Susie for dinner. He loved to run at the old athletic facility with its tall trees and carefully groomed grass. Across the soccer field he went, stopping to kick a few imaginary goals, then onto the football field to score a few touchdowns. It was a sport he had learned to watch on American television but had never played himself. He took the long way around the polo field, where a few solitary riders were letting their horses amble slowly back to the barn, then up a dirt road that followed a little stream, across a wooden bridge and finally back toward the track stadium. It was idyllic. "I need a coaching job at a college like this," he said to himself. "Exactly like this."

Later that evening he met Susie at Gino's.

"I'm going to miss this place," she said, showing her ID to the waitress again. "The food I mean. If I come back here to graduate school and take the usual seven years to get a Ph.D., maybe they'll stop asking me for this card."

Sean remembered the name of the wine they had drunk in New York. "They won't have it here," Susie warned, and they settled for a good Barola, the most expensive wine on the list.

"Well, we'll leave in style," he said. They talked around the subject that was most on their minds, their summer plans. Sean had never described in detail to Susie just why he was so interested in Andy Grimes's work, but he did so now. He told her the entire story, the true version, beginning with the Bradsford race and including his meeting with Blackburn.

"But you don't know the secret?" she asked, a look of amazement on her face. "You haven't found out?"

"No, of course not, or I wouldn't still be looking."

"I'm glad you didn't say or I wouldn't still be coming up here," she said with a smile.

"You know that wouldn't be."

"So you're not using this thing yourself? That's not why you suddenly got to be so good?"

"I didn't suddenly get good," Sean said acidly. "I was sixth best in the world at the last Olympics, and I've just gotten steadily better, and it all came from hard work."

"I know, I know, I was just kidding you," she said, reaching over and taking his hand. "Do you have any idea what it was that he discovered?"

A tray of appetizers arrived, and Sean began serving them both as he continued. "The only thing I can tie it to is this business of getting more oxygen to the tumors. That was Grimes's main interest. But everybody tells me it's a whole different problem trying to get more oxygen to people's muscles when they're exercising. And you know, I can almost understand when Blackburn explains it. What he says sounds strange at first, I guess because I've never been taught to think that way. But when he puts it in simple terms, it all makes sense."

"Well, it's the job of a good teacher to be able to explain it," Susie said.

"That's easy to say, but I don't think it comes naturally to everyone. Anyway, I'm determined to learn this stuff, even if I do start with almost no background." He said it forcefully. "And Blackburn is a really good teacher. I don't know how I can repay him."

"If you find something of Grimes's that they've overlooked, it should make them all happy. It would be a credit to all of their labs."

"I guess. It's funny though, Blackburn himself doesn't think there is anything to find. Of course, I never told any of them about Grimes's running, that's part of my agreement with Beth Markham. If they knew, I'm sure they'd be a lot more curious. It's just too bad I didn't start this before all his lab people left."

"I wish I could do something to help," Susie offered, wiping a spot of tomato sauce from her chin with a napkin.

"There are so many things it could be. He could have stumbled upon some new hormone or some stimulant, or something that works in some way nobody knows anything about. It could be almost anything. Unfortunately my whole investigation's going to come to a stop for at least the time I'm in Colorado. Then I'll have to decide what to do next."

Their main courses finally arrived. The conversation turned to Susie's upcoming race.

"I should be all right. I'm not as fast as I was in February, but I've managed to get in some good work during the past two weeks." She was staring down at the food. "You know what they say, you always run on the training you did two weeks ago." Sean had heard it often enough, but he had never believed it. "It'll be strange not to be running competitively," she said, "but I think I'm ready to give it up."

"You don't have to. There's a great coach at Oxford, and I'm sure that he'd be delighted to have you. Jim could clear it in a minute."

Finally she looked up and met his gaze. "We've been over this before. For you this is a profession, but for me it's just fun."

"I'm telling you, though, it could be useful."

"No, Sean. And we aren't going to talk about it anymore."

Their plans for the summer had pretty much taken shape. Before going to England she would spend a month at her family's summer house in Maine. It was in a small costal community visited by the same families for years. They formed a tight little group. Many of them were from Philadelphia, but Sean doubted that they moved in his social circle.

"Good thing I can't visit, I'd probably use the wrong fork."

"They're just summer camps," Susie teased. "There are never more than four forks at one place. Anyway, it's beautiful there, and it's a chance to see the usual aunts and uncles and cousins and all the people I've known since childhood. This will probably be the last old-fashioned summer before all the people in my year go off and get jobs or do other things. It just seems like the end of a whole period of my life." She sighed. "I'm going to miss it."

"Your family must be very proud of your running, especially your father."

"Not really. He would be if I were a son. Then it would matter. It might even lead to some important business connections. But to have a daughter who was a track star . . . " She shook her head. "Now to play a nice game of tennis at the country club, that would be different. He *is* getting better, though. He could even imagine my having a serious career. And there's now a woman partner in the firm."

"But it sounds like your family is very close, very supportive."

"They are for most things. And since I didn't have a mother and was the youngest of the next generation, they always babied me."

"Like me with all those sisters."

Susie nodded. "I think they were all surprised when I just quietly went along doing as well as all the others, getting into the same schools, winning the same awards. It's always expected of the rest of the family, but when I did it, it was unexpected. As if it were impossible to believe that I'd turned out all right, the bratty little girl who sat on top of the big table on the veranda demanding ice cream and screaming at bedtime. When my cousin played quarterback, everyone was at Grenville for every game. Maybe if I kept running . . . "

"It would be very hard to ignore all the publicity and a big gold medal."

"Don't, Sean. You know I'm not going to do that. But wait until you meet them."

"I'm not sure that I want to after all that, I'd be too terrified." Sean pretended to shiver.

"They'll be in awe. You're so different they won't know what to think. None of them is the best in the world at anything. 'Susie brings home an alien wearing a strange gold amulet, no doubt possessing wondrous powers.'"

"I'm not sure I like that description."

"I hope it's appropriate," she said nervously.

"We're never going to see each other," bemoaned Sean. In early June he was to leave for a six-week course in Boulder, Colorado, given by the university for track and field coaches. Then it would be off to Sweden for the World Championships in August.

"We'll just have to find ways," Susie said. She reached across and squeezed his hand.

"I'll be in Europe in August and September. Somehow I'll find a way to get to England. Christmas would be much too long to wait"

"It certainly would be," she agreed.

"Of course you could always come back for the New York Marathon. After all your apartment is right on the route. You could wave at me or throw some water on me."

"From the penthouse?" she asked.

"That might be fun."

Later they sat outside of her dormitory, kissing in the car, neither wanting to leave. Sean felt awkward. Should he suggest they both go in? She hadn't asked, and she would ask if she wanted to, he thought. Or maybe she didn't know whether she should. How did you ever get to feel comfortable in situations like this? Finally, she pulled away from him.

"As soon as I'm settled, I'll send you my address and my phone number. I'm going to go. Don't get out of the car." She leaned over and kissed him one more time, opened the door and started for the dorm. Then she stopped and came around to his side. He rolled down the window. She leaned in and kissed him again.

"See you," she said. "Go find fifteen seconds in Colorado."

Sean sat for a moment looking through the windshield but seeing nothing. "I think I'll find thirty seconds," he said aloud to no one, then started the car and drove back to Helen and Jim's.

As usual, Helen was still up.

"That's the girl I should marry," he said.

"Be careful, Sean. I wouldn't want you to get hurt. Susie's not like most people you've met, and she has her own agenda."

Chapter 17

The six weeks Sean spent in Boulder, Colorado offered him his first chance to train at high altitude. It was becoming such a popular practice with distance runners that he wanted to try it. "This is really different," he said to himself during his first training run. "My heart rate is so high I can't count it. Tomorrow I'll wear that cardiac monitor." His running performances were incomparably worse for the first two weeks, then began gradually to improve. He did non-aerobic exercises, weight lifting and short sprints, to maintain his strength during a time when his overall mileage was reduced.

The training was just one of his reasons for going. The other was to attend the popular course for track and field coaches offered by the Sports Medicine Institute. It was taught by some of the more famous coaches in the world and had guest lecturers from the nearby Olympic Training Center. There was a strong emphasis on exercise physiology, which Sean hoped would be useful in solving the Grimes mystery.

Altitude training was a natural point of departure. The explanations seemed easy to understand after his session with Blackburn. The atmospheric pressure was lower at higher altitudes, since there was less air piled on top of you. Lower oxygen pressure made it more difficult to fully load the hemoglobin. The body's first response was to simply make the blood go around faster, and this was good training for the heart. But the most important adaptation, which took several weeks to occur, was an increase in the percent of red cells in the blood from forty-five to more than fifty. *So even if the hemoglobin isn't loading as well, it's compensated for because there's more of it, more capacity, more buckets,* Sean thought, recalling Blackburn's expression.

More recently it had become possible to stimulate the body's own production of excess red blood cells using the natural hormone, erythropoietin. It was now produced synthetically through genetic engineering and called EPO. The potential for cheating seemed to grow and grow, but fortunately there were some natural limits. While a small increase in red blood cell concentration might be good, higher values, greater than fifty-five percent, made the blood too viscous and harder to push through the blood vessels. It could even be dangerous, leading to strokes and heart attacks. "If the blood doesn't go around well, it doesn't matter how much oxygen is in it," the instructor emphasized.

Sean attended a series of optional lectures on unique considerations for women in sports. It was in part because of Susie. He found that he missed her terribly. He was even more upset when Jim called with the news of her last race.

"No, no special problems, no tactical mistakes. She just didn't have it at the end. Just ran out of steam."

"Easy to understand," Sean said. "Her training during the past two months, really since Washington, has been totally haphazard. It's a wonder she was even close."

"Still, she took it badly."

"Maybe I should have been there."

"She had enough pressure," Jim said. "That would have made it worse."

Sean was the only man at the special lectures. He found them to be interesting and sometimes a little embarrassing, for example, when they discussed menstrual problems particularly among the distance runners. He learned that the female hormones are stored in fat, and that the endurance athletes with their extremely low proportions of body fat often fail to have menstrual periods. 'Amenorrheic' was a new word to Sean. Susie certainly fit the profile. The discussion of the illegal uses of male hormones was particularly fascinating. Again there seemed to be an endless number of ways to cheat.

There were humorous moments as well, like the heated argument over the choice of bras for high jumpers. Sean refrained from expressing an opinion. All in all, he was glad that he had taken the elective. In his club he coached young women and at times felt uncomfortable designing their training programs. At Grenville Jim coached both the men's and women's teams, although he did have a female assistant. Sean could imagine himself in a similar situation in the future.

Sean stayed two weeks beyond the end of the formal courses. There were few distractions except those of his own making, and he was enjoying training again after his initial acclimatization. During the last week he visited Pike's Peak—he had not adjusted to that altitude— and the cliff dwellings at Mesa Verde. By then he was ready to try running at sea level.

Sean stepped off the plane in Stockholm feeling better prepared than ever before. After "coming down from the mountain" as Bob called it, he had devoted almost a month to speed work. They flew to Sweden just three days before the world championships. It was all part of Higgum's grand strategy for the Olympics.

"Sure, missing those lucrative races earlier in the summer will be expensive," he told Sean, "but this is a special year with a very special goal. We want to win the world championship. It's time to establish yourself as the best, to throw down the gauntlet. Then we let all the others worry about you. Let them change their training plans and alter their racing schedules. It will do them more harm than good."

"Well, I have another goal too," Sean replied. "I want the record. I want to show the world what I gained in Colorado." "And show Susie too," he added under his breath. He knew that he could do it. Bob Higgum knew it too.

The evening of the race was perfect for running, cool and dry. A half moon shone in the sky above the rim of the packed stadium. Sean had to pick his way through the mass of television cameras to reach the starting line. Four of the world's top six 10K runners were there. Chandi Kipu was the best of the Kenyans. He had won three of the earlier summer races, but not against this quality of competition and only with the help of two countrymen, all three clearly supporting one another. Today only one helper was running; the other had failed to qualify.

Next to him was Pedro Alvila, a Mexican who trained with the group now dominating the marathon. Sean would have Pedro's training partners as rivals in New York in not quite three months.

"Bet they're not out running 10K's right now," Sean said to himself.

Then there was Paulo Rossi. He had narrowly lost to Alvila two weeks earlier, but Higgum, who had studied the results and films of the races, thought that Rossi had saved himself for this one.

This field will be better than the Olympic final, Sean thought, *after you take into account that some favorites are always upset in the heats*. He felt ready for any strategy.

In the flash of countless bulbs, they were off. No one wanted the lead. Even the second Kenyan was back in the pack. *I wonder what his instructions are*? They ran as a group, smoothly, easily, with a minimum of jostling. All were professionals. All could bring out the strong-arm stuff if needed, but not at this point in the race.

"It's much too slow," Sean said under his breath, as he ran along comfortably in fourth place. By the second mile nothing at all had happened except that Sean's chances for a world record were gone. He could already feel the disappointment although the race was not a third over, and there was work still to be done. Making up his mind, he increased the pace and went for the lead. The pack followed stringing out only slightly. Finally the second Kenyan dislodged himself from the group and went after Sean.

Well, now I know what he was told to do, thought Sean. But he had so little concern that he simply ignored him. *If he wants to come up here and hassle me, he'll get one good elbow in the ribs real quick.* But the Kenyan stayed his distance. Sean began to open the lead. He wanted to push the others just a little beyond where they were really comfortable.

The panic will set in at about the four-mile mark, he thought. *Then there'll be people bursting out of that pack like fireworks*. But to his surprise nothing seemed to change at four miles. Sean increased his speed. He was more than a hundred yards ahead of the pack. The Kenyan was half way in between and beginning to falter. His race was over.

They must all be crazy, or else they have a very mistaken impression of what I plan to do. He almost smiled as he ran. *Or they know and have decided to race for second. If Rossi can keep them in the pack, he'll win. He's the best sprinter. Maybe the second Kenyan was sent out to try to pull Rossi. If so, it didn't work.* At about five miles the pack began to break up. Kipu was making a move, and Alvila chose to run right on his shoulder. Rossi came out of the pack as well but was content to stay about ten yards behind, and others trailed out from there. Sean increased his speed accordingly so that the three had not shortened the gap on him at all. They obviously knew it, and Sean could imagine how it made them feel.

Kipu came up on his failing teammate and used him to bump Alvila. Sean happened to look back at that moment and saw it clearly. *Boy, that's taking a chance,* he thought. *People have been put down for less than that.* Sean felt totally in command. The track was indeed fast, and he was so relaxed that he allowed himself to ponder on how one would design such a surface tuned to the frequency of their steps, almost like a trampoline. At five and a half he increased his speed again. Rossi made his move. He passed Alvila and was running down Kipu. "I'd swing wide," Sean said out loud. "He's just liable to reach over and punch you."

But Rossi was no schoolboy. He had given the second Kenyan an elbow in the side as he passed him while the former was still recovering his balance from the collision with Alvila. Now he came right alongside Kipu, elbows flying, almost daring him to do something, then cut him off and began to open a lead. Sean loved the idea of being a spectator. He had always liked the feisty little Rossi, and he liked him more now, but not enough to let him gain a yard. The race had been decided long ago, but Sean wanted to send Rossi the message that he could sprint just as fast. He went to a full kick and crossed the finish line with the Italian almost half a lap behind. It was not the world record, but it was the fastest time of the year. Kipu held on for third but, as Sean had anticipated, was put down to fourth because of the flagrant foul.

Rossi was the first to congratulate him. "Is race to dream of," he said in his broken English.

Sean thanked him. "I enjoyed the elbow," he said with a grin.

"Ah, you see. He ees a little sheeet. Pedro should have kick him, but I do it for him." He grinned back.

Bob Higgum was showing more emotion than usual. "FTY, that's the message we wanted to send." Sean could only smile. "That's seven years' hard work, and there's more in there yet. And worth a little money too." He punched Sean playfully on the chest.

"I really wanted that record," Sean said.

Bob shook his head. "Don't worry, don't worry."

"No, but I really wanted it. I had it in me today. This just wasn't enough. I should go on to Holland and . . ."

"No," Bob interrupted him. "We're not going to change the training schedule. Let the others change theirs. Go to England. Go see your girlfriend." Bob never talked about Susie. When Sean looked startled, Bob added, "Of course I know where she is. Did you think I wouldn't? It's my business to know."

"Have you heard anything about her?" Sean asked.

"Sure, and she's the hottest runner in Europe. Well, I heard from Jim who hears it from Hopwell."

"You mean she's competing?"

Higgum laughed. "Hopwell can't believe it. Can't believe Jim let her go."

"Hopwell's supposed to be good."

"Not bad. Tough. Ambitious. Smart." That was high praise indeed from Bob. "The first day she was there your little darling ran a 15:28 in practice."

"What!"

Bob was laughing so hard he could hardly control himself. "It was at the trials for the new students for the college team." He laughed until the tears rolled down his face.

"That's unbelievable."

"Well, I guess she made the team," Bob said between sputters and coughs. "That's the best present Paul Hopwell ever got. Now let's see what he can do with it."

Sean flew from Stockholm to London. At Gatwick he rented a car and drove to Oxford skirting the main part of London to the south. He had spent very little time in England despite having grown up so close by. Although he had never been to Oxford, he had no difficulty in finding Susie's apartment building. He was early and had time to stop for flowers. He could see her hurrying down the hallway in response to his ring and could not remember ever having been so glad to see someone. They ran into each other arms. The flowers barely survived. When she finally noticed them she said, "Just like our first date."

"First date in England," he said. "You look wonderful, as always."

"And so do you." She led him into her apartment. It was small and dark with a low, skewed ceiling. There were only three small windows, but they provided a magnificent view of the backs. She poured some wine from a bottle that she had opened in advance, and they settled on the one couch. "And congratulations. It was all over our papers. They're mad about running here."

"I really wanted that world record."

"But it was FTY. You need competition for the world record, Sean. Sounds like there wasn't any." She kicked off her shoes and tucked her feet under her.

"It was easier than I thought, considering who they were."

"Hopwell thought it was unbelievable. He went over to see it. He always goes. Did you know he was there?"

"No, and Bob didn't say anything. I've never met him and wouldn't even have recognized him. He and Bob have a little rivalry between them."

"I suspected as much." Susie laughed. "He kept muttering about this endless supply of Irishmen that make Higgum look good."

"I think Bob's the one who makes the Irishmen look good."

"Anyway, he was telling all the runners that he'd never seen such a lopsided victory in a field of that quality, that you just played with them."

"That's an exaggeration."

"The funny thing is that he didn't know that we were, umm, connected."

"Are we connected?" Sean asked.

"Well, we're beginning to," she paused to search for the word, "adhere."

"So that's what this is, an adherence."

"Oh, you." She punched his arm. "Anyway, I couldn't resist. I said, 'I know him. He comes up to Grenville to train with Jim when Bob's too busy for him.'"

"You didn't."

"Yes, I did. His mouth just dropped open."

"He'll be wondering about Jim's methods, considering what I've been hearing about you."

"Well, I thought I might just run a little bit more," Susie said.

"Yeah, yeah. You must have trained like crazy. And I thought I had a good summer. Did you really do a 15:28 in practice?"

"Yup," Susie said affecting a Southern drawl. "I shur 'nuf did. Just little ol' me."

"But that's crazy."

"I thought I might just announce my presence."

"The others must have felt like they were in the wrong race."

Susie laughed. "It was a tryout for new students to be accepted into the club. That's what they call the team here. I must say, I haven't seen most of them again."

"How's Hopwell as a coach?"

"He's all right. We sat down and worked out some plans. He's very pushy. Do you know he tried to get me into the Worlds?"

"Really?"

"Yes. Then he was embarrassed. He bragged a lot about how he had so many friends he could do it. I didn't want him to, and fortunately the officials there didn't go along with it. They wouldn't accept his word on a practice run, and I think they were pretty fully committed anyway. But he pays close attention to what I do. I'm sure he thinks he has a live one here."

"I'll say he does," Sean said. "Think of what you could have been doing all along."

"Now, Sean, we don't talk about that."

"But something made you change your mind."

Susie took a long sip of her wine, then said, "It was losing that last race. I just felt that I'd let everybody down. I didn't like the feeling, and I didn't deserve it. I shouldn't have to perform to please others. I'm not a pet monkey. But I had the feeling anyway. There was the team, and Jim, and even Rev. Becker. He came down, said it was the only time he'd ever rooted against his alma mater. I'm sure he thought it was the last time he'd ever see me run. Then he tried to comfort me, told me he understood what I was doing, all that sort of thing. Well, I could see how disappointed he was. And then there was you." She grimaced.

"But we had discussed all that. You didn't have to do it for me." He took her hand in his.

"Yeah, right. And you even tried to warn me that I was going to get beaten, but I didn't listen. You're such a perfectionist. You'd never get yourself into a situation like that. It's what you were trying to tell me in New York, I realize now. Anyway it took me about a week to get over it, and then I started two-a-days for the whole summer."

Sean whistled. "That's too much."

"It doesn't seem to have been." She smiled.

"But you have to cut back."

"I have. Hopwell's taken control of that. He's big on quality, not quantity."

"Well at least you'll have a little time left over to study. I can't believe that still isn't the most important thing for you."

"Oh it is, but now I'm determined to do both."

"Is it much more difficult here?"

"The work isn't harder, but all the labs really take time."

"But aren't you taking mainly courses in government?"

"No, almost all are science."

"Environmental studies?"

"There isn't much of that here. Most are basic biology."

"But why the change?"

She shrugged. "Oh, I don't know. It was a last minute thing, and it did create some problems. The courses I wanted aren't offered in my college. But it's all straightened out now. Tell me, have you learned any more about the Grimes thing?"

"I really didn't have time to work on it, but I guess we can be sure that no one at the Worlds was using it."

"I'll bet there wasn't any secret. Or if there was, it died with him. Don't let it distract you from your training. Maybe you should just forget about it."

"Well I'm not going to think about it now. We have just three days, and then I go back to work on the marathon."

"We'll make the best of them," she said and threw her arms around his neck.

Chapter 18

Sean preferred marathon training. No more quarter mile and half mile sprints. Now five miles was a short run. He had mixed feelings about leaving Europe without pursuing the world record, and he often thought of his decision as he ran. *A few victories and a world record . . . this plan to run the marathon is going to cost me . . . maybe a cool quarter million.* Well, they had known all that when he and Bob developed the schedule almost two years earlier. All he could do was to put it out of his mind and enjoy the training.

What he couldn't put out of his mind was the Grimes mystery. He was beginning to wonder whether the secret had died with the professor. Certainly no one at the Worlds had used anything. Maybe he would learn more when Beth contacted Ann Grossman in Seattle after the start of the semester.

The bad news began arriving in late September, first with a phone call from Beth. He took it in the weight room of the St. Vincent's gym.

"She never arrived."

"What!" He wiped the perspiration from his face with a towel

"I called the Molecular Biology Department office. The secretary put me right through to the chairman. He was really nasty. Said she sent a letter at the last minute saying she wasn't coming. There was no return address, just a Grenville envelope. He assumed she was staying here. Then he went on to tell me what he thought of our school and what I should tell her when I saw her."

"Didn't he realize that you were looking for her too?"

"I guess he was too excited. She was supposed to teach a course and just left them stranded."

"Well it wasn't your fault. I hope you told him where to go."

"I never think fast enough in those situations. And I was trained to be too polite."

"Well, it sounds like another dead end," Sean said to himself after Beth hung up. He went back to the Nautilus machine and started his knee raisers with uncharacteristic energy. *Damn, every time I think we're making progress there's some setback. Where the hell could that woman be? And what do we try next?*

Then it was Bob's turn to bring bad news. A Chinese runner named Han had set FTY in the 10K, breaking Sean's time from the Worlds. Actually two runners, the other named Ho Dak, had beaten his time.

"Who the hell are they?" Sean asked.

"No one seems to know. The Chinese News Agency just gave the times and the home provinces. It's hard to believe. But we'll find out soon enough."

Two weeks later came word that Han had broken the world record by six seconds. There was little additional information except that he was twenty-two years old, too young they agreed, and that his "wonderful accomplishment was attributable to hard work inspired by his love for his country and to new training methods developed in harmony with the teachings of the party."

"Crap."

"We'll see if they submit the time," Bob said. "I wonder what kind of documentation they have? Anyway, we have to take it seriously. Everyone thinks something is funny, though. Distance runners just don't come out of nowhere. Sprinters maybe, but not 10K'ers."

"Yeah, remember those Chinese women swimmers and their East German coaches."

That afternoon Sean ran quarter mile sprints.

"Now they're going to try it outside of China, in Stuttgart," Bob announced a week later, "so the rest of the world can admire them."

"I never should have switched over," Sean said. "I should have stayed in Europe. Then I'd be ready for them right now."

"This is no time to panic. They're not going to dictate our training, that's something we do to others, we don't let it happen to us."

"I'm not panicking. I just want a fair chance at them."

"You'll get it in Sydney."

"I want them before that. I want them right now. I'm going to Germany."

Bob argued against it. "You may not win."

"I have to see those guys. Maybe we can fool them and learn something." Sean knew that this was the way to win the argument. Bob was always willing to lose a battle to win the war.

Sean arrived three days before the meet, long enough to adjust to the time change and to have several practice sessions on the track. It was his first trip to Stuttgart, home of the Mercedes, the Porsche, and the Stuttgart Ballet, a beautiful city with a magnificent sports arena. The composition track was considered to be one of the fastest in the world, the prizes were generous, and the meet always drew top-flight runners from around the world. Only the date, in mid October, kept it from being the premier European venue. Many of the top runners didn't want to extend their seasons so late in the year. For Sean the race was dangerously close to the New York Marathon, but Bob felt comfortable that he could finish New York in a time that the Irish National Olympic Committee had promised would guarantee a slot in the Olympics.

Sean was relaxing in the infield after his morning workout on the Stuttgart track. He sat in a folding chair dressed in sweats with a towel draped around his neck when a Chinese man timidly approached. He was short and slight and wore thick glasses. His dark suit, made of inexpensive material, didn't exactly go well with his new western-style running shoes.

"You Sean Rourke, famous Irish athlete?"

"Yes, I'm Sean Rourke."

"My name Lin Pao. Very big fan." His pronunciation was atrocious, but he spoke slowly, and Sean was able to understand him.

"Are you with the Chinese team?" Sean asked. This fellow hardly looked like an athlete, more like a young schoolteacher.

"I am assistant, not athlete."

"A coach?"

"No. Keep records on computer. Have records of all great runners. That is how know of you. Have all performances for last five years. Feel you are old friend. Always want to see win."

"Except against the Chinese." Sean laughed.

"Only loyal to hope for own country first. Is job too."

"So you keep records of all the top runners?"

"Yes, yes. Even younger one, promising one."

"It's like spying."

"No, no," he denied it vigorously. "Only have results from newspaper or runner magazine. No spy. Is just to show to regular coach, who runs good, what results. They say very helpful."

"I'll bet it is."

"Learn some new things too. Like some runner never do well in rain. Some not good on certain ground . . . surface."

"High tech comes to track and field," Sean said sarcastically.

"You must do same thing. American computers much better."

"Lots of the big teams do, but not my little country. I live in America, but I'm the enemy at Olympic time. I've never even been to their Olympic training center."

"Chinese have new training center in Wuyi mountain, high up, good for runner."

"Yes, and new German coaches. Not good for anybody."

"German coach very strict. Help old Chinese coach to learn better."

"Help them to learn to cheat," Sean said harshly.

"Chinese don't cheat. Athletes win fair. Practice very hard," Lin protested.

"If they listen to the Germans, they'll be cheating. How about your women swimmers who were caught last winter?"

"That was mistake." Lin Pao was becoming agitated.

"It was a mistake on the part of the East Germans. They thought they were smarter than they really were. They've been out of this for a couple of years. The lab people are a jump ahead of them."

"Embarrassment to Chinese people. You not see those swimmers again."

"Well, we'll see how your secret weapons do Thursday night."

"We have no secret weapons."

"You have three runners nobody ever heard of before, who are about to break world records. Where were they hidden?"

"Chao Lee ran in last Olympics. Did well. Not as well as you. I know. It is in the computer. But he train very hard."

"I know him. He may be straight, but how about the others?"

"All countries have new young runner. Try to hide. America too. It very important do well in Olympics. Atlanta get Olympics because of bad American publicity about student strike."

"You mean Tiananmen Square was a little student strike." The conversation was becoming more heated.

"America not know. You not there. I student then. Not about politics. Hooligan student want bigger stipend. Will not listen, then blame government for trouble. Lies. Next time Beijing get Olympics. Very important then for Chinese win. Do same thing as Americans." His English was deteriorating as he became more excited.

"If there are any great runners hiding around America, I haven't seen them. I doubt if they'll win any medals in my events."

Lin Pao laughed sarcastically. "You try fool Lin Pao, but computer has all record."

"Well, you must have some that I don't have."

Lin Pao smiled thinly. "You know secret American runner. He beat you."

All of a sudden Sean was very interested. "Who beat me at my distance? What American?" he asked Lin Pao, hoping he would accept the challenge.

"Root," Lin Pao answered.

Root! Grimes! How could this person know about him? And how much did he know? Then in a flash a horrifying possibility occurred to Sean. Suppose the Chinese had Root's secret. Grimes's lab assistant, had she gone back to China? These runners might be using Grimes's discovery right now. Could the East Germans have killed him and brought their new stooges to Germany to show up the rest of the track world in their old country? He needed more information.

"Oh, Root, Nancy Li's friend." It was a real effort for Sean to appear calm.

"Nancy Li?" Lin Pao's blank stare was genuine.

Damn, I should have learned her real name, Sean thought. *There must be ten million Li's in China. This is going nowhere. Better try a more direct approach.* "And you're telling me you expect to see Root compete against you in Sydney?"

Lin Pao was taken aback by the fury of the question. "Mr. Root very good. Surely must run."

"There is no *Mr*. Root. And you know it."

"Yes, yes, have picture." He realized as he said it that he no longer had the picture. Was this a trap? Had they planted the information as a test of his loyalty? He was perplexed. But what he heard next shocked him even more.

"It was *Doctor* Root, and he's dead. And I think your people killed him."

Lin Pao staggered back.

"And the Americans know about it." Might as well put some real fear into them all. This Pao was obviously an agent sent to question him. Well, he'd give them something to worry about. "They think they're about to catch the people who did it," he lied. "When the world learns that your government murders track stars they don't think they can beat, you'll all be barred from the Games, and there won't be an Olympics in Beijing until hell freezes over."

Lin Pao's mouth hung open. Sean waited to see the effect of his words, then rose, turned his back, and walked away.

Lin Pao stared after Sean, feeling more and more distraught. He had been enjoying his wonderful trip to Germany so much. He had found the special wine Schultz wanted, which had been harder than he expected. And he had found a jacket with Mickey Mouse on the breast pocket. That had been fun. But now this. Why had he ever tried to speak to Rourke? And this was one of his heroes. "I made up personalities for them, and I always thought he would be a gentleman. But that was foolishness. He insults my country. Accuses us of cheating." Lin Pao could hardly bring himself to repeat the words. The few athletes he knew directly would not cheat. He felt certain of it. Is this the way the rest of the world thinks of us? Do they all think of each other like that?

But as he was becoming more indignant he remembered Sean's comments about the women swimmers. What had really happened last winter? It was seldom mentioned in his country. The official explanation was that they had accidentally used some harmless drug that they did not know was proscribed. But was that the truth? Would they have been banned from competition for two years on the basis of an accident? And Sean's comments about the Germans. Were Germans training the women swimmers? He had to have more information, but who would know? Perhaps he should speak to Yan Tse, the head coach of the Chinese team.

And then he thought of Root and almost immediately wondered if he had said too much in his attempts to show off his system and to try to hurt this Irishman who had not responded appropriately to his friendly gesture. Root was dead Sean had said, murdered by Chinese, his own countrymen. Had he heard correctly? His English was not that good. Was there a real man who had actually been killed? Or was it like killing a story. But what about the picture? But the picture had disappeared from his file. And the way the Germans were so interested at first, and then after a while Schultz didn't care. Had Schultz figured out that it was all an American trick? Or had Schultz arranged to have him killed? And Sean had become so angry. Was he pretending? He said the Americans knew and the police were about to catch the people who did it. Could the Americans know about him? Could they think he was involved? Was he to blame because he had found Root and told Schultz? Suddenly Lin Pao shivered in horror. Could the Americans make the German police arrest him while he was in Germany? The Americans, he imagined, could do anything. He had waited with such anticipation for this trip, and now he only wished that he were back in China. Should he tell anyone of this? He could never go to Schultz. He must tell Yan Tse. The old coach would never have been involved in this himself, and Lin knew how much Tse resented the Germans. Why did they need these German coaches anyway? Yes he must talk to Yan Tse, but in private. He had visions of his room being bugged, even in this hotel, luxurious beyond anything that he had ever experienced. Was his imagination running away with him? But he knew from his uncle that there were listening devices in those Beijing hotels that were designed for foreign visitors. Why should it be any different here?

Lin Pao approached Yan Tse later that same afternoon as the Chinese team finished its abbreviated workout. "Master Tse." He addressed him with the ancient title of utmost respect. "I have had a most unnerving experience and I must speak to you of it in the strictest confidence."

"Certainly Lin Pao, my old friend. What can have caused you so much concern? Let us sit here," he motioned to two chairs in almost the same spot where Lin had spoken with Sean.

Lin Pao told his story uninterrupted except at the first mention of Root when Master Tse interjected, "Did you not previously tell me of this Root? You have never mentioned him again." Lin was impressed that Yan Tse would remember the incident related to him so casually months earlier. When he finished describing his encounter with Sean, Lin went on to express his concerns and doubts.

"Do you know that Mr. Rourke has withdrawn from the race tomorrow?" Tse asked.

"No." Lin Pao was shocked and disappointed. He had vacillated between wanting to see his former hero perform at his best and wanting his countrymen to humiliate this barbarian.

"He claims that he will run a marathon on October thirty-first in Dublin to qualify for his country's Olympic team at that distance. It is too close for him to do both."

"But surely he had intended to run here?" Lin Pao asked.

"That is what everyone thought. I do not know the significance of this change. He must run the 10K in Sydney now that he has won the world championship. Does he fear our runners so much? It is true that Lin Han and Ho Dak are running better than we had ever expected, and Chou Lee is always a threat. I will use him to pace the others."

"Perhaps Rourke really believes they are cheating and that he has no possibility of winning. But this cannot be true, Master, tell me that it is not true. You know the authorities here in Stuttgart would love to detect cheating and humiliate their old rivals, and they would humiliate us at the same time. This cannot be permitted."

"Well, the Germans have made mistakes before, but we shall see."

"You refer to the women swimmers, Master Tse."

"Those coaches were so successful in East Germany years ago. They cheated but were never caught, although everyone suspected them. But times change, and the methods of testing have become much better. The Germans who were responsible for the embarrassment of our swimmers are no longer with us." His meaning was quite clear.

"But these other Germans will also be found out. We will be disgraced again."

"Time will tell, Lin Pao. Time will tell. It is not the same with the men. If they try something, it will have to be much different."

"Why is that?" Lin Pao asked.

"It is much easier to improve the performance of the women. One just gives them male hormones and hopes not to be detected."

"How is it possible?"

"Perhaps you should ask that question of our German friends." Yan Tse permitted himself the faintest smile. "There are ways. One could make a new male hormone, very powerful in very small amounts, so that it could not be detected. Or one could use a hormone that disappears very rapidly, use it to build muscle strength in the women but stop in time before testing at the races. This is more difficult now that there is random testing throughout the year."

"And it is for this that we have these Germans?" Lin Pao said with scorn.

"They have much to teach us besides how to cheat. After all," Tse said with a smile, "they have given us you and your wonderful computer system."

Lin Pao was almost to the point of wondering whether he was glad of that or not.

Tse rose slowly from his seat. "We have leaders who want success very badly," he continued. "They do not all share our principles, and they would be glad to look the other way if the Germans use some improper method to achieve this success. But our leaders will not tolerate a repeat of the fiasco of the women swimmers. Even Germans can disappear in China, especially these Germans who will hardly be missed in their homeland. You must tell no one of our conversation. Do not be disillusioned about Mr. Rourke, who is an honorable gentleman and a worthy competitor. I have watched him for years, and he is reaching the pinnacle of success. He is coached by an American, the finest coach of distance runners. I have studied his methods. He too is entirely honorable. These men represent the best in our sport."

Yan Tse strode away in the direction of the locker rooms, but Lin Pao remained behind and walked slowly around the outside of the track pondering the Master's final remarks. He felt better having talked to Yan Tse but was still left with a number of deep concerns. The world was not as simple or as honorable as his computer data would suggest. It was true, although he had never thought of it explicitly, that this Irishman was coached by an American. Was he not undermining his own country's chances? Why would he be allowed to do such a thing? Could it be that the sport itself meant more to these individuals than national loyalty? *I cannot understand such an attitude,* he thought, *but I do not participate in these sports.* He turned, looked to the right and left, then stepped over the low barrier and reverentially set foot on the empty track. At first he tiptoed, silently, carefully placing one clean white running shoe before the other. Then he skipped and ran a dozen steps, feeling the springiness of the magic surface. Embarrassed, he glanced around to see if he had been observed and then slowly and with dignity walked a complete lap.

Chapter 19

Sean's plan was working to perfection. He had hoped his last minute entry in the Stuttgart meet would force the hand of the Chinese. Knowing that he was the competition, Sean reasoned, they would use whatever illegal tricks were at their disposal. And the more chances the monitoring laboratories had to test the Chinese runners, the more likely they were to be exposed. After his conversation with Lin Pao, Sean felt sure that the Chinese would not be holding back.

While he had suspected that something illegal was being done, he had not made the connection to Grimes until his conversation with Lin Pao. *What's his role in this*? Sean wondered. *In some ways Pao seems so incredibly naive. He obviously said more than he intended and then tried to cover it up pretending that he didn't know what had happened to Root. But he didn't seem to recognize what's-her-name Li. Well, by stretching the truth a little bit I hope I at least caused them some worry. And now I don't even have to run.*

Half of Sean's mission in Stuttgart had been accomplished, but there was still one thing that remained to be done. He wanted to get a close-up view of the Chinese runners in action.

From his hotel room Sean dialed the offices of *International Running News* and asked for the senior editor, Ralph Hooker.

After listening to his old friend's expressions of surprise and warm greetings, Sean came right to the point. "I need a favor and I have something to swap."

"Must be a big one," Ralph said.

"I think the Chinese are up to something."

"So does everybody else," Ralph answered. "I hear you're avoiding them. Don't want to make people think you're afraid."

"No, I'm under a lot of pressure to qualify in the Dublin marathon. You know, it's only a little more than a week away. That's just too close, and anyway since August I've been marathon training. My original plan was to do New York."

"Boy, that switch will cost you some money."

"It's probably for the better. Some people are starting to forget that I'm Irish."

"Well, what can I do for you?" Ralph asked.

"I want to be at trackside when the Chinese run."

"Did you ask the organizers?"

"I didn't ask them because I didn't want them to say no. I want to be a special reporter for *IRN*, in fact, I want to be your photographer. Credential me and they can't keep me out. Nobody would interfere with any of your people. The *News* is just too powerful."

"That's a little bit of dirty pool," Ralph protested.

"Not that much. You've used runners before to cover events when they weren't competing, and for expert commentary and editorials. Hell, I've done it a few times for you myself."

"I guess that's right, but in this case it makes me feel that we're part of a spy plot."

"You are. And my part of the deal is that when this story breaks I'll give it to you first."

"You really think you have a lead that nobody else has?" Ralph asked.

"I know it," Sean insisted, "and it's yours as soon as I can tell you about it."

"Well, I'd like to see those bastards nailed, they're a disgrace to the sport, and I'd love to be the person to do it. I think you've got yourself a deal, old buddy. Do you even have a camera or do I have to provide one of those?"

"Get me a fancy one and a couple of lessons on how to use it. I'd actually like to take a few pictures of them. And there's one other thing you could do."

"But I've already made my bargain," Ralph reminded him.

"Ah, but this will add to the value of the thing you just bought."

"Okay, what is it?"

"Somebody from the *News* will be an official steward, that's almost always the case."

"Yes, let me see who it's going to be. Uhh, I can't remember right now . . ."

"Doesn't matter," Sean interrupted. "I just need him to find out something."

"More spy business, huh?"

"I want him to look at the urine samples and see if some of them are pink."

"Pink?"

"Yes, red, pale red. Usually they all drink so much Gatorade that it's practically the color of straw. I want to know if it's a little red."

"But, Sean, they can't be taking something that's coming out in their urine. Anybody would spot it in a minute."

"Just trust me and see if you can find out. That shouldn't be too much trouble, and he ought to be able to get a look if he plays his cards right. He could volunteer for that part of the job. Somebody has to do it."

"Okay. If that's what you want, I'll see if I can arrange it. But it doesn't make a lot of sense."

"Trust me, and get me a good camera."

Ralph Hooker was as good as his word, and the race organizers didn't seem to show any signs of surprise when Sean showed up the next day with his press badge. At race time the infield was filled with coaches, training assistants, aides and track officials, and an enormous number of reporters. Most of the members of the press were clustered around the start-finish line, but for what Sean wanted anywhere would do. He picked a relatively open spot halfway down the second straight, took a few practice shots with the camera, and waited for the race to begin.

Sean noticed the three Chinese runners loosening up together. Lin Pao was in their midst. Despite what Pao had told him, Sean still assumed that he was a coach or trainer. In fact Pao had been brought only as a translator, since few of the other members of the Chinese contingency spoke fluent German. It took Sean a few minutes to recognize the elderly Chinese man dressed in an ill-fitting, dark, western-style suit. It was Yan Tse, for years the titular head of the Chinese track and field program. "Maybe that little bastard, Pao, has pushed him aside," he muttered.

Sean studied the competitors. The German, Hans Schneider, was his country's leading 10K runner. The Stuttgart race would be mandatory for him. Kao Katanya, one of the promising new Kenyans, was not yet top three in his own country, but he would be soon. Sean knew he was determined to win a spot on his country's Olympic team. Then there was the Belgian, Francois Dryx, past his prime but still formidable. Injuries had ruined his year. He had not made the finals in the Worlds, but this was a chance to redeem his season.

The race began, and at first Sean allowed himself to just enjoy the strategy. After all, the runners would pass his position some twenty-five times, more than enough to pick up elements of their style and record them for future use. Chao Lee went to the front and set a fast pace. *He was ordered to do that,* Sean thought. *That doesn't suit his style at all. In fact, he's a person who should be moving up to the marathon. Instead he's sacrificing himself for the others.* It wasn't quite like being a rabbit. It was a more sophisticated role. Katanya was on his heels. *Being sucked into the trap.*

Schneider and the other two Chinese were in the middle of the pack, and Dryx, as usual for this point in the race, was in the rear. There was little change for the first three miles. The pace was very fast. A *lot of them won't be able to keep this up*, Sean thought, *but now they're stuck, and they have to try. By the fifth mile they'll be dropping like flies.*

Sean concentrated on the two other Chinese runners, Han and Dak. They were almost hidden in the pack, but he was in no hurry. He knew the group would stretch out soon enough. At four and a half miles Chao Lee began to falter. "Predictable," Sean pointed out to a stranger standing next to him. "He just can't run like that. That's not his strength."

Katanya went past. There was nothing else for him to do. The horse in front was dying. Runners were falling out of the middle pack. Dryx passed three of them, but he was not gaining on the leaders. Schneider stayed with the two Chinese runners. Eventually this threesome began to gain on Katanya. At five miles, they increased their speed and passed Katanya, who began to fade badly. Then the two Chinese began to open space on Schneider. Dryx passed the Kenyan. He was fourth but trailing Schneider by a good twenty yards. Sean began snapping pictures, pausing between shots to study the runners. The two Chinese were continuing to increase their lead on Schneider.

This race is over. Sean treated the two Chinese as if they were one runner. The whole Bradsford scene eleven months earlier came back to him as if it were yesterday. Would he have recognized it if he hadn't talked to Lin Pao? There was something about the way they ran, something that reminded him of Blue Man. They just weren't breathing hard enough.

Han inched ahead of Dak. They weren't exactly running easily, they were putting forth tremendous effort. Sean could see the pain in their faces. This was a command performance, an all-out effort, no cruising at the end. This was a race for time. It would not be enough to win. They had to impress the German fans. But they just weren't breathing hard enough. Han finished first to thunderous applause, followed by Dak, Schneider, Dryx and the also-rans. Chao Lee staggered over the finish line more than two minutes behind. The time? It was a meet record, and it was fastest time of year, but not a world record. It had beaten Sean's time at the World Championships, and this performance before international judges was authentic. "Not exactly the same conditions," Sean murmured to himself defensively, "but probably better than I could have done today with all my recent marathon training."

He had remained behind and was repacking the photographic equipment that the *News* had provided when Lin Pao approached. Sean could see him coming and tried to think up some snappy retort to what he was sure was going to be a comment about his lack of courage.

"See you in Sydney, turkey" was the most elegant thing he could come up with on short notice. But Lin Pao's greeting was a surprise.

"A thousand pardons, Mr. Rourke, if I have disturbed you in our conversation. I have told Master Yan Tse about it. He says that you and your coach, Mr. Higgum, are most honorable gentlemen. I hope I was not the cause of your not running today."

Sean was taken aback. It was not what he had expected. "No, I have been told by my Olympic committee," he said, slightly stretching the truth, "that I must qualify for the marathon by running in Dublin in just ten days. You will soon have it on your computer."

Lin Pao looked amazed. "You will not do ten kilometers?" Sean began to shake his head. "You will do impossible double?"

"We are thinking of it," Sean answered, "but the final decision hasn't been made."

"Then I will wish you good fortune, but of course I must hope for the success of my countrymen. Not all Chinese are alike."

"That is true everywhere," Sean replied. "I admire your loyalty."

"Perhaps we will meet again." Pao extended his hand.

The celebration at the training center in the Wuyi mountains was held several days later. They knew the results, of course, but had waited for Lin Pao to return with the tapes.

"He is the most useful of them all," Jurgen said.

"You only think that because of the wine." Schultz laughed.

"Ja, to find eight bottles of Grauberg Moselle, and even the correct year. I told you he was dependable."

"He must have learned useful habits during his year in Hamburg, like where to find good wine."

"Ja, and it goes so well with the trout," Jurgen said, "that we may have to send him back for more."

Lin Pao had never before been in the guest dining room, and he had never spoken to Reinhart Jurgen. It was an honor to be invited, but still he approached the meeting with trepidation. In this country honors were sometimes followed closely by misfortune. He had resolved to tell the Germans nothing about his meeting with Rourke. Was he being disloyal? Did they deserve his loyalty? Did they have the best interests of his country at heart? No, he would give his allegiance to Yan Tse, his own countryman.

Even the small glass of the precious wine, which had been poured for him, would not seduce him into joining the German camp. Actually he didn't even like it. Why had he been asked to go to so much trouble to bring it back? *It's sour, and you can hardly taste the grapes. Not like Red Dragon which is really good. But if it enhances my position here, it will be a small price to pay.*

The Germans watched the tape over and over, with no attempt to conceal their satisfaction. Han and then Dak ran past Schneider, then ran backward at double speed, then passed him yet again. Then came an endless stream of questions. How did the crowd react? How about Schneider, did he congratulate them? You could see on the tape that he had. How about the German coaches, how did they react? The reporters, the other competitors . . . ? Lin Pao tried his best to give an accurate impression of the whole event, but the subtleties that seemed so important to them would have been difficult for him to convey even in his native language. Finally came the question he dreaded most. "Was ist's mit Rourke?"

"He will run a marathon in Ireland on Monday."

"Then he came just to spy," Schultz declared. "I hope he saw good."

"They say he planned to run. I myself saw him practicing on the stadium track. But then we were told that the Olympic Committee of Ireland required him to qualify in Dublin."

"Can you believe this, Schultz?" Jurgen raised both hands in the air in a gesture of resignation.

"Nein. The brave Irisher is afraid," he laughed as he answered.

"But, Herrn, to not run Stuttgart and now to miss New York, he will lose so much money. He would never choose it unless forced," Lin noted.

"Hmm. True, Pao. These runners do everything for money."

"Can he possibly train for both distances? Do you think we have frightened him out of the 10K in Sydney?" Schultz asked them both.

Jurgen turned to Lin Pao. "We will be most interested in the computer report from Dublin." It was clearly a sign of dismissal, and he left with a great feeling of relief.

"You know, I did not even mind his accent tonight," Jurgen said laughing.

"They must take us back now." Schultz was up, pacing the room.

"They will never take us back."

"But you saw how well it worked." He was becoming more excited. "You saw how they destroyed Schneider. What can his coaches say against us now? They must resign."

"No. No. They will never do it. And besides we have gone too far now to bring everything back to Germany."

"We can forget what we have done here. Leave it behind or destroy it. The second phase will be far superior, and we can carry it out better and faster in Germany, with real scientists. I wish to work with our own athletes, not these foreigners. Did you not see, there were no blacks within four hundred meters, none of the vaunted

Kenyans? We have proved what we can do. We can win everything. They must listen."

"Manfred, my good friend," Jurgen said, "you must give up this foolish dream. Everything has changed. They will never listen. They do not want to hear. It just doesn't matter as much to them now. We can never go back. Our satisfaction must now come from the athletes we have, whoever they are and whatever their country. That is our role. We must do our best. And I intend to enjoy beating everyone, including Germans, especially Germans."

Chapter 20

With a few telephone calls Sean completed the arrangements for Dublin, a room for himself, and as a surprise one for his parents, at the Shelbourne Hotel, a change in airline tickets, and finally a call to Hugh Downey, a friend on the organizing committee of the marathon.

"I can't believe it," was his reaction. "You know, we don't have the kind of money you demand."

"I think that I should be able to qualify for my own country's Olympic team without demanding any money." Sean laughed.

"Of course, there's no trouble at all getting you in. We accept anyone right up to the time of the race. For someone like you, we'd even accept you after the race started, in case you wanted to give the others a little handicap," Hugh joshed.

"I'm not that generous."

"Well, the two fastest will be about 2:20, if it's a very good day. This isn't New York or London. No thousands of people trying to get in by lottery. No big prize money. We hope to get two thousand, mostly local people, mostly just recreational runners, maybe twenty from your new country."

"It's not my new country," Sean protested.

"I know. Just teasing you a bit, lad. There'll be some American tourists, maybe some students. It's great fun."

"Anything I should know about the course?" Sean asked.

"No surprises. It starts at the post office, a big figure eight really, a two-mile stretch you do twice, over on the other side of the square. Only two hills but the second one into Phoenix Park is the killer. It goes up forever, and often there's a headwind blowing down the hill against you."

"I used to run it for practice when I was in Dublin," Sean said.

"Yes, but it feels a bit different after twenty miles. This isn't one of the easier courses around, laddie. Never have been very good times here. But once you've made it that far, there's just a long downhill to the river and about a mile back to the Post Office. I'll be waiting for you with your medal."

"You set up our drinks for us?" Sean asked.

"Yes, just bring your bottles about a half hour before the race. We'll get them out to the stations."

"How do you mark them?"

"A big 'R' will be fine. There won't be that many people up there with you to steal the drinks. Probably won't be more than fifty to a hundred 2:12 marathoners with last initial 'R' running Dublin this year," he joked. "Small time, Sean. Very friendly, lots of fun, and you know the crowd's going to love you. It's okay for me to announce it?"

"Yes, I'll be there," Sean said and hung up the phone.

He had toyed with the idea of going to Oxford for a day or two but realized it wouldn't be wise. On the other hand, he didn't want to be anywhere in Ireland where people would fuss over him. The pre-marathon week was a time to rest, run a little, and eat pasta.

Sean arrived in Dublin four days before the race, checked into his hotel, and walked the several blocks to a medical bookstore near Trinity College. He asked for a physiology textbook and was presented with an enormous and expensive tome. "I could use this instead of my weights," he told the clerk. Back in the hotel room he carefully tore out the chapters on the heart, lungs, and cardiovascular system. Next day he rented a car and settled into his new routine, a drive out into the country, a short run done at eight-tenths speed—six miles on Thursday would be the longest—and the afternoon under a tree with his newly acquired reading material. The hotel was happy to provide lunch. Pasta salad was perfect. A little wine would have made it better, but Sean never drank during the week before a race. The weather cooperated. Beautiful autumn days. Even gray Dublin seemed cheerful.

His parents arrived the day before the marathon. They were a little overwhelmed by the luxury of the hotel. It just added to Sean's aura. They were the typical doting parents, and he was their only son. That evening they ate in the main dining room, and Sean struggled through one last pasta meal.

"We're so proud of you," his mother said over and over again when she wasn't fussing about how and what he was eating. "It's a shame your sisters can't be here. But Bridget with the new one, and Katie so far away now, and the notice so short and all."

"And Mary?"

"Oh, they would never let her out. It's not like some of these new orders, so lax you wonder what it means. Even the clothes, you know."

"But how is she?"

"It seems to suit her just fine."

"The boys at the Dragon Head will all be listening tomorrow you can be sure," his father said. "It's not on the telly, just the radio. But that won't stop them from downing a good few in your name."

"Oh, John, more's the pity, and it's not something to be bragging to Sean about," his mother rebuked.

"But they're real fans of Sean, Liz, and tomorrow's a holiday, so they can start a little early." He turned to Sean. "Remember when you beat that fellow from Galbirne, the one they made so much of?"

"He ran for Trinity," Sean answered.

"But he was from Galbirne, just north of the pub, the Swan, and he was three years senior."

"Two."

"Two and some. And all the papers for him. I never told you how much was bet on that race, son. Thought it would make you too nerved up to run." He laughed. "But you'll never have to buy at the Dragon. It will always be on the house. They still tell that story late on an evening. And how Mattie got those odds, seven to two, I remember it like yesterday, when he came back."

"How you go on, John, and not even something we should hear."

She likes the story as much as he does, Sean thought, *but can't admit it.*

"Anyway, I don't think that Higgum fellow was right making you give up the mile."

"He didn't make me, dad, and he was right. You know, Bob would fit right in with your friends at the Dragon."

"Maybe so. Maybe not. Name's from Cork I'm thinking. Some

good lads there."

His parents were used to eating early at home, and there was no trouble finishing by eight. Sean went to bed.

He woke the next morning to a gray day, the first since his arrival in Ireland. Marathoner weather. The preparations for the start were as casual as Sean had been led to believe. Runners milled about in front of the post office. Some sat in the McDonald's across the street having last-minute glasses of orange juice while their friends and families had breakfast. The restaurant was giving out gold cardboard crowns as a promotion, and half of the runners were wearing them. But Sean was too superstitious for that. He greeted several old school friends among the competitors.

"You look in great shape."

"You too."

"I'll pace you at the start, if you'd like," one offered.

"Thanks. Just run along with me and fill me in on the news."

"He won't be with you for long," another friend joked.

"As long as you, I'll wager," the first one answered.

Word of Sean's participation had brought reporters and photographers, and the attention alerted the other runners. Many came by to wish him luck. In a marathon few runners have a serious chance of winning. Most have their own personal goals, often just to finish. The camaraderie is infectious.

Sean started from the front of the pack and within a mile had settled in with the serious runners, a group of about twenty-five. Surprisingly, there were several rabbits out ahead, but no one paid much attention. He had arranged for his parents to walk across St. Stephen's Green in front of the hotel to see him at the two-mile mark. They waved. Sean had told them he would be back at the same spot in about an hour, and he reappeared right on schedule. Now they would have another hour or so to browse in the center of town and walk the four or five blocks to the finish back at the post office.

For Sean the race turned out to be as comfortable as it was for his parents. He had never run a figure-eight course, and it did seem strange after an hour to be retracing part of the original route. The major test was the hill in Phoenix Park. Yes, it was harder after an hour and a half of racing, but it was there that Sean left the others for good. Across the top of the park, down the wide central promenade toward the statue, loop back up, always misleading, out of the park, and then the long downhill to the river. *Delightful*, thought Sean now just enjoying the run. *Too bad they all don't end downhill. Well, no. Too bad they don't all end downhill if there's nobody seriously chasing you.* Onto the embankment. No followers in sight. Around the bend in the river, then a sharp left turn and three blocks to the finish line.

Sean was surprised at the size of the crowd that had gathered, to a large extent, no doubt, because of him. As he ran through the narrow pathway lined ten deep with spectators, he heard the shouts. "Rourke, Rourke, Rourke. Sydney. Gold, gold. Way to go. Show 'em. Ireland. For Ireland." They were his countrymen, and they made him glad of his decision. He sprinted toward the finish line. 2:12:21. For this day, this course, this competition, a great result. Someone wrapped a blanket around his shoulders. He saw his parents and waved. The crowd parted as he went to meet them. His mother threw her arms around his neck, and when she finally let go, his father pumped his hand.

"It's a national hero you are," she said, hanging onto his other arm.

"Now isn't that almost as good as being a priest?" He could never resist teasing her.

"The lord hears things like that, Sean." She tried to be stern. It never worked.

"Much better," his father answered.

Other runners began to trail in. Finally the lead woman, Megan Riley, arrived in a time that would qualify for an automatic berth in Sydney. Sean had not met her before, in fact, had never heard of her and had not seen her during the race. *How could I have missed her with that flaming red hair*? He thought. She had run a very respectable time.

"Congratulations, teammate." He waited until she had a moment to catch her breath and then gave her a hug.

"That was my best time ever," she gasped. "I really surprised myself and probably a few other people."

"My PR too," Sean told her.

"It was a good day, good weather. The downhill at the end really helps," she said. Sean nodded in agreement.

They had a chance to talk again after the awards ceremony. "I was in my second year at Trinity but dropped out a year ago to train for this," she said.

"You seem much too young for the marathon," Sean answered.

She laughed. "I can't do the shorter distances. I've tried. My legs just don't go around fast enough. But they don't stop. My coach thinks I should be an ultra-marathoner."

"Don't even mention it," Sean groaned, thinking of what it would feel like to run another marathon right then. "That's not my thing."

"Well, it's not mine yet," Megan said. They exchanged addresses promising to be in touch as the designated leaders of their country's marathon team.

On the flight back, Sean had time to ponder the events in Stuttgart. Had it been wise to tell Lin Pao that the American authorities were investigating the murder of Root? He had done it in a fit of anger, and it certainly had felt good, but he could imagine a number of ramifications.

Bob Hooker had called Sean in Dublin with the news that the urine samples of Lin Han and Ho Dak were indeed pale red in color, but Chao Lee's was clear. "The drug screens showed nothing in the urine," he proclaimed. "You're on to something, and I want the story."

"I don't know what I'm on to," Sean had answered. "When I find out, you'll get it first."

Now he was determined to talk to Lou Gurci as soon as possible. Sean was sure that the Chinese were using Grimes's discovery. They knew about Root, when no one else had ever even heard of him, and they had pink urine which passed the screens just as Grimes's urine had. Did that mean they had killed him? Well, if Grimes had been murdered, the Chinese were the prime suspects. Had he found the motive Gurci was missing?

Chapter 21

Sean and Bill arranged to meet outside Gurci's office. This was Sean's first visit to an American police station, and it was unlike anything that he had imagined. The small brick building stood on a picture-perfect village green alongside white churches dating back to Colonial times and a stone library a century younger. It would have been hard to find except for the flags, the American flag and the state flag flying overhead. The big-city police precincts pictured so dramatically on TV seemed to belong to a different world. On the far side of the building, almost hidden from view, were several cruisers. As he drew nearer, he noted three police bicycles and was amused to see that they were chained to a bicycle rack. "I guess you tough cops haven't managed to stamp out all of the crime yet," Sean said with a grin.

"That's the meanest, lowest crime there is, stealing a bicycle from a policeman." Bill laughed.

Lou's office was tiny. They crowded in, exchanged friendly greetings and sat in two plain, wooden armchairs.

"Boy, you really need that new station," Bill said. "Even ours is bigger than this."

"You know it," Lou agreed. "But the referendum passed almost three to one. We're going to be in it in less than a year. Funny, they voted down a swimming pool, couple other things. They could've afforded them all. No trouble. Taxes are low anyway, and people are pretty well off. But they're into law and order. Everybody coming round to congratulate us. Giving us the thumbs up on the street. Man, it's not like the New York ghetto. Here we get whatever we want, the best of everything." He swept his hand through the air expansively.

Indeed, Sean had noticed a mass of computer equipment filling the top of Lou's desk and spilling over onto a makeshift stand.

"So you got something new on Grimes?" Lou asked. "Just give it to me straight like last time. I'm the guy who gets the real story, remember." He laughed.

Sean laughed too. "It's so much easier that way. There are so many versions floating around now I can't keep track of them myself." He started in on the story, the reports of the near record-breaking performances coming out of China, about the Chinese skipping the world championships, then planning to introduce these "characters," as Sean referred to them, in Germany at Stuttgart, rumors of the German connection, the fiasco with the women swimmers, and Sean's plan of entrapment by entering at the last minute and then withdrawing.

"Smart trick," Lou interrupted, "but do you think they're onto you because of it?"

"Oh, they're onto me. I made sure of that. Let me finish." He described his meeting with Lin Pao and the race.

"You could tell something was funny just watching them run?" Sean nodded. "That going to hold up anywhere?"

"I don't know. The average spectator would never notice. I just assume that any professional runner would, but maybe not. You tend to think that somebody who's in your class knows everything you know, but it isn't always the case. Bob Higgum, my coach, trained me to see everything in the other runners. If they shorten their stride half an inch, it stands out to me like a big red sign."

Lou's eyes widened a little, but he nodded assent. "I believe you," he said. "It's like me watching a hundred guys walk down the street in the Bronx, and I can tell you who's carrying. I could just go pull in the ones I want. But the courts would throw it out. If I got some reason to be suspicious, I can pull 'em over. But can I ever convince a judge that I'm so good I just have to watch them? No way. They say you're picking on the minorities or something. True, a lot of them are minorities, but that's not why I'm picking on them. I can tell who's carrying. Anyway, that's not a problem for me anymore. Go on, don't let me stop you."

Sean described the second meeting with Lin Pao and then told Lou about the urine.

"How'd you find that out?"

"Oh, through a friend."

"Hey, remember I'm the guy you tell everything to."

"Even my secret informants," Sean laughed and went on to tell him about the plan he had put into effect with Ralph Hooker.

"So how's the red urine tied into Grimes?"

Sean told him about Grimes's red urine. "I thought I told you about it before, but maybe I didn't. Not trying to hold anything back, you know." He laughed again, "You're the guy who gets the whole truth. But there are things I just don't always remember to tell."

"I usually don't forget things," Lou said, "but I don't remember that. Anyway, it goes along with the doc trying his own invention and then these guys stealing it and bumping him off." His face darkened. It struck Sean that Lou Gurci was a person who kept his anger inside, and when there was enough to come up to the surface it was probably best not to be around, or at least not to be the object of that anger. There was silence. Lou sat back in his chair, his elbows propped on the arms, his fingertips meeting in front of his nose.

Finally Bill said, "What do you make of it, Lou?"

Very slowly from behind the fingertips came, "I think those fuckin' Chinese or their German buddies killed the famous cancer doctor in my town." Sean involuntarily moved back in his chair. Maybe there really were policemen like those depicted on television.

"But we don't know that, Lou," Bill cautioned. "Even if they got the secret from his lab, maybe from that Chinese woman, it doesn't mean they killed him."

"I just know it, Bill." Lou cut him off. "I just feel it."

Sean was inclined to agree, and to support Lou's opinion he went on, "And there's another thing, maybe just as important. You remember I told you about Grimes's lab people all leaving, and how one was going to a new position in Seattle to start in September." Lou nodded. "Well, she never arrived."

"Never arrived?" Lou repeated.

"Beth Markham waited until after the semester started and then called the university, and they said she never showed up. Apparently she sent them a letter at the last minute resigning before she ever started. Never gave a reason. I guess her new chairman was really pissed."

Lou paused before responding. He seemed back under control and spoke very softly. "How do we know she even wrote the letter?"

"We can find out," Bill offered. "I hope the guy wasn't so mad he threw it away."

"What's her name?" Lou inquired. "I can get her stats from the university. We know how to trace people."

"Ann Grossman."

Bill was shaking his head. "How could we ever find these guys, even if Grimes was murdered?"

"That would mean it was a pro," Lou said. "Always thought so. The Chinese always use their own. It's their way. I never saw them hire an outsider. None of their gangs are up here, so that means New York. That's a big help. The old way be to go down and rattle Chinatown. Rattle enough it'd fall out. New way," he added nodding to his computers. "There're maybe a thousand of those funny tires I told you about been sold in the whole country. Checking them all would be a hell of a lot of work. Already did Connecticut, thinking it might be local kids. There were only eighteen, and I found every one. But it took more time than I could spare, especially since I'm doing this on my own. But now I know to look in New York and Jersey. That'll make it easier. And I got a little more incentive now."

"Let me help, Lou. Give me your list. I'll take Jersey. You do New York. And now we know Chinese names get first priority."

"Thanks, Bill. That's going to make it go a lot faster." Lou leaned back in his chair again, "And I think maybe we'll do a little of each way. You know what they say, 'something old, something new.' I'll use my old connections in Chinatown."

Lou rose from his desk. "Okay Sean, you're doing good work. I told you once before you could be in some danger. I think there's less danger because of what you told that Chinese guy. They'd only bump you off to keep the secret. If they think American officials already know what they did, what's the sense of going after you?"

Sean didn't know whether to be reassured by that or not. Frankly he hadn't considered being bumped off at all, so being told that the chances were a little less wasn't exactly good news.

"I guess it warns them a little bit," Lou said. "But hell, maybe it'll make them do something foolish. They might just bump off the guy themselves, save me the trouble. Course then we won't get a chance to question him. Anyway, I want to be informed of anything that comes up."

They said goodbye, and Sean and Bill walked back toward their cars.

"That guy's tough, I was almost afraid to be in the room."

"There's a lot of New York left in him. I think he came up here to get away from that. He didn't like what he was becoming. But you can see it's still there."

"You don't agree with him about Grimes being murdered, do you?" Sean asked.

Bill shrugged. "When I introduced him to you that first time, I told you he was always right, so what can I say?" He changed the subject. "Hey, Sean, you've got to get a new car."

Sean laughed, "Yeah, a hundred thousand miles and parking on the Philadelphia streets. But then I never have to worry about it. See I didn't even chain it to a tree."

Chapter 22

The events in Stuttgart had increased Sean's anxiety to the point where the Grimes mystery was never out of his mind. Finally he came to a major decision, to move to Grenville so he could spend more time discovering the secret of Mr. Root. However, he needed Bob Higgum's blessing to be away for some months. They met in Bob's office shortly after his return from Dublin.

"So you're trading me in for a younger coach," Bob said.

Sean was shocked. It was the only sign of insecurity he had ever seen in Bob Higgum. But when Sean told him the real reason for going to Grenville, Bob was very understanding, in fact he acted as if it were his own idea. He had heard bits and pieces of the story in the past, when Sean was first trying to find Root. But now Sean brought him up to date about his suspicions that Grimes might have been murdered and his concern that the Chinese runners had discovered the secret.

"You go up to Grenville," Bob ordered, "and try to find out what this Grimes was up to. Jim can get you a position as a volunteer assistant coach, same as here. That way you can use their facilities. They'll love to have you, especially when they hear you don't need a salary."

"It's already set. A fancy title but no pay. They'll let me rent one of the apartments for visiting faculty. A few are still empty this year."

"Good. And I'll just kind of mosey around and see what I can learn. Actually I know Yan Tse quite well."

"You know everyone," Sean said.

"Not everyone, but I do know Tse. Right after Nixon opened China, I went over there as part of a sports cultural exchange program. Remember the Ping-Pong diplomacy?"

It had been before Sean's time, and he shook his head no.

"Well, they thought sports figures as ambassadors of good will were less threatening than businessmen or the military or whatever. Their facilities were awful, and the equipment was worse. I even arranged to send them our used running shoes. They had nothing. The things that we would throw out they would kill for. Of course, their feet were so small they used to shove tissue paper in the toes." Bob laughed. "You know, they seem to have gotten bigger over the years. I don't know whether they feed them more, or Tse just went out and found some taller ones."

"They had that one really tall basketball player," Sean noted.

"Yeah, didn't do 'em much good," Bob pointed out. "I guess with all those people to pick from you can get any shape you want. Tse's had some good ones over the years. Remember Chao Lee. You ran against him."

"Yes, and I told you, they used him as a rabbit at Stuttgart."

"I can't believe Yan Tse did that. The way I remember Lee, he shouldn't even have been a 10K man. If there ever was a guy who should have moved up to the marathon—I'll have to tell Tse. That's one thing, he always listened to what I told him. Almost too much. Maybe that's why I liked him." He laughed again. "Course he was a lot younger then. Course we both were. He must be almost as old as I am. Probably gotten just as independent and cantankerous."

"But, Mr. Higgum, you're so kindly and accommodating." Sean could hardly keep a straight face.

"I thought you told me you'd never seen the Blarney Stone. Lousy Irishman."

Higgum had outlined the entire training program right up to Sydney. It would be a challenge. Sean would run a series of indoor 10K's during the winter season.

"You have to do something in the winter," Higgum had said, "and besides, it pays the bills. Everybody's going to be ducking, so we'll ask for extra appearance money. They've got to put on a show if they want to draw some fans. And, of course, I expect you to win every one of them." It was a command.

Higgum's main concern now was the marathon training. "You can come down here on the weekends for the long runs, fifteen or twenty miles, and I'll watch them myself. We'll really build up the endurance and then go back to speed work in July and August."

Sean's base of operations at the medical school was Beth Markham's room or the adjoining office of Dr. Grimes. At first he occasionally sat in the office to read some of Grimes's papers, but as he used it more and more, he became increasingly uncomfortable. The offices of the radiation oncologists, there were twelve in all, were located along both sides of a short hallway. The more senior of them, Sean had noticed, were on the outside wall and had windows. Grimes's office was clearly second only to Kerr's in size and location.

"I don't see why someone doesn't ask to move into this better office?" he asked Beth. "They're going to resent my using it."

"They're trying to recruit a new tenured full professor to replace Dr. Grimes," she answered. "If they moved a junior person into the second-best office, they'd just have to move him out again."

When Sean mentioned it to Kerr, whom he saw regularly, the answer was the same, "When we need it, we'll throw you out. Meanwhile, just use it."

Still it gave Sean an eerie feeling to sit behind Grimes's desk in his chair, this man, whom he had seen only once, but who had started this strange chain of events. When he was tired of his reading, Sean's mind would wander. He could only try to imagine what it must have been like to sit there and do Grimes's work. He envied him his knowledge and his skill, but then Grimes, Sean thought, must have sat in the same chair when he grew tired of his work and daydreamed of being a famous runner.

The department's business office was in the basement. The manager, Frank Costanza, was one of the few people Sean had seen at the medical school who wore the classic chalk-striped, dark suit. Sean described the purpose of his visit using the same story that he generally told within the school. He ended with, "I have Dr. Kerr's permission to speak to people in the department to try to find out whether Grimes really had started some new project that most of the others wouldn't know about, maybe some work he was just doing on the side. We've reached something of a dead end, and several people have suggested that the business office might know about unusual expenditures that would give some clue to the nature of the research."

"I know," Frank said. "I checked with Beth and with Dr. Kerr to be sure they were in on this and had given their blessing. To tell you the truth, we've never had a request like this before. Nobody has ever asked us to try to find out what someone was doing in the laboratory by working backwards from the expenditures. Of course this is a really unusual circumstance. We haven't had a lot of our scientists die suddenly."

"Do you think you'll be able to help?" Sean asked.

"We'll try. Grimes had a number of research projects funded by the NCI and the ACS, but they should all be pretty well described in the grant applications. I think the best thing would be to look at expenditures from his 74 account. That's money which comes directly from the department. We charge things there when we can't seem to assign a cost to any of the grant accounts. Many of the new projects are funded that way."

"Can Grimes do whatever he wants with this account?" Sean asked.

"Well, with some restrictions. He couldn't decide to pay himself a big bonus or something like that. But with someone like Grimes that's never going to happen. Anything he asked for we would buy. We used to joke that someday we'd get an order for a spaceship. We've had some pretty kooky requests, like the $10,000 worth of fish. I never did find out what he did with them. He said something about having a big fish fry."

"Ten thousand dollars' worth of fish! And you didn't have any idea what they were for?" Sean asked incredulously.

"No, not exactly. For the research, of course. It was just a joke about the picnic. I guess the bottom line is we trusted him. We really have to trust them all. I wouldn't have any way of knowing when he sends us a bill from some biotech company on the West Coast whether it's valid or not."

"Could people steal money from these accounts?"

"That very rarely comes up," Costanza answered with a chill in his voice. "Here, let's just check the 74 account for the last couple of years and see where the money went."

They sat in front of a computer screen.

"Okay, let's start with personnel," Frank continued. "Here's Li.

Everybody called her Nancy, but there's her real first name. Try to pronounce that one."

Remembering how he had wanted it in Stuttgart, Sean took out a small notebook and copied the full name, "Xiaojian Li."

"She went back to China," Frank continued. "But see here, she was seventy-five percent on this account and twenty-five percent on one of the research grants. That's Grimes's attempt to apportion her salary fairly. She must have been spending about three-quarters of her time on some project that wasn't funded from outside sources.

"Now here's Ann Grossman. She was a post-doc who went to Seattle. Supposed to be absolutely terrific. Here's her C.V. We have everything on the computer now. Graduate of Stanford, summa cum laude, Ph.D. from Harvard, six years to get it. That's typical. Three years down here as a post-doc before we took her. We had a real problem getting her that salary. Funny, the medical school tells us how much we can pay these people, but it's our money. They don't want bidding wars between the laboratories. Actually I think this *was* a bidding war. Grimes stole her from somebody else, although it could have been she just liked his project more."

Sean looked at the screen. "That's $35,000?"

"Yeah, that's without the fringes."

"But that's not a great salary."

"Well, these post-docs don't make anything. You don't go into basic medical research to get rich."

"But then they must do a lot better when they get these assistant professorships," Sean said.

"Then she'll make $50,000. Considering the brains of the people, the money spent on their education, and the number of hours they work, these have to be the most underpaid people in the country. Anyway, I don't set the rates. The cheaper we get 'em, the more we can hire. Let's go on."

Frank tapped at the computer and continued, "Here's John Neville. He's a 1224."

"What's that?"

"That means he's already hired by somebody else in the university, so they do all his fringe, health care costs, and stuff. See, here, nothing listed for us. Just a payment."

"What were you paying him for?" Sean asked.

"He'd be doing something for us after hours or on the weekend or during his vacation. It's not uncommon. You could pay him by the hour, or you could negotiate with him to do some specific task and just pay him a lump sum. See, he just got a lump sum."

"What kind of thing would he be doing?"

"Well, he probably knows how to do something that no one in the Grimes lab knew how to do," Frank began to explain.

"Such as?"

"Oh, maybe some unusual test, or maybe he knew how to make something they needed. Often it isn't worth the time and effort to train your own people if you're just going to do something a couple of times, so you find somebody like this and ask him if he'll do it for you. That's another advantage of the post-docs earning so little. They always need more money, and you don't have to pay them a very high rate. I don't know anything about Neville, but he's a person you could try to track down. I don't even have a C.V. or an address for him. See, his primary department is Molecular Genetics. They should have a whole file on him, and maybe some of the people upstairs know him."

"I'll have to try to find out some more about him," Sean said. He turned away from the screen. Computers always made his eyes tired.

"All right, those are the main people," Frank went on. "Here's the fish thing. I really get a kick out of this. I wonder what the hell he *was* doing with them. See. Here's the name, Symington's Fish Farm in Evansville. You could call them up and see what they did. I think he said they were trout. I told him I wanted a few of them, but I never got any."

"Now, here's an interesting account that comes up all the time." Frank pointed at the computer screen. "Not very big items. A hundred dollars, two hundred dollars, but there are lots of them in here. They're transfer payments to 094, that's the Biology Department. Somebody over there could probably tell you exactly what we were buying. Here's their number, 2613. Something they did over and over again. Look. It's spaced out over the last three years."

"What kind of thing might that be?"

"Well, almost anything. A lab over there could be doing some kind of test for Grimes, something like that. I can find out and let you know. Might give you a clue. Or you could ask Beth to do it. She's hooked into this computer."

"Okay."

"Now, here's a bunch of payments to biotech companies. I love the names. Here's Creative Genetics. Makes you wonder what kind of obscene thing they're up to." He laughed. "Here's one. Gene Seq. Don't know where they get these names."

Sean noted some substantial amounts, most in the thousands of dollars. "And these would be?"

"Well, again, almost anything. These are bigger items, so they might be making something for you, maybe growing some bugs. A lot of our people farm out things like that. Say you wanted ten pounds of some bacteria. You'd have to get a fermenter and set it up yourself and know what to feed them. This way you send out one little bug, and send along some money, of course, and they'll send you back all you want. Sometimes they make some fancy chemical or something you can't get through the regular stockroom."

Frank paused and tapped the computer again. "Here, see these numbers are all the same, but that's the regular stockroom. They have solutions and glassware and enzymes. I'm not quite sure what enzymes do, but they cost a lot, about a hundred bucks a crack. But that's all handled through central purchasing. Probably a huge computer over there somewhere knows what everybody bought, but we don't even bother keeping track of it."

"So there's a real network of people involved in this kind of thing," Sean said, leaning back in his chair. "It's not like some mad scientist sitting up there in a room all by himself thinking how to blow up the world."

"Hardly. They're all interconnected. That's what's so strange about this whole thing. Everybody up there must have known what he was doing. It's just bad luck that several of them were planning to leave anyway. If you could talk to them, that would be the easiest way to solve this problem."

"I'm working on that," Sean said with a look of resignation, "but so far no luck." He stood up and stretched. "I really appreciate all of the time you've given me, and I think I do have some good leads. It's hard for an outsider to know just where to look, but I'm beginning to get the hang of all this, and everybody has been really helpful."

"I'm happy to do it," Frank answered. "It'd be nice if there was something up there that would have just gotten lost without your efforts. Be a credit to the whole department, and might be worth some money too. I'll track down those accounts and give them to Beth."

They shook hands, and Sean started to climb the stairs back to his, Grimes's, office. *None of that stuff about fish and genetics was in any of the grants I read, and it never came up with Blackburn,* he thought. *Unless Grimes had more than one secret project, it has to be related to the running. That Cindy person said something about a course he took in San Diego, and she and Blackburn didn't know what it was about. Seems like fish should be related more to swimming, maybe to those Chinese women they caught. But we know how they cheated, with hormones. Strange. Well this might be the best lead yet.*

Suddenly he stopped. Thinking of Lou Gurci's favorite expression, he laughed out loud. *Maybe something is "fishy" after all.*

As soon as he reached the office, Sean called Bill. "Do you know anything about a Symington's Fish Farm? It's supposed to be in Evansville. Isn't that right next to Bradsford?"

"Sure, I know George Symington. We get called up there from time to time. Some people think it's easier to catch their fish in his tanks than in the river. What's up?"

"Well, you'll be surprised to hear that Grimes bought $10,000 worth of fish from Symington's."

"He did what?" Bill exclaimed.

"That's right. Paid for by the university. I saw the invoice myself."

"What kind of fish was he buying?"

"Doesn't say. There's just a record for the payment."

"When did he do it?"

"About two years ago. I'm not sure exactly when he got the fish, but that's when the bill was paid."

"I know George well. We could take a run up there and try to find out what was going on. Why don't you come here on Saturday? We'll take the kids. Tom and Julie love to see the fish farm."

"Weekends are just normal workdays for us. Fish like to eat

every day," George Symington explained. He was a grizzled, older man wearing dirty khakis, a plaid hunter's hat, and Wellington boots that seemed two sizes too big. "You kids don't fall into anything. Wouldn't want one of those real big fish to swallow you up." He made a chomping motion with his hands. The children both squealed and jumped back, but they were old enough to recognize a joke. They wandered about the grounds while George explained the breeding procedures to Sean and Bill. Actually the eggs and sperm were milked from the fish and mixed together in a bucket. *Not very romantic*, Sean thought.

Most of the fish were in shallow pools segregated according to size. "So they don't decide to eat each other," George said. "We raise mainly trout, Rainbow and Browns. But that friend of yours, he wanted just the Rainbows. Came to us because we get all our breeders from the state hatchery. Seems they used to give him fish free when he just wanted a few for his research, but they weren't able to supply a couple thousand pounds." Bill whistled. "He wanted to be sure they were all alike, all came from the same line, so's they'd be just like the ones he did the first experiments on."

"Did he tell you what he did with them?" Sean asked.

"No, never said."

"How did you deliver so many? How did you get them down to the university?" Bill joined in the questioning, "And how could he put them in the laboratory? He couldn't take a couple thousand pounds of fish."

"Didn't take 'em down to the university. Delivered 'em to fish markets all around here."

Sean and Bill stared at each other in amazement.

"See, he didn't want the fish, didn't care about 'em. Just wanted the blood from the fish. Now he's a smart fella. We talked for a while about how he was gonna get the blood out of 'em. Told 'em for ten thousand bucks I'd get the blood, but then we hit on a better idea. If I took the blood out, or he took it out, the fish would have to be thrown away. No good for nothing. But you take those same fish down to a licensed fish market, and they can bleed 'em and still sell 'em. So he rigs up this deal. Signs up a bunch of fish markets right around here. I deliver the fish live, and they kill them and does the bleeding for him. Fixes it so everybody benefits. Gets them to pay him about a dollar a pound for the fish. Throws that money in with his $10,000 and gets about $20,000 worth of fish. He got thousands of pounds of fish."

"Do you have that many fish?" Sean asked.

"Oh, we could deliver them all right, all at once if we really had to, but he didn't care about that. Said he couldn't use 'em that fast anyway. Just dragged it out over some months. That way the fish stores could sell 'em. Otherwise, it'd be more than they could handle, and they wouldn't want them. At least wouldn't want to pay for them."

Sean and Bill looked at each other again.

"Yup, that was a good deal. It was a real shame what happened. A nice guy and plenty excited about what he was doing. Couldn't explain it to me real good, it had something to do with cancer. Always said he'd come back for more if everything worked the way he hoped. Musta not 'cause ain't nobody never come back. You'd think somebody would. The wife's got cancer. Okay now, but you know, you just got to sit and hope."

"Who'd you deliver the fish to around here?" Bill asked. "Maybe we'll drop in and try to see what they did with the blood."

"Well, a lot of the fellers. You know Jeff down at New England Fish. He got some. Maybe he can tell you what they did, but I think they just got the blood and saved it until someone come and picked it up. If Doc explained it to Jeff, maybe he understood better'n I did. That's not my kind of thing."

They thanked George, managed to get the children away from a shallow concrete tank where some of the larger breeding population were kept, and started back toward Bradsford.

"New England Fish is right near home. Let's drop off the kids and go talk to Jeff, the owner," Bill suggested.

Fortunately there were no customers in the fish store when they arrived. Bill introduced Sean and told Jeff the purpose of their visit.

"Don't tell me all those fish were stolen." Jeff pretended to be worried. "I knew that deal was too good to be true. Now the police are after me. Don't shoot. I'll come quietly."

"No, there's nothing illegal about it," Bill assured him, laughing. "Sean here's just trying to get a lead on the research project that the fish were being used for. I don't know whether you heard that Grimes was killed in a hit-and-run accident."

"Yeah. I was very sorry to hear about it. Sorry to lose the deal, of course, but sorry for him too. The woman who used to come for the blood, a Chinese woman, told me when she came to pick up the last batch. Said we didn't have to bleed any more of 'em because they wouldn't need the blood. Funny, under the contract, there were still more to come, and George kept delivering them. Said he'd been paid in advance, so I kept taking them. Even kept doing the bleeding, hoping someone would come for the blood. Doc was so enthusiastic, it's a shame to just have it stop like that. Actually we kept the last blood for about six months, frozen. Finally, I just threw it out. Figured if nobody came in that time nobody was going to come for it. And anyway, she had said nobody ever would."

"Just what was it you did with the fish?" Sean asked.

"Just bled them," Jeff said. "See. Doc just wanted the blood. That's what made the whole deal. I bought these fish for maybe a dollar a pound less than I'd pay for the regular ones. Most trout we sell here are dead a couple days. Come in from Idaho, on ice. These were alive. George would bring them down in these big barrels of water. They were absolutely fresh just like you'd caught 'em yourself. There's no comparing the taste. Customers could all notice, so I ended up selling them for more. Now that's a real deal. I buy them for less, I sell them for more, and the customers are happy. I even ate a few of them myself. Damn good. And working here all day, I usually don't want to go home and have fish."

"But how did you do it? How did you bleed them?" Sean persisted. He had an image of rows of fish lined up with intravenous tubes stuck in their . . . Well, where would you stick them in a fish?

"Easiest thing in the world. You just club them on the head like you would when you caught them so they don't wiggle, then you make a little cut in the tail and hang them up. Catch the blood in a pan. He brought these stainless steel pans for us. Wasn't even cruel to the fish. They never knew. Then afterwards I just sold them. Just like absolutely fresh trout. Maybe they even taste better because they've been bled. You know, you bleed a lot of game before you eat it. Course nobody'd ever have the patience to do it in a fish market."

"But what did you do with the blood?"

"We just poured it in a bottle and put it in the fridge. Nothing fancy. Doc said it didn't have to be sterile or nothing. Said they purified some chemical from it, so we didn't even have to be real careful. Just keep it cold, he said. When we got a big batch, maybe a gallon or so, we'd give him a call, and he or this Chinese woman would come out and pick it up. Usually came with one of those Styrofoam coolers to take it back."

"How much did you give him?"

"Oh, gallons and gallons over some months. Other places were doing it too, according to George. I asked Doc once why he needed so much. He said it was going to take a hundred pounds, I can't remember, a hundred pounds, a thousand pounds, some big amount of fish for just one patient. I figure whatever it was, couldn't a been much of it in any one fish to take so many for a single treatment."

"Did he ever tell you what he was getting out of the blood or what he was doing with it?" Sean asked.

"Not so's I remember. Then I wouldn't have understood anyway. He did cancer stuff, you know."

"Yes, we knew that," Bill said.

"Really a shame about him. He was so excited about this. Said that maybe a lot of other fish out there could be even better than trout."

"Oh, really."

"Yeah, he came out here with a list of them one day. Names were all in Latin. I couldn't even recognize most of 'em. The only one I knew was the Tautog. Up in Maine they call our blackfish a Tautog. Turns out, I guess, that's the official name. Funny how all them Maine fellers learned their Latin so good." Jeff chuckled at his own joke. "I was able to help him get a couple of them. They come in live anyway sometimes. Lobster fishermen get them in their traps. They live on the bottom."

Sean had never heard of a blackfish. "So you bled them for him too?"

"Oh, no, no, that's a funny story. He did something to them and wanted to keep them alive for a week. He gave them something, a chemical or a poison. Well, I guess it wasn't a poison 'cause he wanted to keep 'em alive. I've got a saltwater tank here. I told him I could keep them alive, but he said no he didn't want to take the chance that some of this stuff might get out of his fish and into the others, or maybe we'd get them mixed up, and I'd sell one of the fish that had this stuff in it. I told him no way that was going to happen, but he wanted to be extra careful with it. Finally he gets this idea that you could keep 'em in a lobster pot if that's where the lobstermen found 'em."

Sean and Bill stared at Jeff as he went on.

"So one day I got three, real lively, jumping all over the place. He came up and he met with this fella I know. Told him he wanted him to take the three of them and put them in a lobster trap for a week. Said as how he'd give him fifty bucks if one of them came back alive and a hundred if all three of them came back alive. Said he'd be able to identify the fish, so the guy couldn't cheat him. Don't know how he was going to do that, but I guess that was from the chemical. Then he sticks them with a syringe and gives them to the lobsterman. A week later the guy comes back with just one. I guess the biggest fish killed the other two. Started to eat them. They do that. Anyway Doc was so happy he got the one, he gave the guy the hundred bucks anyway."

"So then you bled that one too like the others?" Sean asked.

"Oh no, this was special. Doc did this himself. Came up with a lot of little bottles that had something in them. We clubbed the fish over the head and cut it and put the first fresh blood into the little bottles. Then real quick dropped them in liquid nitrogen. I never seen that stuff before. Looks just like water. Comes in a fancy little thermos bottle. Froze them solid in just a couple of seconds. After he had about half dozen little bottles, he just took the rest of the blood the way we'd always done. Just put it on some regular ice to keep cold. Then we cut open the fish and got the liver, wrapped it up in some Saran wrap and dropped it right in the thermos too. Then we threw out that fish. Told me he didn't want nobody eating it by mistake."

"Did he ever come for any more blackfish?" Bill asked.

"Nope, that was the only time that happened. Said he thought the Tautog might be even better than the trout, but he hadn't done that much work on it yet. I'll tell ya if he found something in fish that was worth a dollar a pound, hell even fifty cents or a quarter a pound, that'd make a lot of fishermen down on the shore mighty happy. The that'd make a lot of fishermen down on the shore mighty happy. The whole New England fisheries is real depressed, just don't get the catch any more, been overfished for years."

Bill looked at his watch. "We've got to get going. Sean and I really appreciate this," he said, extending his hand. "This has been very helpful."

Jeff shook hands with them both. "Listen, if any of you guys are thinking of starting this again you put my name right at the head of the list. This was the best deal I ever had. Fact is, I could make it better for you and still make a profit."

"Well, I hope we can do something like that," Sean said, starting for the door.

"Here, Bill, wait. Let me give you something to take home for Mary. How 'bout a couple a blackfish in honor of Doc." Bill started to refuse. "No, it's okay. It's late and it's Saturday. Nobody's going to come in to buy them now. And blackfish are darn good. A lot of people never eat them, but Mary will know how to cook them." He used a net to pull two blackfish from a tank. "These will go four or five pounds. Real fresh." Jeff wrapped them in paper, put them in a plastic bag and handed them to Bill, who thanked him again.

"Let me know if I can help you in any way. I'd sure like to see this thing go."

That evening as they ate the Tautog, which Mary had poached with vegetables and served with boiled potatoes and tomatoes, Sean kept thinking back over the events of the day. What was he eating that was going to cure cancer? Since so much of the runner's literature was devoted to diet he was familiar with the latest craze for oily fish. But that was supposed to prevent heart disease, not cure cancer, and trout wasn't one of those oily fish. And then it occurred to Sean to wonder what had happened to all that blood. It must have been processed down into some tiny amount of some exotic chemical, he concluded. Now he had to find out what it was.

Chapter 23

Sean had asked Beth Markham to help him find John Neville, the Australian post-doctoral fellow who had been paid for part-time work through Grimes's 74 account. She had arranged for him to meet with Jane Munson, secretary to the chairman of the Department of Molecular Genetics and an old acquaintance of Beth's. They had borrowed the chairman's office.

"He was a great character," Jane was saying. "Handsome, athletic, rode a bicycle everywhere, very romantic, although I'm not supposed to say things like that. Great letters of recommendation from one of the top labs in Australia. He was a little flaky though. People used to joke that he must be on something. I'm sure that wasn't true. It was just that he never settled down. He would transfer from one group to another without ever really accomplishing much, but he'd say he just wanted to learn the techniques from each of the laboratories and find out how they thought about problems. I guess that's okay, but two years seems a long time without actually producing a substantial piece of work. Everybody liked him and said he was good, and he was always willing to help out, in the labs, anything. He even fixed my bicycle. It was new, and it never shifted right, and nobody could figure out why, not even the dealer. In about fifteen minutes he had it working perfectly. 'Tuning, Luv, just tuning,' he said." She tried unsuccessfully to imitate an Australian accent. "Of course he had lots of free time."

"Wasn't he assigned to someone for direction?" Sean asked.

"Well, he came with a grant from the Laver Foundation, so he was pretty much his own person. Everybody knew that he wouldn't be here long. It was just a training thing. I don't think he ever considered living here."

"But he could still be a postdoctoral fellow?" Sean asked.

"Oh yes, he was on a student visa. I think he just liked seeing the world. I don't know if he was ever going to pursue a career in science at all. When he left, he said we wouldn't need a forwarding address, but that he'd be in touch and send us one when he settled down. His plan was to go biking in Europe for a while and just country hop for a year or two until he gradually got back to Australia."

"So no one really knows how to reach him? Or even if he's still alive," Sean added darkly.

"Why wouldn't he be alive?" Jane stared at him curiously. "I never heard of him dying. I suppose he could have without us knowing, but it just doesn't seem possible. He's the kind of person you could never imagine dying."

Sean could imagine at least one reason why he might not be alive, but then if no one else could find him maybe Lin Pao's friends couldn't either. Of course, they had found Root before Sean had managed to find him. They probably had their ways.

"He must have had some family, someone in Australia?" he asked.

"Well, if he did, I'm not sure how to reach them. There is one person who might know, and that's Joan Danner."

"Who is she?"

"She's another post-doc. They were very close friends, if you know what I mean. In fact, I think they might even have lived together for a while. Yes, she'd be the one to know, if anyone would. Although I'm not sure just how friendly they were at the end. I probably shouldn't be telling you any of that, but if you're going to ask her, which I imagine you will, you might be a little circumspect. Joan Danner can get touchy when she's crossed."

"Is she here now?" Sean asked.

"She's probably in the lab. If not, they'll know where to find her." She gave Sean the room number and pointed him in the right direction. "If I do think of any other ways we might find out, I'll let you know." He thanked her and headed off down the hallway.

Sean found a laboratory much like the others he had become accustomed to over the last several months. On the door were the usual cartoons depicting mad scientists or gigantic rodents. At first the laboratories had all looked alike, but now he was beginning to recognize the differences. This one, for example, had no signs or smell of animals as did the Blackburn-Helms laboratory, nor was it crammed with the kind of electronic gear that filled the Sorin laboratory. There were the usual bottles of reagents and test tubes, but most of the equipment, except for a few centrifuges, he did not recognize. Finally he spotted through the suspended shelves a head of short, curly brown hair. Rounding the end of the lab bench he found a woman in the mandatory white coat, who was bent over a low laboratory bench, elbows braced on the tabletop evidently doing something that required concentration and precision. He hesitated to interrupt and finally almost whispered, "Excuse me."

"In a minute," the woman grumbled.

"I'm just looking for Joan Danner," he responded.

"I'm loading a gel. Just wait," the voice admonished sharply. Over her shoulder he could see that she was using what seemed to be a fancy eye dropper to drip a blue liquid into small slots cut into a slab of what looked like gelatin. After minutes, which seemed an hour, she straightened up, seized two wires, a red one and a black one, inserted them into the sides of a small box that held the gelatin slab, switched on an electrical apparatus, and then stood and stretched. It was a totally natural, enthusiastic stretch, right down to the grimace on her face. It revealed a bare midriff and a tiny waist as her sweater rose above the top of her jeans.

"This work is bad for the back and for the eyes," she said. She was about five six and of medium build as the stretch revealed to completeness. Her face was symmetrical, but she would not be called pretty. Her eyes were her most remarkable feature. They were dark brown but clear, almost sparkling. They seemed to say, "I'm very smart, I'm very competent, I'm interested in almost everything, I like what I'm doing, and I don't take any crap." Did they really say all that, or did he just come to realize when he knew her better that it was a good description of her?

"What's up? Coffee?" Without waiting for him to answer she headed for a lounge-like room furnished with an assortment of discarded furniture, a small table, a blackboard, a disorderly bookshelf, and most important, a gurgling coffeepot. Sean introduced himself. She never did acknowledge her identity.

"I'm trying to find Jack Neville," he said.

"I thought you were looking for me," she responded.

"Someone told me that you might be able to help me find him."

"Now, who would tell you a thing like that?"

"Well, actually it was Miss Munson, Jane Munson. She said that he used to work in this laboratory and that, well, you kind of knew everyone who worked here," he lied.

"Oh, is that really what she said? Well, she must have told you that he left months ago."

Sean thought, *I used to be so honest before I started all this investigating business, and it kept me out of trouble.*

He went on, "She told me that you were a very close friend of his, that he had left here without leaving a forwarding address because he planned to travel in Europe and gradually make his way to Australia, so the department doesn't really know how to contact him. She thought that perhaps you would know where he might be."

Joan seemed to like this approach better. She pointed at the machine and the cups to let him know that he could pour himself a cup of coffee if he wanted. He chose not to.

"I did know Jack well, but I don't know how to reach him, and no one else will either."

The way she said it made Sean ask, "Was there some sort of trouble?"

"No, of course not. Why would you ask?"

"It just seems a little unusual that no one knows how to reach a person who was here for a few years and must have had friends and connections."

She seemed to lighten up a little. "Well, you just don't know Jack. He's the kind who would decide to go wander in the outback for a year and then emerge again as if nothing had happened. He's indestructible, and he'll pop up in Australia and land a good research job just as soon as he's ready." Was she a little envious?

"Well, I'm glad that he's all right, ah, I mean, that there's no reason to think that he isn't all right just because no one can reach him, but I'm really sorry because I did want to ask him some things."

"What kinds of things?" she asked showing no hesitation.

"Some time ago he was doing some work for Dr. Grimes over in Radiation Oncology, and I've been trying to find out just what they were up to."

"For some particular reason?"

"It's kind of a long story," Sean said, not really wanting to go through it all again for a person who seemed unlikely to be able to help.

"I still have half a cup, and that gel still has a good forty-five minutes left to run." She was not easily put off, so he told her his medical school version of the story, not including the developments in Stuttgart.

"I heard that Grimes had been killed. I knew him vaguely myself, or I should say that I knew of him. He once sat in on a class that I was monitoring. Funny, I never expected to see someone like that in one of my classes."

"Why not?" Sean asked.

"Oh, it was some basic science, not the kind of thing you'd expect to be of interest to one of the clinicians. Jack left just about the time Grimes was killed. Not that there was any connection," she added quickly. "He hadn't worked with him for over a year, but I remember him mentioning it. It was just a part-time thing to earn some extra money. He liked him. Said he was really smart."

"Everybody seemed to have the same impression of him," Sean said. "You wouldn't have any idea what they were doing, would you? That's what we're really trying to find out."

"No. Normally Jack would have told me about it, but I think he was specifically asked to keep it a secret."

"You mean by Grimes?"

"Oh course, by Grimes. Who else?"

"But why would he do that?" Sean asked.

"Many reasons. He might have had a hot lead and didn't want to get scooped by somebody else. Maybe he thought somebody with a bigger lab could do the work faster. Maybe he thought it was valuable and wanted to patent it."

"But surely it wouldn't matter now that Grimes is dead?"

"Of course it would," she snapped. "The university or someone might still want to protect the idea."

"But even if Grimes had placed some restriction on what Neville could say, certainly he could still tell Kerr, Grimes's chairman, about it. Kerr should be the one to act in Grimes's place."

"You sound like a lawyer."

"No, no, I'm not." Sean shook his head vigorously. "But it's just really frustrating that nobody can figure out what these people were doing, and the people who might know aren't supposed to talk about it."

"Now, wait a minute." She turned away and then turned back. "I didn't say I knew he wasn't supposed to talk about it. I just said I thought that they had an arrangement like that. Maybe they didn't. Maybe if you find Jack he'll tell you all about it. Of course, I've already told you that you're not going to find him."

"Well, it just sounds like another dead end," Sean said with resignation.

"I don't see how you couldn't find out somehow. You can't hide a whole research effort in a university like this. Somebody out there always knows what you're doing."

"What kinds of things did Neville do? What was he good at?"

"He was good at a lot of things. Some of them even involved science."

Sean frowned. "I meant that Grimes would want to hire him."

"I know what you meant," she said sarcastically. "He was in genetics. We all are."

"Did he do anything with fish?"

"With fish? Why do you ask that?"

"Because I found out through the business office that Grimes had spent a lot of money to buy trout blood."

"I can't imagine Jack had any interest in trout except to catch them and eat them. Look, I have to go back. Can't talk any more right now, but you put a problem to me, and I like problems. I'll think about it and see what I can come up with. I just don't believe that you can't find out what the hell those guys were doing." She walked out into the main laboratory shaking her head.

Sean headed for the lunchroom. He planned to stay at the medical school and spend a few hours in the library in the early afternoon before going out for a second training session. It was the last of the good fall weather, and he would do two-a-days whenever he had the chance. Beth and Jane Munson were eating lunch together. They waved him over.

"Come join us. Tell us what happened."

"I sent him right to the lion's den," Jane said laughingly to Beth, "or should I say the lioness's den. How'd you fare? Did she snap at you?"

"Hey, what's all this," Sean said. "She was perfectly pleasant."

"There, you see. He's a born diplomat," Beth said to Jane. "I told you he'd manage to get something out of her. He does out of everybody."

"She was happy to talk between experiments, but I must say she didn't turn out to be very helpful. She has no idea how to find Neville and seemed to take pride in telling me that I'd never find him."

"Well, I don't know who else would know," Jane said with a shrug.

"It seems everybody who was with Grimes has suddenly disappeared, although at least for Neville his disappearance doesn't seem to be connected. He just seems to be that kind of guy."

"And did Joan have any idea what they might have been doing?" Jane asked. Beth had just been briefing her on the problem.

"No."

"Just wait. She'll think of something. She'll find somebody who heard it from somebody who heard it from Neville. She knows absolutely everybody here. And everybody seems to owe her a favor, for helping them with some experiment or setting up some new piece of equipment or something. She's so competent . . . just needs to find a job."

"She has a job," Sean said, but before he had finished he knew what was meant. "You mean she needs to be one of those assistant professors?"

"That's right," Jane agreed. "This is her second tour as a post-doc. Time's passing."

"If she's so good, why doesn't she get one."

"Well," Jane continued, "first thing is there just aren't a lot of openings. Most years we don't have a single one. And she's determined to stay here."

"What's wrong with that?" Sean asked.

"Often it's a better strategy to leave. She'll be more appreciated if she goes somewhere else. And in the new place people will know that she's independent, not just doing something suggested by her advisor. Original ideas mean so much to the people who promote you and give you grant money."

"So she really has to leave?" Sean asked.

"She should. They probably should have pushed her out already, but again she's so useful that nobody quite wants to."

"Sounds like a no-win situation," Sean said.

"Well, what Reynolds says, he's my chairman, is that she needs to do something really great, and that just takes a lot of luck. What she does is very good, but she just needs a big break."

By the time he had finished his sandwich, Sean had changed his mind about going to the library. He wanted to be outside, to be running. He thought of Joan Danner and the big break that she needed. He needed a big break too.

Chapter 24

A few days later Sean met Dr. Kerr in his office. He wanted to give him a brief progress report including what he had learned from the business office and from his trip to the fish farm and also describe the dead ends that he had reached in trying to find Ann Grossman and Jack Neville. He thought it best not to tell Kerr or anyone else at the medical school about his experience with Lin Pao and the Chinese runners.

"I didn't know about the fish, and I never heard anything like that from the other laboratory people," Kerr responded and turned his chair slightly to look out through the large single window, where the last of the fall foliage provided a colorful backdrop. He looked tired. Sean knew that he had taken an early morning flight back from Washington.

"Ten thousand pounds, you said?"

Sean nodded. "Maybe more!"

"Of course, if he was bringing back just the blood, nobody would have seen the fish." He turned back to face Sean. "It's an exciting discovery, because it shows he was working on something we didn't know about. But it doesn't suggest anything to me. He must have been preparing something from the blood, something present in only a low concentration, if he needed so much. It must be some kind of hormone. You wouldn't think it would be a toxin. There are deadly poisons in some fish, but I never heard of them in trout."

"Do fish have the same kinds of hormones that we do? Testosterone, and things like that?" Sean asked.

"I really don't know what kind of sex hormones they have," Kerr admitted. "I never thought about it. Pretty much the same, I'd guess. We could find someone who would know, or we could just go and try to look it up ourselves. But aren't hormones illegal? It's pretty hard to imagine that Andy would have wanted you to try something that was banned."

"How about the kinds of hormones that regulate blood flow? Maybe he found something while trying to find ways to improve tumor oxygenation?"

"That's hardly my field. It's been a long time since I was forced to study comparative anatomy. You don't have to do that anymore for medical school, thank goodness. As I recall, fish had pretty much the same kinds of blood vessels and hearts, although some of them were simpler than ours. I'm sure I never learned anything about their autonomic nervous system." He must have detected Sean's blank look. "That's the part of the nervous system that regulates things like the size of the blood vessels and other functional things inside you like your gut, things like that as opposed to moving your arms and legs. We're definitely going to need to find an expert. Give me a little time to think of who would be best."

When Sean stepped next door to Grimes's office, he found a message waiting from Joan Danner.

"She wants to talk to you," Beth told him. "I'll get her back." She dialed and soon had Joan on the line. "She says how about late this afternoon?" Beth relayed.

Sean shook his head. "Can't. I have the kids this afternoon."

"He says that won't do, but any other time," Beth with hand over the receiver. "She's grumbling. Lunch?" Beth looked at him. Sean nodded. "Okay, I'll be sure that he gets there. Yes, yes, I understand. Goodbye." As Beth hung up, she stared at the phone and said, "Touchy, touchy. And just a post-doc. Wait 'til she's a full professor. You're to meet her outside of her building at exactly twelve o'clock. Precisely, not a minute late." Beth grinned.

"Tough, isn't she?" Sean grinned too.

"She said she must be back at one. Something about a gelatin or something like that."

"Must be one of those things with the blue slots," Sean said. "Okay, I think I can find it by myself."

Joan appeared at five after twelve. Sean couldn't resist. "You're late," he complained.

"I'm sorry." She was obviously surprised. "I started the gels late, but that means," she looked at her watch, "I don't have to be back until five after one."

Sean was tempted to tell her that he couldn't stay after one, but laughing to himself he decided that he'd pushed hard enough. They walked toward a small restaurant just one block from her building. "I'm sorry I couldn't make it this afternoon. I have to coach the kids today."

"What kids?" she asked.

"I volunteer at the Boys' Club. They're mainly minority children who don't have a lot to do when school lets out."

"Well, that's nice of you," she said. "How did you manage to get involved in that?"

"I organized a program when I was in Philadelphia. It was successful, or at least I thought it was successful, and I enjoyed it very much. When I decided to come up here for the rest of the year, I got a couple of the St. Vincent runners to take it over for me. I didn't want there to be a gap. It was just starting to benefit from its continuity, its tradition, with the older runners helping the younger ones."

"You really did that?" she asked.

"Yes, it started when I was a sophomore so that it's been, oh, almost seven years. When I got to Grenville, I heard about the club here and went down to see how I could help. It turns out there was some interest. There will be more interest in the spring when I begin handing out uniforms and running shoes."

"Do you buy those things yourself?"

"Some. Most I get from my own sponsors. For them, it's nothing. They have lots of seconds, most of which they just throw out. You know, a perfectly good shoe, but the color didn't come out quite right. Something like that. You're damn happy to get them if you can't afford shoes yourself."

They pushed through a swinging door into a large single room, nearly filled with customers, most of whom seemed to be students, and found a booth near the front.

"Since officially I'm here to help Jim McBride, he's the track and field coach, I'll be able to get the kids into the Grenville facilities when the weather gets nice again," Sean continued after they had ordered.

Joan was staring at him across the table. Finally she said, "I checked you out. I wanted to see if you were real."

"Don't I look real?" Sean laughed.

"I'm not sure I know what a real world champion is supposed to look like."

"Well, you can have a good long look," Sean said, taking a long look himself. There was something intriguing about Joan that made him want to know her better.

"Maybe I'll just do that," she answered. The food arrived. "Your story just seemed too fantastic, with Paul Sorin showing that picture around the lunchroom, and all that business with Blackburn and Kerr."

"How did you find out all that?" Sean wondered out loud.

"I know everyone, or at least I know someone who knows everyone. You reach that point when you've been here forever."

"Beth Markham tells me that, but she's been here twenty years. You've been here only four."

"How do you know that?" she asked, surprised.

"If you can ask questions about me, I can ask questions about you."

"Jane Munson, I'll bet."

"Well, you see, I'm beginning to know everyone too, and I've only been here for a few weeks."

"What else did you find out from Jane Munson?"

"I'm not the one who said it was Jane Munson."

"Well, what else did you find out from whoever it was?"

"I'm not sure that I should say," Sean teased. She made an exasperated gesture with her hands. "All right. They said only nice things, and always that you were enormously competent."

She blushed, then tried to hide her embarrassment. "We'll see how competent I am with this problem of yours. You gave it to me, and I think of it as a challenge. What I wanted to do was go back over this blood business. Tell me again exactly how it was collected."

This wasn't Sean's idea of a luncheon topic, but it didn't seem to bother her at all. He described the bleeding process as best he could remember.

"And it just dripped into the pan?" she asked. "It didn't have to be sterile or anything?"

"No, that's what the fish person said. Grimes told him that they got something out chemically and that it would be purified later."

"And they didn't quick-freeze it?"

"No, it was stored in a refrigerator. But wait, some *was* put into liquid nitrogen. It came from a different fish, not a trout." Sean told her the story of the Tautog in the lobster pot. "What would that mean?" He paused to take a bite from his hamburger.

"I just wondered if they were trying to preserve the nucleic acids."

"Why does it have to be the nucleic acids that they were trying to preserve?"

"I'm thinking of how this would fit in with what Jack did."

"And the nucleic acids are hard to preserve?"

"The DNA is very stable, but the RNA is fragile," she said between bites.

"What's the difference?" Sean asked.

"You really don't know?" She looked up in amazement. "Oh, I forgot, you probably don't. Well, the DNA holds the genetic code. When you want to use the information to make something, first you make RNA, lots of copies. It's like copying the master plan so every carpenter on the job can have his own set. That way the original is less likely to be damaged. If you want to study a particular genetic sequence, it's easier to find among all the other genes if you trick the cell into making these multiple copies. It sounds from your story as if they gave something to the fish to stimulate it to start making some particular RNA that they wanted to get out and sequence. We'll have to try to find out what sequence they wanted." She stopped talking and began to eat again.

"Would the RNA make hormones?"

"No, not directly. Why do you ask?"

"Well, I was just talking to Dr. Kerr about the possibility that they were getting hormones from the fish blood. You know, sex hormones or those things that improve your circulation."

"They couldn't be that stupid." She had finished swallowing. "Even I've heard of cheating with sex hormones, and everybody must be checking for stimulants. Didn't they take a gold medal away from an American swimmer years ago just because there was some ephedrine in the nosedrops for his hay fever?"

"Yes. Every athlete must know that story."

"But to answer your question, the RNA usually carries the information to make proteins, so it could be directing the synthesis of some enzymes that make hormones."

Sean looked blank.

"You know, most enzymes are proteins," she said with a quizzical look.

"I'm afraid I don't even remember what proteins are."

"Mmm. Mmm." She motioned for him to wait while she finished chewing. "They're made of amino acids. A protein is a long chain of amino acids. There are twenty different amino acids, and the chain can have any sequence at all. You can have a couple of the same amino acids hooked together and then some different ones. Anything."

"How do they get hooked together?" Sean asked, then took a sip of his tea.

"You don't have to know the details. Pretend there's a hook on one side of the amino acid and an eye on the other side. A hook goes into the eye of the first one, another one comes along and puts a hook into the eye of the second one." She hooked the index finger of her right hand around her bent left thumb. "It just extends like a big chain."

"Well, that's very simple, when you put it like that."

"Most of this is simple, if it's put the right way."

"And how many amino acids are in the chain?" Sean asked.

"Hundreds. There's a big range, but think hundreds. If the chain is long enough, it can fold into really complex three-dimensional shapes. It can bend and flip back on itself, do all kinds of things. A short chain wouldn't have all those options. Real proteins can twist into specific shapes to do certain jobs." She continued before Sean could interrupt. "For example, they may fold into a shape just so precise that if some small molecule, for example a sugar molecule, went inside they would twist it in a way that would make it easier for the sugar to come apart. That kind of protein would be called an enzyme. It's a catalyst to help you burn sugar. Without it you couldn't run your 10K."

"Ah. So some could be enzymes, catalysts, to make the hormones?"

"Yes. But I didn't mean to imply that all proteins are enzymes. Antibodies are proteins that are just the right size to grab onto bacteria or viruses. Hemoglobin, the red stuff, is a protein that carries oxygen, and myosin makes your muscles move."

"So many different kinds?"

"It's all in the shape. Only certain chains can twist themselves into certain shapes. They can be classified into broad categories, but in general each one is very specific for each task. As you can imagine, you have many possibilities with a chain that could be a couple hundred links long, having any one of twenty different amino acids for each link. There are trillions of possibilities, too many of them to ever have been made in all of nature."

Sean found that really astounding and said so.

"Well, you come to some weird conclusions when you deal with very large numbers," Joan continued. "My father used to say about Chevrolets that there were so many options you could order that there were combinations that were never made. Not a single car was ever made with some certain combination of options. It gives you a sense of what 'rare' really means, and there are a hell of a lot more protein molecules than there are Chevrolets."

"How do you know all these things about the proteins?"

"Everybody knows. It's freshman biochemistry. But I know more than most people, because I study how the cell folds proteins, how it gets them into these weird shapes." She pushed her plate away. "That's my specialty. There's a great group here, one of the world's best."

"And you're part of that group?"

She hesitated. "I used to be. But I wanted to try to do something a little different, so I switched over to a group in genetics to learn some new techniques to apply to the folding problem."

"So, would that be considered original science?"

Joan looked surprised. "What do you know about original versus non-original science?" she asked a little testily. "Where did you pick that up?"

He didn't want to admit that it was from Jane. "Someone told me that if you stayed in the same place, it was hard to know if you were doing independent, original work, or just following what your old adviser had started."

"Well, that can be a real problem." She had backed off a little, but Sean was in the mood to push.

"Do you think you're going to have that problem?" He looked at her over the rim of his cup

"Everybody has that problem," she said defensively.

"Do you think moving from the one lab to the other will solve that problem?"

"How the hell do I know? I hope so. It doesn't matter. I mean, what it really depends on is what you've done. What really counts is if your work stands out and impresses others."

"You mean the ones who judge you for the grants and the promotions?"

She stared at him. "God, you know more about medical politics than most of the graduate students."

"I'm just a poor runner," Sean said facetiously. "I just listen to what people say and try to find out what's happening around me."

"Well, from what I've heard you're not too poor, and I'm getting the impression that you're not a dumb jock either. But I can't believe that you've actually taken on this project."

"Well, maybe I'm like you," he said. "Somehow it dropped in my lap, and I don't like to think that I can't solve it. With the appropriate help, of course."

She stared across at him, the twinkle in her eyes. "I'll bet you don't like to be told that you can't do something."

Before he could answer, she waved for the waitress. "I must go. If that damn gel runs over, I've had it." They paid. She insisted on paying her share. They walked, almost ran, back to the laboratory.

"Tell me something . . ." He stopped her just as she was opening the door.

"What?"

"Is this RNA stuff colored? Is it red?"

"No, it's not colored. You mean when it's dissolved, of course. The solution would look like water. Why are you asking me that?"

"Oh, nothing in particular."

Joan rolled her eyes. "Yeah, I believe that. Well, we're not going to solve this in one day. Let's pick a time to meet again. I'll tell you about the protein folding, and you can tell me anything else you can remember about this blood business." She ran up the stairs.

Sean walked back to Grimes's office, trying to digest all that he had learned during the day, but his thoughts kept turning to Joan. *She's so feisty and stubborn. Well she'll soon find out how stubborn the Irish can be.* He could hardly wait to see her again.

Chapter 25

Joan and Sean met several days later in Grimes's office. She had chosen the place. "Post-docs don't have private offices," she explained. "All I have is a little alcove in the middle of the laboratory. It's hard to talk there about anything, much less something you might want to keep private." She sat on the couch and looked around Grimes's room. "Now this is a *real* office. I could take this."

"Well, in a few more years . . ."

"Don't I hope?" she said. "And you get to use this? I mean, doesn't anyone else use it?"

"No," Sean explained. "It's being saved for someone they're recruiting. Hardly anyone even comes in. I don't know why. Maybe because of how he was murdered."

"He was *murdered*? That's not the way I heard it."

Sean scrambled to cover up. "No, no, not really murdered. I just meant it was as good as murder. Those damn drunk drivers. I'm out there all the time running, and I can tell you it gives me something to think about." Did that convince her? She seemed a little harder to fool than some of the others. *I've got to be careful about slips like that*, Sean admonished himself. *And anyway I'm not absolutely sure.*

"You promised to tell me about the protein folding," he said, trying to change the subject.

"Yes, I did," she said. "But first tell me why you wanted to know if RNA is red."

"Well it's a long story."

She gave him a skeptical look. "Why am I getting the feeling that I'm not hearing the whole truth about this mystery? That's going to make it a hell of a lot harder to solve."

"It's not that I'm deliberately holding anything back. It's just that I'm never sure what's important and what to even try to remember."

"Yeah, I bet. So Grimes death wasn't really in an accident. It was all a coverup. He was murdered with a red poison."

"No, no, no." Sean was taken aback. "Of course it was an accident. It's just that, ah, well, the first time I went running with Dr. Grimes . . ."

"You mean your old friend Andy, don't you?" she interrupted.

"Right, of course, my old friend Andy. Ah, we were standing there peeing together after the race and his urine was red."

She laughed. "So, you're some kind of voyeur."

"No, no. In the men's room. It was in a firehouse. There was just one long urinal. You couldn't help but notice that the guy next to you was peeing red." It was the best story he could make up on the spur of the moment.

"I wouldn't know about those things," she said smugly.

"Oh, come on."

She grinned. "I'm just teasing you. But that means you think Grimes was using the stuff on himself. You never told me that before. You said he wanted you to take part in some kind of experiment."

"Ah." He knew he had been caught in a lie again.

"Sean, are you telling me the truth? If you don't tell me everything you know, I'm not going to be able to help."

"Well, it's just awkward." Sean toyed with a pencil on the desk, buying time to think of an answer. "I couldn't come up here, where nobody even knows me, and tell people one of their old friends was, well, doing something he wasn't supposed to do."

"How do you know he wasn't supposed to do it? You don't even know what it was, so you don't know whether he was cheating or not. That's what you were going to say, wasn't it?"

"I don't know whether in the strict sense of the word it was cheating, but it was cheating in spirit if he took anything to make him run better."

She paused for a moment. "And I don't suppose you would do that."

"No."

"Then why are you so anxious to find out what Grimes did?"

"Because I don't want some good athlete to use it against me or against anyone else."

"A good athlete?"

"Grimes wasn't a good athlete, just a fifty-year-old man who ran for fun. But if some world class runner got his hands on this thing..."

"Then you'd have to take it yourself," she interrupted.

"No, I wouldn't have to take it myself. I'd just have to keep them from taking it. I'm the world champion, remember, and I didn't need anything illegal to help me do it. You know, asking me whether I'd cheat in running is like my asking you whether you'd make up data in your laboratory."

"Oh, come on," she said.

"Well, it is."

"All right. I apologize."

"I accept. Now tell me how you fold these enzymes."

"I don't fold enzymes. I study how proteins fold."

"Right."

"Ah, where to begin? Well, people talk about proteins having four kinds of structure. You remember I told you that the protein is made up of this big long chain of amino acids."

"Yes."

"That's the first kind, the primary structure. The links of the chain are very strong. They are good, honest chemical bonds. Even boiling won't break those bonds. But the protein wouldn't be very useful if it were just a straight line. It needs a way to fold into more complex three-dimensional shapes."

Joan reached over to the desk, tore a piece of paper from a yellow pad, and began to twist it into a long, thin strand.

Sean leaned forward to watch and said, "Okay, so now we have a tough chain. What would make it fold and stay folded, not just flop around all the time?"

"Well, if the chain is long enough, it can double back on itself. Then some of the side groups can interact in a pretty strong way." She doubled the paper strand into a "**U**" shape.

Sean had been reading about proteins since their last meeting, and he knew that each of the amino acids had a linker on each side to form the chain, the hook and the eye, but then it had another component that projected off sideways, perpendicular to the length of the chain. That's what made each of them unique.

"Some of the side projections are able to attach to each other," she continued. "They might form hydrogen bonds, or two of the amino acids that have sulphur atoms could join together through them. It's like we put a few dabs of glue along here," She pointed to some spots on the **U**-shaped piece of paper. "to cross connect the arms of the **U**. These bonds wouldn't be as strong as the backbone. Most of them would break if you boiled the protein. That's what happens when you cook an egg white, you break the secondary structure of the albumin."

"Hmm," said Sean. He thought he was getting the hang of it. "Okay, so what's the third one?"

"The tertiary structure has still weaker bonds, and it can generate even more subtle shapes."

"There are still weaker kinds of chemical bonds?" Sean asked.

"They're not even really chemical bonds in the strict sense. But, for example, some of the side chains are a little greasy." She smiled.

"Greasy?" Sean laughed. "You mean like the food at that place the other day?"

"Well, put it this way. They would rather be in a greasy environment surrounded by fat instead of surrounded by water."

"But the whole thing's dissolved in water, isn't it?"

"Right. And, so, the chain folds itself around and tries to get all the little greasy guys to make a little clump in the middle, and all the little guys that would rather be near water to stick out into the water."

"This is too clever," Sean said shifting in his seat. "You mean this really happens?"

"Yes, it does really happen. I'm not making it up."

"And the fourth kind of structure?"

"Well, the fourth kind is a little different. It's probably not worth going into."

"But I've come this far, why stop now," he protested.

"Oh, all right. It involves having one of these chains, after it's all folded up, find another one floating around in the solution and decide that the two of them could make some bonds together."

"Hmm. Sounds sexy."

"Very cute." Joan rolled her eyes. "But you can imagine how when these chains are so long, they don't know whether they're grabbing their own tails or grabbing another completely different chain. And all the same kinds of bonds could be used, except of course, the ones that actually make the chains themselves. They could cross-attach with the sulphurs, or the hydrogen bonds, or they could find greasy buddies on the other chain and make a big clump with them. The most famous example is the hemoglobin molecule, the red stuff in your blood that carries the oxygen."

Sean's interest picked up immediately.

"Actually hemoglobin is made of two different kinds of protein chains called alpha and beta. Two of each of them stick together quite tightly to form a clump of four called a tetramer. The clump doesn't usually come apart, unless you do something nasty to it, but the chains can slip back and forth on each other in a way that affects how they bind oxygen. You probably don't know anything about how hemoglobin works, but it's very important that a lot of oxygen load and unload at a precise pressure, and it takes this complicated mechanism to do it. It's a masterpiece of evolution. But I'm sure you aren't interested in all that."

"So what do *you* actually study? It sounds like everything's known about this already."

"No way. We know some of the principles but the beauty is in the details."

"What details do *you* study?"

"Well, and this is the genetic twist, I make mutant proteins. I change the primary chain by just a little bit. I take out one, or maybe several, of the amino acids and stick in others instead, and I see how that affects the protein."

Sean shrugged his shoulders. "There must be an enormous number of possibilities, if there are hundreds of links in the chain and so many different amino acids."

"Sure, but lots of the changes wouldn't be interesting. So you limit yourself to testing ones that are reasonable and that will teach you something. For example I can take out some of the greasy amino acids and put in ones that like water, and see how that changes the shape and function of the protein."

"I'm impressed. So, basically you're solving a big puzzle. It's like a game. I mean you're not sitting there trying to make a new drug or cure some disease. You're kind of having fun."

"Well, now wait." She held up her hands. "It's not just playing. When people understand these basic things, they can go on and do something practical with them."

"So it's like laying the groundwork, like long-range planning. What are you going to do with it?"

"I probably won't be the person who does anything with it. It'll just be more basic knowledge that somebody else can use."

"You just do it with the hope that some day someone will find something useful to do with it?"

"I do it for a number of reasons, that's one, and the challenge, and the fun, and to earn a living." She laughed.

"From what I hear, they don't pay you very well," Sean said.

"That's for sure. But I don't need much."

Sean glanced at his watch. It was almost noon. "Can I take you to lunch?" he asked.

"No, you can't."

"Why not?"

"Because it doesn't cost enough." She smiled. "You can take me to dinner."

Chapter 26

Sean was running half mile sprints. He didn't like the sprints and didn't particularly like running indoors, but the weather was finally turning cold. After finishing the set, he recorded the time in a small notebook. *Damn, those last two were both slow*, he admonished himself. He dressed in outdoor running gear as quickly as possible in order not to cool down and went out the small door at the end of the cage. At least there was no snow. Actually he didn't mind running in snow once it was packed down, but he didn't like slush. *Maybe up to the bridge and back*, he thought. It was a luxury to have a run that wasn't timed. That was his reward on sprint day.

"You can't do any constructive thinking when you're running sprints," he said to himself, "they're too short." What he tried to think about now was Joan. She seemed to be involved in so many different laboratory projects, some by herself and some with other scientists, and then there was "this little mystery," as she called it. He wished that she spent more time on it. But that was just being selfish. Joan seemed completely certain that it would be solved, but he was impatient, and unfortunately his own attempts seemed to have reached a dead end. If she never did find the answer, would he have wasted time believing in her? But what else was there to do anyway?

Joan had invited herself to Gino's because, she said, it was the most expensive restaurant in town. It was hardly expensive by Philadelphia standards, or even worse, New York standards, but still Sean had refused. Gino's seemed to belong to Susie. Instead, they were at a small French restaurant with a bring-your-own-bottle arrangement. There wasn't a great choice of restaurants in Grenville. To compensate, or perhaps to let her know that he had not passed over Gino's because of the cost, he had splurged on a fine bottle of French wine.

"Picking the color in advance kind of limits your food choice," she had said as they entered. But a broad smile spread over her face as the waiter unwrapped the bottle and began to open it. "I can probably find something on the menu that will go with this."

Sean smiled back.

"Do you go to Philadelphia every weekend?" she asked him.

"Almost every one," he said. "It depends on what the team's doing. I'm supposed to help with their coaching."

"Do you have someone there you go to see?" She stared at the menu.

"Yes," Sean answered. "A very sexy man."

She looked up from the menu. "Oh."

"He checks my report card every week, and then he grades me."

"Hmm." She was beginning to recognize when she was being teased.

"His name is Bob Higgum. If they had Nobel prizes in coaching, he would have one."

The wine was served without the usual formal tasting.

"This is really good," Joan proclaimed. "It needs some time to breathe. The purists would probably think we're horrible for drinking it so early."

Sean had learned enough to know what that meant. "I know, but it still seemed the best choice."

"A trick is just to stir it up in the glass," she said. "You can actually beat it with your fork. All the other customers will stare at you, but it'll hurry it along."

The waiter returned and they ordered. As they waited for their food, Sean began to tell her Bob Higgum stories. It seemed a relatively safe topic, and they had decided there would be no science talk for the evening.

"So, you'd like to be the Bob Higgum of Grenville?" she asked.

"I'd certainly like to coach someday, but I doubt if it will be at a place like Grenville. It doesn't seem as if our goals would be compatible. I like to be the best, or at least to have a chance to be the best. Anyway Grenville already has a Bob Higgum. They have Jim McBride, one of the best in the country. It's an interesting thing about a place like this, they have the resources and the appeal to have a coach of that quality even though they're not in the serious business of promoting athletics like all the scholarship schools."

"But how frustrating to never have the chance to develop a top runner. It would be like us not having good students," she said.

"And students who could give only part of their time to the work," Sean added. "The teaching can be its own reward, as with the kids in the club. But that's just for fun. If you really want to measure yourself as a coach, you have to work with the best."

Joan nodded in understanding. "It would be very discouraging if we never had a chance of getting a really good graduate student. The mentors of the grad students and the post-docs certainly get a lot of satisfaction from the good ones." She laughed. "Because they get credit for most of their research work. A big empire of really good students brings in the money and makes you famous. It's part of the game. We recruit the best students and the best faculty just as other places do athletes. It's just as competitive." They were interrupted by the arrival of the food. "Thanks, yes, all set," she said to the waiter and continued, "I don't see why this McBride person would want to stay here under the circumstances."

"I didn't either at first, but maybe I'm beginning to understand. It's a compromise, one I don't think I would make. But anyway it's not true that he never has a good athlete. He had an absolutely wonderful woman runner last year."

"Oh?" She looked up.

"She's a 5K man. I mean a 5K *person*."

"That's a bit of a slip. Does she look like a man?"

"No, no. I'm just used to saying 5K man, 10K man, you know, marathon man. Actually, she was very attractive."

"Oh."

"And she was an absolutely beautiful runner." She was looking directly at him. "Jim said she was the greatest natural runner he had ever seen."

"So, will she win Olympic medals and make Grenville and Jim famous?"

"Well, from what I heard of her in the last few months she may, but Grenville hardly needs to be made famous, and Jim doesn't either."

"But surely she can do him a lot of good. Don't coaches become famous because of their athletes?"

"He's already famous. He'll probably be one of the assistants on the Olympic coaching staff. This is good," he said, pointing toward the boeuf bourgogne on his plate. "How's yours?"

She nodded, took a sip of wine, and went on without answering. "But this has to make him more famous."

She never lets go, he thought. "Look, his reputation is growing all the time because everyone recognizes what a good teacher he is."

"Still, this will certainly help him get a coaching job at one of those athletic factories where he can control all those prize studs."

"I don't think he wants to control a lot of prize studs."

"How do you know?"

"Look, I just think it's better to be here. It's a much more interesting place, and running's the same everywhere."

"Sounds like you're talking yourself into changing your mind. Does he coach you?"

"He helps, but he follows Bob's training program. They're so much alike it wouldn't make much difference."

"So you just do your training and help coach the students and then do your detective work?" She sat back and looked at him carefully.

"That keeps me busy, but I do take a class."

"What kind of class do you take?"

"You'd probably laugh if I told you." He put down his fork and leaned back in his chair. "I had intended taking a biology class, but I got here late and thought I'd never be able to catch up. That was probably wrong. I should have taken it."

"Well, what do you take?"

"A course on athletics in society."

"What!" she said.

"It's really funny. At any other university that would be the biggest gut in the world, full of football players, and they'd be giving them laboratory credit for practice time."

"I would think so," she agreed.

"Ah, but not at Grenville. This is taught in the Classics Department. The prerequisites are a reading knowledge of Latin and Greek."

"You're pulling my leg," she said. "You're always doing that.

I've got to get used to it."

"I'm not. It's the truth. You can look it up in the catalog. Actually, it's very interesting, and it will fit in well with what I plan to do."

"So you mean to tell me that you're sitting there reading original articles in Greek."

"Yes. I was a little rusty, but I'm picking it up." He was staring down at his plate, trying not to betray a laugh.

"Where did you ever learn Greek?"

"Remember, I'm from a very advanced country. I went to a Catholic school, where everyone had to learn Latin. Greek was an elective, and I elected it."

She just stared at him in disbelief. "You *are* pulling my leg. How could you convince them to let you take this course?"

"I just walked in and introduced myself to the professor and told him I was a member of the faculty, I was visiting, and asked if they extended course-monitoring privileges. He said they did and checked the prerequisites. I said I'd be a little out of practice at first and then told him what I did. He was overjoyed. I've already been assigned to give a seminar on the history of the marathon. He's just off the wall about it, having a marathoner who may win an Olympic medal presenting this in his class. Apparently almost every year someone chooses the marathon as a topic."

"I just can't believe this," she said. "But you're not a member of the faculty."

It was a real struggle to keep a straight face. "Actually I am. I'm an assistant professor."

"What?" She could be heard at the next table. "Now I know this whole thing is a joke."

"You can look it up, not in the catalog because it happened too late, but on the Internet. The whole catalog is on the Internet, and that version gets updated all the time, so I'm sure it's in there. You must know how to use the Internet."

"Of course I know how to use the Internet," she said testily. "How in the hell could they make you an assistant professor?"

"Actually," Sean said, "I'm an adjunct assistant professor. Some of them get paid, others are just guests. Mind you, I'm only at the lowest rank."

"Damn it. That lowest rank is what I've been trying to get for five years." She picked up her wineglass.

"I think it's a little joke. It became a project for Jim. He wanted me to have some kind of title, and he suggested this one. I don't think he ever expected it to go through. But it turns out one of the deans is a great track fan, who used to run for the school, so he presented it to whatever committee is supposed to rule on it. When they said it's only for world famous people, the dean played his trump card. The way Jim tells it, he had copies of the New York Times and the Times of London articles on my winning the world championship. He just passed them around the table. They all looked at them and said something like 'What the hell, it'll be fun having him here.' So you see, you're being taken to dinner by Assistant Professor Rourke."

"Jesus Christ. This is really crazy. I must be in the wrong field."

"Well, running isn't easy. It takes a lot of practice, and you have to be very smart."

"I think I'm going to throw this at you," she said dangerously waving the glass.

"It's too good," he said with a smug smile. "You'll have to wait until we're drinking something that doesn't matter."

"I just can't believe it." She shook her head. "Well, I guess I'll just have to call you 'Professor Rourke' from now on."

"That's better than 'Dumb Jock Rourke'."

"Yeah, somehow that never did quite fit," she said. "Now tell me about this girl you fell in love with, the runner."

"Wait a minute. I didn't say I fell in love with her."

"Yes, you did." She smirked.

"Well, I've taken her out a couple of times."

"Yes . . ."

"And I ran a race with her once."

"Did you win?"

"No, I mean we were on a mixed relay team for charity."

"Not that thing in New York?"

"Yes. That seems to have generated a lot of publicity."

"It did. I must say I'm impressed. That was a really good cause."

"Did you go down to it?"

"No. People from here did though. Some went to run, but that's not my thing. Several of the women's groups here supported it. So, is she still here?"

"No. She's in England. Would you like dessert?"

"I shouldn't, but I will. What's she doing in England?"

"Actually, she has a Rhodes Scholarship."

"Ah, sounds like another dumb jock, or do you call them jockettes."

"She's very smart. The problem was to try to convince her to keep running. She was going to give it up."

"You'll have to tell her that wouldn't be wise or she'll never get to be an assistant professor."

"Right," Sean said. "Well, anyway, she lost a race here, the last race of her career in college."

"Against some arch-rival?"

"Yes. She was so furious about it that she just started to train like crazy. She never really had the time for it over here, but now she's on a regular schedule just like the pros."

"Things must be easier over there."

"No. I think she just decided to give it one last try."

"And I'll bet she's winning everything," Joan said.

"Last I heard, she'd had some incredible training times, and they're getting her ready for the big European indoor races in January and February."

"Sounds like they're training a horse."

Sean paused, trying to think of something clever to say. "Well, it's a little bit the same, but these horses talk back to you."

"Some real horses talk back to you," Joan cracked. "Some of them buck you off."

"Yes, well."

"Sounds like you don't get to see her much."

"I go over there occasionally, and she's coming over here for Christmas."

"How many times did you go over there?"

"Once, after I won the Worlds."

"So you've seen her only once since. What kind of relationship is that?"

"Wait a minute." Sean gave her a quizzical look. "Why do you want to know this?"

"Sorry. I'm picking on you. I'm mad because you're an assistant professor, and I shouldn't drag your girlfriend into it."

"She's not my girlfriend."

"I know you told me that before. Of course I don't believe you."

"Okay, well tell me about your boyfriend, this Jack Neville."

"Wait a minute. It doesn't follow that I should tell you about my boyfriend just because you're telling me about your girlfriend."

"Tell me anyway, even if it doesn't follow."

"He was great in bed." She said it in a slightly louder voice.

"What?" He instinctively glanced around to see if she had been overheard.

"He was smart too. Actually, he was very smart, and he was kind of, ah, Aussie like."

"You mean like Crocodile Dundee?"

"No, no." She paused. "Like that tennis player, Newk."

"This was a serious thing?"

"No, it was never serious."

"But I thought you used to live with him."

"Now who's been telling you that?"

"Any good detective would find that out," Sean answered, "but I can't reveal my sources."

"We never really lived together. We both had separate places." She smiled. "We just used them one at a time. You should have bought a bigger bottle of wine."

"I usually don't drink that much." Sean shook his head.

"I'm prepared to drink any amount of this." She held the glass up to the light. "Is it because of the running?"

"I guess a little bit. Before a big race I don't drink at all. Don't ask me why, it doesn't really make any sense. It's just an old habit."

"It's so hard to think of you as a runner. I mean, I know you are. You could be a . . . um . . . a detective, a gentleman detective."

"Oh, I was thinking more of being a Greek scholar," he said.

"No, really. I've got to see you run."

"I give demonstrations at least once a day, twice on some days."

"Yes, but I'll bet they're at five in the morning."

"No, only in the summer, but I'll be running in New York toward the end of January. You could come down. Really, it's not far."

"I know where New York is."

"Okay, but I mean, it's easy to get tickets. They give me tickets.

You could come down and watch."

"You're not afraid I'd make you nervous."

"There'll be about fifteen thousand people there," Sean explained.

"Ah, so I'm just like any of the other fifteen thousand people."

"I didn't say that," he said.

"So you wouldn't try to impress me."

"If I impress Bob, then I'll impress you."

A big smile spread across her face. "You really are fun to tease."

He looked her straight in the eye. "You are too."

Chapter 27

Yan Tse was quite amazed to hear from his old friend, Bob Higgum. He had known him for almost twenty years, since the friendship exchange program. Even at that time, Tse was considered to be the dean of Chinese track and field coaches, and while Higgum was several years younger, Tse had always looked up to him as his teacher. When they had first met, Yan Tse was forbidden to travel outside of China, but over the years the restrictions had been relaxed, and he had even managed to visit Higgum in the United States. Now they more commonly saw each other at international track meets, although paradoxically as Tse began to travel more, Higgum, using the excuse of advanced age, began to travel less. Still, when they met, it was almost as if they had not been apart at all, almost as if they were resuming the same conversation in mid sentence.

Yan tried to remember when he had last received a letter from Bob, a rare event indeed. This one was even more puzzling because of its brevity and because of the possibility that it contained a secret meaning. The message said simply "Chao Lee should run the marathon. An honest effort would certainly bring rewards." It was signed "Bob," and there was nothing else in the envelope. The first sentence was not a surprise. Bob Higgum often gave unsolicited advice, and besides Yan Tse had been thinking the same thing himself. If it had not been for the meddling Germans who seemed for reasons he did not understand to want Chao Lee to continue training for the 10K, he would have already made the change himself.

It was the second sentence that baffled and perplexed him, in particular, the word "honest." Yan Tse's English was not good, but he recognized that this was a word with more than one meaning. Which one had Bob Higgum intended?

Usually he chose to keep his own counsel, but in this matter he felt the need for assistance. Thus he approached Lin Pao whose knowledge of English, at least written English, was superior to that of anyone else he knew, certainly anyone whom he was willing to take into his confidence. Lin Pao read the brief note and was immediately disturbed. He opted for the more sinister interpretation.

"It is true that an honest effort can mean a worthy, wholehearted, laudatory effort, but I think in this case it was the writer's intention to admonish that the effort not be dishonest. Higgum is the coach of Sean Rourke. Surely he knows everything that Rourke knows. You are convinced that he remains a close friend?"

"I am certain," Yan Tse insisted. "If your interpretation is correct, then this is a timely warning from an old friend, and I shall accept it."

Chao Lee was called in to see the Master that same afternoon. Yan Tse did not waste words with his runners.

"I have decided that you will run the Olympic marathon."

Chao Lee was surprised and overjoyed. "Thank you, Master Tse, thank you." Chao Lee bowed from the waist. It reminded Yan Tse of the days before the revolution.

"Here is an outline of the program for the next nine months and a detailed schedule for the next four weeks. Most of your training will be here in the mountains, but some will be on the coast, in case it is warm and humid in Sydney in September." Chao Lee nodded vigorously, continuing to bow up and down. Yan Tse waved him to stop.

"I will not always be with you when you are not here, and I must rely on you to carry out my plan exactly as it is written." Chao Lee continued to bow. Tse knew that the admonition was unnecessary. Lee was a dedicated athlete who would never lose for want of preparation or effort.

"Go and begin. And stop bowing, it is no longer done." Chao Lee bowed again and left. Actually, being bowed to did not make Yan Tse feel uncomfortable. He smiled to himself. It would take all his resources to withstand the German invasion, but now there were signs that an old ally was entering the fray.

Chapter 28

Joan was surprised, pleasantly, when Sean asked her if she would like to go to the Metropolitan Opera in New York on the twenty-ninth of December.

"What are they playing?" she asked, never intending for an instant to turn down the invitation.

"Cosi Fan Tutte. It's a new production."

Joan brightened immediately. "You mean with that new Italian soprano?"

"Yes."

"That's the hottest ticket in New York. How did you ever manage to get them?"

"I arranged it quite a while ago, through a scalper. The same scalpers who do the athletic events do things like the opera. That's how I knew one. I couldn't have gotten them for any price if hadn't owed me a favor."

Joan looked him right in the eye. "Sean, these were for the woman from Oxford, weren't they?"

"Yes. She'll be running in Amsterdam, and it's just too close to break training."

"Oh."

Sean had been crestfallen when Susie told him over the phone that she would not be returning for the holidays. He had been so looking forward to seeing her. And it seemed clear that she didn't want him to come to Europe.

"But why did Hopwell have to pick this race?" he had asked her.

"He says the best people will be there, and it's a chance to compete against them once before the big London meet."

"Tell him no."

"I can't do that. If he's going to be my coach, I have to listen to him. And anyway that's not fair. I wouldn't ask you to interrupt your training," Susie snapped.

"But you were the one who just did this for fun. You were going to give it up."

"Well if I'm going to do it, I'm going to do it right. And I shouldn't have to apologize. I feel as if I'm always apologizing, if I don't run, if I do run."

"I didn't mean it like that," Sean said.

"Oh, I know. I'm just mad at everything. I wanted to come back too."

They had not spoken since.

"She really couldn't do it," he tried now to explain to Joan. "She wanted to."

"I'm sorry. I think I know how badly you wanted to see her."

"We can drive down in time for dinner," Sean suggested, "and back afterward."

Joan thought for a moment. "It'll be awfully late. One of us will just fall asleep at the wheel. I have some friends in New York. They'd be happy to let us stay over, and we can come back the next day."

"But I don't want to inconvenience anyone," Sean protested.

"No, no. We do it all the time. Nobody would ever stay in a hotel. It's too expensive. Oh, this will be so exciting," Joan proclaimed. "I've never been to the Met. I've hardly ever been to an opera except the ones they try to produce here. What do you suppose we have to wear? Will it be very fancy? I'll have to get a clothes consult on this one."

The trip was much anticipated and was a frequent topic of conversation. One day when they were in her small office she announced, "I found out that there's a restaurant right at the opera."

"But that must be just sandwiches and things," Sean said, recalling the European theaters that he'd visited. "We should go somewhere nice."

"No, no," Joan argued. "It's supposed to be very nice, and you're right there so you can't be late. Apparently they shoo you out the door after the main course, and you come back at the intermission."

"Well, I don't know." Sean hesitated.

"I'm sorry, I'm spending all your money without even asking you. It's probably very expensive."

"Oh, we can afford it. We can take out a mortgage." He laughed.

"We don't have anything to mortgage," she said.

"I'm the one who suggested a fancy restaurant. I'm just not so sure what one would be like at the opera, but if you want, we can try it."

"How much money do you earn running?" Joan asked.

Sean thought he was used to Joan's directness, but the question took him aback. "Now that's not the kind of thing you ask somebody."

"It's the kind of thing I just asked someone."

"Well, I manage to get by and not to starve."

"I've noticed. Do you get thousands of dollars when you win these races?"

"Mmmm."

"Tens of thousands of dollars?"

"Mmmm."

She just looked at him.

"It depends on the race. We're not paid like the professional basketball players, but if you're good you do all right. At one of the big European races last fall, after the World's, the first prizes were pounds of gold. Just a gimmick, but worth a lot of money. I could have done really well financially, but instead I went off to train for the marathon. Crazy, some people think. It *will* have been crazy if nothing comes from it, but it's what I wanted to do. The one I just can't get over was that trial for the American marathon team for Atlanta. A hundred thousand dollars to win the trial."

"Wow! A hundred thousand for one race."

"Well, that's really unusual, but it was just a trial. I have an immigrant visa. I should have taken out citizenship and run the damn thing."

"Would you have won it?" Joan asked.

"Probably. I'd certainly be favored over the other American runners. I won't be the favorite in this Olympics by a long shot, although I'm hoping to surprise a few people."

"But then you sell shoes and things too," she said.

Sean had visions of himself helping customers try on shoes.

"Yes, and I always tell people not to get them too tight, especially in the toes." He reached down and pinched the front of his shoe.

"Oh, you."

"It's true. I do have contracts with some manufacturers, and if I win a gold medal I'll get more, and they'll pay more."

"Do they pay a lot now?"

"A good bit more than winning the races."

"Really!"

"They have very complicated systems. What they pay depends on how good you are. So when I set FTY, that's fastest time of the year for anyone anywhere running the 10K, I began to get bonuses every month for as long as my time held up."

"And did it hold up a long time?" she asked.

"I'm still getting it. Actually some runners broke the time in the fall in Stuttgart, but everybody thinks they cheated."

"They cheated?" she repeated. "Why don't they just throw them out?" She flipped her hand backward in a tossing motion.

"Nobody can prove it yet. They're Chinese runners. The Chinese have been doing a lot of cheating recently. Anyway, most of my companies that have this system just consider that my time still stands. And then, of course, winning the World's, that earned some big bonuses."

"It's really worth that much to them?"

"There's an awfully big market for running clothes and sports drinks and shoes and things. And it's the recreational runners who buy all that stuff, and they all run the longer distances." She looked a little puzzled. "Well, you don't see your average forty-year-old businessman doing hundred yard dashes back and forth across his front lawn. He's out there jogging three, four, five miles, so he identifies with somebody like me and wants to run in my shoes. There are more than 20 million runners in this country alone."

"Are your running shoes any good?" she asked.

"I use them. I can just buy them off the shelf, don't need any special fitting."

"They make you *buy* them?"

Sean laughed. "No, no, they don't make me buy them. They give me so many I can't remember where they all are. Funny though, I never wear them except to run."

"Every fashionably dressed person on Fifth Avenue is wearing them," Joan pointed out.

"That's great for the company, but for me they're just work shoes. I guess it's because when I was a kid a good pair was a real luxury. They last only about five hundred miles, and I never wanted to waste a single step. I used to have a name for each pair. When my sisters wanted to tease me, especially Mary, they would hide them. So I kept them locked in my closet. Mary's a nun now, doing penance for those past sins, no doubt.

"Anyway, what I meant was that I'm easy to fit, so if I'm somewhere and happen to need a new pair I just buy them. When I told the company I won the World's in a pair that I bought, their advertising guys went bonkers. There's actually going to be a whole TV ad with me walking into a store and asking for their shoes, putting them on and winning the World's."

"You must have done that on purpose."

"No, it just happened. You wouldn't believe how much more the same shoes cost in Europe."

"So, you're going to be on television?"

"Soon. We've already taped four ads. My favorite has me with one of my kids, a little black girl. She steals the scene. It tells how to get a pamphlet with advice on setting up running clubs. Very public service like." She was staring at him. "How did we get onto this in the first place?" he asked.

She laughed. "I wondered if you could afford the restaurant at the Met."

"Ah, yes." He laughed too. "Well, you call them and make the reservation, and I'll try to figure out some way to pay for it."

Opera Day was cold and clear. Sean hated to drive into the city, but there was no other good way to get there. At least there was no snow on the ground, and none was in the forecast. There was less traffic than usual during the week between Christmas and New Year's, so they made the trip without any unexpected delays, and Sean had no difficulty finding a parking garage near the apartment where they would be staying.

"I feel bad about Kathy and Bill," Sean said in the elevator. "Here we are planning a fancy evening and leaving them at home."

"Oh, they're not here. They're off at her parents. They go there every Christmas."

"So, they just let us stay here by ourselves?"

"I have a key. They always stay with me in Grenville. She's often up there. She's still working on a project with her Ph.D. adviser. Actually, they're happy to have someone look in on the place." Joan opened the door. "Look at it. There's Christmas paper everywhere. She does everything at the last minute. You can just see her wrapping things as they're tearing out of the house, probably late for Christmas dinner."

They left their bags at the apartment and decided to walk the short distance to Lincoln Center. The Met glistened like a jewel at the far end of the plaza. In size and brightness it overwhelmed its neighboring concert halls on either side. It towered over the dry fountain seeming to proclaim that winter could not dull its spirit. The magnificent Chagalls added just the right touch of color behind the glass facade. Joan squeezed Sean's arm. "Do you think you could ever come here so often that you wouldn't feel like this?"

He laughed. "That would be a nice challenge."

They could see the restaurant from outside, suspended in air off to the right side of the double spiral staircase. For the occasion Joan had been transformed from "laboratory rat," her own description of herself, to elegant New Yorker. Sean noticed that she was in the same uniform that Susie had worn to dinner on Central Park South, but the black dress was distinctly less stylish, and the pearls were about half as large.

The food was delicious, the wine was outstanding, and the service was impeccable and perfectly timed so that the entrees were completed just before the first curtain.

The opera lived up to its billing. The production was crisp and new, and the performances were first-rate. They returned to the restaurant at the first intermission for dessert. Ordered earlier, it was there waiting at the table with the coffee.

"This was a good idea," Sean admitted.

"I don't know why you were so reluctant."

"I don't either." Sean had thought she was unusually reserved during the first part of the evening, but as the opera went on she seemed to return to her old feisty self.

At the second intermission they had champagne on the balcony behind the boxes looking down on the gaily dressed audience talking and drinking on the multiple layers of the horseshoe shaped antrum.

"Makes you want to live in New York," Joan said. "It's just so perfect."

When the final curtain fell, they stayed and applauded until the house lights went on, then got their coats and walked slowly across the plaza reluctant to leave.

Back in the apartment Joan began setting up a futon on the living room floor.

"How are we going to do this?" Sean started.

"Well, you and I are both going to sleep here. We wouldn't want to mess up their bed." The only bed, in the adjacent room, was in total disarray.

"Do you really think . . . ?"

"Do I think we should? Of course I do. Your heartless girlfriend has chosen to stay in London, and my heartless boyfriend is off somewhere probably bicycling across Europe."

"But he isn't your boyfriend anymore."

"That's true. He isn't. But I could have borrowed him for the holidays, and anyway you keep telling me that she's not your girlfriend even though I don't believe you."

"So are you borrowing me for the weekend?" Sean asked.

"I was thinking more like a . . . well perhaps a four-week affair." She began turning out the lights.

"I'm not sure I want a four-week affair," Sean said.

"You can decide later whether you don't want a four-week affair because that would be too long or because it would be too short." All the lights were out. "Anyway, you could have a four-week renewable affair."

"Well, I'm not sure." She was standing directly in front of him and put her arms around his neck.

"Sean," she said, "Cosi Fan Tutte."

"I never know quite what that means."

"Loosely translated it means 'everyone's doing it.'"

He was lying in bed, or rather on the futon, it felt like being on the floor, with Joan cuddled up next to him almost completely covered by the blankets. It was very early, and he was trying to remember whether he had been asleep at all. Maybe between the third and the fourth, or . . . He had completely lost count. This wasn't what he had planned. He thought of Susie. Should he feel guilty? Where was she anyway? Certainly he and Joan weren't in love. Joan just aggressively went after what she wanted, and she seemed to know what she wanted, or at least what she wanted him to do, and she led him to it, nicely, he thought. But a four-week affair! Renewable! What kind of thing was that, even to say? It had to mean more to her than that. Joan began to stretch, the long, luxurious stretch that he had seen once before. Then she squirmed over on top of him.

"Oh, I'm going to be sore," she said. "But, what the hell."

Chapter 29

The university was finally returning to normal after the holiday, but still it seemed to Sean that little progress was being made on the Grimes's mystery. Joan felt certain that she would somehow solve it, but Sean had difficulty sharing her optimism. His frustration and anxiety were growing. The investigation of the fish purchases had reached a dead end, and there seemed to be little hope of finding Jack Neville. And despite Lou Gurci's confident prediction, Ann Grossman's whereabouts remained unknown. She seemed to have vanished from the face of the earth.

Bill, who was in almost daily contact with Gurci, described the search, when Sean visited Bradsford for the New Year's holiday. "We have a good bit of information on her, except where she is or what happened to her. Grew up in New York, father died, mother retired to Florida and died about two years ago. No other relatives. When she left Grenville, she closed her bank account, that's not unusual. But her credit cards are still open and haven't been used for months, that's very unusual."

"How about her letter of resignation in Seattle?" Sean asked.

"They still have it, and it looks authentic. They got it in August, which is what made them so mad. It was on Grenville stationery, so no other return address, and they did throw away the envelope, so no postmark. We're trying passports now, but they don't always record your number when you leave the country."

"It would be too much of a coincidence for her just to have left," Sean said. "After Grimes, I have to think the worst."

With no other leads, Sean and Beth Markham began to screen some of Grimes's other expenditures that had been identified by the business office. They selected a half-dozen different accounts, the larger ones and those with a repetitive pattern of usage. In her free time Beth was to try to trace down the original purchase orders to see if the exact nature of the products could be identified.

Sean's first race of the winter season was in New York City the following week.

"Here's your chance to see me run," he told Joan, as they were having coffee in the medical school cafeteria. "The 10K is scheduled for three on Saturday afternoon in Madison Square Garden. It'll be on television."

"You mean I don't get to come down and see you in person?" Joan asked.

"Of course you do. I'm inviting you. I just meant the time was set for the TV coverage. We can go down together. They'll pay for everything. Hotel room. We'll go down and back in a limo. It's always written into the contract."

"I've never been in a limousine," Joan admitted. "Will it come right to my door?"

"Absolutely. They'll carry your luggage. You can bring ten suitcases if you want."

"I don't have enough clothes to fill one suitcase. I'll just make them carry my knapsack. Can we go to the opera again, when you've finished work? How long does this job take?"

"Oh, not long, about half an hour including the awards." Sean laughed.

"The hourly wages sound very good."

"Yes, and it comes with room and board. We'll go down Friday and stay 'til Sunday."

"This is terrific." Joan had just been helped into the car by the chauffeur. "This must be why you keep that old wreck of yours. You're planning to be driven around in limousines all your life."

"It *is* time to get rid of that thing," Sean agreed. "I've had it for seven years, and it was used when I got it. But then, I never have to worry about where I park."

"Yes, but you could get killed in it," Joan said. "Tennis players get new cars when *they* win tournaments. You just took up the wrong sport. I've got to find myself a tennis player with a fancy car." Sean didn't want to tell her that every winner at the World's had received a Mercedes. He had given it to his parents, the first good car they had ever owned.

"Where's that switch for the divider?" She found it, and the window separating them from the driver slowly rose. Joan sat back and gave Sean a self-satisfied smile. "There, that's much better. Complete privacy."

"Joan!"

"What else is there to do all the way to New York City?"

"But . . ."

"Don't tell me there's no sex, like no drinking, before the races."

"Well, some people think that you should, or, I mean, shouldn't."

"But is there really any truth to that?"

"Oh, I don't know. I just never have in the past."

"That's just because you never had anybody so persuasive or so good," she said. "Anyway, it could be an experiment. Better to find out now than the night before the Olympics."

The race went as planned. Sean surged directly to the front, and the others were content to follow. He ran a painstakingly slow first three miles, picked it up a little between three and four, and then ran away.

"It actually took you less than half an hour," Joan said, as they waited for a cab outside the arena.

"It always does. I wouldn't be worth much if it took more."

"I was so scared in the beginning," she said, looking up and putting her arm through his. "You know, those others stayed right up there with you. I thought that any one of them might win."

"That's the way it was planned."

"Were you doing that just to show off for me?" she asked.

Sean laughed at the question. "No. I don't have the luxury of showing off for anyone. That strategy was picked by Bob Higgum. He wants me to work on speed at the end of the race, and he wants to send a message to the more serious competitors. Otherwise, they might think I've lost some sprinting ability because of the marathon training."

"Did this send the message?"

"Well, the whole time was slow. But, yes, it probably did. The last mile was very fast."

Since they were going to the opera, they decided to eat there again. "It just seems like less hassle, and it's about as good as anywhere," Sean said.

"So now you're the one that wants to go there," Joan teased him. "I'll bet from now on every time we go to the Met we'll eat at that restaurant."

"Could do worse."

"You like old habits, don't you," she said.

"If they're good ones."

They saw a spectacular performance of The Flying Dutchman.

"I don't see why they have to die," Joan said, as they walked back to their hotel. "He was supposed to have been saved if he found a woman who really loved him."

"I think the implication was that his soul was saved, and they were happy in heaven," Sean answered.

"To hell with that."

Back in Grenville the following Monday Sean took Helen and Jim to Gino's for dinner. The McBrides had spent the Christmas holidays in California, and Sean had not seen them for several weeks. Jim received his usual greeting at the restaurant. It seemed to Sean that they had shaken hands with most of the employees before they managed to reach their table.

"Slowest time of the year and slowest night of the week, and still it's packed," Jim said to Sean.

Food and wine arrived without being ordered. Occasionally Sean was required to say "Yes" to the question, "How you like a some nice . . . ?"

No menus appeared. "Most of this stuff's not listed," Jim explained.

"Tell me about your trip," Sean said. "Why California?"

"We have several sets of relatives there," Helen answered, "so it was a chance to visit them, and it was a chance to take a look around, to think of what it might be like to live there."

"Oh. Is there something going on that I don't know about?"

"Well, we've been keeping it secret for a little while." Jim looked away. "You know the job at Cal Central is opening. Mason is finally retiring, and they asked Grenville for permission to talk to me. It's by no means settled. In fact, I'm not even sure I'm the leading candidate."

"Do they have to ask Grenville?"

"They were being very formal," Jim answered. "Probably because it's Grenville. If it were one of their rivals, well, they just steal coaches back and forth without saying a word. But Grenville's different. And also, they're probably sure that Grenville would never say no to them just talking to me, or to letting me go. It's just not that kind of place."

"Boy, that would be a change. That's one of the real athletic factories."

Jim nodded. "It's the big time. There'd be plenty of pressure to win. Of course, you'd never have to worry whether the athletes could read or write."

"It makes me nervous," Helen said, putting down her fork and giving Jim a worried look. "You could be out of a job if you didn't produce in a year or two."

"It's not that bad," Jim reassured her.

"I thought you liked it here?" Sean asked.

"I do, but there are lots of frustrations. This would be different, a chance to coach the very best. Maybe it was getting ready to work with the Olympic team, or working with you the last few months, that made me think I'd just like to spend my time with people at that level. It's a different kind of coaching."

"Is Bob behind this?" Sean asked.

"He's recommended me, and you know that's going to carry a lot of weight." Sean nodded his agreement. "But, hey, I haven't made up my mind yet. There are many good things about Grenville, and besides, Cal Central hasn't offered me the job."

"They will, or at least they should. You certainly deserve it."

"Thanks. It'll be awhile before anything's decided. Hey, how about Susie," Jim suddenly changed the subject.

"What about her? What's she done?" Sean asked.

"I thought you people were in close touch," Helen said.

"I haven't heard from her since before Christmas. She was supposed to come over here, and then she changed her mind at the last minute."

"Hopwell entered her in Amsterdam."

"How'd she do?" Sean asked anxiously.

"Second to Greta Myerling in 15:30. Beat some biggies."

"That's a great time, not as good as that crazy run at Oxford, of course."

"No, but that was outdoors," Jim said. "This was her first big time race indoors. It takes a few tries to get used to the conditions. I thought it was fantastic."

"She's certainly improving rapidly," Sean agreed.

"It was just a matter of work. She never really had the time to put her mind to it here. That's an example of the frustrations at Grenville. Classes must be easier in England."

"They shouldn't be if she's taking all that science."

"Oh, I bet they don't care what those Rhodes people do," Helen broke in. "She probably just goes to interesting lectures and drinks the college's port."

"Well, if that's the secret," Sean said, "I'll have to start drinking port myself."

"Apparently Hopwell wanted to give her experience to get ready for the big London race. Sounds like they're all going to be there. That'll be the real test."

"I may have to go over for it. I haven't seen her as much this fall as I'd hoped." He thought of Joan and all the time he was spending with her. He always expected to feel guilty about it, but he never did.

"Now don't you go chasing her," Helen admonished. "I'm afraid you're going to end up disappointed."

"I don't think Sean will be disappointed, honey. I think she'll run very well."

Helen rolled her eyes. "Ugh, men are *so* stupid."

Chapter 30

"Boy, you guys will have a real orgy," Joan said. It was a Sunday morning several weeks later, and they were having breakfast in her bed.

"I don't know whether we'll have an orgy or not." Sean was taken aback. He had just told Joan that he was going to London to see Susie race.

"But if you're madly in love with her, and you've seen her only once in six months, what else would you do."

"I never said I was madly in love with her, and besides . . ."

But Joan wasn't listening, she just went on. "Of course, I guess you'll have to wait until after the race. That makes more sense for women. But I told you it wouldn't make any difference for men, and I was right."

"Then why should it make a difference for women?"

"Well, they're just different." She laughed. "And we know they do all the work. At least some of them do." Sean never knew how to react to this kind of banter. "Anyway, I expect you'll be in bed with her the night after that race."

"This is crazy," he said.

"No, it's not. There aren't any exclusive rights in this four-week contract."

"What four-week contract?"

"Our four-week contract, and it's almost time to renegotiate it."

"But why on earth are you so anxious for me to go to bed with her?"

"Well, you're crazy about her, and I want to keep it that way."

"I don't understand."

"That will guarantee that we don't become too serious about each other."

"Oh," said Sean, frowning. He still couldn't follow Joan's logic.

"Yes, otherwise, I might not be able to renew the contract."

"This is absurd."

"No, it's not, Sean. You and I don't figure in each other's long-term plans, but that doesn't mean we can't have some fun while she's off in England. So you see, dear, it serves my purpose to keep you interested in her."

Why did I say that? Joan thought after he had left. *Couldn't be that I feel the tiniest twinge of guilt for stealing her boyfriend while she's away? I never have in the past. And it's not as if they're married. If she really cared, she would have come back. Serves her right. Anyway this gives her another chance. And I really don't want to get involved with anybody right now.*

Susie's race was on Saturday. When Sean had called her, she seemed almost alarmed that he was coming. He was surprised and upset by her reaction. It was not the kind of welcome he had expected. But after she had extracted a promise from him that he would not attend the race, "No hiding in the back or anything. I'll be too nervous as it is," she had seemed delighted that she would see him. "It's been so long, and I miss you. When that damn Hopwell decided that I had to run in Amsterdam, I thought I would shoot him."

In London the weather was raw, cold and cloudy with only occasional "patches of bright." Sean was staying in a hotel in Knightsbridge. It gave him a choice of a number of running sites including Hyde Park and Kensington Gardens. Around the perimeter of both was about 10K, and the distances could be increased by running the interior paths.

Susie hadn't anticipated that the race would be on television, on one of the new satellite channels that were popping up all over Europe. Sean was delighted to learn he would be able to watch it in his hotel room. He wondered if that would have made her nervous as well.

Sean had run the 5K many times. In some ways it was his favorite distance, with more room for strategy than the mile, but still short enough so that every move was critical. He felt sure that Hopwell would have a precise plan for Susie. The field was indeed outstanding, Chenkova from Russia and Klara Heinz and Greta Myerling, who had beaten Susie in Amsterdam. It was odds on that one of these women would win gold in Sydney. *The Eastern Europeans need the money*, Sean thought. *Otherwise, you'd never get a field like this.*

The television coverage was crude, but it was better than nothing. *Must be a few remote cameras somewhere high up and then a single hand-held unit at trackside.* Sean could recognize Susie, but he desperately wanted a close up. He just wanted to see her.

At the gun Susie went right to the front. She opened a small gap so that she could run by herself and set a blistering pace towing the pack along.

"No, no!" Sean practically screamed into the television set. "For God sake, listen to Hopwell." But she was running easily and beautifully. It reminded him of the first time he had seen her at the Washington meet where she had breezed to victory while working on her thesis between heats. But this was a different level of competition. The first mile time was unbelievable. The announcer was going mad, and the pace never slowed. What had Hopwell told her to do? Runners began falling out of the back of the pack. Chenkova, a strong runner with a weak kick, tried to keep the gap from becoming too large. The contrast in their running styles could not have been more striking. Susie glided whippet-like over the ground while the Russian pounded the boards, seeming to expend double the energy. At two miles she was through. The pace was under world record time. The announcer was practically screaming the splits into the microphone. Sean was standing in front of the television set, shouting encouragement to Susie.

With three-quarters of a mile left, Myerling made her move. Heinz was still in the pack which had by now reeled in Chenkova. At a half mile, Myerling was still twenty yards behind. Sean cursed the coverage. He wanted to see the faces of the runners. He wanted to study their strides. "At least with the damn cameras so high there's no distortion. You can see exactly who's gaining," he consoled himself.

With a quarter mile left Myerling was ten yards behind. Heinz had done nothing except come to the head of the pack, but the two leaders were pulling away. Everyone in the building was on their feet. The announcer could hardly be heard over the roar of the crowd, but Sean didn't need him. Susie's stride never changed. Perhaps her pace quickened slightly, but she had run from start to finish unbelievably at almost exactly the same rate.

With two hundred yards to go, Myerling, realizing that she could not overtake Susie, slowed slightly to ensure her second place. If Susie saw this concession, it had no effect. She glided down the last straight and through the tape as she had throughout the race and ran across the infield to where Hopwell was throwing his arms into the air. The letters "WR" flashed beside the time. It was the indoor record, but from the looks of it, thought Sean, the outdoor one would go in the spring.

"Awesome," he said out loud. It wasn't one of his favorite slang words, it just seemed to be the most accurate description. The other runners were congratulating her now without much enthusiasm. Myerling was just shaking her head, almost in disbelief. Finally a close-up. An interview. A few inane questions.

"Will it be on the news?" Susie asked the interviewer. He nodded, and then she waved into the camera.

"Thanks, Jim. Hi, Sean. I'm sorry I wouldn't let you come."

"What did you mean by that?" The interviewer asked.

"My boyfriend came to London, but for luck I wouldn't let him attend the race." Then she laughed into the camera. "Now I guess he'll never be able to come to see me run."

Sean was ready to kiss the television screen, but by then it was filled with a male high jumper.

Chapter 31

The day Sean returned, Joan invited him over for dinner. "Now I want to know absolutely everything that happened," she said, as she led him into the kitchen. "I read about the world record. It was in our papers. You must have been off the wall."

"I was. She's the most beautiful runner. I mean, she runs beautifully."

"Yeah, yeah. This must mean that she's better than you. You don't have a world record." Sean hadn't quite thought of it that way.

"You're right, actually," he said, as he sat at the kitchen counter. "Interesting. She was too polite to point it out to me."

"I just wanted to be sure that she got all the credit she deserved. I trust that now she'll have all these shoe contracts and juice contracts and things and make even more money than you do. We need equal opportunity for women in this field." Sean shook his head. "Well, how will she be able to support you if you break a leg or something?"

"I'm not sure Susie would know whether she had another million in the bank," Sean said snidely.

"Ah, she has desirable characteristics that I didn't know about." She reached into the oven.

"This isn't a home made meal," Sean complained as the pizza emerged.

"You know I don't cook, but I did reheat it myself. Here." She handed him a bottle and a corkscrew. "Open the wine. I'm sure it'll be good even if you didn't ferment it yourself. So, what else happened?"

"What do you mean?" he asked innocently.

"Well, did you go to bed with her or didn't you?"

"Of course I did."

"And did she think you were better? Practice makes you better, you know."

"Joan!"

"I'm just asking."

Sean had spent most of the return flight thinking of the differences. Not that he and Susie didn't enjoyed it, but everything with Susie seemed formal or mannered or structured. Maybe they just weren't together enough to really be relaxed, or maybe, Sean liked to think, it just seemed that they were doing something that was more important to both of them. Sean had always thought that sex would be more closely related to love. That was before he had met Joan. But then he could never quite figure out how he felt about Joan, except that he was sure her idea of a long-term relationship was measured out four weeks at a time.

"I really thought you might not do it," Joan said, as she sat down across from him.

"Oh."

"But I'm glad that you did."

"Why?" Sean frowned.

"Well, for all the reasons I gave you before. I mean, if you really love her you shouldn't lose that just because you have to be apart."

"Don't tell me that underneath that tough exterior there beats a romantic heart."

"Ha." She pointed at the platter. "Don't take all the ones with pepperoni."

"You know, I almost thought I'd have to come back and tell you that we hadn't gone to bed."

"You mean you had to talk her into it? What kind of woman is she?"

"No, no. I thought she was having her period."

"They say those seventy-pound runners don't have periods," Joan said sarcastically.

"Well, we were up in her hotel room. It was a mess. And I went into the bathroom and there was a pair of pants hanging in the shower that still had some bloodstains on them."

"How did you even know what they were?"

"I have sisters, and we had only one bathroom where I grew up. Their things were all over."

Joan had a strange look on her face. She usually ate quickly, but now she nibbled at the edge of her slice, staring at the remaining pizza. "So you bravely pushed forward, no pun intended, and she really was having her period."

"No."

"How do you know?" Joan was demanding.

"Well, wouldn't I know. Wouldn't it be a mess?"

"Hmmm," Joan said. "It must have been from the day before, or at least two days before if you didn't see any signs of it." Somehow this didn't sound to Sean like the Colorado class in women's athletic training. "How long had she been in that hotel?" Now it sounded like an interrogation.

Sean tried to think. "Just the day before I got there."

A strange look, half triumph, half glee, came over Joan's face. "The lousy bitch cheated!" she shouted across the table and threw her crust onto the platter.

"Wait a minute," Sean shouted back. "You have no right to say that."

"She pee'd red. She pee'd red, Sean. Didn't you tell me Grimes pee'd red?"

Sean felt himself flush with anger. "She did not. You can't say that. It was blood. I saw it. You're just saying that because you're jealous." He was sorry before the words were out of his mouth. There was a silence.

"I am not jealous," she said very quietly. "You're so besotted that you can't look at the data."

He was draining his wineglass and pouring himself more. Everything that he thought to say sounded foolish.

"Just look at it, Sean. She didn't even win in college, right. I know you think she's a beautiful runner, but she never won a collegiate championship. She lost her last race. You told me so. She was going to quit running, and then suddenly in six months she's the best in the world. You know about these things. You know about coaching. Can anybody possibly do that?"

"But this is different," Sean protested. "She was a wonderful runner. She just never had time to practice. Even Jim McBride said she was the greatest natural runner he's ever seen."

"But, Sean, you're a great natural runner. Everybody at that level is a great natural runner. I know how hard you work, even if you joke about it. How many of those stupid half-mile things do you do every week, that you always complain about. And Higgum, you told me he picked you out as a natural marathoner when he first saw you, and that was eight years ago. It took you eight years, and maybe you're the best now, but you still don't have a world record. She can't be any better than you are." It was the most ingratiating thing she could think of to say.

"I can't believe it," Sean said. "That wasn't some magic red hormone in her pants. It was blood. I mean it looked like blood. It was even, you know, brownish red." He was staring at the pizza thinking to himself what a gruesome thing to say, but it didn't seem to be bothering Joan at all. She seemed to be a million miles away.

Slowly she rose from her chair and began to move aimlessly about the room. "Maybe it *is* blood," she was saying to herself. "Maybe it *is* blood."

"It was blood. I know it."

"No, no." She snapped her fingers. "Maybe Grimes's secret is blood."

"We know it comes from blood."

"No, no. Stupid. I didn't mean you. I mean, we're all stupid. We missed it."

"Missed what?" Sean asked.

"Look. How many damn fish did he buy?"

"Twenty thousand dollars' worth."

"And how much blood did he get?"

"Gallons," Sean answered.

"And we all assumed, since they needed so much blood, that whatever they were purifying was present in tiny amounts. Suppose it wasn't there in just tiny amounts, but that they needed lots of it."

"But what could it be, if we wouldn't recognize it when there was so much of it around?"

"The thing that was staring us in the face. The hemoglobin." She paused and then slapped her forehead. "And that's what the RNA was for. Uh, I'm so dumb, I can't stand it."

"What RNA?" Sean asked.

"From that funny fish. Jack was playing with hemoglobin sequences. It's classic, the hemoglobin gene was one of the first ever sequenced, and they invented the RNA technique to do it."

"Wait, wait. Explain that to me again."

"You give the fish something to make it anemic. That's what Grimes was injecting into them. Over the next week the fish makes new red blood cells like crazy. In the red cells it makes loads of hemoglobin, and to do that it makes loads of the RNA from the hemoglobin gene."

"And that's why they quick-froze the Tautog blood in the liquid nitrogen, to save the RNA?"

"Right. Come on, we've got to get to the library right now before it closes. I can't stand to wait 'til tomorrow morning."

She began stuffing the remaining pizza, including the piece that had been on Sean's plate, into the garbage pail. "And here I was counting on a nice night in bed. I was sure you'd need one by this time." She got her coat from the hall closet, then returned to the kitchen, where Sean was still sitting at the table staring at the spot where the pizza had been. She came over and stood behind him and put her hands on his shoulders. "I'm sorry," she said. "Suddenly it doesn't seem like a lot of fun to tease you about your girlfriend. Let's go find out about fish blood."

"How could you give fish blood to humans?" Sean asked, as they drove toward the medical center. "You can't give blood from other animals. You can't even give it from most humans. Don't they have to be just the right type?"

"You certainly couldn't give the whole blood. It would be rejected, or worse. But there must be some way to do it. I've read somewhere that they were giving hemoglobin from cows or pigs to humans, trying to use it when human blood was short."

"But how could you do it?" Sean insisted.

"I don't know, Sean, it's not my field. Be patient. We'll find out. There are people who try to make artificial red blood cells."

"Artificial ones?"

"Yes, they make them out of some kind of lipids, fats, and put the hemoglobin into them."

"But how could Susie know how to do that? She doesn't know anything about biology."

"Maybe she got somebody to do it for her. Isn't she rich? Maybe she bought a lab. Maybe she bought a few scientists."

"I just can't believe that. And how could she even find out about it? How would she know to try?"

"How much did you tell her?"

"I can't remember exactly." Sean shrugged. "Something. Not very much."

"You can't remember?"

"Well, I don't tell everyone the whole story. I don't think it's appropriate especially when we don't know exactly what Grimes had in mind. It's like defaming him after he's dead."

"That's silly, Sean. How could you defame Grimes? What did he do except get himself hit by a car?"

"That's just it. I don't know what he was doing."

"You know what they say, 'Liars need good memories.' Maybe you told your Susie girl friend more than you told me, and it was enough for her to figure this out, or for someone else to figure it out if she wasn't able." She crossed her arms and looked over at him. "It would be nice to hear the whole story for once."

"What's the plan?" he asked as they entered the library.

"We have just about an hour before they throw us out, so we'll have to work fast. We'll look up a few of the standard textbooks on hemoglobin. I'll be the reader, and you'll be the runner. You're good at that." She laughed.

"I think I'd like to be a reader too." Sean always relied on the reference librarian, but Joan went straight to one of the empty computer screens, punched in a password, then "Hemoglobin" and "Text." A moderate-sized list, about twenty titles, began to scroll down the screen. Joan chose three, written in English and with recent copyright dates, and pushed the print button.

"I'll get this one," she said, circling the first name. "You find these other two, and we'll meet over at that table." She nodded in the direction of one of the reading rooms and disappeared. Sean turned to the desk to ask for help. When he finally returned with the only one he could find, she was deep into her text and frantically scribbling notes. As he approached, she tore off a sheet of paper and handed it to him.

"Find this and copy it. It's an article. You know what that is? It's in a journal. Just copy this one article. It's from the nineteen-thirties. It'll be filed over in the B-Wing with everything older than ten years."

Sean glanced at what was written and gave an involuntary start. It began with "Root." "What's . . . what's this about Root?" he asked, pointing to the word.

She glanced up. "It's the author. That's the one you want to copy. Hurry up. We have only half an hour. Get one of the stack people to help you find it. Can you copy? Do you have a copy account number?" Sean shook his head. Beth had always done it for him.

"Here." She fished out a plastic card. "Take this, and ask them to do it for you." Sean was still staring at the piece of paper in amazement. "What's the matter?" she asked.

"It's Root. That's Grimes."

"What do you mean, that's Grimes?"

"That's what he called himself."

"Is this some other damn thing you haven't told me about? I'm getting sick of this. Please just get the article copied, and we'll talk about it afterward. Run. Please," she said and laughed.

"Shhhh," said someone at the adjacent table. "Quiet."

An hour later they were back in the small cubicle that served as her office. For once no one was working late in the laboratory, so they were not interrupted.

Sean told her the whole story. The mysterious Blue Man named Root, the two thousand dollars, discovering Grimes's identity, the strange circumstances of his death, and his own suspicions of the Chinese and the East Germans. Joan sat and listened in silence.

Finally she said, "That explains a lot. Sean, why didn't you tell me all this before? We might have gotten here a lot sooner."

"I made a deal with Beth Markham. Without her help I wouldn't have gotten anywhere. We agreed upon a story to tell in the medical school that wouldn't embarrass Grimes's reputation."

"Why should this embarrass Grimes? He didn't do anything wrong, except, I guess, he ran under an assumed name. Imagine, he picked the name Root. He must have had a sense of humor, or at least he wanted to give credit to the right person. But you don't even know if what he did was illegal."

"It was unsportsmanlike."

"I thought professionals took advantage of every trick that wasn't illegal or couldn't be found out."

"Some do," Sean had to agree.

"And besides, he gave back the money. I think you're right, he just wanted to try it out on himself, and he never knew there'd be anybody good in the race or any money involved. After all, who ever heard of that race? It wasn't as if he used it when he ran the New York Marathon."

"Beth and I kind of feel the same way," Sean said.

"So the story about him wanting to try it on you, there was no truth to that at all?"

"No, I never spoke a word to the man in my life. But by now I feel that he's my best friend."

"Maybe that's not the right choice of words," Joan said.

"Okay, but now it's your turn. Tell me what the hell Grimes did. And who is Root?"

"It's after midnight. I was counting on spending the night with you but not like this. Let's go home. I'll tell you in the car what I found out. It's going to take me a little while to put this all together."

"Well, it started again," Joan said with relief, once they were in the car. "It would have been damn cold to walk."

"You must want a ride in a Porsche awfully badly. You've been picking on this thing for weeks."

"How about just a nice Toyota. At least get something with the modern safety devices. What good will it do you to have saved money if you're dead?"

"My family will be rich. I have lots of insurance."

"What good will that do me?"

"Well, you won't have to worry about negotiating these four-week contracts," Sean pointed out.

"Touche."

"Anyway, tell me what you found out," Sean pleaded.

"It seems there's a hemoglobin in fish called a 'Root-effect' hemoglobin. It's not in all fish, but it's in trout. The figures in the textbook were actually from trout blood. It sounds like—and this is kind of strange—that the fish have many different hemoglobins. That's really weird, but that's what it said. I was reading pretty fast."

"What's so weird about that? We have a lot of hemoglobin."

"But it's all one kind."

"Well, but, but how about all the different blood types?"

"No, no, no. Wait. Wait. Boy, you're the perfect example of 'a little knowledge is a dangerous thing.' First of all, the blood types have nothing to do with the kind of hemoglobin. They refer to markers that are on the wall of the red blood cell. The hemoglobin inside is the same, no matter what type you are."

"So all humans have exactly the same kind of hemoglobin?" Sean asked, wanting to be sure that he had heard correctly.

"All normal adults have the same kind. Fetuses have a special kind. And there are diseases where the hemoglobin is different. You've heard of sickle cell anemia."

"That's the disease black children get?" Sean asked. "One of my kids had some mild form."

"It comes from having an abnormal hemoglobin. Remember the thing about the protein chains, the chains of amino acids?"

"Of course." Why did she think he couldn't learn anything?

"Okay. There's a protein chain in the hemoglobin. Actually there are two different chains. A particular change of one of the amino acids in the beta chain causes sickle cell anemia. It comes from a mutation. You know I make deliberate mutations, so I can change the amino acids one at a time to study protein folding. This mutation alters the hemoglobin so it forms clumps and deforms the red cell into the shape of a sickle, which clogs the blood vessels."

"Ah."

"Anyway it sounds as if in some species of fish the normal adult has a lot of different hemoglobins. The main one in trout, the one that has this Root effect, is called hemoglobin IV."

"So there are at least four."

"Yes, but the article implied that there are even more, maybe seven or eight. I didn't know any of this before tonight."

"And what's so special about the Root hemoglobin?" Sean asked.

"It's funny," she said scowling, "but when you put it in acid, it loses its oxygen-binding sites. Then they come back when you take it out of the acid. I just don't quite get what Grimes was up to. It's not like it's a Bohr effect, or maybe it's kind of like a huge Bohr effect."

"What's a Bohr effect?" They had pulled up in front of her apartment.

"I've had enough hemoglobin for one night. Let's go screw."

"That's the most romantic invitation I've ever had," Sean responded.

"Well, you can always turn it down."

Joan propped herself up on her elbow. "Now I've got it. I've figured it out."

"But it's one-thirty," Sean protested.

"I always think better when I'm in bed with somebody."

"You mean you figured it out while we were . . ."

"My subconscious does it. I was giving you my undivided attention."

Sean shook his head.

"Anyway, don't you want to know what it is?"

"Of course I do, even at this hour." He grabbed a pillow, folded it in half and put it behind his head. "So, tell me."

"When you exercise and you're not getting enough oxygen, your muscles make lactic acid. You've heard of that?"

"Sure, it's in all the running magazines." Sean was always proud to be able to show that he knew a little of the science. "If you don't have enough oxygen, you can't burn your sugar completely and efficiently. Instead, you use a kind of alternative pathway and get some of the energy out of the sugar, but you make lactic acid in the process."

"And I'll bet tumors do the same thing when they don't have enough oxygen." She was talking more to herself than to Sean. "That must have been what got Grimes interested in it. People must have measured how acidic it is inside tumors. When this hemoglobin goes to a place that's acidic, it will just dump its oxygen like crazy. It's a very clever idea. Now it all fits. He found this out while he was thinking of oxygen delivery for his cancer treatments, and I'll bet he just decided he'd be his own guinea pig. And why not try it out while he was running. He was a runner anyway."

Sean was wide awake by now. "But who is this Root? It sounds like *he* really discovered it."

"That article was from the thirties. Root must be long dead. Apparently he found this weird effect in fish blood, and his name's always been associated with it. But from the textbook it sounds like people don't believe his original explanation of it anymore. Of course, that's not surprising. Think of it. He found it sixty years ago. They couldn't even have known the structure of hemoglobin then."

"And nobody's ever thought of using it before this?" Sean asked incredulously.

"Most people probably never heard of it, and I guess the ones who did never thought of what to do with it. It shows how narrow we are, and how much there is to be gained by crossing fields."

"That's what you're trying to do in your own work."

"Yup. Look, we have our big break now, but there's still a lot we don't know about this. I think we should split up the work. You can stop being a runner and become a reader." She tickled him in the ribs. "I'll find out all about the hemoglobin, the structure of it, and why and how it does this thing. That's kind of in my line anyway. You find out about packaging, how you could give it to somebody, how you could wrap it up. The science of that should be easy."

"It doesn't sound easy to me."

"No, I don't mean it would be easy to do, but easy to read the papers. They won't require a lot of sophisticated background knowledge. You could ask Blackburn. I'll bet he knows all about it, but he just didn't make the connection either."

"Actually, I never told him about the trout blood. It came up after I spoke to him."

"Then it may ring a bell. Maybe he'll even know how Grimes was using it."

"I won't be able to get to him right away. I have to be in Philadelphia next week for a race. But there's a woman, Cindy Helms, who used to work with Blackburn on all these hypoxia things. I met her just as she was leaving for Penn, and she invited me to come talk to her if I had questions. That's when I was still living there. I'll give her a call and make an appointment."

"So she got that job. Have fun."

"Do you know her?"

"A little." She was sitting on top of him. "It's too late to go to sleep now," she said with a smile. "It's time for me to do a little more inspired thinking about science, and I'll need your help."

Chapter 32

Sean was glad to be back in his own apartment in Philadelphia. Despite the cold he opened all of the windows and set about to clean it. He needed time to think, and frankly he was glad to be away from Joan. She was always ready to think for two, but he didn't always find that helpful. For example, she was so sure that Susie was using this hemoglobin, but that had to be just an emotional reaction, he thought. How could Susie have solved the mystery in such a short time, and then made it work? Sean still didn't know how the hemoglobin was used, and obviously Joan didn't either. When had he told Susie about it? He couldn't even remember. Was it at Oxford? Or was it at that last dinner in Grenville? But she could never have done all that in four or five months while she was in England. But why had she suddenly changed her plans and begun to take all those science courses? Basic science courses she had said. It just seemed impossible.

Then he had a horrible thought, suppose she had learned it years before. Didn't she say that she knew someone who had worked with Grimes? Could she have been using it the whole time she was at Grenville? No, that was impossible, he reassured himself, quickly counting up the years. That would have been before Grimes even tried it himself. And she was a great runner when she was still in prep school.

And besides, the strength of her running was in her beautiful natural form. She wasn't winning because of superior physical conditioning. Or was she, with this new funny running strategy? He only wished that the television coverage had been better in her London race. But would he have recognized the subtleties that he had noticed in Grimes and in the Chinese? Would he have even been prepared to see it even if it was right in front of his face? Well, he would be next time, and now he just had to arrange to see her run again.

The race was the following evening. Sean had bought tickets for everyone in his club. He missed the youngsters, some of whom he had known for the full six or seven years. On his visits to Philadelphia, he had managed to run with some of them, but it was not the same. Now was their chance to wildly applaud their mentor, no matter that the race was never in doubt. It was almost a carbon copy of New York. In the last two miles he simply ran away from the others.

Sean had arranged a massive spaghetti dinner at a nearby restaurant for after the race. There, he and the two undergraduates who were taking his place went over the report cards of the students. Doing well in school was a requirement for club membership. But the real fun was in going over the running results, the small triumphs, the improvements, and even the disappointments.

Sean had planned a twenty-mile run with Bob, Bob in the car of course, for the morning after the race. It was part of the new "burn fat" training regimen. *A little more of that pasta and I'd have defeated Higgum's plan*, he thought as he left the restaurant. Inducing lipases was all the rage, running when you're hungry, learning to burn fat more efficiently. *That would be a good thing to ask Joan about. She needs something to keep her mind busy in bed*, he thought peevishly. *Well, I'll do the long practice run tomorrow with no breakfast.*

Higgum picked up Sean the next morning, and they drove toward Fairmont Park. In the car they reviewed Sean's training plans for the next several weeks. Finally Bob mentioned Susie.

"Your friend in England is really stirring things up," he said and laughed. "You're going to have to set some records, or she'll think you're just second best."

"I know. She's really sharp right now. I went over for the London race."

"So that's where you were."

"As if you didn't know," Sean said.

"Jim McBride is walking on air. It couldn't have happened at a better time. He wants that Cal Central job."

"We talked about it. He told me you recommended him."

"I did, and that will count a little bit." False modesty thought Sean. "But training a world record holder will count a lot. Everybody knows she's *his* runner."

"Hopwell deserves some of the credit."

"Very little."

"You eh, you don't like him, do you?" Sean asked.

"Oh, I don't dislike him, much. It's just that he's so pompous. And anyway I grew up not liking Brits. He doesn't like me, because I'm Irish, and because I was one of the first to recruit Europeans to American colleges. Half of the best English runners train over here now, so they're not with him."

"But he's good?"

"Yeah, sure. If he weren't, I wouldn't dislike him." He chuckled.

"Well, he must have helped Susie, she certainly improved while she was over there."

"Some, maybe. But you don't make distance runners in three months. No, this is the best thing that could have happened to Jim. He's going to get that Cal Central job now. And he should. He deserves it."

It had occurred to Sean that Higgum might be pushing Jim too hard. Having one of his boys at Cal Central would extend his web of influence even farther.

"You're sure that Jim has made up his mind? There are a lot of attractions to a place like Grenville. Jim really likes it, and I can understand why. If I were there, I'd try to develop a good program even with all their restrictions."

"But you're not Jim, even if you're always being compared. Do you know that people think he's from Ireland?"

"He is. His family just made the trip a little earlier than I did."

"They just assume all my runners are from Ireland, except Okabi of course." Bob laughed. "Anyway I'm glad you and Jim have had the chance to get to know each other better. He's as competitive as you are, maybe more so, but never had the big victories as a runner. He still needs to prove himself at the top level in something. For him that's going to be coaching, and he deserves the chance. He'll do great things with all that Cal talent. You'll prove yourself on the track, then you can do whatever you want. I could see you coaching at a place like Grenville, pulling off upsets, all the big programs not ever wanting to compete against you, afraid of you and your amateurs." Higgum smiled his self-satisfied smile. Sean smiled too.

They reached the southern gate to the park. Higgum was in the mood for blood. "You have a hundred minutes for twenty miles," he told Sean. It was a figure that would be near world record time if extended for the full marathon, twenty-six miles.

"A hundred and ten," Sean negotiated.

"A hundred and five," Bob counter-offered.

"I'm sure we can reach some agreement. I'll see you at eight miles and then at the bridge." Sean waved and started down the path into the park. When he got back to the apartment he was exhausted, but he knew that he had gotten even more out of this run because of the race the day before. "No pain, no gain." He said it so many times it was a joke. He relaxed in the tub.

What would have happened if Beth had never sent the two thousand dollars? I'd be living here in this apartment. I never would have met Susie. I never would have met Joan and wouldn't know anything about fish or hemoglobin. My running probably wouldn't be much different. But ignorance isn't bliss. I'd be a setup for the Chinese. What am I going to do about them? I can't let them take all this away from me. Not after all this work. I can't let them win by cheating.

The next day Sean met Cindy Helms in her new office. She proudly showed him around the laboratories.

"What luxury," he said. "All this is yours?"

"Mine for as long as I put it to good use. And look, a real live post-doc of my own." She introduced a dark-haired woman in jeans, who seemed so busy she hardly had time to acknowledge him.

"You people just clone one another," Sean said.

"Yes, that's the general idea," she said as they entered her office. She pointed for Sean to take a chair opposite the desk, and they both sat down. "Now what's this you want to know about hemoglobin. Didn't Joe explain it all to you? I'll have to tell him he's losing his touch as a teacher."

"No, no, don't do that. He gave me so much time and was very helpful. This is a little different. I'm trying to figure out how you could use hemoglobin from another animal to make blood for a runner. I'm not sure I put that very well, but suppose you had a super kind of hemoglobin and you wanted to put it into a human, could you do that? Could you use it to make one of those blood substitutes they talk about?"

"Yes," Cindy said, "but is there such a hemoglobin?"

"There just might be," Sean said. "Do you know Joan Danner?"

"The woman from Grenville, a post-doc in Genetics?" Cindy didn't seem pleased to hear her name, Sean thought, or was that just his imagination?

"I met her in a roundabout way after you left, and she's been helping with this mystery."

"Why would she be putting her nose into this?"

"It sounds as if you don't like her," Sean said. "Isn't she good?"

"No, no, it's nothing like that. I don't know her very well, but you're right, I'm not very fond of her. Yes, she's supposed to be very good. What does she have to do with this?"

"She had a friend named Neville who worked for Grimes."

"The Australian, the bike racer?"

"Bike racer?" Sean tried not to show surprise.

"Oh, he won some race, not a big one." She laughed. "Well it was big. It was one hundred miles, to raise money for the American Heart Association. Tom and I did twenty-five. You could do just part. There were some good people in it, but he won by a lot."

"Well, I think she used to go out with him."

"She used to go out with everybody," Cindy declared.

Sean was a little taken aback, but he covered. "Well, I'm not interested in that. I just wanted to find this fellow Neville, but apparently he's gone. I told Danner a little bit about the story, and meanwhile, again after you left, I found out that Grimes had ordered a lot of fish blood."

"Fish blood?" Cindy repeated.

"Well, no one could quite figure out why, but then she—you know she seems very smart to me—she got the idea that there was some special kind of hemoglobin in fish, and that Grimes could be putting it into those animals with cancer."

Cindy leaned back in her chair. "Come to think of it, they were doing something with blood, but I never knew what they were using it for. And I never saw any fish around."

"You wouldn't have. The fish were bled somewhere else."

She frowned. "I'm trying to remember. They were passing it through columns, that's a way to separate things."

"The hemoglobin?"

"Could be. They were doing it with a lot of blood because as I recall, there were three columns in the lab, huge, the biggest columns I ever saw."

"So maybe they were mass-producing something," Sean suggested.

"Possible," Cindy agreed.

"So now suppose there was a fancy hemoglobin in the fish, and you got it out of their blood and you purified it, then how would you use it."

"Well, there are a number of things that have been tried. If you had a very pure preparation, you could put it right into the bloodstream, just like you were giving a regular transfusion."

"But somewhere I learned that the hemoglobin isn't supposed to be just dissolved in the plasma in the blood. It's supposed to be in the red cells."

"You have a good memory," Cindy said, smiling. "Maybe we'll make a scientist out of you after all. The truth of the matter is that people have used just plain hemoglobin dissolved in saltwater as a blood substitute. It's called 'stroma-free hemoglobin.' That means the hemoglobin has been taken out of the red blood cells and removed from what's left of them, the stroma. But there are some problems."

"Like?"

"The hemoglobin itself when it's dissolved is small enough so it can go through the kidneys into the bladder. When it's inside a red cell, that's millions of times bigger, it's not excreted."

"So it would come out in your urine?"

"That's where things always end up when they go through the kidneys." Cindy laughed.

"And it would be red?" He could hardly conceal his excitement. "The urine would be red?"

"Certainly," Cindy said. "Pinkish or red. How red would depend on how fast you were making urine and how much hemoglobin you were given."

"And this wouldn't cause any harm?"

"Not if you were careful. The big disadvantage would come if you wanted to keep the hemoglobin. You'd be losing it steadily. It wouldn't last very long, maybe a few hours."

Long enough for a 10K race, thought Sean.

"But in terms of the kidneys, it turns out not to be harmful, if you don't let yourself get too dehydrated. You runners are very careful about that. If you stopped putting a lot of water through your kidneys, you would get a high concentration of hemoglobin, and it might begin to try to make, how should I put it, clumps. That could ruin the kidney, because the clumps could be the wrong size and clog the ducts. That's putting it in laymen's terms, of course."

"Well, I'm certainly a layman." Sean smiled.

"But you could prevent the clumps if you just made sure you drank lots of water, even more than usual, so you were putting out urine continuously. Of course you might pee in your pants, if you were making all that urine and couldn't get to a john right away." She laughed again. "And it could be very red, even with all that water, if we're talking about giving someone enough hemoglobin to make a difference in oxygen delivery."

Sean was so excited by this news, he could barely contain himself. But he knew he had to appear calm, since Cindy only knew the official "medical school version" of the Grimes story.

"Tell me, why are people interested in this stroma-free hemoglobin if it doesn't last very long in the blood stream and has this risk of harming the kidneys?"

"Well it's still experimental, but the goal would be to use it in emergencies. For example, since blood type, you know, the ABO system, stuff like that, is all carried on the red cell, you wouldn't have to worry about cross-matching for transfusions. Anybody could take the hemoglobin," Cindy explained.

"And anybody could take fish hemoglobin?"

"Probably."

Sean thanked Cindy profusely and promised to be in touch. He was so excited about what he had learned that he decided to cut short his trip and return to Grenville at once.

Chapter 33

Sean called Joan as soon as he was back. They met in Grimes's old office. He wanted to tell her in person what he had learned.

"So that's it!" Joan exclaimed when he had finished. "They were taking stroma-free hemoglobin, and that's what was making their urine red."

"It's all beginning to make sense, and you know, they wouldn't pick that up in the testing because runners often have blood in their urine."

"They do?" she said with surprise.

"Yes. With strenuous exercise you can pass a little blood through the kidneys. It's not very much, but it's enough for those sensitive tests to pick up, so they just ignore it," Sean explained.

"But you'd think they'd pay attention if there was a lot."

"The most obvious source of a lot of blood would be an irritation on your, um, on your private parts."

"You mean your penis," Joan said laughing.

"Well, I was thinking of both sexes. You know, during a long run you get irritated, chafed from the clothing you wear, even when you grease up. I'll bet it's worse for the women. And of course, some of the women runners could be having their periods."

"I thought we agreed they didn't do that," Joan reminded him.

"No, that's unusual. Anyway, for all those reasons the testers would just pass up a little hemoglobin."

"Very interesting, very interesting."

"Now let's hear what you found out," Sean demanded eagerly.

"Okay. Ah, first let's talk about this Bohr effect first. Remember I mentioned it the other night? You said you didn't know what it was."

"I don't think I've ever heard of it."

"Remember, someone, maybe Blackburn, told you how important it was that the hemoglobin load and unload oxygen at the right pressure."

Sean nodded.

"Well, there are several things that can change the pressure at which the hemoglobin works, including how much acid is around. Most places in the body, except the stomach of course, aren't very acidic or basic. They're near neutral. When the blood leaves the heart it's a little bit basic. Out in the tissue where it picks up some of the waste products of metabolism it becomes more acidic. If you make the blood a little more acidic, the hemoglobin loads and unloads oxygen at a higher pressure."

"Higher pressure?"

"Yes, but think what it really means. If it takes higher pressure to load it, that means the oxygen will come off more easily."

"So it comes off more easily in the tissue," Sean said.

"Right. Now you take the blood back to the lungs, you make it a little more basic, and the hemoglobin works at lower pressure, that means lower pressure to load, easier to load. It's called the 'Bohr shift' after its discoverer."

Sean was grinning from ear to ear. "Let me be sure I've got it. This just seems too clever. More acid out in the tissue means it's easier to unload there where you're supposed to unload, and less acid in the lung means easier to load where you're supposed to load."

"Ain't nature grand? Now before we stand around congratulating ourselves on how clever our blood is, let me tell you that this effect is small. It goes in the right direction, but quite frankly you could get along fine without it. It just doesn't make a lot of difference."

"That's kind of disappointing. Why even have it if it's not going to help?"

"Well, that's not quite the way a good biologist would look at it," Joan explained. "We have lots of things in us that don't seem to make sense right now, but remember you're just looking at one point in evolution, a single frame in a whole movie. Some things, like your appendix, were useful and are going away. This Bohr shift would be more useful if it were bigger and maybe it's just coming."

"You mean a million years from now the hemoglobin will have changed and will work better?"

"Why not?"

"Then the runners will be better. Bob keeps telling me this is the year to get that gold medal." He faked a worried look.

"Yeah, yeah," she scoffed. "Maybe we'll evolve wings before we evolve better hemoglobin. Anyway, it turns out that the fish are a little bit ahead of us in this game."

"You mean their hemoglobin changes more when you make it acid?"

"It really changes! You know that there are four spots on the hemoglobin to bind oxygen and that all four of the spots load at about the same pressure."

"Right," Sean said.

"What happens with the fish hemoglobins, the particular fish hemoglobins they named after Root, is that when you put them in acid, the sites almost seem to disappear."

"Disappear?"

"Yes, and guess what happens to the oxygen when those sites disappear."

"I don't know," Sean answered, with a puzzled expression on his face. "I guess it comes off."

"Right, it comes off. Like you turned a pocket inside out. It just gets dumped."

"So you mean that the oxygen just dumps no matter what the pressure is?"

"Almost. The missing binding sites are really still there. They can load or unload just like they always did, but only at such a high pressure that for all practical purposes they're gone. It's like the world's largest Bohr effect. A hundred times bigger than a Bohr effect. More than a hundred times bigger."

"That's amazing."

Joan fidgeted in her chair as she became more and more excited. "If you're *unloading* where it's acidic, you know in the capillary with the lactic acid," Sean nodded, "lots of oxygen will come off at a very high pressure. But when you *load* oxygen in the lung where it's basic, it's just as easy with this fish hemoglobin as it is with human." Finally she got up and began to pace about the room, "Do you see what this *means*?"

"Well, I'm getting it. I just don't think about these things as fast as you do."

"Didn't Blackburn tell you all about hyperbaric oxygen and why it doesn't work very well? The pressure is high, but there's not enough quantity of oxygen. Right? Not much dissolves in the plasma, in the saltwater."

"Right." Sean nodded his head vigorously

"And the problem with normal hemoglobin is that even though the quantity of oxygen is adequate, the pressure is too low to push it out into the tissue."

"So you're going to tell me this is the best of both worlds." Sean was becoming excited as well.

"You got it."

"I don't understand how the fish have this and we don't." Sean was suddenly more subdued. "Aren't we supposed to be more advanced than they are?"

"Well, they can swim underwater better than you can." She laughed while answering.

"Because of this hemoglobin?"

"No, no. I'm joking. This hemoglobin has nothing to do with swimming underwater. They swim under water because they have gills. Some fish don't even have this kind of hemoglobin."

"It just seems we should have fancier hemoglobin than fish," Sean protested.

Joan looked at him in amazement. "You're taking this as if it were an insult from nature or something, Sean. We work just fine."

"But if we came from fish like some of you people believe, then why did we forget how to make this Root hemoglobin?"

"Maybe when we were separating from the fish, they still didn't know how to make it. See, they learn faster than we do, and you think you're so smart." She was teasing him again. He shook his head.

"Listen," she continued. "These changes are driven by what some people call evolutionary pressure. If you really need this thing, and it's going to be useful to you, then you're more likely to select for it."

"You mean if all the people who didn't have it were dying out..."

Sean was still shaking his head.

"If the only humans who were allowed to reproduce were the fastest runners, we might all have Root-effect hemoglobins," she said and laughed. "Or we might just evolve big brains instead and take the Root-effect hemoglobins from the fish."

"Yeah, pretty smart of Grimes, wasn't it?" Finally Sean was smiling.

"I never heard anybody say he was dumb."

"You think the fish just swim faster because of this hemoglobin?"

"I don't think anyone knows exactly what they do with it. There is one interesting theory though, that the deep-sea fish, you know the ones that would never come to the surface in their whole lives, use it to fill their swim bladders."

"The thing that creates the buoyancy?" Even Sean knew enough biology to know about swim bladders.

"Yes, fish have a bubble in them that lets them regulate the depth at which they float. It turns out that around the swim bladder is a special organ, not like anything we have, that makes the blood more acidic. If enough oxygen came off at a really high pressure, it could diffuse into the swim bladder space and form a bubble. This hemoglobin acts like an oxygen pump. In the lungs where it's more basic it loads at low pressure. In the tissue where it's more acidic it dumps at high pressure."

"That could really happen?"

"It sounds strange, but that's what they say. I have a few more things to learn about this, but we're pretty far along toward solving this whole mystery. Now we have to make some decisions about what we do with what we know."

"Well, first we've got to tell Kerr. That was my promise when he allowed me to look into it and asked everyone to cooperate with me. I presume that this thing could be important, and that someone should pursue this research, and the right people should get credit for it. It might even be valuable. Kerr was concerned that the university's interests be protected."

"He would be. Of course he's right, and it could be very valuable. Any place in the body where oxygen was in short supply would become acidic. That's the only thing you really need to make this system work. So, it might be good for heart attacks, strokes and all kinds of things as well as for cancer."

"And runners' muscles making lactic acid," Sean added. "It might really work." He paused. "I think maybe we know for sure that it does work."

"Now we've also got to figure out what to do with these people who are using it, although I hate to bring it up."

Sean knew she wasn't referring just to the Chinese. "We still don't know for sure whether Susie's using it," he insisted. "You just guessed that."

Joan rolled her eyes.

"We can't say that she did it if we can't prove it."

"Sean, I'm going to leave that one entirely up to you. If it isn't illegal to use hemoglobin, maybe you should just congratulate her on how smart she is."

"Don't be sarcastic," he said. "You know how I feel about things like that. Even if it's just unsportsmanlike."

"Yes, and I can imagine how much you're going to dislike poor sportsmanship if it costs you a couple of medals and a million bucks."

"Well," Sean was exasperated, "we've got to go one step at a time. The first thing is to find out whether she was really using it."

"I already know, but maybe *you* have to go find out."

"Now that's not fair."

She put her hands up, palms facing him. "Hey, I said before, I'm staying out of it."

"I wonder if I should tell Jim about my suspicions? Oh, shit."

"What?"

"He's being considered for a coaching job, one I think he really wants. He's probably going to get it, in part because of Susie. Not that he doesn't deserve it anyway, but to have one of your runners break a world's record . . . that will surely give him the edge."

"Uh-oh. And if they find out she cheated, they'll think he was in on it."

"Damn," Sean exclaimed and banged his fist on the desk. "I've got to go back to England."

"Just what are you planning to do there, daily underwear checks?"

"That might be fun," Sean said matching her sarcasm.

"I thought you'd enjoy it."

"I'll be able to find out, but not like that."

"Why don't you just confront her with your suspicions?"

"No, no. I couldn't do that."

"Why not? Are you afraid of her?"

"No, I'm not afraid of her. But I don't want to offend her."

"If she has nothing to hide, she shouldn't care," Joan said.

"That's not the way people are."

"Well, this sounds like a universal problem." Joan was obviously enjoying his discomfort. "What are you going to do if your wife is, ah, working late in the laboratory with some handsome post-doc, and you're just a little suspicious?"

"I'm not married, and who said if I were that my wife would be working in a laboratory?"

"You're not generalizing properly," Joan admonished.

"Maybe not, but I'm making my point. Anyway, I don't know the answers to these things. In this case, I'd just like a little more evidence before I confront her. I guess that's a measure of how much trust I have in her."

"Well, what are you going to do to find out?"

"There are a couple of things. First of all, I have a friend over there. He'll be able to check the urine after the races and see if it's red."

"Oh, great! Now you've hired a private detective to follow your wife."

"Why the hell are you being like this?" Sean exploded. "Why don't you just try to help instead of trying to make it harder? It's hard enough as it is."

Joan was taken aback. "I'm sorry," she said. "I guess I was enjoying your dilemma. Maybe I just like dilemmas, but I shouldn't be enjoying it when it's causing you so much pain. Maybe I'm enjoying it because she's the one causing the pain, and I'm just trying to amplify it."

"Oh?"

"Anyway, what's the other way you're going to find out?"

"I just have to watch her run."

"How can you tell from watching her?"

"I can tell. When you do this for a living, you learn to watch subtle things about runners. Maybe most people couldn't tell, but a good pro could, or at least any good pro who had reason to suspect something."

"You mean they run a different way?"

"All the people I know who've used this, and that's just Root, Root-Grimes, and the Chinese . . . there was something funny about the way they ran."

"And Susie? Did you notice it when she ran?"

"Oh, the stupid television coverage was so bad, there weren't enough close-ups. I couldn't tell. But I probably would have been blind to it anyway."

"Well, that's an admission."

"I'd have to be there when she ran."

"What's so different about them?"

"At first I couldn't put my finger on it. But it all makes sense now, they just don't breathe hard enough."

"They don't breathe hard enough," Joan repeated.

"Yeah. You can see how much work they're putting out, and you can see how much pain they're in from doing it, but they're not breathing hard."

"And you can recognize that?" Joan asked with amazement.

"I can. I did, even before I knew what they were up to."

"But what does it mean?" she asked

"It means their conditioning is out of balance. See, when you're well trained for some specific sport," Sean explained, "every component of the machine is being pushed to the maximum. The heart, the lungs, the muscles, they're in perfect balance. With these people one part is working much better than the others."

"The breathing part," Joan said.

"Sure. Look at it this way. I'm in terrific aerobic shape."

"Of course, you run 10K's and marathons."

"But if you put me on a bicycle, I couldn't even get out of breath. That's not because biking is easier, it's because I don't do it regularly. Even though I use my legs in my business, the leg muscles that you use for biking are a little different. I don't have enough of those muscles, developed the way they should be, to challenge my heart and lung capacity. It's the same in reverse for the bikers. They probably couldn't get out of breath running. You know, the bikers, like Jack, are in absolutely terrific aerobic shape, but they wouldn't have the running muscles to even test . . ."

"What did you say?" Joan interrupted. "About Jack?"

"Oh, somebody told me he was a bike racer. You never mentioned that."

"Who told you that? He wasn't a racer. He just biked for fun."

"Sounds like he was very good."

"That's silly. You're the only athlete in my life. Anyway, what you were saying is that when these people are cheating they give a big boost to their aerobic system, and they don't have the muscles to keep up with it."

"That's exactly right," Sean continued. "And it's going to be of most help to the middle distance people, the milers, perfect for Susie's 5K, my 10K. I don't think this Root hemoglobin would affect the 100-yard dash people. Hell, that takes nine seconds. You hardly need to breathe. You go into a big 'oxygen debt,' as they call it, but seconds later you stop running, you start panting, and you pay back the debt." Sean was thinking out loud. "It probably won't help the marathoners either."

"But that's the hardest thing of all," Joan protested.

"But it's not hard breathing. Good marathoners don't get out of breath, except at the end when the sprint, of course. Marathoners run out of the other fuel. They run out of sugar, glycogen. That's why they have all these funny training schedules. Anyway, I think I could pick out the people who are using this Root hemoglobin."

"So, you have to go watch Susie run, and you have to hope she's using it that day."

"I'll get her running schedule from Jim and go over there again when I can. And I'll get my friend to check the urine. One way or the other, I'll find out for sure. I just hope I'm not sorry when I do."

Chapter 34

Reinhardt Jurgen smiled to himself as he watched the crane lower a second stainless steel fermentation tank onto the floor of the new laboratory. There was such satisfaction in seeing a project finally begin to take shape, but in this case it was tempered by the realization that it might not be in time. Some things were so much more difficult in China.

"Well, if it turns out they came too late, we can use these good German vats to make good German beer," Manfred Schultz joked.

But Jurgen was not in the mood for humor. "If we had not wasted so much of the virus trying to determine what it was . . ."

"Some of the laboratory record books must have been lost by the Chinese agents."

"That should not have happened. They were specifically instructed to bring everything. Now there is barely enough virus left to seed the cultures. If the virus does not grow in time, there will be only what remains of the original supply, scarcely enough to treat Han and Dak. We may have only one chance."

"If we were at home, or even in America, we could simply contract with someone to grow the virus for us. 'Biotech' companies, they call them." Schultz used the English word.

"Never!" Jurgen almost shouted. "It must not leave our laboratories. Those companies cannot be trusted. If they kept a sample of the culture, our secret would be lost without our even knowing it."

"We could use the hemoglobin again. It worked well. You were correct, they suspect nothing, even though it should be so obvious."

"But we stretch our luck. Eventually they would find out. No, the hemoglobin was a useful test, but now we must move on. The virus will be foolproof. They will never detect it."

Chapter 35

The next weekend Sean went to the Midwest, to the "pot of gold race" as Bob Higgum called it because of the amount of the appearance and prize money. He won the 10K as expected. It was becoming monotonous.

"Just remember, they're the junior varsity," Bob had said. "The real competition is all hiding."

But the money was good. As Sean looked at the check he thought, *I could live on this for a year.*

To celebrate, Jim and Helen had invited him to dinner on the evening of his return. Jim kept him up to date on Susie's running. Apparently she had lost the next two races.

Jim told him the times. "They're good, but not near her world record."

"Well, you can't do that every day," Sean said, "and she lost to very good people. The Europeans have really turned out the top women. I can't even find someone decent to race against."

"Yeah, it's a lot different when they're hungry. The women don't get nearly as much money as the men, and there are a lot of those eastern Europeans who were just unleashed. Boy, they want to make it fast."

"I don't blame them," Sean agreed. "Some of them have had their whole careers controlled by their governments. Now when they're nearing the end, they're desperate to get something in the bank before they're too old and nobody wants them."

"That's going to happen to everybody," Jim added philosophically.

"I know. I really felt sorry for Abi at Bradsford last year. But the men who started when I did should be pretty well off. That last race was like stealing. It wasn't even a good workout."

"Yeah, there have been big changes over the last ten years," Jim agreed.

"And you'll be a famous coach some day," Helen burst in.

"Well, I think of that sometimes."

"No, it's true. Jim tells me all the time. He probably wouldn't admit it to your face, but he thinks you're more like Higgum than he is. And you know, in your sick little circle," she moved her hand in an arc to encompass them all and laughed "that's the highest flattery."

"I'm not sure we like being called sick," Jim protested. "We're just, um, what do you call them, not camp followers, but, um, groupies. We're Higgum groupies."

Sean laughed too. "Well, I don't think that's quite the word. But one of these days the old man won't be around anymore, and we're the ones who have to carry on his tradition. We really do hope to be just like him. In fact, we are." He pointed his finger at Jim. "You're just like him. If you go out there to Cal Central, you're going to have one of the best teams in the country. How's that going, by the way?"

"Just between you and me, and Helen," he said, looking at his wife, "I think I'm going to get it. I shouldn't say that because I don't want to jinx it."

"That's terrific." Sean was genuinely pleased for his friend's success. He looked at Helen. "So now you'll have to learn to cook TexMex."

"Blah," was Helen's response. "I wonder what New England boiled dinner tastes like by the side of a pool."

Ralph Hooker called two days later to say that Susie's urine was not red. "You're going to owe me for this, buddy. I need a story."

"I appreciate it very much," Sean assured him.

"Now, look. You have to give me a little something. This woman trained with your friend, and you're the guy who knows about this red urine. What's up? What's her connection to the Chinese?"

Sean had a moment of panic. "Look, Ralph. I trusted you. Not a word of this. She has no connection to the Chinese at all. It's just worth checking anybody who's setting world records."

"Yeah. Why do I have such a hard time believing you?"

"Remember. We had a deal," Sean reminded him.

"I remember, but that doesn't mean I can't use things that I find out for myself."

"I don't think I'd accuse Susie Fredricks of something in print, Ralph. Do you know who her father is? He runs one of the biggest law firms in New York."

"Oh."

Sean could tell that had stopped Hooker in his tracks. "I don't know how the Chinese are about libel suits, and, hell, they're probably guilty, as you and I are going to be the first to tell the world, but things are different in New York City. The only question would be whether Fredricks bought the magazine and fired all of you, or whether he sued you and got the magazine that way."

"Okay, okay, no need for that. I just smell something big, and if I'm helping, I'm entitled to it."

"That was always the deal," Sean said.

Sean was surprised by the arrival of an invitation from a faculty committee to discuss the track program at Grenville. He knew that he had to talk to Jim before the interview. Jim was not at all upset.

"They're not asking you to evaluate me behind my back," he told Sean. "They know all about my interest in the Cal Central job, and they've made it clear that they'd like me to stay. They're aware that the chances are against it, though, and are getting ready to search for somebody new. Since I haven't resigned yet, they can't call it a search committee, but that's what it is."

"You think they're interested in me as a candidate?" Sean asked.

"Of course. How could they do better?"

"It would be a real change. I'm not sure how it would work out."

"You should give it a try, it's perfect for you. Take it when they offer it to you."

"It's bad luck to say that in advance."

"Did they offer you the job right on the spot?" Joan asked after the interview. It was early evening, and Sean, exhausted from his afternoon workout, perched on a stool waiting for her to finish an experiment in the otherwise deserted laboratory.

"No. They're just supposed to be studying the situation in case Jim does decide to leave."

"Why would you want the job?" She didn't look up from her

work.

"I don't know whether I do. I've drawn up a balance sheet in my mind. I like the place, the traditions and everything. It kind of reminds me of home. And I like the students. But there would never be very many good athletes." The thought was uppermost in his mind, having just shared the practice track with the varsity runners. "Maybe I'd like that kind of challenge. It would be so much fun to knock off some of the big powers. But it would be really frustrating when they were kicking your butt. I hope it's not because I'm afraid of the challenge at a big track school, where you have to win, and there are no excuses. I don't think so."

Was she listening, or was he talking to himself? He always enjoyed watching her in the lab. She worked with such efficiency, moving with grace and precision. Even if he didn't know what she was doing, he knew she was doing it right. *It's like watching a great natural runner,* he thought.

"And after all, it would be a demotion. I'd have to give up my assistant professorship. They're just for visitors." He knew he could always get a response by mentioning the position.

"Bah," Joan grumbled over her shoulder.

She really is attractive, Sean thought, *even when she wears old blue jeans and a dirty lab coat. Of course wearing that skirt today means she wants to be taken to one of the better restaurants. We seem to spend most of our free time together. If it weren't for this blood stuff, I'd never even be thinking of Susie.*

"Seriously, I don't know whether I want it or not, or how it would fit into my plans for the next several years," Sean continued.

"What *are* your plans?" She finally looked up.

"Well, to keep running, barring any severe injuries, for five or six more years. Maybe with some luck I could still reach the Olympics after the next one."

"But you're practically doing the same amount of work now, and you're training just the way you normally would." She peeled off her gloves and moved out of sight behind an incubator.

"I'm certainly not doing all the work, and I don't have the responsibility." He got up and began to wander between the benches, following her. "If I have to be away to train or to race, I can just go. But with the right help and the right scheduling I think it could be done.

They'd also have to agree to go along with the exposure in the commercials. There's no way I would consider giving up that much money. I'll have to show you some of the rough versions. Anyway I do like Grenville, maybe for the same reasons you do. Sometimes I think I should give it a try, if they offer it to me of course."

She turned and stared at him, and he could almost feel her mind working. "But they won't offer it to you unless Jim gets his job in California."

"Of course not."

"And he won't get his job in California if someone finds out that his prize runner, or prize ex-runner, has been cheating."

"I could just see that coming."

"Well, that's a real moral dilemma," Joan said, beginning to put things away for the night. "Surely you're not going to stop your investigation."

She's enjoying this, thought Sean. *She just loves it.* "Now wait a minute." He rose to the bait. "We know that she hasn't had any blood or any red color in her urine in her last two races."

"What the hell, she lost those races."

"Boy, you're just determined that she's guilty, aren't you."

"Just the facts, just give me the facts," Joan insisted. "Her urine's clean, she loses. Her urine's bloody, she wins."

"But I never actually saw red urine, just those stains."

"Oh, come on. She's smart. She doesn't have to win every race. And besides she probably knows you're suspicious."

"How could she know I'm suspicious? And anyway, *you're* the one who's suspicious."

"Jesus, Sean." Joan turned quickly and pointed at him with the automatic pipetter she held in her right hand like a pistol. "She got the idea from *you.* Either she knows you'd be suspicious or she thinks you're stupid. Which do you prefer?"

Sean had the feeling she was right, but he didn't want to admit it. "Well, what am I supposed to do, go over to London and wait for her to win one?"

"Tell her you're coming over and that you're going to be very upset if she doesn't win for you. That will work. She won't want to disappoint you."

"You really *are* enjoying this."

"Oh no, Sean, I appreciate your problem. I'm just a seeker after the truth like any good scientist."

"Crap."

"My, what nasty language you use." She began to gather her things.

"She really bothers you, doesn't she?"

"No, no. I just don't want anything to interfere with honesty and fairness in track and field," she pronounced self-righteously.

"All right. I'm going to take you up on it. Meanwhile, we've got to schedule a meeting with Kerr, and who else should we have? Maybe Blackburn. Should we have Cindy Helms come back up?"

"Let's leave her in Philadelphia."

"You don't like her either, do you?"

"She's the one who doesn't like me." Joan began turning out the lights.

"And does she have some reason for that?" Sean asked, still following her about the room.

She stopped before the door and turned back to face him. "I used to go out with her husband."

"Well, she must have gotten over that. It sounds like she won." He smiled.

She smiled back. "I went out with him after she'd 'won,' as you call it."

Chapter 36

Sean was at the fieldhouse when the call came from Lou Gurci.

"Hi. Bill told me how to get you. Hope they didn't have to drag you off the track."

"No problem," Sean assured him. "I was just out there cheering on the kids. What's up?"

"I need to know if there's anything you want us to try to find out from this guy."

"What guy?" Sean was temporarily at a loss.

"The guy who whacked Grimes."

"You mean you've got him? You've arrested him?" Sean could hardly believe the good news.

"Not exactly. Is there anything you want me to find out from him? Anything that might help you solve this mystery. He's not going to know much. Just a hired hitter, but you never know. Maybe somebody let something slip. Help you figure out what Grimes was doing."

"Oh, I haven't had a chance to tell you, but I think we've got the thing solved. I mean, I think we know what the secret was. We don't know everything about it or just how he used it, but we should be able to figure that out."

"That's great." Lou sounded genuinely pleased. "You're a smart fellow."

"I don't get the credit, I just finally tied up with the right scientist down here, and she figured it out. It all makes sense now, the red urine and everything."

"Is it big?" Lou asked.

"I think so. The doctors seem very excited about it."

"That's good. I just thought it was going to be."

Sean had been thinking while they were talking. "You could try to find out who was behind this."

"Hey, we're sure going to do that."

"Oh, I didn't mean that. I didn't mean to insult you." Sean was embarrassed for having asked it. "Like Lin Pao. Did Lin Pao put him up to it? And a couple of other names."

"Wait a minute. Let me write them down. Lin Pao I think I got already. He's the guy you talked to in Germany, right?"

"Yes. Okay, here are a couple others. Lin Han . . ."

"H A N. Yeah."

"Ho Dak . . ."

"D A C K?"

"No, no. D A K and Chao Lee."

"Bet I can spell that." Lou laughed.

"And Ann Grossman, try to find out what happened to her."

"I won't forget that. Okay, anything else you can think of, you got to get to me in the next day or two. Let's make it the next day. Say tomorrow noon, last chance."

"I can't think of anyone else, but if I do I'll give you a call."

"Okay, I'll let you know what we find out, and that was good news about the invention."

The more Sean thought about it, the stranger the conversation seemed. Surely there'd be plenty of time to question this person and maybe to "plea bargain"—was that the right term— for more information?

Almost a week went by before they managed to meet. Lou Gurci was already seated at a table in Sparky's with a glass of beer in front of him when Sean arrived. Bill followed in a few minutes.

"Not too busy tonight," Bill greeted them. "What's the matter, Sparky's food gone to pot?"

"No." Lou laughed. "It's the only night of the week there's no basketball or hockey. Guys stay home, keep the family happy." They ordered beers and food and passed the time.

Finally Lou said, "What we say here don't go out." Sean nodded. Bill didn't bother. "First off, the guy didn't know any Lin Pao or Dak or Lee or any of those others. And he never heard of this Grossman. Course she could have been hit somewhere else."

"And you're sure he was telling the truth?" Sean asked.

Lou glanced up from his plate. "They usually are about that time." It had an ominous ring to it.

"How did you find him?"

"We got him pretty much through the computer. Anyhow, couldn't have gotten him without it. Bill here played a big part. Remember he had Jersey?"

Sean nodded.

"I narrowed it down to about twenty-five names from the tires." Bill continued the story. "Looked through all the people who sent back the warranties, searching for a Chinese name. Then I thought, 'Don't be dumb, this guy isn't going to send back the warranty.' So then I went through the ones who didn't send back warranties. The wholesaler keeps a record of the shops that sold them. I checked every shop. Only one had a customer with a Chinese name. And they kept the serial number of the car they put the tires on. I found the guy who had the car registered. Turned out he bought it from the original owner, with a little minor fender damage. One thing led to another."

"The guy was a little hard to find," Lou interrupted. "So then we turned old-fashioned." He stopped for a swallow of beer. "I still have some connections down there. Let the word out. Let the word *leak* out, if we have to come get him, bunch of guys are going down with him. Takes about a day. They give him to a friend of a friend, you know. Turns out this fucker's a low level hitter for a bunch of drug dealers. Not worth anything. Expendable to them. We make sure everybody knows we don't want to pump him for no crap on them, just on a little free-lancing he's doing on the side."

"Did he confess?" Sean asked.

Lou drank some more beer. "Yeah, he did confess."

"Is he going to be able to identify the people who hired him?"

"He's not going to be able to do anything. But he gave us some names."

"What do you mean?"

Bill interrupted. "I think he means that he isn't with us any more."

"What?"

"You know," Lou paused, "you know that saying, 'He's having dinner with the fishes.'"

"What did you do to him?" Sean stared wide eyed.

"Hey, I wasn't there." Lou shrugged. "No way these guys would ever turn him over to cops. They don't work like that. It was a big favor that they'd pump him a little. But turn him over . . ." He looked at Bill incredulously.

Bill nodded in agreement. "Couldn't take the chance he'd sing. Probably could have fingered them all. They'd never let us see him."

"Way we heard it," Lou picked up, "they gave him to a different bunch of dealers. He hit a couple of their guys once. They was looking for him anyway. Just a matter of time. Good that we got there when we did."

"Jesus!"

"Look," Lou said, "this asshole came to my town, he whacks one of my citizens when he's out running on a road. No," he said, shaking his head from side to side, "no, that doesn't happen. And the guy he whacks is a cancer doctor. He got this damn discovery that nobody knows what it is. Sure I'm relieved that you guys found his invention, but how much time's been lost? More than a year. I mean, suppose he was going to cure cancer. How many guys die a year of cancer?" He was looking at Sean as if he expected an answer.

"I don't know. A couple hundred thousand."

"So say this was going to work and it was delayed a year, then the damn guy killed a couple hundred thousand people."

Sean started to say, "Well, I don't know . . ."

"Look, suppose it worked for one in ten. So then he killed, what, fifty thousand people."

"Well," Sean said, "we don't know whether it will work at all."

"So, he killed one person. He killed the wrong person . . . In my town. He probably killed twenty others, too. But this was the one that made him fish food." Lou's anger overflowed. He held his glass in one hand and the beer bottle in the other and alternately clenched them as if he wanted to crush them in his bare hands.

Sean was dumbfounded.

Bill didn't seem disturbed or startled. Turning to Sean he said quietly, "There's nothing we could have done. If we had him, of course he would have been treated properly. The guys who did it had been after him anyway. We were damn lucky to be in time to get some questions answered."

"But how would you know people like that? Why would they do you a favor?"

Bill wagged his finger at Sean and said quietly, "It's best not to ask."

"No. No. It's okay," said Lou, now seeming calmer. "One guy, I saved his life. Pulled him from a restaurant after a fire bombing. Gang war. 'Tongs' they call them. The world would be better off if I had let him burn. I thought maybe he'd sing. No way. He's worse than any of them. But he never forgot."

Sean didn't know what to say. Finally Bill broke in. "Did he finger anybody, Lou?"

"Yeah." Lou said. "They're sneaky little bastards. Leave a real crooked trail. We did some big-time arm twisting. Fellow could lose a liquor license. You know, some of them restaurants down there, some of them have cockroaches in the kitchen. We got to inspect them more often." He laughed and laughed, and Bill finally joined in. "Bottom line," he finally continued, "we traced it back through three contacts to an attache, a cultural attache in the Chinese embassy in New York, name of Zeng, George Zeng. Don't sound right, but that's it."

"What will you do to him?" Sean asked almost not wanting to know the answer.

"Can't do much. Couldn't prove it. Diplomatic immunity anyway. We told the Feds. They could hassle him. They could throw him out of the country. Then I guess they'd throw out one of ours. Nothing you could do officially." He laughed again. "Course, accidents do happen. Fellow like that, comes from a country, well, not like ours, not used to the big city, maybe don't watch out for cars, maybe he don't know the city, goes to the wrong place. Bad people down there, he could get mugged." Lou was just shaking his head slowly. He'd stopped eating.

Sean didn't like what he had heard, but he was almost afraid to say so. Lou could tell from his expression that he was upset. "Look, you may not like this, Sean, I don't like it either. I came up here because I didn't want to be involved in this kind of crap no more. Some places in the world life is cheap." He paused. "Some places close to here it's cheap. But it's not cheap in my town. In my town it's very expensive, like an eye for an eye." Lou drained his beer.

"And that Pao fella, I don't know if it leads back to him. Maybe you'll find out sometime, but I can tell you for sure that this guy didn't know him, and I'm never going to get to sweat the guy at the embassy, so if you think Pao's dangerous, keep your guard up. But maybe he's not involved. That last conversation he had with you, if I remember it right, it was a little wacko. Maybe Pao's clean. Anyway, we won't talk about this no more."

Suddenly Lou's mood seemed to change completely. "Let's eat up and get the pie. Sparky always has homemade pie on Monday." He was already waving for the waitress.

Chapter 37

The meeting with Kerr and Blackburn was easily arranged. They sat around a small table in a conference room near the radiobiology labs. Presenting the science was to be left to Joan, but because of his promise to Beth Markham, Sean was determined not to reveal the whole story. Joan was perfectly happy to forget she knew that Grimes had won a race and passed some red urine, but she took great pleasure in pretending to be upset that they would not mention the role of Susie's underwear in the discovery.

"It's the great red panty coverup," she must have said a dozen times.

"Look if we don't know for sure, we don't have the right to bring it up," was Sean's standard answer.

"Well, you're going to bring it up about the Chinese, and you don't know for sure about them."

"They're less likely to sue us for defamation of character."

"Oh, bull." But finally she agreed.

Sean spoke first, explaining the discovery of the fish purchase and how Grimes was interested only in the blood. He told them about the unknown Chinese runners with their East German coaches, about the race in Stuttgart, and about the urine that was red but still passed the toxicology screens. He reminded them of the missing lab books and the Chinese research associate who had left suddenly, presumably to return to China. Sean gave Joan the credit for thinking of the fish hemoglobin and left her to tell them the rest of the story.

Blackburn and Kerr sat in rapt attention while Joan presented what in essence was a scientific seminar.

If I hear this about five more times, I'll be able to give it myself,

Sean thought.

Blackburn had been taking notes, but when Joan described the change in oxygen binding of the Root hemoglobin in acid he stopped, and a grin spread across his face. He recognized the implications immediately, even faster than Joan had, for this was directly related to his own interests.

"Grimes, that SOB. You know he was going to spring this on me some day. He'd present it like a quiz. He always did that. Who the hell would ever get the right answer? How do you suppose he discovered it?"

"And he never told you anything about this?" Kerr asked with disbelief in his voice.

"Not a word," Blackburn assured him. "But he was like that, good at thinking up wild ideas. He knew most would never work out, so he'd just putter along with them until he thought they looked promising."

"Well, he certainly went beyond that in this case," Kerr pointed out. "Maybe he wanted to keep it absolutely quiet, thinking of the patent rights. This could be very important."

"You're right," Blackburn agreed. "I wish they didn't have patents on anything, it just ruins the kind of free exchange we used to have. But as long as they do, our school might as well get its share."

Joan sat down, and Kerr rose and began pacing. "Speaking of patents," he said, "we must get this to the university attorneys. Someone's going to have to know enough to write it up." He looked questioningly at Joan.

"It's going to be hard to patent without the original data," Blackburn said. "We could try to duplicate some of this stuff as fast as possible, just enough to minimally support the claims. The Chinese could be a problem."

"Oh I just hope they try to file," Kerr pronounced angrily. " But they won't. They never honor our patents anyway, and they won't be so crazy as to try to gain rights elsewhere. Even so we really do have to hurry on this." He turned to Joan, "Would you be interested in being involved in this project? I'm sorry I'm not really familiar with what you do right now, but you can see this is kind of an emergency. Perhaps you could help out for a short period of time."

Joan clearly was surprised. This was not at all what she had expected. While she hesitated, Kerr pressed. "What do you think, Dr. Danner? Will you help us?"

"It's nice of you to ask," she said, "but this really isn't my field. There are many people here in the medical school who could do a better job."

"But you have a head start, and it just seems right that if you unraveled the mystery you should have a chance to work on it." It obviously didn't occur to him that not everyone would want to work on this particular problem.

"I'm sorry," Joan insisted. "It's not my kind of research, and it would mean a delay in my own work, possibly a long delay, because I don't think this problem is going to be as simple as you think."

"I can appreciate that," Kerr said, "and I guess I'm asking you for a favor. What department are you in?"

"Molecular genetics."

"And you're on the faculty? Do you have a heavy teaching load right now?"

"Actually, I'm not on the faculty. I'm a postdoctoral fellow, and no, most of our teaching is done in the fall."

"What do you work on?"

"I use techniques of molecular genetics to study protein folding."

Kerr looked blank. "What is that?"

His question delighted Sean, who grinned so broadly that Kerr turned to look at him. "I asked her the same question myself," Sean said. "I always feel so ignorant whenever I ask someone in this place what they do."

"You shouldn't. There's an awful lot that goes on in this medical school that I don't understand, and that includes protein folding. Look," Kerr said to Joan apologetically, "I've really put you in an uncomfortable position. It was selfish of me to think that our interests are more important than everybody's else's. If you could help, we would really appreciate it. If you can't spare the time from your work, we'll understand."

"I'd like to help," Joan said. "You must know that. It's just that this field is so far from my own that I'm not sure what I would contribute. A few good protein chemists would put you way ahead."

"We'll get them too if we need them. But I've said enough. Think it over. Either way we really appreciate it. You and Sean have done a great piece of work here."

He turned to Sean. "I must say, when you first came in here I never thought this would lead anywhere. For you to be so persistent, I never could see why you were, but to be so sure that Grimes really had something and then to put it all together like this, it's just magnificent. You should have been a detective. When we get this sorted out, you can be sure that we'll see to it the right people get the credit and the other kinds of rewards that go along with it." He pumped Sean's hand and patted him on the back. "You really did it. You really did it. Shows I just didn't have enough faith."

"But you did have faith," Sean protested. "You let me pursue it, and I'm sure it wasn't always convenient for everyone who helped."

"True, I guess. But you get the credit and Dr. Danner here, of course."

After the meeting Sean suggested to Joan that they go to the small restaurant under the art gallery where he had first eaten with Beth. "It's better than our usual lunch counter," he said, "and we need to celebrate."

After they were served, he reached across the table and touched her cheek. "You were terrific. I guess you do things like that all the time, make those scientific presentations, but I've never seen it. I was really proud of you."

"Oh, Sean." Her face flushed.

"You could see how impressed they were. But I don't understand why you didn't take Kerr up on his offer?"

"Now don't start."

"But why not? You said yourself. It could be a very important project."

"I haven't said no."

"But you're going to, aren't you?"

She carefully put back a piece of tomato that had fallen from her sandwich. "Well, it's not the kind of research I want to do."

"Why don't you tell Kerr you'll only do it if you can run the whole project, and you want to be an assistant professor?"

"He'd never do that. And anyway it's not my kind of project."

"But you can do anything."

"Flattery, flattery," she said.

"Mmm." He held up his hand as he swallowed a mouthful of pasta. "It's not flattery. I'm the outsider who comes in and hears everything. I know what people say about you."

"What do they say about me?"

"That's what they say about you. You can do anything."

She blushed again. "Oh, I probably could learn the things I'd need to do that kind of work, but it's not what I'm interested in. It isn't even molecular biology."

"Sure it is. All those things about the proteins and the mutants. Isn't that molecular?"

"All right, it is somewhat. But that's not what they're going to do now. They're just going to purify a lot of that hemoglobin and stuff it into animals."

"Well, everybody wants to know how the hemoglobin works. You could make mutations in it, just like you do now for your own proteins. And it will get you your promotion. You know he would do it."

She slowly put down the sandwich and picked up her wine glass. "But it's not what I want."

"I just don't understand why."

"Well, first of all, it's a clinical department. I'm a basic scientist, and basic scientists should be in basic science departments. That's where my collaborators are, that's where I want to teach, and it's the teaching that brings grad students and post-docs to your lab."

"But they have basic scientists in Kerr's department."

"Yes, but then people always wonder whether you're second-class, whether the clinical departments hire second-class basic scientists."

"But if you're not second-class, people will be able to tell. If you're doing good work and publishing, why would it come up?"

"Some people wouldn't even pay any attention to your work."

"Well, then who cares about them," Sean said, waving his wine-glass in an agitated manner. "They can't be the better people. Why can't you have the courage to be in any kind of department that you want?"

She didn't like to hear that. "Oh, that's not the most important reason. It's because I have a project that interests me, one that I've worked on for a long time. I didn't pick this hemoglobin project. It just arrived one day. It arrived with you," she said and finished the sandwich with one large bite.

"But it could be a great project. You said so yourself."

She threw up her hands. "But it would be a compromise. Don't you see, they want me to do something that's interesting to them, not to me?"

"Look," Sean said, "You know it's important. Wouldn't you get special satisfaction out of doing something that might help patients? Did you think I was going to say runners?" He laughed. He had to do something to break the tension.

"That's an old argument. Who's to say that when I discover something basic, it won't have even more significance for the long run?" She ran one hand through her curly hair and drummed the other on the table.

"Bad pun. But this way you could see the results faster. It seems like a reasonable compromise," Sean suggested.

"Why are you so interested in having me compromise?"

"You know, I ask myself that sometimes." He stared into her eyes.

She looked away. "You go off to London and do panty checks."

"I don't have to do panty checks. Ralph Hooker's boys do it for me. I just have to watch her run."

"Well, whatever. Go do it, and I'll think about this. In the meantime order some more wine," she said. "This is supposed to be a celebration."

Chapter 38

Sean flew to London and took the train to Oxford. He had booked a room at the Randolph and from there followed Susie's unnecessarily elaborate directions to their meeting place in a garden behind Magdalen College.

"So that I can throw myself on you without making a spectacle of myself," she had said.

"It's hard to resist an invitation like that," Sean had answered, and when they met she demonstrated what she had meant. It was early May, and the warm weather and a rare sunny day had filled the river with scores of punts. They walked arm in arm along the bank talking and laughing, but Sean couldn't help thinking how his expectations of a year before had changed so dramatically. Now he felt closer to someone else, and he had come here to learn if Susie were cheating. The Grimes mystery, which had originally brought them together, was never mentioned.

"Are you really coming to the race tomorrow?" Susie finally asked.

"Nothing could keep me away."

"But the last time when you stayed away I set my record."

"Yes, but I've stayed away since then, and you haven't always won."

"I know." She obviously thought that an explanation was expected. "I think it must be the way we train. It's the way Hopwell does it. We never point for anything. We just race all the time." She seemed to sag as she said it. "I'm in something at least every two weeks. You don't do that. You do three or four races in a row and then won't do anything for two or three months. I mean no races. You certainly do something." She squeezed his arm.

"People use both systems. Some feel the best training is to actually race. It guarantees an all-out effort, but I don't think it's necessary if you have really disciplined runners who will carry out the training schedule the way you design it. Bob knows I do that down to the last couple of seconds on every run. Maybe Hopwell's students are less disciplined. This may be his way to be sure that they're really putting out."

"Well, it does the opposite with me. I just can't get terribly excited about all those races."

"I'll bet it has the competition a little baffled." Sean laughed. "That's always good strategy."

"I guess so," Susie agreed.

"It'll be interesting to see what Hopwell will do as the important races get closer. Will he rest you before the Olympic trials?"

"I don't know." Susie seemed puzzled. "That's an important question we haven't discussed. At some point I'll have to shift over to the American coaches. Should I trust Hopwell's methods and stay with him right up to the trials, or go over maybe a month early and go back to Jim? Presumably if I'm lucky enough to get through the trials, Jim will be the one coaching me as part of the U.S. team."

"Yes, it's been decided. He'll be with the women distance runners." Sean paused and then shrugged. "I don't know what to recommend. Be sure Hopwell knows your real goals, and that he's not just using you over here to win some races for him, like to beat Cambridge, without planning ahead."

"He wouldn't do that," Susie assured him.

"I don't think so either, although Bob would certainly point out that he's an English loyalist." He laughed.

"Anyway," Susie announced, "the plan is to go for pasta, and then I'm going to disappear. Much as I hate to, we'll just have to wait 'til tomorrow to go to bed." She laughed. "That's why I insisted on meeting you out here. I didn't trust myself. I want you to be proud of me tomorrow, on the track, I mean."

Sean had a seat in the front row. The weather had returned to normal. It was cool and windy, and there was a threat of rain. The women's 5K was in mid afternoon. Sean crouched low and pulled up the zipper of his jacket as he glanced at the sky and hoped the race would begin soon.

At the start, a rabbit went to the front. Susie went too. "Oh no," was Sean's initial reaction. "Hasn't Hopwell taught her anything?" But the race soon settled into a pattern. The rabbit gradually opened a larger and larger lead over Susie, and Susie continually increased her lead over the pack. This was an open meet, but the prize money was small, and it had not attracted the highest quality runners.

Susie ran with monotonous regularity. At about a mile and a half the rabbit began to tire noticeably. Without waiting to be passed, she simply ran off the track. At the second mile the pack began to break up as some runners tried futilely to close the gap. It was hopeless. Susie just ran on like a train. Each time she passed, Sean strained out of his seat to be inches closer. He wanted to be in the infield. Susie ran with a kind of fixed stare on her face. She wasn't breathing hard, but then she certainly wasn't being challenged. He just couldn't make up his mind. She rolled on toward the finish line.

Hopwell has no strategy at all, Sean thought. *She might as well be a windup toy. No getaway at the start, no sprint at the finish.* Susie crossed the line in an outstanding time, almost matching her indoor World record. As soon as the others had finished, Sean hopped over the low concrete restraining wall and ran across the track to Susie. An usher followed him briefly, but when he saw the two of them embracing, he just smiled and turned away.

"Oh, you're not supposed to be here," she said, recovering from her surprise. He wasn't about to tell her why he was there, although hugging Susie should have been reason enough.

Sean had never before met Paul Hopwell, but Hopwell had recognized him at the track meet and invited him to use the university's facilities for training while he was in England. Sean took advantage of it every day. They were sitting by the track, Sean recovering from his morning workout and Paul watching his students. He was tall and thin, with sandy hair, and a regal, almost pompous bearing. He looked like a barrister to Sean, but his conversation was relaxed and informal. By now he had learned that Susie and Sean were "close," as he put it.

"She's a beautiful runner," said Hopwell, who clearly had the same appreciation of form as did Sean, "but I find her so difficult to coach."

"How so?"

"It's not that she isn't perfectly cooperative. In fact, she's overly concerned to do everything that I suggest. Jim McBride must be a tough taskmaster." He laughed.

"No, I think it's just Susie." Sean laughed too. "But then why do you think it's difficult?"

"Because, and think of how this hurts my ego to say it, nothing that I plan seems to make any difference."

"What do you mean?"

"Well, we do speed work, but it doesn't seem to make her any faster. We do some endurance work, but I don't see any change. We've done a little weight work. I've never been too enthusiastic about that, but I must admit it's added to her strength. But otherwise she just goes on her way. I've given up planning race strategy. She says that she just feels most comfortable running at the same pace throughout the race. She can't seem to settle in during the middle laps, and because of that she doesn't have an effective kick. In the races she lost, she tried hard but simply didn't have it. Now we're doing quarter-mile intervals two or three times a week. That's my equivalent of shock therapy."

"But she runs some exceptional races," Sean protested.

"Quite," Hopwell agreed. "Yesterday was superb, and the London race, of course, speaks for itself. It surprised me. I didn't think she could do that well. Then she was down for a month or two. I don't know what it was. It occurred to me that she'd gone stale, perhaps needed some time off, but nothing seemed to help. Then all of a sudden she began to steadily improve. The last few practices were very impressive and then this race." He was shaking his head. "Maybe it's a female thing. I'm hopeless with that."

"So am I," Sean admitted.

They chatted about Sean's own racing. "Well, I've made the marathon team. The winner of Dublin gets an automatic place, and the other two are determined by committee. I suspect I'll be in the 10K. That's also selected by a committee."

"Oh, they certainly don't have anyone who could match you in either event." It was flattering, and it was the truth, Sean knew.

"We haven't finally decided whether to do one or both. The

schedules are out now, of course, and there are seven days between the 10K final and the marathon. It's not as bad as it might have been."

"At least the weather should be good, not like that beastly Atlanta."

"Tell me." Sean smiled ruefully. "I wilted at about four miles. This time the marathon's in the evening, timed to finish at the closing ceremonies. It's such a great tradition."

"It would be wonderful to win it, but that's a very hard double," Paul Hopwell warned. "Personally I think the marathon is for older runners. You should have at least two more good tries. I would train for the 10K and not run the risk that you'll be prepared for neither. Don't let Higgum push you into something impossible."

"He wouldn't do that," Sean said defensively.

"I'm sure he thinks you can do both. At least the 10K is first. Bob and I have had so many disagreements over the years, there are people who think we don't like each other. Nothing to it. We don't always see eye to eye, but he's one of the great coaches, and he's going to be missed when he retires."

Hopwell had given him good advice, Sean knew. He liked him and his concern for Susie and left feeling assured that Hopwell had her best interests at heart. On the flight back, there was time to think. A message from Hooker confirmed that no runners in the Oxford race had red urine. Still, Sean felt uneasy. He dreaded having to describe his uncertainty to Joan, but try as he might he couldn't convince himself that all was well. There was something strange about Susie's running, although it wasn't as extreme as what he had noticed with Blue Man and with the Chinese. And she really hadn't been out of breath when he had reached her on the track not fifteen seconds after the finish.

And how did he feel about her? It was certainly hard to say goodbye. A year ago he would have been ready for a serious relationship. Of course that was before he had his suspicions, or before Joan had hers, or before he even knew Joan. But anyway, they were his suspicions too, no matter if he was always arguing with Joan about them. How much did these doubts influence the way he felt about Susie, and how much did his feelings for Joan affect the way he felt about Susie?

At times like this he wished that he had never heard of Grimes, but then he would never have met Susie, or Joan, and there would be Chinese runners getting ready to win *his* Olympic medal. Something *had* to be done about that.

Chapter 39

Joan met Sean's connecting flight at Grenville's tiny airport. It was so small that she could drive almost to the gate.

"I didn't expect to be picked up," he said, pleased and surprised.

"This way I can be sure we go directly to one of my favorite restaurants. Now tell me everything, while I drive."

In the car, Sean told her what had happened. As he had anticipated, Joan interpreted his doubts in the least flattering way for Susie, and he told her so.

"Sean, they're your doubts. You're the one who was there."

"But she ran really well, and the urine wasn't red, and they even did blood tests," he protested.

"You told me that already. But you said you could tell better just by watching."

"Well, I can't, or sometimes I can, but I couldn't be sure."

"So she found some way to stop the hemoglobin from coming out through the kidneys."

"But this time they took blood samples too."

"Is that so unusual?" Joan asked with surprise.

"They're doing it more and more. It's because of people taking this EPO, the stuff that makes you produce more red blood cells. When they spin down the red cells, to see how many you have, shouldn't they also see the hemoglobin still in solution."

"Very good," said Joan, reaching over and patting his hand. "You really are beginning to learn this stuff. Things that are truly dissolved, like the stroma-free hemoglobin, don't come down in a regular old centrifuge, so the plasma on top would be red instead of the usual straw color. But nobody would pay any attention."

"Why not? It should be so obvious." Sean complained.

"Because everybody who collects blood knows that sometimes a few of the normal red blood cells break and leak hemoglobin. It happens all the time, if the needle stick isn't clean, or the blood is pulled out with too much suction. It's so common that the laboratory technicians wouldn't even notice."

"It just seems everyone's always ignoring the hemoglobin," Sean said with despair in his voice.

"It's easy to overlook the obvious," Joan explained. "Hemoglobin's all around anyway, so it's hard to be surprised to find it. If it's in the urine, you blame menstrual periods or abrasions, if it's in the plasma it's from sloppy blood collection."

"Right. If they were cheating with some weird drug that wasn't normally around, you'd know something was wrong the minute you found it."

"Anyway they have to be packaging the hemoglobin somehow, or it would leak out through the kidneys."

"But how could Susie have done it?" Sean asked.

"She hired someone." Joan took both hands off the wheel to shrug. "She's rich."

"No, no, I meant how *could* it be done."

"I don't know, yet, but it's good to hear you admitting the possibility. I trust these suspicions kept you from doing anything rash, like getting engaged."

"I wasn't about to do anything like that," he said. Then he looked over at her. "Would you have been upset?"

She kept her eyes on the road. "Yes, but I would never admit it. You're becoming a habit, a nice habit. Sometimes I think you're just on loan, but it's going to be hard to give you back."

"Maybe we should skip the restaurant," Sean suggested, reaching out his arm and running his hand down the back of her neck.

The next day Sean worked out on the Grenville track under Jim's supervision. When he had finished, they sat in the second row of the stands, and Sean gave a very different report of his visit to Oxford. He described Susie's magnificent performance but never told Jim of his suspicions. Only Bob and Joan were party to that information. He often wondered about his decision. If Susie were doing something illegal and she were discovered, Jim's reputation would certainly suffer. Some would think that she had been doing it when she ran for Grenville, others would suspect Hopwell. What if Hopwell were involved? But that seemed highly unlikely. The common connection was clearly his investigation of the Grimes mystery, and there was no way that Hopwell could have known about that.

"I never saw what Hopwell described to you," Jim said after Sean had told him about their conversation. "She didn't train enough because she was always busy with something else. One year, it was her junior year, she seemed to have less going on. She trained more and she was better, just as you'd expect. And then this other thing about the way she runs the races, she didn't do that here. In fact, she was very intelligent about pacing and strategy. That's the way she is. You only have to tell her something once. And she had a good kick at the end of a race. Certainly she could have used more work on it, and that would have been in my plans if she had stayed here. I like Hopwell's idea about those quarter-mile repeats. Boy, he's a tough coach."

"If she makes the Olympic team, I guess she'll be assigned to you."

"Yes, I'll have the women distance runners," Jim said, "but obviously I'd be happy to coach her for the trials if she wants. There's nothing in our agreement with the Olympic committee that forbids us from coaching people for the trials whom we've coached in the past. It's really her choice. But it sounds from the results of the last race that Hopwell is finally getting things turned around."

"Yes," Sean agreed. "Funny thing is he can't seem to figure out what's made the difference."

* * * * *

Bob Higgum was sent to Tokyo in June to scout the Chinese runners. Rumors had circulated for weeks that they would be competing there. The Americans were as concerned about the Chinese as anyone else, and to them cost was no object.

Bob and Sean had talked about it in Philadelphia at a final coaching session before the trip.

"I don't know why they think I'd be so good at detecting cheating." Bob laughed.

"Because you've been around so long you've seen almost everything. And you have so many honorary positions with all of these international committees that no one would ever try to stop you from sticking your nose in anywhere."

Sean had been keeping Bob Higgum up to date on all of the developments in the Grimes mystery and on his suspicions about Susie.

"I was suspicious before you were," Bob said. "Nobody develops that fast in this field."

Sean had described for him the breathing of the runners. He had managed to obtain a tape of the Stuttgart race, and they studied it together.

"Good pickup! You were really well trained." Bob laughed as he said it.

"I was. But it was even more obvious seeing it live."

Few subtleties escaped Bob. And there was no doubt that he would find someone in Japan to check the urine.

Sean hurried back to Philadelphia the day Bob returned. They met in the St. Vincent's gym.

"It was great," Bob told him. "You know I don't usually like to travel, so I told them my price was a first-class air ticket. That was smart. It was the longest flight I've ever been on, nonstop from New York. The plane was one of those special 747's, and I was in the upper cabin. Never been up there before, and I was the only one."

"The only one?"

"Going over I was absolutely alone. Coming back there were two other people in the whole cabin. There were more waitresses…"

"Stewardesses," Sean interrupted him.

"…. than there were passengers, and the seats converted to beds. You could completely stretch out."

"Remind me to demand that, if I'm ever asked to go over."

"Oh, the Tokyo organizers are dying to have you. Big money there, and they won't worry about the air fare."

Sean could hardly wait to get through the pleasantries to find out what had happened. He already knew the results of the race. Han and Dak had finished one, two. Not a world record but dangerously near on a track not noted for being fast. *This is getting too close for comfort*, Sean had thought when he saw the results in Runners' Weekly. *They're going to beat me if we can't stop them, and we're running out of time.*

"It was very interesting, very interesting," Higgum continued.

"You're dragging this out on purpose to torture me," Sean teased him.

"Okay, well right. Their urine wasn't red."

Damn, Sean thought. *Another mystery. The Chinese know how to do it. And Susie knows too. Joan was right. It must be something completely new.*

"How about the running, Bob? What did you think of the running?"

"I think I saw what you saw, but it's subtle. It certainly wasn't easier to spot live. It was more obvious on the Stuttgart tape."

"No, something's changed," Sean said. "It was much more obvious when I first saw it, but then the last time with Susie it was harder to tell."

"Your description is good, though." Bob complimented him. "The Chinese runners just didn't breathe hard enough. They didn't seem to have this strange look of pain that you described, no more than anyone would. But something wasn't right. I think I noticed the breathing best after the race. Right after, it looked like they were just not as short of oxygen as the other runners. They didn't have the debt to pay back and weren't standing there gasping. That fits in with the way you think this stuff works, doesn't it?" Sean nodded assent. "But what do you think of the urine not being red? Isn't this hemoglobin supposed to leak out through the kidneys?"

"We're trying to figure out how they can stop that from happening, but so far no luck."

"Well, let me tell you some other things I learned. I had a pleasant little chat with Yan Tse."

"He was there?" Sean was suddenly much more excited.

"Yes, and your old friend Lin Pao was with him. The excuse was that Pao's English is better, but I've never had any trouble communicating with Tse. In the old days I would have thought he was a policeman, undercover, CIA type, but Yan Tse used to have a way of letting me know when they were around. This Lin Pao seemed to be in his confidence."

"I don't like it at all," Sean interjected.

"Now, now, don't be too hasty. He's an old friend. You have to be more trusting."

"In this case that's kind of hard, especially having seen what they did to Grimes."

"There are good people and bad people in every country, Sean. Yan Tse finds himself in a very strange situation."

"He told you about it?"

"Of course he did. There's a new training camp in the Wuyi Mountains. They're all training at altitude, even the sprinters. Get all that extra iron in them, make them too heavy to run." Bob laughed. "Quite a few Germans are in the camp. They're called 'special trainers.' The big boss is named Jurgen. I'm sure I've heard of him. They have a lot of authority, and the Chinese are afraid to cross them. They're playing all the usual games but can't force them on the athletes. Some, like Chao Lee, have refused to take part. And since there's so much national pride involved, the Chinese won't let the Germans appear in public. So Yan Tse is still the coach and makes the final decisions. The Germans hand him these trained athletes and try to tell him what he's supposed to do with them. He says they've recommended some of the craziest training schedules he's ever heard." Bob laughed again. "Of course, since Yan Tse prides himself on being one of my pupils he doesn't take any of their advice at all."

"So why doesn't he put a stop to it?" Sean demanded.

"That's a little beyond him for now. The Germans were brought in by some high government officials, and they expect results. If they don't get them, some heads are going to roll, and that's literally roll. Yan Tse has to pretend to be cooperative so that if things don't work out they can't blame him. He's a real survivor. I don't try to teach him that part of his game. He's better at it than I am."

"Oh, I don't know. You've survived a few wars yourself."

"My wars weren't quite life and death. Anyway apparently it's going to be death if these guys get caught cheating. The politicians don't care if they cheat, as long as they don't get caught. This fiasco with the women swimmers . . ."

"What about that?" Sean asked eagerly.

"Nobody knows what happened to *those* special trainers." This time Bob's laugh was ghoulish. "But ever since then the remaining Germans haven't been quite so cocky."

"Does Yan Tse know what they're doing to the runners?" Sean asked.

"No. Apparently the Germans don't have to tell him, and I guess Yan Tse doesn't want to push them directly. Again, because if they get caught, he doesn't want to share any of the blame. It's a nice little division of responsibility, and I don't think Yan Tse wants to change it."

"But he must have some idea."

"Well, he thought they were blood doping. He says they brought blood to Stuttgart. Of course, Yan Tse couldn't complain a lot about that, since it's not illegal."

"But we know what that blood was," Sean reminded him.

Bob nodded. "I don't know exactly what you told this Lin Pao fellow in Stuttgart, but he's still very upset. I'm convinced Pao and Tse don't know anything about Grimes. Otherwise, they wouldn't bring it up. Pao still thinks Root is some famous American runner. He doesn't know whether or not to believe you, that he's dead. He can't seem to get it through his head that we couldn't just hide a runner in this country. Yan Tse knows what it's like over here, since he's actually visited, but he doesn't know what to make of the whole thing." Bob abruptly changed the subject. "Let's set the record right now. Maybe at the Penn Relays."

"What!" Sean exclaimed. "That's not even a good track, and nobody will be there."

"It'll be that much more impressive. I've got a line on a good rabbit. You don't need anyone else. You're as disciplined as a machine. Jim McBride tells me you've actually done it in practice."

"Ah, maybe." Sean didn't want to admit it.

"I figure it'll force these varmints to be a little more aggressive and show their hand." *Varmints*, thought Sean. *I haven't heard that word in years. He must have taken up watching westerns.*

"Okay, let's do it." Sean said it with a determination that brought the slightest smile to Higgum's face.

Chapter 40

As soon as he returned to Grenville, Sean shared the news from Tokyo with Joan. He was unable to hide his anxiety, as they discussed it in the hospital cafeteria. "They're up to something different, not just giving the stroma-free hemoglobin, but something completely different."

He went back to the line for two more cups of coffee, while she guarded the table. As he sat down again, he asked, "What do you think Jack Neville did on this project? Wasn't he in molecular genetics, same as you?"

"That's a good question. He sure as hell wouldn't have known which end of the mouse to put the hemoglobin in. Every now and then I think about that and wonder."

"And you don't have any idea what he was doing?"

"I've already said he wouldn't tell me anything about it."

"But I thought you always talked science in bed?"

She glanced up at him. "I don't always talk science in bed, but it's a nice time to talk about it, if you're ever so lucky as to go to bed with a good scientist. Ever again, I mean."

"Well, then what did you and he talk about."

"We'd just kind of lie there and whisper sweet nothings to each other like you and Susie do."

"I meant scientifically. I don't care about the other."

"Well, I don't either," she said. "Actually, we talked about mutations."

"You were planning on having some children and wondered whether you could cross an Australian with an American." Sean couldn't resist.

"Oh, that's not even funny." She crumpled her napkin into a ball and threw it at him. “We talked about how to make mutations. It used to be much harder to do. You know, Sean, it’s been ever so long since I enjoyed his company.”

“I know. You’ve been stuck with poor substitutes ever since.”

“No, they weren’t all poor substitutes.”

“All right, all right, you win that round. What about the mutations? Seriously.”

“Well, seriously, they were much harder to make in those days. I gave him several schemes. Now it’s relatively easy. You just do it with PCR.”

“With what?”

“Oh, you know, the thing in the O.J. case. Anyway, that’s not important. You may just be right. I hate to admit it. He must have been making mutants of something for Grimes. I guess I must have thought that at the time, but I had no idea what Grimes was doing. Now that we know, it must have been hemoglobin mutants.”

“But the mutants are bad,” Sean said. “Didn’t you tell me that sickle cell anemia comes from a mutation?”

“It depends on what mutations you make. You could design anything, good or bad.”

“You mean, you could make any genes you want.”

“If you were willing to pay for them, sure.”

“And the genes could tell people to make fish hemoglobin?”

“No, no, that’s just science fiction. You can’t turn people into fish. Hmmm,” she stopped. “But there are so many possibilities. How the hell will we ever figure out what Jack was doing?”

“I know,” Sean said. She looked at him. “Remember way back in the winter when we were at a dead end.”

“I wasn’t at a dead end,” Joan protested, “I just wasn’t thinking about the problem full time.”

“Right. Anyway, I went back to some of the things that I learned from the business office.”

“And?”

“And there were a lot of other accounts. Some were to companies with ‘genetic’ and words like that in the name.”

“Oh.” Joan suddenly became more interested.

“I asked Beth Markham to go over them and make a more detailed list, to try to find out what they were. Maybe if you knew what they were buying or what they were having made, you'd be able to figure out what he was doing."

"You are pretty smart for a dumb jock," she said. "Maybe I *will* let you go to bed with me even if you don't know any science."

After lunch Joan and Sean returned to Grimes's office to talk to Beth Markham. They passed Kerr in the hall.

"Sure you're not still working on this?" He smiled at Joan. "Sure you couldn't be tempted with a very attractive offer? I'm prepared to be a nudge if I can't succeed any other way."

"We'll see," Joan answered.

"I'll take that answer as encouragement," Kerr said and continued down the hallway.

Joan and Sean went into the office, and Beth showed them the list she had prepared. It had been forgotten in the excitement of the realization that the fish blood was the key to the mystery.

"The first one is this company in California called Gene Seq," she said. "The requisitions just say sequencing. I called them to ask what they were for, and they absolutely refused to talk about it. The woman said they were sequences of DNA, and they were not available to anyone except the person who had supplied the DNA to them. I didn't think we supplied DNA to anyone."

"Damn it," Joan exclaimed. "If Grimes had just used our sequencing lab, we'd be able to get his sequences." Sean and Beth stared at her.

"Look, if you're playing with DNA, at some point in the game you have to determine the sequence of the nucleotides, the bases that make up the code. You both know about that, surely. If you're working with a new gene, the first thing to do is determine the sequence. If you've been trying to make a gene, or make some mutations in a gene, then the final test is to go back and sequence it again. You can sequence by hand in your own laboratory, but it can also be done by machine. Not every small lab wants to invest the money for their own sequencer, so now there are companies that will do it for a fee. You send them some of your DNA, and a couple days later they send back the sequence."

"Sounds like a good idea," Sean said. "Why did it upset you so much?"

"Because the outside companies are sworn to secrecy. Some of these sequences can be worth a fortune. The companies claim that they actually destroy the information and all the leftover DNA. I've always suspected that some of them have a backup record, but they certainly aren't going to give out the information to someone who just calls and asks."

"Wouldn't they give it to the university under these circumstances?"

"Yes, if they really did still have a copy. So, Beth, maybe you should ask Dr. Kerr to write an official letter saying that he's authorized to represent Grimes. Tell them as little as possible, and see if you can't get those sequences from them." She turned back to Sean. "See, if he'd just done the damn things here in one of the university shared facilities, it would be much easier to get them."

"Maybe it was part of his strategy to keep it secret," Sean suggested.

"Maybe," Joan had to agree, "but it's going to make our job a lot tougher if we can't get them." She turned to Beth. "What else do you have?"

"There's more. Here's one, another California company, just a couple of payments but they're big. The requisitions say 'plasmid' preparation."

Joan looked over Beth's shoulder. "A plasmid is just a piece of DNA that serves as a convenient carrier for your genes. You can put it inside cells or bacteria for cloning. Probably Grimes's new genes were put into these plasmids. But all that money!" She let out a low whistle. "He sure was making them in large amounts. Hmm. Okay, what's next?"

"Well, I think this is another company. It's called TransMouse."

"I can't believe it!" Joan cried and slapped her hand on the desktop. "I can't believe they did this much and nobody knew about it. Well, nobody ever said Jack Neville had only one talent." Even Beth Markham caught the meaning and smiled.

"But what does this company do?" Sean asked.

"Their name's TransMouse," Joan said sarcastically. "What do you think they do? They make transgenic mice." She turned to Beth. "Okay, how many did they make?"

"Well, we paid them $4,000 three times."

"God, they made three of them."

"What are they, and why are they so special?" Sean insisted.

"Don't you see? They put their gene in a line of mice. In fact, it sounds like three genes, provided they all worked," she said mainly to herself. "But, of course, most of those companies don't charge you if it doesn't work."

"But what are they?" Sean was becoming exasperated.

"Look, they want to put their gene in a mouse, but not just one mouse, they want to put it in a whole line of mice so that all the mice that descend from those mice will have the gene. It's kind of the ultimate genetic engineering."

"But what kind of gene?"

"Hemoglobin genes. What else would they be putting in them?"

"Okay, okay," Sean admitted. "That was stupid of me."

"This means they probably had at least three genes they thought would work. They never would have wasted the money to make transgenic animals if the genes weren't right."

"Why are they so hard to make?" he asked.

"Well, the really amazing thing is that you can make them at all. The way they do it is to get a fertilized egg from a mouse and use a tiny micro-pipette to inject it with the new DNA. Then they put the egg into a female mouse who's ready to carry eggs anyway. They put in a lot of eggs because most of them don't work. When the pups are born, they test them to see if any have the new gene."

"But they put the gene in all of them." Sean wanted to be sure he understood.

"Yes, yes. But most times it doesn't take. To be passed on, the gene has to somehow get incorporated into the DNA of the mouse, the DNA that came from the mother and the father. Sometimes by luck it does, it just kind of attaches itself and goes along for the ride. If it doesn't get broken up along the way, and a lot of other bad things don't happen to it, and it finally gets incorporated, then it can be there forever."

"Ah."

"Then you need a couple of mice," Joan continued, "and you breed them back to each other again and again. With a little bit of luck you eventually get out a number of them, a whole line of them, that all have the gene, and they'll always have it, forever."

"So it's like making a new species?"

"It's not really making a whole new species. They still look like mice and have long tails and eat cheese. But yes, they're slightly different from any other mice that have ever existed in the past."

"Different because of the gene?"

"Yes, and what the gene makes. You can bet that those little mice are all running around making fish hemoglobin. What the hell do you suppose happened to them?"

"Wouldn't they still be at the company?" Sean asked.

"No, no, that's not the way it's done. Usually the company just sends you all the pups, and you keep them in the university's animal farm."

"So you think they might be here at Grenville."

"They might be. Unless that Li woman killed them all."

"Could she get into the animal farm?"

"Not necessary. She'd just send down an order that they didn't want them anymore. The keepers wouldn't even think twice about destroying them. They do it all the time. Otherwise, you have to pay maintenance costs for the animals, and their little hotels are very expensive. Anyway, we'll have to look into it. Beth, you could do that. Check and see if there were boarding charges."

"Oh, no," Beth protested. "Do you have any idea how many animal boarding charges are generated in this department?"

"I forgot that you people have all those animals with tumors. Well, see what you can do. Ask them if there are any strange mouse lines over there. Get Blackburn or one of his laboratory people. They must know."

"Could you do this in humans?" Sean asked.

"Not unless you got to them when they were still eggs. You'd have to plan ahead. Maybe for the Olympics of 2024." She laughed. "And then, of course, a lot of other things would have to go right too, but you may be on to something. Okay, what else?"

"Well, actually the largest number of requisitions was from our own Biology Department, an account number 2613. All I could find out was that it's a nucleic acid synthesis laboratory."

"Oligos!" Joan shouted before Beth could even complete her sentence. "I know that account number better than my own telephone number. Finally some luck!"

"Oligos?" Sean asked.

"Oligonucleotides. For PCR primers. That's great. We'll be able to get the sequences. They're kept in a computer in the Biology Department, and I'm sure that damn Chinese woman wouldn't have access to erase them."

"What are they?" Sean persisted.

"'Oligo' is short for 'oligonucleotide.' You're the Greek scholar. It means 'few.' And nucleotides are the building blocks of DNA. Oligos are very short chains of DNA."

"But why do we want them?"

"I'll explain it to you later." Before he could interrupt, she added, "It's not because you can't understand it. It's really very simple, but I'm sure Beth has no interest in learning about it."

"I'm sure I couldn't understand it," Beth said.

"Oh, anyone can understand it." Joan dismissed the protest with a wave of her hand. "What else is on the list?"

They went over a number of other accounts that seemed less interesting.

"There are still a few more that I haven't tracked down yet," Beth said. "I've been busy with my regular work, so I didn't pursue them all. But I have some time now, and I'll get back on it if you'd like."

"Please do," Sean said. "It certainly sounds as if some of these are going to be helpful. In the meantime, if you could get Kerr to write that letter to the sequencing company maybe we'll be lucky, but somehow I doubt it." Beth gathered her notes and left.

"I'm going to see some friends in the oligo lab," Joan announced. "I'll bet they keep copies of all of the original requisitions with the sequences on them. If not, the sequences will be in the computer that controls the synthesizer. When you send over a sequence to be made, someone types it into the computer, cross checks it a couple of times, and then the machine makes the oligo. When they send you the oligo, they send back an actual copy of your requisition and a copy of what was typed into the computer. That way you can compare them to make sure that the transcriber didn't make a mistake."

"Is it really that crucial?" Sean asked.

"One typing mistake is one mutation."

"Oh!"

"Now I just hope the oligos are cross-filed in that computer by Grimes's billing code. They must be. Judging from the size of the bills, they made hundreds of them for him. It's going to take me some time after I get them to try to sort them out."

"We haven't much time left," Sean reminded her anxiously.

"Don't push me. I'll do it as fast as I can."

"Will you recognize what sequences they are?"

"Good God, no. Who could ever remember something like that?"

Sean shrugged.

"They're in code, nothing but a sequence of A's, G's, C's and T's all in some particular order," Joan said, "but impossible to memorize. No, if we're lucky there will be some indication on the requisition that says what the oligos were for. Otherwise, it's going to be a lot of searching of the gene bank."

"You have to explain this to me," Sean said.

"I know, but I'll have to extract a big price. Remember the bottle of wine that you bought the first time we ever went out to dinner, at the French restaurant that doesn't have the liquor license?" Sean nodded. "I'll have one of those, please. And I'll have the dinner to go along with it too, of course."

Sean laughed. "Coming right up. But you get only half the bottle. I get the rest of it."

Chapter 41

"Funny we've never been back here," Joan said after they had ordered.

"Too expensive. I save it for first dates, when I'm really trying to impress someone."

"It's not so . . . oh, you," she said, feeling silly for not having recognized the joke.

"And of course when I'm buying some expertise."

The waiter opened the bottle Sean had brought and poured.

"It *is* the same wine."

"Wasn't that the deal?"

"I guess so." She suddenly seemed sad.

"What's the matter?"

"Nothing. Oh, I don't know. It's nice to do something special that we've done before."

"I guess twice doesn't make it a tradition, but we could work on it."

"It's just as good as I remember," she said, sipping the wine. Then she suddenly brightened. "Okay, a deal is a deal. If I have to work for it, if no one will buy me a bottle otherwise . . ."

"You know that's not true," Sean protested.

"I know, and besides I like to talk science, in case you hadn't noticed. But not another word about it until we order and our food arrives. I'm going to enjoy the wine."

"Deal," said Sean.

When their dinners arrived, Joan spread a cocktail napkin beside her plate and placed a pen on it, then she picked up her fork.

"The oligos, that's what I don't understand," Sean said between bites. "What do we do with them?"

"Okay. First about DNA. You know how it contains information. It's the cell's master blueprint. And the information is in a code. One of the things it has to encode, maybe the most important thing, is how to make proteins. And of course your friend hemoglobin is a protein."

"Two different proteins clumped together, right?"

"That's right. Now since a protein is a long chain made of amino acid building blocks, what better way to code for it than another chain. The DNA molecule is a chain made up of four kinds of building blocks called nucleotides or bases named A, T, G, and C. Since there are only four, and there are twenty amino acids counting the rare ones, we have to use several nucleotides to code for one amino acid."

"That's like Morse code, where there are twenty-six letters to encode with just two possibilities, dot and dash."

"Exactly. If we used two nucleotide positions we would have sixteen possibilities, four times four, any of the four letters in the first position matched with any of the four in the second position. That's not enough. So nature uses three. Each triplet is called a 'codon.' It's like a word with three letters. There are now sixty-four possible words, four times four times four. That's more than we need to represent all twenty amino acids, so some codons can be used for instructions, for example, 'TAG' is a codon that means 'end the protein chain.' And we can have some redundancy, 'TAT' and 'TAC' both stand for the amino acid tyrosine."

"It's really very simple, isn't it?"

"Yes, and very precise. Sometimes a change in a single nucleotide can change the message. For example 'TGC', just one different from TAC, would put a cysteine in the protein chain instead of the tyrosine. And cysteine is one of those amino acids that has a sulfur and can form the special cross links, remember, in the secondary structure of the protein."

Sean nodded and sipped his wine.

"So if you replaced tyrosine with cysteine, the whole shape of the protein could change, and the function as well. That's a *serious* mutation."

"Okay, so where do the oligos fit into all this?"

"Remember, the oligos are short chains of DNA, maybe twenty, maybe even fifty nucleotides long, but not thousands or millions like genes. It's possible to make these short chains chemically in a machine, and that's what Grimes was buying from the Biology Department."

"But what are they for?"

"Patience, patience." She paused to eat, and Sean fidgeted. "You can use them to copy DNA or to make mutants. Normally the DNA in a cell comes as two strands wrapped around each other, you know, the famous 'double helix.' One has the code in a form that's ready to read, and the other has all the same information but in a slightly different form, kind of like a negative in photography. To use the DNA, either to read the code to make protein or to copy the DNA, the two chains have to come apart. In a cell, there are certain switches to make this happen at the right time. But if you want to do it in a test tube, all you have to do is heat the solution of DNA to almost boiling. This will overcome the stickiness that holds the two strands together in the double helix."

She had her pen out and was trying to draw on the napkin. It kept slipping, and she speared it with the little finger of her left hand, which also held a piece of French bread. The indistinct diagram that emerged wasn't helping Sean's understanding at all.

He moved a silver vase, that held a single rose, to the edge of the table and reached across to flick a large crumb from a DNA strand. "Wait, wait." But there was no stopping her.

"Now the oligo is designed to match a short stretch of one of the chains. In essence it's a small piece of the opposite chain. If you add the oligo to a solution of the separated chains and cool the mixture, the oligo will find the right spot and stick to it. So picture what that's like. There's a long single strand, thousands long, the normal DNA, and for a short length, about twenty links long, there is a partner chain, the oligo, trying to form the double helix, but then it just ends."

Sean waited while she swallowed another bite.

"In cells, there are enzymes called polymerases whose normal job is to make the DNA chains. They need a supply of the building blocks, of course, and they need a pattern, which is the opposite chain. When these enzymes come upon a chain that terminates before its partner, they assume that it was damaged, broken, and they set about to fix it by extending the shorter chain until it reaches the end of the longer chain. See, the oligo, just a little piece of DNA you can make yourself, is fooling the system into copying a very long chain. That's why the oligo is sometimes called a primer, because it primes the reaction."

"This whole thing is amazing," Sean said, shaking his head.

"It gets better. If you design another oligo to stick to the opposite single strand partner, you can copy the other chain as well. That's how PCR works. You need an oligo which sticks to the positive chain at one end of the gene you want to copy and another oligo which sticks to the negative chain at the opposite end. Of course you need the gene you want to copy, but it can be a tiny amount, as little as one molecule! And you need a supply of nucleotide building blocks and the enzyme. The original double helix comes apart when heated. Then you cool the mixture, and the oligos jump on their corresponding strands. When you get to a temperature the enzyme likes it extends the oligos. Quick as a flash there are two full new chains, a new negative chain made on the positive template and vice versa, and they're all wrapped together with their partners just like the original double helix. But there are twice as many. You can do the same thing again, heat and cool, doubling every time, two, four, eight, sixteen…"

She had returned to the napkin, and it soon was covered with intertwined double strands. "It gets big really fast. Thirty doublings is almost a billion times. That's why it's called Polymerase Chain Reaction. Not because it makes DNA chains, but because it's a chain reaction. It just runs away."

Sean had long since finished eating, and he kept trying to say something so that Joan would have a chance. "Like a nuclear reaction, a melt down or a bomb?"

"Exactly. You can see why the forensic people would be interested. It was all over the papers during the O.J. trial. We drop our DNA all the time, in every hair, every cell we shed. You can take a single DNA molecule and amplify it until you have enough to analyze and match to the suspect."

"So Grimes used this to make large amounts of some gene, presumably some hemoglobin gene?" Sean asked.

"Yes, and also to make mutants. Remember the oligo becomes part of the final strand. If you put a change, a different nucleotide, in one position of the oligo, it would end up in the final DNA. It would be a mutation." She drew an X in one of the oligos on the napkin. "And having just one of the twenty nucleotides not match perfectly wouldn't keep the oligo from sticking to the right spot on the original gene and priming the extension."

"And you could do the whole thing again to put in more changes?"

"Absolutely. It just takes time and money, and not too much of either. Now, it's important to appreciate that an oligo that is twenty or so nucleotides long will be very specific, like a fingerprint." She began to draw circles around another of the oligos. By now the napkin had the appearance of a New York city subway car from the seventies, but Sean had the point.

Joan hurried on. "Remember a particular oligo is one possibility in four times four times four, done twenty times. That's one in a trillion. There are a trillion different possible oligos that contain twenty nucleotides. So your oligo isn't going to land on just any piece of the DNA, it's going to stick to a very specific short stretch out of all the DNA. If there is no such stretch, that provides an almost perfect match, say at least eighteen out of twenty, it won't stick at all."

She switched to circling a short stretch of one of the long DNA strands, then threw down the pen with finality and obvious satisfaction, and pronounced in triumph, "That's why you can copy or mutate the exact gene you want. And it's important to us because by finding the oligos that Grimes used, we'll be able to identify the genes he was working on."

"So that's it. That's what this is all for. We're, *you're* going to find the genes."

"We'll match the oligos to their full genes from the gene bank. That will tell us what genes Grimes started from, and the imperfect matches will tell us what changes, what mutations, he was trying to make."

"And, as you said, a particular twenty-long oligo is so unique..." Sean mused. "It's like doing his experiment in reverse."

"Exactly. We'll try to find out what genetic sequences match the oligos. We start off with some clues."

"Like what?" Sean asked.

Joan's picked up her glass, swirled the wine, leaned back in her chair, and began to outline her battle plan. "First of all, they're related to hemoglobin somehow, almost certainly, so most of those primers are going to match parts of the genes for the different hemoglobin proteins, or maybe the genes for switches that regulate hemoglobin production."

"But won't it take forever to look through all of that."

"We'll do it by computer."

"So you'll put the sequences for the genes for the hemoglobin proteins in the computer and then go searching them?"

"Something like that. We don't even have to do all the work ourselves because lots of the hemoglobins genes, certainly the ones from humans and mice and common animals, have already been sequenced and put in the gene bank."

"You know, I have a vision of shelves in a bank vault stacked with blue jeans."

"Oh, Sean." She giggled. "No, of course that's not what it is. It's a registry of almost every gene that's ever been sequenced. Searching the bank used to take quite a while, but now that we have super-computers it's almost instantaneous. You send the request over the Internet, and the answer comes right back. As fast as Beth can find the oligos, we'll know where they fit."

"It sounds easy. It sounds too easy." Sean shook his head.

"Well, there's plenty of room for complications," Joan admitted. "First of all, Grimes may have been working with gene sequences that aren't in the bank, like the Tautog hemoglobin gene. Obviously they were determining the sequence for themselves and keeping it secret. And then even for common hemoglobin genes, if they made lots of mutations, things that no one else has ever made before, there might not be many good matches."

"Does the match have to be perfect when you use the gene bank?"

"Ah, I was just coming to that." Joan waved away the waiter who was approaching with the dessert cart and went on without a pause. "No, it doesn't have to be perfect. Oh, I'm sorry. Did you want some? You never do. Anyway, you can tell the computer to search and allow any number of mismatches, for example, to find any sequence in the bank that matches a twenty-long oligo with five or fewer mistakes. But when you increase the number of mismatches you will accept, the specificity goes down, and the search finds many sequences in the bank that you're not interested in at all."

"You know, this sounds to me like it's exactly in line with your interests. You told Kerr you wouldn't take his position because it had nothing to do with your kind of research. But that doesn't seem to be the case anymore."

"Let's not get into that. I'm not sure this wine beats the '82 Lynch Bages, but I don't think I'd leave any of it in the bottom of the bottle."

"Joan, do you think that the Chinese found a way to put these genes into their runners?"

"I really didn't want to think about it, but I guess we must. If it's been done at all, the Chinese certainly didn't develop the technique by themselves, because there's an American who's doing it too."

"You mean Susie," Sean said. Joan nodded. "I'm not sure what I think about Susie having funny genes running around in her."

"Now, wait a minute," Joan said. "Even if they are in there, it's not likely that they're in her germ line."

"Her germ line?"

"Yes. With the transgenic mice, those animals pass on the genes to their offspring. But I told you, you could only make one if you happened to come upon the mouse when it's still an egg. Since we didn't know Susie when she was an egg, it seems unlikely that anybody managed to get the genes in there. Too bad." She laughed. "I'll bet you were thinking of breeding the perfect runner." Sean looked horrified.

Joan reached out and covered his hand with hers. "I'm sorry. I'm very sorry. That was really crude of me."

"The whole thing just sounds so awful." Sean shook his head slowly from side to side with a mixture of wonder and sorrow. "Why are such things possible?" he continued to himself. "Why don't these scientists just leave well enough alone?" Then he paused. "No. No. I'm not going to get trapped into that kind of thinking."

Joan had never stopped, becoming more and more cheerful and enthusiastic. "Anyway it certainly looks like Grimes made some genes that he thought were going to work, or he wouldn't have tried to make transgenic mice."

"I just can't believe it," Sean said, trying to slow her. "How did they do all this?"

"You know, it's all just sitting there waiting to be done. All this is possible. You just have to put it together. Grimes was smart enough to think of it, and he was smart enough to get a couple of people like Jack and Ann Grossman to do it."

"They were really good?"

"Well, I've told you Jack was. He could never stick to anything, but he was certainly smart. This project would have really appealed to him. I'm surprised he didn't run off with all this stuff. What the hell, maybe he did."

"You don't really believe that?"

"No, I don't think so. In fact, I think he was through with this project before they ever got anywhere near this far. I think this has to be Ann Grossman's work. She was even better. She was the only person here that I was afraid of."

"Afraid of?"

"In the great competition to land the perfect assistant professorship. Thank God she decided to go to the West Coast. If they picked anyone else over me, I'd be claiming foul, prejudice, favoritism, anything. But if they picked her over me, I'd just go congratulate her. Now nobody can even find her." They both had the same thought at the same time.

"Do you think those damn Chinese killed her too?"

"I don't want to think about that. Too bad we can't order another bottle of wine. We'll just have to go home."

"Sounds like you're planning another four-week renewal."

"Perhaps you'd like to reduce the term to two weeks or one week if your negotiations with Susie are entering a critical phase."

"Something is certainly entering a critical phase."

"How do you think you'd react if you found out for sure she was cheating?" Joan asked.

"I don't think there'd be a lot of choice."

"There'd be all kinds of choices," Joan insisted. "For example, could you marry her?" Sean looked at her. Was this a serious question or just the start of some intellectual game? "First of all, I don't know whether I'd marry her anyway, whether she cheated or not."

"Well, suppose you would if she hadn't cheated, would you still if she did cheat?"

Sean thought for a long moment. "No," he said, "to be honest with you, I wouldn't."

"Isn't that a little harsh?"

"I guess I can't imagine being married to someone I couldn't trust."

"Suppose she came and told you about it before you'd ever actually caught her?"

"I don't know," Sean answered slowly.

"Suppose she admitted that she made a mistake and said she was sorry?" Joan was sitting up now, on the edge of her chair. "Suppose she said she did it for you because, she wanted to impress you?"

"I just don't know," Sean protested defensively, "and anyway, nobody ever . . ."

"Nobody ever does anything for a single reason."

"Well, she didn't have to impress me. I was already impressed."

"Hell, you were more than impressed. You were smitten."

"Well, perhaps I've been 'unsmotted' or whatever the word is."

"Couldn't you forgive her?" Joan asked. "I know how important it is for you not to cheat, but you should be able to forgive anything. That's very important in a relationship."

"Maybe I could forgive her, but I might not want to marry her."

"But that's not really forgiving. That's just coming to terms with it with some conditions."

"I never win these arguments with you." Sean protested.

"This isn't an argument."

"Well, what is it?"

"I was . . . I was just trying to make sure that you thought about this."

"Did you really think that I hadn't thought about it?" Sean asked looking her straight in the eyes.

"It's very important to me that you do." She returned his gaze. It was the look he had come to love.

Chapter 42

Joan was not pleased when she wasn't invited to Philadelphia. She knew that something special was planned even though Sean refused to talk about it. *If Susie were here, I bet he would ask her,* she thought.

"We'll have a special celebration when I get back," he told her.

"You're sure there's going to be something to celebrate."

"We'll see."

The relays were an institution in Philadelphia. Competition took place at all levels, and many well-known athletes had begun their careers at this meet. While most highly paid professionals were unlikely to attend, there were always a few who found it convenient for their training schedules or who were running for old times' sake. The event was heavily supported by the local running community.

For this occasion Sean wanted everything to be exactly right. The pre-race ritual was to be the same as it had been so many times in the past. As usual he had gone to Philadelphia several days before the race to help coach the students in his club. As promised, Bob had found a rabbit of Olympic quality, a 5K specialist who would almost certainly be in the upcoming games and who was delighted to be part of a serious attempt at a world's record. They planned a pace for the first three miles that the rabbit could easily maintain. Sean would run directly behind him, taking advantage of the little draft that there was at this speed. The rabbit would go farther if he could but would pull off the track as soon as his pace began to falter. They prayed for good weather and no wind.

When Sean awoke Saturday morning, he knew it was a day to run. It often seemed to him that all of the attention to details, all of the worrying over trivia, was nothing more than an exercise to keep the mind occupied for the day or two before the race. But regardless of the routine some days were better than others. Perhaps it was determined by chance. Some days everything was just right.

Bob believed in meticulous preparation. Four of his own timers were stationed at equal intervals around the track. He himself was in the infield, the maestro about to direct a carefully orchestrated performance. The other runners were aware of the record attempt and would allow themselves to be passed on the inside. Everyone wanted to be part of a record.

The weather was fine, sixty-five degrees, overcast, little humidity, no wind. Sean made sure that he had warmed up adequately. He could hardly contain himself. It was one of the advantages of having a rabbit that in your excitement you could not start too fast. The rabbit and Sean were given the inside of the track, the gun sounded, and they were off.

Sean simply followed the lead runner one stride behind. It was so carefully programmed that each of the interval timers had a sheet with the ideal time for the runners to pass on each lap. They sat with their stopwatches and simply shouted out the gap between the ideal and the actual time. Plus four. Minus one. Plus two. It was like watching the dashboard computer in an automobile rally. Sean had time to think about the role of the rabbit. This was a runner who would labor for another's glory, but if the attempt were successful he would barely share in the triumph. Sean wondered if he could ever play that part.

World records have their own significance. In a sense they belong to mankind rather than to an individual, and it is its own reward to contribute in some way. Rabbit and Sean were on schedule at three miles, and the rabbit continued. He managed another half mile. As soon as he began to slow, Bob Higgum waved him off the track.

On the next lap when Sean passed the rabbit, still doubled over in the infield gasping for breath, he realized how much effort the other had put into their combined attempt. It only made him feel that much more responsible for accomplishing their goal. On schedule at four miles, running easily. On schedule at four and a half, starting to hurt. On schedule at five, this was meant to hurt. After five and a half he was allowed to do what he wanted, but when he reached it Bob was there to shout, "Wait, wait. One more lap." It meant one more lap before he could sprint.

Sean felt better than Bob could know. He increased the pace a little, but not as much as he would have without Bob's admonition. And now at five and three quarters came the same shout from Bob. Sean kept the pace steady, refusing to look at the time although he had the ideal splits memorized. When he passed Bob the last time, "go, go, go," replaced "wait, wait, wait."

There was slightly less than a lap to go when he made his move. For the first time he heard the roar of the crowd. He knew they were standing. What he recalled afterward was how silent they had been throughout the race. For the first twenty-five plus minutes, the entire meet had come to a stop. Everyone knew exactly what was happening. It was as if they were watching a tennis match: no one wanted to interfere in the slightest with the plan. Even his normally rowdy students were hushed until the last lap. The other runners had pulled far to the outside. Sean clipped the apex of the last corner. He could see the tape being stretched across the track just as the last of the back markers passed the finish line. He could hear Bob for the thousandth time saying, "There's no sense leaving anything on the track." He leaned into the tape, stretching for every tenth of a second. The roar was even louder. Fans stormed onto the track. The other runners could barely finish. He bent over gasping for breath, almost not wanting to look back at the clock. Finally, he straightened and turned. On the scoreboard "WR" flashed beside the time: *12 seconds*. He searched through the crowd of well-wishers to find the rabbit and insisted that they take the victory lap together.

The party Sean threw for his students that night was even more boisterous than the preceding year's. And for the first time Bob Higgum attended. For Sean, the most fun was going over each runner's performance and handing out the awards according to his own system. It was arranged so that virtually everyone received some special designation. For many it was the high point of the year. Every one of the runners received a written training plan prepared by Sean to get them through the summer. And there were gifts, shoes and other running gear supplied by Sean's companies, that always seemed to be won by the youngsters who needed them most.

It's a start, a chance to give a little bit back, thought Sean exchanging handshakes, hugs, and high five's as they left the restaurant. *Their lives are so different from mine. I was just as poor, but it was so secure in my village. Everybody knew me. It would have been hard to get into serious trouble. These kids live in hell. It's a wonder any of them survive. But no one dropped out of school this year, and it looks like everyone will pass, and I get to go to three graduations.*

Near the end Bob whispered in Sean's ear, "A world record deserves a day off. You can do the twenty-five-mile run on Monday if you don't want to do it tomorrow."

"You sure know how to ruin a party," Sean answered. "We'll do it tomorrow, but we'll start an hour late."

On Sunday morning they learned that in the Chinese National Games, Han had run the 10K two seconds faster. Sean's heart sank. It rebounded only slightly when he heard that the time would not be submitted because it was wind assisted. His sense of urgency was turning to desperation. *Either I find out what they're doing, or I run a hell of a lot faster.* The long practice run was completed in two hours and twenty minutes, with Higgum at the check points *suggesting*, then *ordering*, finally *pleading* that Sean slow down.

Chapter 43

It was a beautiful Saturday in June, and Joan and Sean had decided to drive to a small country inn for the weekend.

"You look very pretty," Sean said to her as she was getting into the car.

She turned crimson. "I'm supposed to look sophisticated, not pretty."

"You look very chic and pretty."

"It sounded like a real date, so I bought a new dress. I buy one every year whether I need it or not, just blow half a month's stipend."

"I keep reading that The Miller's Inn has the best restaurant in the state, so it seems the right place for a celebration," Sean said.

"I'm still mad at you for not inviting me to Philadelphia."

"Hey, I have the right to be a little superstitious."

"It must have been so wonderful. Did Higgum go wild?"

"He did. And the kids too, even more. But I must say, it was less satisfying than winning the World's. That was a real race against real competition. This was more like a training exercise, except for being an all-out effort. It was all preprogrammed, not spontaneous. So many people worked on it. And they knew, and I knew, that I could do it. It was like an automobile race with all those mechanics in the pit, only I was the race car, or maybe the driver. Like I was on the outside driving my body. And we were all hoping that nothing would go wrong, no flat tires, no rain, no wind."

"But it was such an accomplishment, something that no one has ever done."

"Oh, I don't mean to put it down. It was great, and it will bring me more fame and money than anything I've done up to now. But it was different from what I expected. I always dreamed of doing it while barely winning a brilliant strategic race against the best people, where we all broke the record. Of course now the Chinese have put a bit of a damper on it."

"But, Sean, if they had the wind blowing them around the track, why shouldn't they be able to run faster. It means you're still better, and you have the official record."

"I do have the record, but that doesn't mean they wouldn't have beaten me. It's a rule that if the wind's blowing above a certain speed, no records can be set," Sean explained. "And if you were running in a straight line and had a tailwind, it would certainly help you. But when you're running around a closed track, a circle or an oval, you're going to face the wind some of the time and have it at your back some of the time, and in a situation like that, the wind always hurts you more than it helps you."

Joan thought for a minute. "It stands to reason. So why don't they let them have the record?"

"It's a tradition. You can imagine that the wind could gust or change direction in ways that would help the runner."

Joan laughed. "Or you could be running in a tornado that was spinning around. It'd blow you right around the track." Sean laughed too.

"Anyway," Joan said, "you must have made tons of money."

"Well, not prize money. That's why nobody could believe I'd do it at that meet. But the bonuses on my contracts for being the new World record holder are, shall we say, substantial."

"Then you can buy a new car. This one's so bad we should have brought mine."

"Yours doesn't even start."

"That's just because it doesn't get used enough. Anyway it's the best that I can afford, and it brought you back from the airport."

The next morning at breakfast they sat by a window looking out over a mill pond surrounded by willow trees. "Now this inn would be something to buy," Sean said. "It's so perfect, it doesn't seem real. Someone must have painted it here. We could chuck everything and run this restaurant."

"Hmmm," she said. "That would be a change of plans in a lot of ways."

"One of us would have to learn to cook," Sean pointed out.

"I'm very good at reheating."

"I don't think the clientele would like that."

"Maybe we could just keep the chef they have."

"I think he's the owner," Sean said.

"Oh well, it seemed like a good idea. I guess we'll just have to find out what the Chinese are doing, so you can still earn your living by running."

"Have you been making any progress on the gene thing?"

"Some, but we're sure not getting any breaks. The sequencing company is sticking to its story that they don't keep the sequences. The animal people can't find the transgenic mice. They think they got an order to destroy them. And the most stupid thing of all, the oligo lab doesn't keep a cross reference by the name of the person who places the order."

"Now you're going to give me the good news." Sean had to laugh despite his disappointment.

"Well we haven't been sitting around crying about it. We're looking for the oligos by hand."

"Uhh."

"It's tedious but not impossible. They have a record of every oligo they've ever made. What it means is someone, Beth in her spare time, sits down and goes over each order looking for Grimes's billing code. Actually, there aren't that many, about ten thousand over the period when he was ordering them."

"She has to search ten thousand of them? She'll go crazy."

"It's not fun, but it's not that hard. She goes through them as fast as she can run down a column of numbers. She does a couple hundred and has a cup of coffee and does a couple hundred more. It's getting done. She sends them over as soon as she has a few."

"Did you find matches? Did you find sequences that the oligos matched?"

"Oh, yes," she said. "Many, many. Beth has found more than a hundred oligos already, and there are still more to come. Most of them match in the globin genes. It's certain that they were trying to make mutants in both the alpha and beta globins."

"They're the two protein chains in the hemoglobin, right?"

Joan usually didn't eat in the morning, but now she contented herself by stealing from Sean's plate. She spoke between nibbles of bacon. "Right. They're quite similar. Each one is 140-some amino acids long and has a place that can hold on to one iron atom. Then the iron atom holds on to one oxygen molecule, that's where the oxygen binds."

"Got it." Sean nodded agreement.

"Now four of them get together, two of the alphas and two of the betas, and kind of wrap themselves around each other and form a stable clump. Remember, we said that when the proteins fold up, sometimes they join with several others, always trying to form those weak bonds and to put the greasy guys on the inside and the water-loving guys on the outside."

This bacon would definitely go on the inside, he thought. Joan had just stolen another piece and was licking her fingers.

"That's what you called the fourth kind of structure," he said.

"Exactly."

"And the whole clump is one hemoglobin molecule." Sean wanted to be sure. "And that's why you say it can bind four oxygens. Really, one's going on each of the globins."

"Right."

"Don't you want to draw it?" Sean suggested, thinking that might distract her from his plate.

"No, no, there's nothing to draw." She waved away the idea and in the same motion took another piece. "This clump is very sophisticated. The interesting thing about it is that little things will make it change shape, and then it will function differently."

"I don't follow." Sean started to interrupt.

"People call it an 'allosteric' protein. That means 'other shape'."

"I know that part of it. I'm the Greek scholar here."

"I forgot." She laughed. "You know all of the things that my usual students don't know and then, of course, you don't know many of the things I expect them to know."

"But . . ."

"Anyway, Sean, let me finish. The hemoglobin molecule changes shape in a very special way as it binds more oxygen. So suppose it has no oxygen on it at all, then it has a certain shape."

"Okay."

"And one oxygen goes on somewhere, on one of the four binding sites."

"Okay."

"That causes a little change in shape, which makes it easier for a second oxygen to bind, and so on until all four sites are full."

"What's so strange about that?" Sean asked.

"It's strange because for most chemical reactions it gets harder and harder as you push them to completion. But oxygen binding to hemoglobin works just the opposite. As soon as you get it started, it gets easier and easier to push it to completion, that is, to fill all the binding sites."

"And that's good?"

"It's good because it makes the hemoglobin load and unload oxygen over that narrow range of pressure. Remember, hardly any oxygen goes on until you reach a certain pressure, and then boom, it all goes on. That's what makes it a good transport system."

"So that's how it works."

"Yes," Joan said. "Now the other reason we're so interested in these changes in shape of the hemoglobin molecule, these allosteric properties, is because they are responsible for the Root effect."

"Ah."

"In this case, the important thing is making the solution a little acidic."

"Right."

"That causes a different change in shape which makes it very hard to get any oxygen on, or looking at it the other way around, makes it very easy for the oxygen to come off. In a Root-effect hemoglobin the acid locks the protein in the shape that doesn't bind oxygen as well."

"And that's because there's something different about the alpha globin and the beta globin in the fish hemoglobin, right? They're mutants of the human hemoglobin," Sean said.

"It's not fair to say who's a mutant of whom, but many of the amino acids are different."

"But somewhere hidden in all the differences in the amino acids are those that make the fish hemoglobin have a Root effect and the human hemoglobin not have a Root effect?"

"Correct. And obviously Grimes's team was trying to find out which differences are important so they could change human hemoglobin to have a Root effect. The way they were doing it was making globin chains that were partly changed. So maybe they'd start with a human globin and change five or ten amino acids at a time until finally they got a Root effect."

"And that's what the primers were for?"

"Yes. You should eat faster. The eggs really will be better warm. The story gets even more interesting. Some of the oligos Grimes ordered corresponded to control elements for the hemoglobin gene."

"What are they?"

"We haven't talked about this a lot, but way back you may remember that I told you that we had to pry apart the double helix to get the strands out to do the PCR reaction."

"There was a picture, very helpful. If you could draw it again..."

"Not necessary. Not necessary." She waved dismissively and launched another successful predatory attack. "They also have to get pried apart if you want to read the code. Now, most of the time in our cells, because we're so fancy and complicated, most of the DNA isn't being read at all."

"Why not?"

"It's not needed. For example some of the DNA contains messages for how to make the things you need to be a liver cell, but if you're not going to be a liver cell, you're going to be a blood cell instead, those messages are all turned off."

"And how do you do that?" Sean asked.

"If we knew that, maybe we could just turn off all the ones that cause cancer."

"Sounds like a good idea? He tried without being obvious to maneuver his fork into a defensive position, as she reached out and broke off a piece of his toast. "You're sure you don't want me to order some for you?"

"No. No. I never eat this early." She swallowed the toast and continued. "The regulation can be very complicated, but for hemoglobin it's fairly well understood. Most of these genes have control elements sitting around them. There are things called promoters and enhancers, which when they become active, cause the hemoglobin gene to be read more often. We've learned that Grimes had oligos for these regions, so you have to think that they were using PCR to make them too."

"And what does all that mean?" Sean asked.

"To me it means that they were going to make a functional DNA construct that had the regulators and promoters along with the gene, so if they put it into a cell it would turn on and make hemoglobin. It just kind of confirms what we suspected when we heard about those transgenic mice. Chances are this construct worked. Remember the bills we found for those plasmid preparations. That was probably it. And they were making it in large amounts."

"What do you suppose happened to it?" Sean asked, already knowing the answer.

"I think it took a trip to China."

"God damn it." Then he paused. "And don't tell me, but a little bit of it probably stayed home."

"Probably."

"You know, Joan, this project sounds more and more like your own research, genetics and mutants and how they influence the shapes of these proteins. Maybe you should reconsider Dr. Kerr's..."

"Maybe we shouldn't talk about that."

"But you obviously like this problem. When you talk about it you get so excited and go on and on."

"I do *not* go on and on, I just try to answer your questions. And we are *not* going to talk about my changing projects."

"Okay, okay, but we do have to hurry on this."

"You really are worried about them, the Chinese, aren't you?"

"Of course I am. It's really frustrating. It's like being in a bad dream where burglars break into your house, and you can't do anything about it, and you have to sit there and watch them steal your things. We've got to stop them."

"Well I still have to figure out just how they're getting the DNA into people. You can't just feed it to them." She laughed. "And I am trying my best."

"Perhaps you need more incentive. I could let you have the last piece of my bacon."

"Harrumph."

Chapter 44

Susie had arrived in New York during the first week of July, eight days before the United States Olympic Trials in Sacramento. Sean was meeting her for dinner Sunday night in New York, but after that he was strictly forbidden from seeing her or from attending the trials.

Walking into the lobby on Central Park South, he thought of Yogi Berra saying 'It's deja vu all over again.' It was just one year and two months since the New York relay race. This time the voice over the intercom said, "Will you please send him up, George," and the doorman directed Sean toward the elevator.

As it rose, the events of the year passed through his mind. How could one ever have predicted something like this? He got off the elevator and rang the bell of the only door he saw. The penthouse seemed to occupy the entire floor. The door opened, and Susie threw herself into his arms and kissed him. When they managed to pull apart, they were both gasping.

"You need aerobic training for that!" Susie exclaimed.

Sean nodded. "If we do that again, we may not make it to dinner."

"Dinner first. Here, help me with these." She turned around and handed back the two ends of the strand of pearls. Then she withdrew them. "No, wait." She disappeared into a side room and returned with a single strand of what Sean thought were the largest diamonds he had ever seen. "Grandmother's." She resumed her position. He fastened the clasp and a clever little safety chain. She turned. They were dazzling on her dark blue dress.

"We'll never make it to our favorite restaurant. We'll be mugged." Sean laughed.

"No, we won't," she said. "Remember how fast we are. We can

be there in, um, fifteen seconds."

"You 5K people must do more speed work than I do." Sean laughed again. "But do you have endurance?"

"We'll see about that later in the evening."

Franco greeted them at the door. It was as if they had been there just last week. "Your father told me that you have set records and that you will be in the Olympic tryouts."

"Yes, in just six days," she said. "I'll be here for three of them, so you'll have a chance to stuff me with pasta."

Franco laughed. "It will be our pleasure. And, Mr. Rourke, it's so nice to see you."

How could he possibly have remembered? Sean wondered.

"Mr. Rourke is now the world record holder in the 10K run," Susie said proudly.

"Aha, I must say I knew that," Franco said. "Congratulations. And must we stuff him with pasta too?"

"Well, it doesn't have to be an emergency stuffing," Sean answered. "Fortunately, I've qualified, so I have a few weeks to relax."

"Would you like to be here?" Franco pointed to what obviously was the most desirable table. "Or would you like to be hidden?"

"I think we should be here," Sean replied. "We tend to fight when we're hidden."

"Oh yes, I remember." Franco laughed again. "It was terrible. Everyone was talking about it." He thought that was just hilarious.

"Besides," Sean added, "I think that Susie deserves to be seen."

"I could not agree with you more." So they were ushered to a table in a far corner that offered a commanding view of the entire restaurant.

"I could never tire of this place," Susie said.

"It's easy to see why, and I don't think they could ever tire of you."

"I hope not." It seemed to Sean that she suddenly looked very sad. The champagne arrived. They toasted Sean's record and Susie's upcoming races.

"Hopwell has been very pleased with my progress," Susie told him. "The training was going so well that I just decided to stay there until the last minute. We outlined a day-by-day schedule to lead right up to the trials. Jim agreed with it all. If I'm successful, of course, Jim will be coaching me with the team. Hopwell thinks I can do even better than I did in London."

"It'll be easier outdoors. I still can't get used to the indoor tracks even though I've had so much practice on them. But watch out for the heat. California is going to be a lot warmer than Oxford."

"Hopwell wants me to hold back in the preliminaries. The way they're running it, the first two finishers in each heat will be guaranteed a spot in the finals, and then there'll be some others picked on the basis of time. I guess it's the fairest way, although every now and then a person makes the finals who might not deserve it, because they were lucky enough to be in a slow heat."

"It's a compromise," Sean agreed. "Some people just don't run well when they're not pushed."

"Anyway, in the final, of course, I have to go all out. Three will make the team."

"Relax, Susie, and just enjoy it."

"Easy for you to say, you're in."

"I know. But in all honesty you're a sure thing. There aren't three people in this country who are better than you."

"I hope not," Susie said, "but I am nervous."

They ordered from the same waiter who had helped them the last time. "And have you selected a wine?" he asked.

"No, no, I've learned to leave that up to you," Sean answered.

The conversation turned to Sean's schedule. "Well, who knows what to do?" he said. "I'm going to Colorado in the middle of the month. I'd like to run at the higher altitude for about three weeks. Then I'm going 'down under.' I've rented a house in the suburbs. Sydney will be such a big adjustment, not only the time change, but the season, early spring. It could be cool. Hard to imagine after Atlanta, but perfect for us. Records are going to fall. Oh, I may get to carry our flag."

"Oh Sean, how wonderful," Susie almost squealed with delight.

"I guess it's wonderful to be considered an elder statesman, I'm one of the few on our team who's been to an Olympics before. Just wait 'til you experience the thrill of marching in with your team—of course yours is huge—and then of watching them light that fire from the torch."

"Sean, don't you dare say that. It's bad luck." She put down her glass and crossed her fingers.

"Oh, that's silly. You'll be there, and you'll love it. Then we'll have five days after the opening ceremony until our first trials. They're both on the same day."

"Let's hope it's a good one."

"We won't get to celebrate too much," Sean continued. "You're on again two days later, and I go the day after that."

"I don't see why you men need more rest," she teased him.

"Oh, that's about the usual. It's 10K after all. The whole thing should be fun."

They were progressing through the meal. It was as good as he had remembered. "I write down the names of these things when I get home," he said, waving his glass. "My mind goes blank when I see an Italian wine list."

They chose not to order dessert, which simply meant that huge plates of homemade ice cream and cookies arrived instead, together with a dessert wine. As they left, they were surrounded by Franco and members of the staff, who enthusiastically wished them good luck.

"I'm stuffed," Sean announced. "I don't think we could break twenty seconds getting back to the apartment."

"Perhaps with the right incentive," said Susie.

"Did you really think I wouldn't want to watch it," Joan asked, "or that I'd let you watch it by yourself?" Much to Sean's disappointment, the heats of the women's trials had not been televised, but the final was being shown in prime time, and he and Joan were sitting in front of her television, waiting for the race to begin. "I should drag you to bed," she said, "and then if you wanted, you could watch her over my shoulder."

Joan had been dreading the day, but now that it had arrived she felt a sense of relief. Before it was like sparring with a phantom, but now her rival was here. Well, not exactly here, but she seemed more real back in the United States than she had in England. And just when had she become a rival?

That kind of snuck up on me, she thought. *I wouldn't have been telling him to go to bed with her, but it didn't matter to me then. Of course he didn't have to listen to me. And then we—he—wouldn't have found the red urine. Well sometimes these things just have to work themselves out. And maybe it was a good strategy after all. Not the one I would pick now, but . . .*

"Don't you want to know what she looks like? You've never even seen her."

"I'll force myself to look. Actually, nothing could keep me from watching. I feel I have a stake in this. Actually, maybe several stakes. Actually, a stake in . . ."

"I sense a horrible pun coming," Sean broke in.

"All right, all right. I'll stop." The women were warming up on the track, and the announcer was identifying them by their numbers and their lane assignments.

"She's really thin, isn't she," Joan said. Sean looked at her. "I'm sorry. I didn't mean to criticize. I'm just commenting that she's really thin, even compared to the others, and they're all really thin."

"There aren't a lot of fat distance runners," Sean answered.

"It's no wonder they never have menstrual periods. It is strange though," she was muttering, "why the lack of hormones doesn't seem to influence their libidos."

"Joan," Sean warned.

"I'm teasing. I'm teasing. It's my right to tease." Then she turned serious. "You know, she *is* elegant. She even looks elegant in that silly suit."

The runners were positioned. Susie had drawn lane three. Sean didn't know enough about the others to have an opinion about what would be a reasonable strategy. Anyway, Susie was on her own. Hopwell was not there to coach her, nor was Jim McBride. *Of course, if she runs the way she did the last time I saw her, strategy won't come into it at all*, he thought.

The gun sounded, and the group surged forward. Within the first half mile Susie had found a comfortable position on the inside, away from the pack. The two runners ahead of her were setting a blistering pace.

"There she is in third," Joan pointed out unnecessarily. Sean nodded. "She does run beautifully. It's just the way you described her. She's so smooth. Do you know whom she reminds me of?" Sean shook his head. He was barely listening. "You, she reminds me of you."

That caught Sean's attention. "No," he said. "I don't look like that."

"You probably don't know how you look."

"Actually, I do. I've spent hours studying myself on video tape."

"That must be an interesting experience."

"Interesting and not usually pleasant, because Bob is there telling me all the little things he doesn't quite like."

"Ugh," Joan said.

Except for some swapping in the back of pack, the runners held position for the next mile. *Fast*, thought Sean, *fast. Record pace.*

"Why doesn't she go?" Joan asked. "Why doesn't she run faster?"

"Wait, wait."

"Oh, I know, it's just like you. It's the same thing you did when I watched you."

"Not quite. That was practice. This is for real."

"That wasn't for practice. That was for thousands of dollars."

"This is for real," he insisted.

Somewhere beyond the two-mile mark the leader began to fade. The second-place runner passed her. Susie passed her. The pack began to string out. Susie was in her machine mode, no emotion, no effort, so smooth. Slowly she began to narrow the gap. "Ah, nice, nice. She's running at just the pace she wants," he said.

Joan was absolutely beside herself. "She's got to get going. She's got to get going. Make her go faster. Oh, you can't make her go faster. Faster, faster," she began shouting at the television.

Sean had to laugh out loud. "Calm, Joan, calm. She's gaining. There are more than two laps left. She's going to do it. Don't worry."

"But all those others are coming up too." Actually, the others had gained not at all. That illusion was created as the pack broke apart. Now it was obvious to everyone that Susie was closing, and rapidly. "Oh, you were right. You were right," Joan admitted. "She is. Oh, get her Susie. Get her."

In contrast, Sean was sitting quietly on the end of his seat barely whispering to himself, "Yes, yes."

With a lap and a half to go Susie had the lead, and she extended it with every stride. It was almost imperceptible, but she was increasing the pace.

"Oh, she's going to win! She's going to win!" Joan shouted.

"The record, the record. We want the bloody record."

Joan suddenly realized that there were bigger stakes. "What is it?" she demanded. Sean quoted the time. Actually it was flashing in the corner of the screen. The time on the race clock was relentlessly drawing closer.

Now Joan had something else to cheer for. "Run, damn it, run. Get that record."

Susie was on the last straight, smooth, no obvious kick. "Is she going to do it, is she going to do it?" Joan shouted into Sean's ear. All he could tell, even with his practiced eye, was that it was going to be close. They switched to a head-on shot.

"Damn it, not that," Sean shouted at the TV. The cameraman must have heard because he switched back to the perpendicular view. Neither of them said a word until the finish. The clock stopped. It was two seconds short. "WR" flashed on the screen.

"Yes," they both stood simultaneously and hugged each other, jumping up and down. The announcer was ecstatic. Susie was being mobbed. Sean and Joan stopped and looked at each other.

"She looks nice from a distance," Joan said softly. Sean just nodded. He didn't know what to say. He had never before seen Joan cry.

Chapter 45

Sean was in Grimes's office waiting for Joan when Joe Blackburn walked in unannounced, carrying a large cardboard box.

"Heard you were leaving, and I might not get to see you again before the big event."

Sean got up from the desk, and they shook hands. Blackburn collapsed into the couch which gave out an ominous groan.

"Wanted to wish you good luck, and I brought a little present," he continued.

"I'm just going to Colorado for a few weeks to train at high altitude," Sean explained, "but I expect to be back."

"Anyway, I wanted to see you. A year ago, when we first met, I was maybe not as helpful as I could have been."

"You were very helpful. I learned a lot."

"To be honest, I thought you were nuts. Still would today if it happened again. It's hard for specialists to admit that amateurs can make contributions too. So I owe you an apology."

"No, no." Sean tried to protest, but Blackburn went on.

"You came here to find something for your running, not just to help us. Well, here it is." He reached into the box and pulled out a plastic transfusion bag, which he tossed over the desk to Sean. It contained a dark red, dry powder. "That's what all this was about, the fourth hemoglobin of good old Oncorhynchus mykiss, more commonly known as the Rainbow trout. Just add water and stir."

Sean stared at the bag in disbelief. The fine powder fell from one end to the other as he raised it to the light. He had thought about it for so long, but never imagined holding it in his own hands, never even imagined what it would look like. It had been a concept, not a real material. But here it was, the thing that had cost Grimes his life.

"Everything you need is in the box. Enough for six units. The dry form is stable forever. It's sterile and pure, and it's safe in dogs. That's all I can say about it. This batch comes from our first production run. Somehow it never got included in the inventory, just sort of disappeared." Sean continued to stare, speechless. "You didn't tell us too much about the Chinese, but I gather they were using it to beat you. This sort of levels the field. Not like cheating if they are too. Only fair." As Blackburn spoke he became more excited and more short of breath, but he hurried on, clipping his words. "No insult meant. Not your thing, then chuck it."

He struggled to get out of the deep couch. Sean rose too, and they stood facing each other. "Not into sports. You probably never would have guessed. But really pissed about Andy." He looked Sean in the eye and put his hand on his shoulder and shook him. "I want those bastards beaten *bad.* Don't care how, whatever it takes." Then seeming embarrassed either by the show of emotion, or by what he had done, he turned and left the room.

The open box lay on the couch. Sean went over and sat beside it. Inside were six bags of saline and the remaining five of the red powder, lengths of plastic tubing, and sterile needles. There was even a professional tourniquet. "He's thought of everything," Sean said to himself as he toyed with its Velcro catch. "It would be so easy . . ."

He got up and went slowly to the window, staring at nothing, in his mind still seeing the flustered Blackburn. *How much emotion it must have cost him to do this! But it's crazy. I would be caught. And anyway most of the others aren't cheating, and the records . . . It's not right.* He turned and hefted the bag that had been lying on the desk.

Meanwhile, Joan had been intercepted in the hallway by Kerr.

"Come in, come in," he insisted, motioning toward his office. "Tell me what you're up to. I've heard all kinds of rumors." Seeing no avenue of escape, she reluctantly followed. He closed the door behind her, waved her to a seat, and sat behind his desk.

"Sean tells me that you're in the midst of another very nice piece of detective work and that this one is a little more in your line."

"Yes, surprisingly it is," Joan admitted.

"I understand that Grimes had set off on a little genetic engineering project, and he made some hemoglobin genes and even made some transgenic mice with them. It never would have occurred to me that he knew anything about that field, but then he was always surprising me."

"It is amazing how much they managed to accomplish," Joan agreed. "Not to take anything away from him, but he recruited a couple of very good people. It just shows what you can do if you have the right kind of setup."

"And you know I'm going to try to recruit another very good person and give her the right kind of setup."

"I suspected that." She laughed.

"Just hear me out. If you don't want to, that's obviously perfectly all right, but I think you might be missing a good opportunity. I can understand why you didn't want to be involved in the part of the project that we've been doing up to now. By the way, it's going pretty well. Blackburn has hired two protein chemists to really push the work along, and they've already developed an acceptable method for purifying the hemoglobin. There are still some tricks to learn about how to use it, but he seems to feel that in a month or so they'll actually be testing it in the tumor systems."

"That's really moving."

"We're hurrying for all the obvious reasons. It's such a shame that we don't have Grimes's notes; it would have saved us so much time. Anyway, it looks like you've uncovered a very different aspect to the problem, and the genetic engineering is going to require a whole new team with different expertise. Now, recognizing that, I wonder if you'd reconsider our offer. It seems to me that this is right up your alley."

"Somewhat. But I still think it would be better for me to be in a basic science department where I can work on any research project I want."

"You know, I've heard that argument before. In reality, very few people have that luxury. What you can do anywhere depends on what you can convince some funding agency to support and what the department needs to fulfill all its teaching responsibilities."

It's true. I wish it weren't, but it is. It depressed her to have to admit that her options were more limited than she would like. She stared at her hands as he went on.

"Something you should think of is the satisfaction you can get by working on research that is closer to the final application. You may, if everything works well, have the opportunity to see the benefits of what you've done on real patients. Not everyone gets to experience that, but I can tell you it makes up for a lot of compromise."

"I don't doubt that," she answered softly. "I don't doubt the importance of that kind of research or its rewards. I'm just not sure that I'm the person to do it."

"All I can do is make the offer. Assistant Professor, all of your start up costs for three years, and a laboratory remodeled to suit your specifications. You'll have to make out a budget: personnel, supplies, equipment. How much space will you need? You'll get everything that you ask for that's reasonable. We'll negotiate a salary. You probably know the going rates, but I'll tell you in advance that you won't be disappointed. What have I forgotten?"

Joan sat listening, almost wishing she weren't hearing. She didn't know what to say. Obviously Kerr had done this before, probably many, many times.

"I guess what I need most is time to think it over."

"I wouldn't let you make a decision without thinking it over. Consider the advantages and the disadvantages and cut the best deal you can. I'm quite flexible, and I suspect you're a very tough negotiator."

"Thank you. Thank you very much." She wanted to run from the room in terror. They shook hands, and Joan went next door.

"We heard you were waylaid," Sean said with a smile.

"He must have been tipped," Joan said accusingly. "He seemed to have planned our conversation in advance."

"Who would have told him that you were coming by?" Beth said grinning.

"Did he try to convince you to accept a position in this department?" Sean asked innocently.

"You know he did."

"No, I don't know it, but I was sure that he would sometime."

"Well, it was a great offer, assistant professor, all the trimmings. Many people would do anything for an offer like that."

"But not you?" he asked.

"I don't know. I just don't know what to do, and I almost wish he hadn't made the offer. While I was listening to it unfold, I thought maybe I should turn and run from the room." She laughed.

"The ostrich approach." Sean laughed too. "But wait 'til you hear what just happened to me!"

They started into the office.

"Wasn't that Blackburn I just saw leaving?" Joan was staring at the bag Sean still held.

He motioned to the box and handed her the unit of hemoglobin.

"That's not what I think it is?"

"Yes. He just walked in and gave it to me. Said he wanted the Chinese beaten because of Grimes. He was trying to help."

By now Joan had retrieved several of the bags from the box. "You're not going to use it?"

"No. I can't. Funny, that was easier to say when I didn't have it. But the answer is still the same."

"Not even tempted?"

"Only by curiosity. Maybe try it in practice, just to see what it's like. I'd love to know. But I won't. I'd be too scared. We'll just have to get them some other way."

"Well then let me tell you what I've come up with about the genes." As she spoke she carefully placed the bags of hemoglobin back in the box. "This project *is* getting more interesting. I think I know how Grimes could have gotten the genes into people. This isn't my field so it took a little reading and talking to some people who do similar things. But now it all makes sense, and as usual it isn't even that complicated."

"You mean I'll be able to understand it?"

"Even you," she said, sitting in a chair by the desk. "The goal here is to have the fish hemoglobin made in some of the human red blood cells. You don't need it in all of them, twenty or thirty percent of them would be enough to get the effect you wanted."

"Okay." Sean nodded and sat behind the desk.

"You probably know that the red blood cells are made in the bone marrow. And over your lifetime, you make millions and millions of them, because they wear out and more have to be made. A red blood cell lasts about a month, unless you're bleeding, of course." She laughed. "When it starts to wear out, it's caught in the spleen and chewed up, and some parts like the iron can be used again, recycled."

"Got it."

"Now, in the bone marrow, there are things called stem cells. They're a kind of basic cell from which the other blood cells are derived. The most basic of all of these stem cells is called a *pluripotential* stem cell. You're the classics scholar, so you know that just means they have the potential to do a lot of different things."

"Yes."

"The most important, is that they can make more of themselves, one of them can make two and two can make four and so on."

"Just like the cancer cells," Sean noted.

"Yes, kind of like the cancer cells. They're immortal. And presumably, if everything worked well, and there were no screw-ups, you could grow a patient's whole bone marrow from just one of these cells."

"Really!"

"They serve as a reservoir, so you can never run out of the various blood cells. Usually they divide and make more of themselves, but as needed, they switch over to make the final products, white blood cells, or platelets for clotting, or the ones we're interested in, the red blood cells."

"Hmm."

"When they do that, they basically commit themselves to serve their new role and eventually to die. To become a red cell, they must turn on the hemoglobin-making machinery and fill themselves with hemoglobin. That's when they make all the RNA with the sequences for the globin chains, remember, the stuff Grimes was getting from the Tautog."

"Ah, and that's what starts the clock ticking, and then they have about a month to live?"

"Yes. When they get enough hemoglobin in them, they leave the bone marrow and circulate in the blood carrying oxygen until they wear out and the spleen grabs them."

"I'm following you," Sean assured her.

"Now, if you wanted to put the recipe for a fish hemoglobin into a person, and you wanted it to stay there for a long time, you'd have to put it into the pluripotential stem cells. From then on, as long as that reservoir was feeding the whole system, every cell would have the fish hemoglobin gene. And eventually when it came time to make hemoglobin it would make some fish hemoglobin. If it still had its human hemoglobin genes, it would make some of that too."

"Wouldn't this gene end up in the platelet line and the white blood cell line as well?"

She nodded. "Yes, but it would never get activated there. That's why it was important for Grimes to put the regulators into the DNA constructs. The hemoglobin regulators only get activated when the stem cells decide they're going to go into the red blood cell line."

"Ah."

"When Grimes was making the transgenic mice, his fish hemoglobin gene was going to be in every single cell in the mouse, but only the red blood cells were going to turn it on, providing of course that he made his DNA construct the right way so that all the control elements were intact and functioning."

"This is really clever." Sean was grinning from ear to ear.

"Isn't it? So, now, what you have to do is get some of these stem cells and put in the DNA."

"Can you do that?" Sean asked.

"Yes. The cancer treatment doctors often do it. Some chemotherapy severely damages the bone marrow. A simple strategy is to take stem cells from a patient, keep them alive outside of his body, give him the chemotherapy, do a lot of damage to the bone marrow, but then when the chemotherapy has left the body, give back the stem cells. So ways were developed to purify the stem cells either from bone marrow or even just from the blood. Sometimes the stem cells leave the bone marrow and just wander around in the blood vessels. So you could take some blood from a vein, separate the stem cells, and even give back the rest of the blood afterward."

"And that really works?"

"It's actually being done now in cancer treatment, and it's much less expensive, and less painful, than trying to get out bone marrow."

"Okay," Sean said. "So now we have the stem cells. How do we put the DNA in them?"

"Well, there are three or four different methods. I don't know yet which Grimes actually used. One way is to put your whole DNA construct into some virus that infects stem cells. Then you just incubate the virus with the cells for a while, until it gets inside. When the virus is trying to put its own DNA into the stem cell, it's going to carry along the thing that you made."

"But won't the virus kill the stem cells, or at least make them sick?"

"The virus can be altered so that it isn't harmful. You can selectively damage the part of the viral DNA that's necessary to let it divide and grow more viruses and kill the stem cells, but not damage the part that's necessary for the virus to get into the cells or the part that's carrying your DNA construct."

"Then how do we get the stem cells back in the bone marrow?"

"Simplest thing of all." She leaned back in the chair as if her work were done and waved her hand in a dismissive gesture. "We don't even have to put them into the bone marrow. We just inject them into a vein. I told you the cells go in and out of the marrow all the time. You just hope that some of them will go back, and that you haven't damaged them too much with all the manipulating you've been doing."

"And so that's all there is to it?"

"That and a lot of luck," Joan said, crossing her fingers.

"And then once you've done it, these genes would be in the people, and they would make this fish hemoglobin, or whatever you put in, *forever*?"

"Well, pretty much forever."

Sean stared at her wide-eyed. "It almost sounds like science fiction."

"None of this is impossible. Five years ago it would have been. But in another five years it will be absolutely routine."

"Unbelievable," Sean said. "So you think the Chinese could do all this?"

"Oh, yes, I certainly do. We don't know how much Grimes and his team accomplished. They may have finished preparing the DNA, maybe even put it in a virus."

"And the Chinese could get the stem cells?"

"Of course. It's a big mistake to think that their science is primitive."

Sean threw up his hands. "So, now these people, all the ones who've done this, are going to make the fish hemoglobin in their own red blood cells, where it's supposed to be. It's going to function correctly, it's not going to leak out of their kidneys, and they're going to make it forever."

"That's probably right," Joan agreed.

"You know," Sean was thinking out loud, "this would explain why lately they haven't looked so strange while they're running."

"I don't follow you."

Sean got up and began to pace the room. "Well, when they were giving themselves the blood, I mean the stroma-free hemoglobin, before they did the gene thing, they certainly weren't doing it every day. They probably weren't even doing it when they were training. They just did it for the races."

"Yes." Joan had a puzzled look on her face.

"Remember how I described it to you, they were like people whose training was a little out of balance. Their breathing ability was way ahead of their muscles."

"Ah, I see. But if they had the hemoglobin in them all the time, the muscles would catch up."

"Right. If they could practice every day with their new super oxygen delivery system, eventually they'd develop the muscles that could take full advantage of it. So after a couple of months, maybe just weeks, we're not going to be able to tell just by looking at them whether they're using the Root-effect hemoglobin or not. That must have been why when Bob saw them in Japan the effect was so subtle. He congratulated me on my good eye, but when I first saw them it was much easier to recognize that something was wrong. His eye for these things has always been better than mine."

"Very interesting."

"But how the hell could Susie have done this?" Sean asked. "I mean, how would she know how to do it, not how could she make the decision to do it on herself, although I must say I'd like to know the answer to that too?"

"Didn't she study some science at Grenville?"

"At first, but then she changed to . . . Wait. At Oxford she changed back. She's taking all science courses. There was a big fuss about her switching her schedule at the last minute."

"You never told me that. Still, she would need an insider somewhere. If she got the DNA constructs, and they were all ready to put into stem cells, she'd be nine-tenths of the way there. She'd have to get somebody to harvest some of her stem cells, but the rest is trivial."

"But who could do that?"

"In lots of hospitals it's almost routine. The doctor just orders it. Very simple. The blood bank draws some blood, puts it through its purification system, and stores away the stem cells. If you found a blood bank technician who was not totally honest, and you offered him the right amount of money, no questions asked, ten thousand maybe."

"So you really think she did it?" Sean asked her.

"I think that it would have been possible for her to do it."

"But what would *make* her do it? To change her body *forever*." Sean shook his head. "For what? To win some race. Her. With *her* life." He paused, then went on. "Okay, I can see some poor Chinese peasant with nothing else . . ."

"Being rich doesn't make you honest, Sean," Joan interrupted.

"I know that. But she was so, *so special*. She had everything. And she ruined it." He turned back to Joan with a sardonic smile. "Hell, the poor Chinese runners probably didn't even know what was happening to them. In Germany right now some of those old trainers from the cold-war times are on trial for giving male hormones to women swimmers without their knowledge. The swimmers were just kids. What did they know? And in East Germany I imagine you did what you were told."

"They're all crazy," Joan said sadly.

"But we have to do something about it," Sean exclaimed. "Once these people have practiced for a while with the hemoglobin in them, they'll be unbeatable."

"Well, there are still ways of detecting it."

"How?" Sean stopped pacing to stare at her.

"You'd have to get some of their blood, then take out the hemoglobin and characterize it. Most of the hemoglobin in them is going to be human hemoglobin, so you'd have to separate it and identify some that wasn't normal human."

"Isn't that going to be hard? Could you even do it?"

"Oh, sure. You could do it by electrophoresis. That's how they diagnose sickle cell anemia. You put the hemoglobin on a piece of wet paper and run an electric current through it. Different hemoglobins will have different electric charges because of the changed amino acids, so they will move to different spots on the paper. But the sports labs wouldn't normally do such a fancy test unless you told them to do it. The real question for now is, do you blow the whistle on them?"

"If I don't I'm going to lose, and so are some others who deserve a fair chance to win. And this could spread to other sports. But if I do, it's going to ruin Susie and probably take down Jim McBride and possibly Paul Hopwell as well."

"Susie deserves it," Joan interrupted, "although emotionally you'll have a hard time dealing with that one."

"No, I won't. If she's guilty, she should get what she deserves. But the other two are innocent, even though most people won't give them the benefit of the doubt. It will cost Jim his new job. I don't know what Grenville will do. They're so honorable they'll probably believe him, although it strikes me that this isn't the kind of place that likes even a hint of scandal."

"And, of course, if Jim doesn't get his new job there won't be an opening for you at Grenville," Joan added.

"Well, the coaching position is the least of my concerns. I wouldn't compromise myself for that. I'm not even sure I'd take it if they offered it to me. Would I compromise myself to help a couple of friends who don't deserve this trouble? Maybe."

"You have a lot to think about," Joan said, "and remember, even if you decide you're willing to lose, you still represent your country, and there are other runners who will be representing their countries who won't want to lose because someone cheated. You have a responsibility to them."

"I know. I know." There was a resigned look on his face, but then it changed to an ironic smile. "Whatever happened to the good old days, when all I had to worry about was hitting the practice splits on time to keep Bob happy? I'm going to Colorado and ignoring all this nonsense."

"Now who's the ostrich?" Joan said with a laugh.

"Yeah, well."

"When are you going, not that I'm going to miss you, of course?"

"Day after tomorrow. I'd like to be up there for about three weeks. But it doesn't hurt to come down for a day or two if I have to. I told you that some of my teammates are going to be in the house too."

"I think you did," she said.

"Mainly distance people. It'll be good to have someone to train with, and it'll be good to get to know them. I feel so out of it since I don't live over there, and they have voted to make me the captain."

"Captain of the whole team?"

"Yes, of the whole delegation. It means I get to carry the flag."

"Sean, that's a terrific honor."

"It is, but it reminds me that I haven't done much to support the team. They must think I'm an elder statesman."

"Right, really elderly," she said.

"Anyway, there's a nice mountain near the house, about eighteen hundred feet. I plan to run up it about ten times every morning. Maybe now I better make it twenty."

"Yuck!"

"How would you like to come too? You could get a car and follow me up and throw water at me."

"Well, that might be fun," she said. "But I don't know. There's some unfinished business here. Somebody has to stay home and work."

"But you're coming to Australia for the Games? I have a house there too."

She shook her head vigorously. "No, nope, I'm not."

"Why not? I'm inviting you."

"Because, that belongs to somebody else. You're going to have enough on your mind without me being down there. I just don't think I should. When it's all over, then, well then you'll come back. Especially if you're going to work here."

"Yes, I guess so."

"Anyway, it'll be on television, won't it? Maybe I'll even watch. Or, maybe I'll ignore you and just go to a movie."

"Just don't attack the television set. Don't throw anything through the screen." He wiggled his finger at her and laughed.

"Now what are you going to be doing to make me throw something through the screen?" she demanded, as she started to get up.

"Maybe losing."

"Well then, don't lose."

"Gee, I never thought of that. Say, what are we going to do with this stuff?" He motioned toward Blackburn's box.

She picked it up and winked at him. "I can store it in my lab, in case you change your mind."

"Don't even joke about it."

Chapter 46

Beth Markham appeared in Joan's lab a week after Sean had gone to Colorado. It was five o'clock, and, as promised, she was dropping off the last of the oligo sequences on her way home.

"I think this is it," she said as she handed a folder to Joan. "I've gone over and over the lists. Some were put on the wrong billing code by mistake and then corrected later, but I managed to get them too."

"Thanks, I know how much work it was, and we really appreciate it."

"I hope it's going to help," Beth said and laughed. "I'd hate to think I turned all those pages for nothing."

"One way or another it will. It hasn't produced a big breakthrough yet, but when we sit down to try to reproduce Grimes's work, we'll need these primers. Too bad, we'll have to make them all over again. It's a lot of money."

"It's more than ten thousand dollars," Beth confirmed.

"I know. They seem to have vanished from Grimes's lab. At least no one found them when it was being cleaned out. I suppose someone just threw them down the drain."

"Are they easy to get rid of?"

"Oh, sure. Each one is just a couple of drops of solution in a small test tube. You could stuff a hundred of them in your pocket and take them with you. In fact, that's probably what actually happened to them. They took a nice trip to China."

"Wouldn't they spoil?" Beth asked.

"No, they're very tough."

"Well, I have all the original order forms now, so if someone would like to work on this project again I could have them made. I think it takes just a couple of days to get them."

There's no mistaking her meaning, Joan thought. *She and Sean and Kerr, they're all involved in this. They're ganging up on me.* "I'm sure someone will want to do it someday," she answered, "but who knows who that someone will be."

Beth left, and Joan put the list in front of her computer. It had been a long day, and it was going to be longer. She would try to run the new sequences through the gene bank at odd moments, while waiting for a gel to run or a centrifuge to stop. She was in a foul mood. The PCR reaction she was using to make a mutant for one of her other research projects wasn't working, and she couldn't figure out why. "You can calculate these damn temperatures by every one of their formulae," she said to herself, "and it still doesn't work. It all comes down to trial and error."

She remade the mixtures for another attempt, using a slightly different annealing temperature. "That's the temperature at which the little oligo will stick on the long chain of DNA," she said and then stopped herself. "Damn it, you're not explaining something to Sean. You act as if he were here even when he's not. He isn't the center of the universe." But indeed it seemed that he was. She knew how much she missed him, but she didn't want to admit it. *I didn't used to get myself into situations like this, and I don't like it. I wasn't supposed to fall in love with him. He isn't even a scientist. What will we talk about when this is over? But we never seem to have trouble talking.*

"If I were smart," she said out loud as she dropped mineral oil into the PCR test tubes, "I'd mix up a big batch of these solutions, since I'm probably going to have to try twenty different temperatures before the dumb PCR reaction works. But then," she rationalized, "that would mean admitting that I didn't think it was going to work this time, and I don't like to do that." She started to load the tubes into the PCR temperature cycler. "When you worry more about the fall-back positions than you do about getting it right the first time, you're in trouble." She turned on the cycler, heated the solutions for the first time, and added the enzyme. It would be on automatic for about an hour and a half, freeing her to do other things and hopefully to have a few moments for the oligos.

Every time Joan used the gene bank she was filled with amazement. Her routine for each oligo was first to search all of the recorded hemoglobin sequences and then to search the entire gene bank. At the second request, there was the slightest pause, less than a second, before the results began to appear on the screen. The fact that there was a pause rather than an instantaneous response always reminded her of what had been done. Millions and millions of bases had been searched for a match sequence. "What would it have taken to do it by hand, a thousand graduate students a full year?" The first oligo matched a short stretch of the human hemoglobin beta chain in all but one of its bases. "Another oligo to make a mutant," she said to herself and recorded her finding for future use.

"Ooops." She ran to the power supply for a gel and turned it off. "Got to pay attention. I almost lost that one." She unloaded the gel and photographed the bands of DNA on a view box. "It's getting so I can't keep track of four experiments at the same time anymore. I must be getting old, or else I have too many distractions in my life." She used a razor blade to cut out a small sliver of the gel, which contained a fragment of a gene, then melted it, cooled it slightly, and added an enzyme that would digest the starch gel into small fragments, freeing the DNA.

Back to the computer. Another oligo. Not in the known hemoglobins. Not even with a thirty percent mismatch, not even with fifty percent mismatch. Still not there. Not in the gene bank. *It must be from one of those weird fish, or else they were doing something totally different.*

It was time to get the finished PCR reaction mixture, put it on a gel, and see if any DNA had been made. Back to the computer. Another oligo to make hemoglobin mutants. Back to the gel. No PCR product. "Shit," she said. "Have to make more of the PCR solution. Should I make tenfold? No, I'll make just enough for one more run. Sometimes it just feels good to be stubborn." She restarted the temperature cycler, then went back to the computer. It was approaching midnight.

Another seventeen-hour day and no dinner, she thought. *But, what the hell, I'm getting four-fifty an hour. Not bad for a Ph.D. and two fellowships*. There were three more oligos. *Might as well do them and catch the last shuttle.* Another oligo for making mutants.

This time three changes in the alpha chain. "There has to be a pattern to this," she said aloud. "That's my next project. Damn, I don't want this to be my next project. But I have to admit it is getting interesting." Next oligo. No matches.

Got to hurry. Ten minutes 'til that shuttle leaves. Her apartment was on the far side of the university but directly on the route of a shuttle bus that ran between the medical center and other parts of the campus. Regular service ended at one A.M., but for security reasons the campus police would come at any time to accompany you to your car or to drive you home if you lived nearby. *I hate to call them again*, she thought. *I do it so often.*

Last oligo. No matches in the hemoglobins, but many matches elsewhere in the gene bank. *It's in a lot of things. I'll have to sort these out later.* As she glanced at the long list of names rolling down the screen, one match stood out: "HslTK," thymidine kinase, an enzyme.

"Huh?" she said out loud. "That's really weird."

Five minutes to one. Computer off. Quick look around the lab. All the enzymes in the freezer, none left out on the benchtops where they would decay overnight. All the water baths full. No gels running. PCR machine cheerfully cycling away. Out with the lights. Down the stairs. Onto the bus. "That was close," the driver complained, anxious to be off on his last run. She was too tired to bother answering.

A half hour later Joan was propped up in bed, a slice of leftover pizza on a plate in her lap and a glass of red wine on the nightstand beside her. Don Giovanni was on the stereo. Since Cosi, she had been on a Mozart kick. "I think I like this one best," she said to herself, "but ah well, they're all good." They had reached one of her favorites. She smiled and sang along. "Ma in Ispagna son gia mille e tre." She repeated it with the singer. "How could he have slept with one thousand and three women?" she wondered aloud and reached for the wine. "And just in Spain, not counting all the other countries." She saluted him with the glass. "I thought I was doing all right until I bogged down with the last two, Jack and now Sean." It seemed she'd been with Sean forever. "Can't be only six months. Jack, that was more than twice as long. I'll have to dump them all. I need more variety." She said it without enthusiasm.

"It's a wonder Giovanni never caught anything. He could have gotten syphilis, which would have been a real problem then. Of course no one had AIDS in Giovanni's time. Now I guess there aren't any others that we can't cure except maybe Herpes, but even then there's that Gan . . ." She stopped, then sat bolt upright spilling the wine. In the background Donna Elvira denounced the villainy of men. Zerlina sang. It was Dawn Upshaw, her favorite soprano, but she didn't hear. "Oh, God! Oh, let it be true, oh, just let it be true. Ann Grossman, wherever you are, you're so damn smart," she said out loud. "You'll have your revenge on those Chinese bastards. Yours and Grimes's. And *I'll* make sure of it."

She leapt from the bed, put on the clothes that were still in a heap on the floor, grabbed her keys, and hurried down the stairs, out of the apartment building, and into the unreliable car. "Start, start, damn it. You need a new battery. No, you just need to be driven more often. Start and I'll buy you a battery. Start just this once." It started. She raced through the deserted campus toward the medical school, but as she drew near she drove more slowly. She could hardly stand to know. Suppose it weren't true. She parked illegally right in front of the main entrance. Who would care at three in the morning, and so what if they towed it? She showed her identification to the guard and told him the rooms that she would be using. *Security*, she thought, but had to admit that it made her feel much better about being there at that time of night. When she reached the lab, she was relieved to find people in the next room. She waved to them. "Another all nighter?"

She turned on the computer and sat and stared at the blank screen for what seemed like minutes, almost afraid to begin. Finally she called up the "Match" subroutine.

"Which seq?" the computer asked.

She typed in the code for the last oligo.

"Match to which seq?"

She took a deep breath and typed "HslTK," the thymidine kinase gene of the Herpes simplex virus. Her finger wavered for a moment over the "enter" key, then pushed.

"Shit," she groaned and turned away. Slowly she rose to her feet, then forced herself to look at the screen again. The summary data showed a poor fit, about fifty percent. Was it just a chance mismatch? She turned her back on the computer and walked slowly out into the dimly lit main laboratory. The lights of the PCR temperature cycler winked at her. Its work over for the night, it held the precious newly synthesized genes. "Come and get them," it seemed to say. "Come and see what I've made." Instead, she stopped before the electrophoresis boxes, stacked on a tabletop stained blue from countless spills of the dye used to mark the DNA. Absentmindedly she began arranging the gel trays as if preparing for the next day's work. Then she paused and rushed back.

"I've got to see the actual match for myself." Without bothering to sit, she leaned over the keyboard and typed the request. The two sequences optimally aligned began to appear on the screen. Before the first line had been completed, she sprang back, throwing both fists in the air. "Yes, yes, yes!" The last half of the oligo was a perfect match for the beginning of the TK gene. The first half "hung in the breeze." It wasn't meant to match! It wasn't meant to make mutants! It was meant to be a linker! The first half of the oligo would match the end of some other piece of DNA, serving as a strut, connecting it to the TK gene. "And don't I know what you were meant to connect, my lovely little oligo. You must match one of Grimes's weird hemoglobins."

She was so excited, she couldn't sit down. She just stared at the screen, and then she remembered Ann Grossman. It was as if she were seeing into her mind. "When you follow someone's line of thinking, it's a special kind of intimacy," she said to herself. "It's almost as close as you can get. Maybe it *is* as close as you can get. Maybe that's why I talk science in bed. But it shouldn't have to be science. It could be anything that you have to think about together. It's like suddenly realizing what the poet meant." She reached for the phone and dialed. It seemed to ring forever. Finally a sleepy voice with a thick Irish accent answered.

"I'd like to speak to Sean Rourke," she demanded.

"He's in bed. It must be after, where's the bloody light. It must be after one o'clock. We're all in bed, damn it."

"Get him. I have to speak to him."

"He won't want to get up. He's running tomorrow."

"Listen, don't argue with me. Tell him this is Joan Danner. Tell him to get up. You can take my word for it. He'll want you to."

The receiver banged against something. A minute later she recognized Sean's voice.

"Joan? What is it? What's wrong? It's almost two o'clock."

"Oh, I just called up to see how the training was going and to be sure that you were getting your rest."

"What . . . Joan?"

"You may congratulate me, my dear. I've *got* it."

"Got what?" He was suddenly wide awake and as excited as she was.

"I found out about the genes they used and how we can knock them out."

"Knock them out!" Sean repeated.

"Yes, yes." She was beside herself with excitement. "All we have to do is give them a pill."

"And the genes will be knocked out?"

"All the cells that have the genes, the ones that make the Root hemoglobin, will be killed."

"My God, you can really do that?"

"Yes, Sean, yes! The problem is solved. We can get rid of it."

"But what do we have to do to them?"

"Give them a pill. Slip it in their water or something. I'll have to find out exactly. But it won't hurt them. They'll never even know it happened."

"It just sounds too good to be true. How did you ever figure it out?"

"You can thank Ann Grossman, or Grimes, or both of them. Whoever decided."

"But how does it work? What is it?"

"Sean, I can't tell you over the phone. It's too complicated. I know, I know, you could understand it. But if you think it's late there, what do you think it is here? I've been up since six yesterday morning."

"Since six!"

"Well, this came out of the last of the oligos, that Beth brought on her way home. I was busy and didn't get to them right away. Just as I was leaving at about one A.M. I found this strange match but didn't make the connection. Then I went home and listened to a little

Mozart. Everything in life is in Mozart."

"You're teasing me," Sean protested.

"No. I'll tell you all about it when you come back, but I just had to let you know tonight. Otherwise, who knows, you might be lying out there in the mountains having nightmares about Chinese runners."

"Oh, I wanted to know right away. But we've got to get this stuff into the Chinese."

"We'll solve that tomorrow," she said.

"Bob. We must tell Bob. Joan, I'll fly to New York tomorrow. Why don't you meet me there, and we'll go to Philadelphia. He'll know what we should do with it. Do you know how to get this poison?"

"In a drugstore." Joan laughed.

"What?"

"Never mind. Listen, call me tomorrow when you've made your flight reservations and don't call too early."

"I miss you."

"Me too," Joan said. "I mean, I miss *you*."

"I . . ." Sean started.

"Enough. Don't say any more." Then she hung up.

"I guess I expected to find an ogre," Joan said.

"And instead you've found a leprechaun." Bob Higgum laughed. "And I expected to find a mad scientist, and instead I've found a very beautiful young woman."

"See. I told you," Sean said. "He can be charming. He just doesn't want anybody to know it." They were in Higgum's office in the fieldhouse at St. Vincent's.

"Sean tells me you've solved the whole puzzle and you know how to stop them."

"I think so. It's all based on circumstantial evidence, so we won't know if I'm right until it either works or doesn't work, but I don't think that I'm wrong."

"Can you explain it to me in a way that I can understand? Be really simple. If you think he's slow," he nodded at Sean, "wait 'til you try to teach me."

"It is simple. Sean has told you about the fish hemoglobin that carries the oxygen better?" Bob nodded assent. "What the Chinese have done is to teach their own bone marrow cells, some of them, to make this hemoglobin instead of human hemoglobin and to make it inside their own red blood cells."

"Nice trick, that," said Bob.

"Yes," she agreed. "To do this, they take out some cells from the bone marrow and infect them with a virus. The virus carries the gene to tell the red blood cells how to make the fish hemoglobin. Then they put the bone marrow cells back into the runner . . ."

"And he makes blood like a fish," Bob interrupted.

"Kind of. He makes fish hemoglobin in human red blood cells."

"So they don't have red urine anymore," Sean interjected, "the way they used to when they took hemoglobin from a fish and put it in their own bloodstream."

"I see. And now Sean tells me you've found a way to get rid of these cells that make the fish blood. Fishy blood." Bob laughed at his own pun. "Something fishy in these runners."

"I think so," Joan said. "You see, the people who designed this virus meant to give it to patients. They wanted to be able to control the cells that had the foreign gene, especially if the gene turned out to be harmful. They wanted to be able to get rid of it. Just in case."

"Sounds like a smart precaution," Bob said.

"It's going to be a standard thing when people start to do so-called gene therapy," Joan explained. "There's always going to be some risk, and you'd like to be able to stop the experiment. For some kinds of treatment, you might not need the genes after a while, and since there's probably always going to be some disadvantage to changing around someone's genes, it'll be better to just get rid of them."

"So the wise doctor put in a suicide pill for these cells?" Bob asked.

Joan laughed. "Pretty much," she agreed, "except we have to give the pill from the outside. What they put in was an enzyme, Sean's favorite kind of protein, called thymidine kinase, not from a human, we have it too, but from the Herpes virus. The human version and the Herpes version both do the same things in real life, they put a phosphate group on one of the building blocks of DNA, it's one of the hooks that holds the chain together. But the enzymes are a little different. The Herpes version is less precise. It can be tricked into putting the phosphate on a drug, called Ganciclovir, and turning it into a poison. The human version of the enzyme isn't fooled and won't make the poison. That's why, for example, they can use this drug to treat Herpes infections. It will kill all of the bone marrow cells that have the Herpes version of this so-called TK gene, and Grimes put it in his virus right next to the gene for the fish hemoglobin." Sean was grinning from ear to ear.

"So we have to give the Chinese this medicine?" Bob wanted to be sure.

"That's right," Joan said, "and I guess that's why we've come to you. The medicine is harmless if we don't give too much, and it wouldn't really do anything to a person who isn't carrying the virus."

"In case you just wanted to drop it in the punch bowl at a reception for the Chinese athletes," Sean interrupted.

"Well, that's right," Joan said. "You wouldn't have to worry about giving a little bit of it to somebody else, and the only harm that this would do to the people who had the fish gene, besides preventing them from making fish hemoglobin, might be to make their red blood cell counts go down a little bit until all their other normal bone marrow cells, which never had the gene put in them, could multiply and make up the difference."

"In the meantime," Sean pointed out, "they might not even run as well as usual."

"That would be like poisoning them," Bob said, "which we wouldn't want to do." He paused, then added, "Usually. But, of course, the only people who would be poisoned would be the people who brought it upon themselves."

"Yes," Joan said, "and it wouldn't really be much of an effect because they'd start making new normal bone marrow cells as soon as the bad ones began disappearing. It would be a continuous process."

"A continuous process?" Bob looked puzzled. "Does that mean we have to get to them early?"

"Yes," Joan answered, "unfortunately. In fact, the red blood cells that they've already made won't be poisoned. They don't do anything except run around holding their hemoglobin. We would want to do this a couple of weeks before the races. Actually, it would be best to do it a month or more before the races."

"And you have this stuff?" Bob asked.

"Yes. Most drugstores carry it. You can give it by mouth, or you can give it intravenously."

Sean interrupted, "It's good that it works by mouth, because I don't think we'll get them to line up for intravenous injections."

"Well, that *is* a relief," Bob said. "Yan Tse is going to have to do this, and I had visions of concocting some story for him about having to vaccinate all of the Chinese athletes before they could enter Australia because they carried Fu-Fu fever or something." They all laughed.

"Do you think Yan Tse would really do this?"

"He's an old friend and a very practical one, Sean, a real survivor. He's been through more in his life than any of us. And at heart he's a businessman. He has assets and liabilities in the favor book." Sean could only shake his head. "Now, young lady," Bob continued, "from you I need the medicine, and I need instructions, like how much do we give one of them if we can be sure of the amount. If we're not sure, how much can we give without killing them. And if we really do have to put it where others could get it by accident, like in the bottled water or the tea or something, how much should we put in so we don't hurt innocent people who happen to drink it."

"You're sure you don't want to just kill them all," Sean said jokingly, but Bob took it seriously.

"No, no. There are friends over there. This may actually help Yan Tse to get rid of those Germans. But when this is done we're going to owe some big debts. I think I know how we can pay them back."

When Sean stepped out for a moment, Bob turned to Joan. "Sean needs a good girl. I know he likes you."

Joan did not take kindly to being referred to as a girl. "He already has a girl," she snapped.

"She's too skinny."

"What!"

Bob Higgum laughed. "At my age you can say anything you want, but I was just teasing. Not about you. About her. Being skinny isn't the reason that she's not the right girl."

Joan was sitting there amazed, trying to think of an answer, when she was saved by Sean's return.

Chapter 47

Two years earlier Lin Pao had looked forward to the Olympics with eager anticipation. His first trip to Germany had been wonderful, and Australia would be a whole new adventure. But ever since Stuttgart the prospect had filled him with dread. Even his hope, baseless as it turned out, that Mickey might accompany the team to Sydney could not dispel his anxiety.

Why couldn't she go? Her situation seemed so strange. In almost a year and a half, he had never known her to leave the training center. She had resisted all his invitations with the excuse that she was needed for the athletes. If this were true, why wouldn't she be needed during the Games? It didn't make sense. Maybe she just didn't like him. But she seemed friendly enough. The jacket from Germany had been a big hit. She often wore it. And by now he knew that there was no boyfriend in America. She had visited Disney World herself while she was a postdoctoral fellow working with a famous cancer specialist who was killed in an auto accident. Strange, if she were training to be a cancer doctor why would she be working here? She never talked about what she did.

He was sick of this matter with Root. Why had he ever stumbled upon him? And Rourke. And now this Robert Higgum and the accusations, and yet Yan Tse clearly believed them. What bothered Lin more than anything was the thought that his own countrymen could have been involved in murdering an American athlete, and, even worse, one who was a doctor. It was unworthy to cheat at sports, and if they had, he hoped that they would be found out and punished. But to commit murder, if this ever became known! He remembered his naive fear that he might be arrested in Germany and turned over to the Americans. But he had done nothing, although to an outsider he might seem to be just another part of the conspiracy, providing information, another cog in the wheel.

He was relieved to feel that he was in Yan Tse's confidence, for Yan Tse had survived any number of upheavals, even the great cultural revolution. *He will survive this too*, Lin Pao thought, *and I shall survive it with him.*

Lin Pao almost never visited his uncle, but finally after thinking about it for weeks, he had decided to do so. His uncle, he knew, spent most of his time in Shanghai, just an overnight train ride away, and the meeting was duly arranged. The sleeping compartments, even in the first-class carriages, were primitive beyond belief. Having seen the railroads in Germany and Japan, Lin considered this train to be an embarrassment for his country. What must visitors think? True, the scenery along the route was spectacular with its terraced rice paddies and the occasional water buffalo and the beautiful mist-shrouded mountains. But it hardly made up for the crowded filthy conditions and the danger at almost every station from thieves and pickpockets who would literally reach into the windows that were left open because of the lack of air conditioning. He slept hardly at all on the train but fortunately was able to find a room where he could wash and make himself presentable before visiting his uncle's office.

Lin Pao's parents were dead. His uncle, Dao Zhen, was the older brother of Lin Pao's mother. Like Yan Tse, he was a survivor, an early Revolutionary and a ranking party member. He had finally found himself on Deng's side, and this had probably cost his sister her life during the last cultural revolution. But when Deng finally came to power, Zhen was poised to reap his rewards, and the rewards were far beyond Lin Pao's wildest dreams. His uncle was a senior member of the Economic Ministry and had managed to have himself placed in charge of the private investments of the Army of the People's Republic, whose main activity now seemed to consist of selling used military equipment in the Middle East and becoming the leading entrepreneur at home. The army even owned Shanghai's largest discotheque. Mindful of the changing tides of power in his native country, Lin Pao's uncle had fortunes stashed in safe havens around the world. He was prepared to flee at a moment's notice, but for now he made the most of his position.

Zhen's luxurious office was in the old British financial district and offered a panoramic view of the river. The setting went with his clothes, finely tailored in Hong Kong, but the man himself seemed so humble. He sprang from his chair with an agility that belied his years and greeted Lin Pao warmly. He felt an obligation to him that went beyond the usual strong familial bonds in China, because of the responsibility he felt for the death of Lin's parents.

"I hear wonderful reports of your work at the Training Center," he said. Lin Pao had no idea that his uncle knew what he was doing. "You know," Zhen continued, seeing the surprise on his nephew's face, "I have eyes and ears everywhere. It must be much more interesting and in the long run much healthier to be in the mountains than to be here in the Economic Ministry. When you are young, you should enjoy yourself and not be concerned about material things. It is enough for me to worry about them."

Lin Pao dutifully expressed his gratitude to his uncle and described his activities and his living conditions.

Zhen listened patiently, and only when Lin fell silent did he say, "You have come to tell me something or to ask my advice, but now you are reluctant to do so. You should not hesitate. I will help if I can."

Lin told him the story of Root and Yan Tse and the Germans, and of his fears of a repetition of the fiasco of the Chinese swimmers, and finally of the accusation of murder of the American. Throughout his recitation his uncle sat almost motionlessly with no hint of expression other than attentiveness. He was framed against the magnificent outside view, but Lin Pao's eyes never left his uncle's face. It was small and round and seemed to be covered with wrinkled tissue paper rather than skin. The crooked nose was a family legend, broken during the long march and never reset, as the story was told. Outwardly he seemed such a gentle and passive person. Those who knew him did not make that mistake.

At the mention of the murder, Zhen began to shake his head slowly. "I have little contact with sports," he said finally. "But even I know of the swimmers. It is imperative that we enlarge our business in the outside world, to Japan and to the West. These episodes hurt us for they play into the hands of our enemies." He spoke softly but there was no mistaking the intensity. "If this can be corrected, quietly, with no publicity, and in a manner that will satisfy those who have been offended, we will all benefit." Then shaking his head again, "Do you know who has committed this murder?"

"No," Lin Pao said.

"You must try to find out and report to me. I have some influence at the training center. You may not know that it was constructed and is managed by the army."

A number of questions flooded into Lin's mind. He asked the one that was most important to him, "Is that the reason I was chosen for my position?"

"No. But it is how I know that you have been doing so well. Now you can be of service to me. Be careful. But be assured there is sufficient power at your call."

"It is an honor to be asked."

"Avoid attention and return to the center as you came, by train. It is abominable, but it is best that you go back the same way. First, have a good dinner and go to the theater. My aide will arrange it and any other form of amusement you like. It will be an acceptable excuse for a healthy young man to have come to the city, and what is more natural than to pay one's respects to an aging uncle." Lin Pao rose and bowed to his uncle, but Zhen came around the desk and shook his hand.

"I am old, but I am very modern."

Lin Pao had just returned to the training center when Yan Tse arrived with a letter from Bob Higgum. "I cannot understand it," he said.

Lin Pao read the letter slowly. "A man is fortunate indeed when he finds a simple, harmless medicine that will solve all of his problems. It must be used in a timely fashion without delay, or the results cannot be guaranteed. If there is some question about the best method of administration, please do not hesitate to call."

"Medicine must be a metaphor for some form of action," Lin said.

"No, no." Yan Tse shook his head. "He sent medicine."

"He sent it?" Lin made no attempt to hide his astonishment.

"Yes, here." He held out to Lin Pao a small bottle filled with white capsules. "He sent twelve bottles." On the outside was a label giving the name of the drug, 'Ganciclovir,' the size of the tablets in milligrams, the chemical formula, the name and address of the manufacturer, an expiration date, and the admonition that it be used only under the direction of a physician.

"It seems like a regular drug." Lin Pao turned a bottle in his hands. "But it could be a substitute."

"The bottles were sealed," Yan Tse assured him. "Of course, it is still possible that they do not contain the original drug."

"But even if that is true, there must be some meaning to his choice of this label."

"We must find out what this drug is used for," Yan Tse said.

"He is inviting you to call him," Lin Pao suggested.

"Yes, but I think only in an emergency."

"May I beg to differ? He would assume that you would not know how to administer the drug. I think he wants you to call. Perhaps with this message and something he might say in person, we would know his true meaning, while it would not be obvious to someone who overheard."

Yan Tse paused, then said, "I think you may be right, my friend."

"Can you speak to him directly," Lin Pao asked, "in the United States?"

"Yes, that can be done now, but I would prefer not to do it from here. We should go to the hotel resort for foreigners. They have a direct dialing system, and I have Bob Higgum's telephone numbers."

"Are those calls monitored?"

"I do not know, but I think not. When the system was first established, all conversations were recorded, but when the foreigners learned of this they refused to do business. I have been told that it has been stopped. But let us assume the worst and take precautions."

"Mr. Higgum must have anticipated this," Lin Pao said, "and have a way of delivering the message."

"I think you are right," Yan Tse agreed. "You will come with me and listen, so that I do not miss any of his words."

Lin Pao knew that Yan Tse spoke English quite well and did not need his help. He had been accorded a great honor, to be so trusted. With it came great responsibility as well.

Two days later they visited the hotel under the guise of hearing a Western rock-and-roll band in one of the several nightclubs. *Why will*

Mickey never come here with me? Lin thought sadly when he heard the music.

They reached Bob Higgum on the second try. After an enthusiastic greeting Bob said, “I was so sorry to hear about your condition, and I know how you must have picked it up, you old devil.” He laughed. “Not slowing down a bit, even at your age. Well, anyone who’s infected should try to take at least six capsules. Three would help, but six would probably cure them. You can mix it in water or tea or punch to hide the taste, although it’s not too bad. And it’s perfectly safe, so if the wrong people should take it by accident, or even your children, although I know you will be cautious, they will not be harmed in any way.” Then he laughed again. “I probably sent you much too much, but there’s enough to treat many people in case some of your close friends have the same problem. It happens that way sometimes.” Yan Tse thanked him profusely.

“Not at all. Not at all, old buck. Get yourself cleared up. We wouldn’t want you spreading any of that in Australia.” Bob laughed boisterously. “I’ll see you in Sydney. Remember it’s always been a sailors’ town. Those Aussies know how to make visitors feel welcome. We’ll have a great old time. I’ll find the best places.” They hung up.

“What can this medicine be used for?” Lin Pao wondered.

“It must be for a venereal disease.” Yan Tse laughed. “What a superb cover Bob Higgum has devised.”

“Do you really think that it is what the label says it is?”

“We can ask him in Sydney,” Yan Tse said, “but for now we know what we must do.”

Chapter 48

On his way back to Colorado, Sean stopped in New York to see Susie for one last time before she left for Australia. They were having dinner in a small French bistro on the Upper East Side. The entrees had arrived.

"I limit myself to eating out about twice a week," Susie said, "and the rest of the time I cook. And I don't go near our favorite place. Too many calories, and I don't have the willpower to say no."

"And the training?" Sean asked. "How is it going?"

"Very well. I'm following Hopwell's program, but I've been over it all with Jim, and he seems to agree."

"You must be getting used to the heat," Sean said. "New York is terrible in August. It will be much cooler in Sydney."

"It should be. I'm hoping for that usual boost you get every fall when the weather suddenly cools."

"If that track is as fast as they say it is, no records will be safe," he said.

"I can't wait to get there and try it. I think I'll be the first of all the competitors to arrive. But I have a nice place to stay, and it'll give me plenty of time to adjust."

"Yes. One week would be enough, and you'll have three, more than three, weeks."

"Mmm, good," Susie said, tasting the wine.

"It's so much easier to remember the names of the French ones compared to the Italians."

"It's not hard to remember this one. I keep thinking this might be the last good bottle of wine before the games. This might be the last good meal in New York before the games. This might be the, well, last of lots of good things before the games." She smiled.

"I know." Sean laughed. "You get into a real countdown mode."

"You mean, you're doing the same thing?" Susie asked.

"Yup."

"I thought maybe you'd get over it when you were an old pro. I worry about everything, as if there's some little mistake I could make that would ruin all of my training, or some little detail that I'm going to overlook."

"The nail for the horseshoe. I used to do exactly the same thing. The secret is to shove all of that into one corner of your mind and use the rest of it to focus and to relax."

"Easier said than done."

"You should be relaxed. You've got those others right where you want them."

"I don't feel that way," she said.

"You've got the world record."

"You have the world record too."

"Always try to imagine how the opposition is feeling. They're so uptight, they're the ones who can waste all their energy worrying about tiny little insignificant details."

"You really think so?" Susie wanted reassurance.

"Sure. They're all trying to second-guess your strategy, wondering how you're training. I bet they're all moving to Sydney early, just because you are. You can have fun misleading them. Ride around on a bicycle. They'll think you're secretly cross-training, and they'll all have bicycles by the next day." He laughed.

"Who would even know if I had a bicycle?"

"Believe me, Susie, there are people who know exactly how you're training."

"No," she said putting down her fork and staring at him in amazement.

"Absolutely. This is serious business."

"So they're *spying* on me."

"Well, in a sense, but I'd hardly call it that."

"It makes me feel as if I'm in a goldfish bowl."

"That's part of the price of being good," Sean said, "and famous."

"So if I invite you back home, people will know?" Susie asked.

"Some people might expect it, but no, I don't think we'll end up in the scandal sheets in the morning. That's for tennis players at

Wimbledon."

Sean tried to persuade Joan to join him for several days in Colorado.

"This might not be the right time," Joan protested.

"Why not? It'll be nice. The mountains are really beautiful. Some of the leaves may even start to turn. It's been colder than usual, but not bad."

"I didn't mean the weather. I just meant perhaps you should be training by yourself."

"You could help me if you'd like. You could drive me back down after I run up my favorite hill, and if you don't want to, well, you could just be there."

Finally she agreed with one condition, "There'll be no serious talk."

"About what?" Sean asked coyly.

"You know about what. About the future."

"So, we'll need a list of censored topics?"

"Yes, and I'll make it up."

"You drive a hard bargain for the privilege of wining and dining you in a beautiful spot."

"You're not going to be wining and dining. You're going to be training."

"Well, we still have to eat and drink."

In Colorado Sean was up each day before dawn. He loaded his water bottles into a rented Jeep and distributed them along the road leading to the mountain peak. Then he drove back down to wake Joan.

"And what am I supposed to do?" she asked on the first day.

"Well, you drive the car up the road to the top of the mountain, get me and drive me back down. That way I save bus fare."

"Why don't you run down? It would be much easier."

"Easier to be injured," Sean said. "No, you drive me down, and then I turn around and run back up again."

"What? You must be mad."

"Not mad, just hungry."

"And here I thought this was a nice cushy career you'd picked for yourself."

"Right. When people see you in the stadium they all wish they could run as you can, but not many of them would want to be with you on the third time up the mountain."

"Or the first or the second," Joan agreed. "And you do this every day?"

"I do it in the morning, and then late in the afternoon, when it starts to cool, I kind of cruise around in the valley. There's an old silver mine. I could show you how to drive over there. I'll run, and you can meet me later with the wine. It's a spectacular spot to watch the sun go down."

"Now that sounds better," Joan said.

The mountain road included multiple switchbacks and occasionally was almost flat, providing a welcome respite. For the first ascent of the morning it was in the shade for most of its length. Sean carried a floppy hat in his hand and wore it only where there was sun. At first the temperature was almost comfortable, but then it rose rapidly even in the shade. Sean drank copious amounts of fluid and poured water over his head. Even so, the heat and the altitude sapped his strength, and during the later runs he arrived at the summit almost unable to stand. Perspiration poured from his body and soaked his running gear. His head band could no longer keep the sweat from his eyes, and they burned from the salt.

"This is a big help," Sean said, reaching for a fresh towel, as Joan drove back down the mountain."

"But you've done enough for today."

"Why? Is the Jeep getting tired?" He laughed. "Ten repeats. On time. So it is written, so it shall be done."

"Yeah, yeah. I know." She threw up her hands.

On the last night they sat, arms around each other, on a rocky ledge overlooking the old mine while the moon rose slowly over the eastern rim of the valley.

"We have to come back," Sean announced. "When I stop running, I want to learn to ski. They would never let me do it now, too risky. Actually it would be a perfect place for a . . ."

"Sean, don't you dare." She pulled away.

"It's funny. Normally we never talk about anything very serious, but as soon as you tell me we can't, then things seem to come up all the time."

"That's the rule for now," she said. "Go to Sydney and do what you have to do."

"You're sure you won't come with me?" Sean asked.

"No. What you have to do down there you have to do by yourself. We've talked about it enough in the past. Now you have to make the decisions."

"I know," he agreed, with resignation.

Joan looked away and said quietly, "And you'll have to decide about Grenville."

"We're still negotiating. There are a few complications."

"What kinds of complications?" Joan asked, trying not to hide her anxiety.

"Well the university isn't used to having their faculty or their coaches appearing ten times a night on television, and they're not quite sure that they want that kind of publicity, not that the university would ever be named. I was very straightforward with them. I told them that if I couldn't do the advertising I was not interested at all. Let's not kid ourselves, there's an enormous amount of money involved. There's so much money, they wouldn't even have to pay me. I could take the money from coaching and give it to the Boys' Club. It's not a Boys' Club, you know. It was just called that originally. It has both sexes."

"Thank goodness." Joan feigned relief. "Actually, I knew that. But I hope you didn't tell them you'd work for nothing. That's not a good bargaining strategy."

"Oh, it's not a bad strategy here," Sean said. "They already know what I earn. One of these ads is worth way more than their President's annual salary."

"That's obscene," Joan said, then paused, "but I think I like it."

"There are some other considerations. For the next few years I'll need time to train and compete and do these other things. That means they'll need another senior coach, one who could handle the administrative things, really a co-chief. It would be good to have a woman, a heptathlete would be perfect, she'd know how to coach all those field events."

"So you're going to have a woman boss?"

"There are so many smart answers to that, I don't know which one to choose. How about, 'don't I already.'"

"I wonder," Joan said, giving him a sly look and squeezing his arm. "So, is this a done deal?"

"Not quite," Sean answered. "I think they'll agree to everything, and then I have to decide. Of course, I told them they have to put it all in writing."

"You did?"

"It's the only way. They did seem a little surprised, as if I didn't trust their good faith, so I just said to them, suppose the director of athletics gets hit by a truck. Who will ever remember what he promised? There's really no answer to that except to write it down."

"That's good."

"Listen, when you go to negotiate with Kerr, you remember it."

"Wait a minute. Who said I was going to negotiate with Kerr? Anyway, I thought I knew how to negotiate. I've been practicing it in my mind long enough, but I must say I didn't think about getting it all in writing. You really think I should demand that?"

"If you're not interested in his position, what difference does it make?" Sean said and drew her closer to him.

They were silent for several minutes. Finally he said, "It's hard to believe the time's come."

"It seems we've been waiting for Sydney ever since we met," Joan answered softly.

"The frustrating thing is having so much of it beyond my control. We have no idea if Yan Tse was successful. We don't even know if he tried."

"Bob seemed sure that he would," Joan said. "Still, it must be hard to hurt the chances of your own athletes. After all he *is* their coach."

"It sounds as if he's the kind of person who would rather lose honestly than win by cheating. And it may be the only way for him to get back control of his team," he added cynically.

"I just hope he was able to do it right away."

"How long do you think it will take to work?"

"The Ganciclovir will kill the infected stem cells almost immediately. The problem will be the red blood cells that have already been made with the fish hemoglobin. They can last well over a month. They'll drop at a rate of about two or three percent a day, once new ones are no longer being made."

"So they could still have some when I run against them."

"Yes, but it'll get better every day that passes. Of course it will take a little time for their normal stem cells to get back up to the usual level, so they may be a little low on normal red cells, and that too will help us."

"But if they found out what was happening they could make it up with a regular transfusion."

"Sure, if they found out. But that would just be normal blood, anyone could do that."

"Do you think they'll find out?"

"Hard to tell." She shrugged. "It will be a gradual change. They would have to be monitoring the levels of Root-effect hemoglobin in their blood, using that electrophoresis technique we talked about. I just can't imagine they would bring that kind of equipment to Australia, so they'll be operating blind the last few weeks just when their performances are starting to decline."

"We hope."

"We hope."

He leaned over and kissed her.

Chapter 49

The teams marched into the stadium in alphabetical order. As they waited in the staging area the nervous tension and the anticipation were at a fever pitch. Participants tried to relax, tried to delay the moment when they would succumb to the awe inspired by the tradition. A gallows-humor mentality prevailed.

"Rourke, you've got to use that staff to defend us," one of Sean's teammates shouted above the clamor. Another: "Do you know we're in the midst of the Iranians, the Iraqis, and the Israelis?" Another: "We're a real buffer state. Maybe we should go and hide behind the Italians. Maybe they'll cook something for us."

Finally it was their turn. They waited in the dark tunnel, and then to the roar of the crowd Sean, carrying the Irish flag, led them into the stadium. So many Irish had emigrated to Australia that the two countries were forever bound together. The Irish team was a great favorite.

Everyone must have seen an opening ceremony, Sean thought. It was perhaps the most widely televised spectacle in sports. This was Sean's second Games, and he hoped for two more. It was an honor to be chosen to lead the team. His emotions were much the same as they had been in Atlanta. He felt the pride of being among the select few and then the humility when he realized that the select few were not so few. True, the massive teams from Germany, Russia, and the United States, and the Australian team, last to enter, dwarfed his own. But it was more than that. It was the realization that so many athletes in so many different sports had spent the same time and effort and had the same hopes and dreams that he had.

The lighting of the fire always brought tears to his eyes. It had when he was a child, watching the ceremony on television, it had at the last Olympics, and it did again. *Perhaps because I'm a runner.* The thought of the torch being carried mainly on foot all the way from Greece struck a personal note.

During the administration of the oath Sean thought of Susie and wondered what was going through her mind. *How must she feel about herself?* She was undetectable in the midst of the vast American team.

In Grenville, Joan was up early to watch. She desperately wanted to be there. She had that feeling of having been involved in the preparations for the party and then not having been invited. "That's silly," she said aloud. "I was invited, but it's better that I'm not there. Maybe there'll be another chance sometime, but then, maybe there won't."

By agreement, Susie and Sean saw little of each other during the ensuing week. Their preliminary heats were scheduled for Thursday, and by chance they followed immediately after one another, the women's 5K first and then the men's 10K. He had talked to her by phone, and they had lunched together on Tuesday.

"Serious eating starts today," Sean had said, sitting before a large bowl of pasta, "and I haven't had a drink in more than a week."

"I have occasionally," Susie admitted.

"I'm sure it doesn't matter. It's just my habit." They talked about relaxing and mundane things like how to be there on time for the race.

"Remember that time when the American slept through," Sean reminded her.

Susie nodded. "Every competitor everywhere must remember that scene, with that awful commentator asking him over and over again how he felt."

Neither of them was using the official housing. Years ago there had been pressure to have everyone stay in the Olympic village, but that was largely forgotten now in the days of the million-dollar athletes, some of whom even came with their own bodyguards. *I guess some of the spirit has been lost,* Sean thought. But he certainly had no intention of staying in a dormitory and running the risk of being disturbed by someone celebrating an earlier victory.

Sean had no contact with the Chinese. Their designated practice times on the track were widely separated, and neither he nor Yan Tse nor Lin Pao had attempted to establish contact. Bob Higgum had reported a thumbs-up sign from Tse, but as he warned Sean, "who knows whether they really managed to do it, or whether it worked. Better to assume that they still have their fancy fish blood. One way or the other, this isn't going to be easy."

Sean and Bob had been over the list of runners they considered to be contenders so many times that he felt he knew them as if they were family. Kipu, Alvila, and Rossi, all of whom he had beaten in the World championships were the best. Sandri from Morocco, who had missed the entire season with an injury, would have been in that group based on past performance, but now he was an unknown. The rumors were that he had returned to his previous form. Matsu was the new young Kenyan sensation. "Is there no end to them?" Sean asked himself. "How many of them will be in the marathon, at the front of the pack?" Hans Schneider was improving constantly. Losing to the Chinese at Stuttgart had seemed to inspire him. Dryx was back again, suddenly rejuvenated. A horrifying thought flashed through Sean's mind: *Suppose some of these others have the blood.* He dismissed it. But then, of course, there were the Chinese. Dak and Han.

"We'll see how they all look in the trials," Bob said. "But don't worry. You're the best. You're top dog until someone knocks you off. You have the record. The others all know that, and a good many of them know they can't beat you. They don't know what to make of the Chinese or whether the Chinese can beat you. They're all waiting for a showdown. Their best hope is that you'll run yourselves out of it, and they'll pick up the pieces."

"You really believe that's what they're thinking?"

"Almost all of them. All the smart ones," Bob said and laughed, "because that's the way I'd be thinking. The Kenyans won't. They feel they can beat anyone."

The assignments for the trials were released on Wednesday. Sean stared at the list. He had drawn Alvila and no one else that he recognized.

"Do you really think these are picked at random?" he asked Bob.

"Supposed to be."

"Well, I can't complain about my luck. The two of us should be in the finals."

"The top two from each race will be in the finals, but, as you know, they'll pick six more based on time. You know what that means. Those others in your race are thinking they have to make it on their time, because they don't expect to beat you or Pedro. I've seen favorites lose in situations like that, usually because they took it easy and then got caught in the end. There's to be no loafing. You and Alvila go out there and destroy them." Bob was speaking with uncommon vehemence.

"I almost wish I'd drawn one of the Chinese."

"You'll get your chance soon enough. And this way maybe we'll learn something useful."

"Probably not about Dak. He's in with Rossi and no one else. They'll just walk."

"They could get too cute, just like you and Alvila," Bob cautioned.

"Not Rossi."

"No, not likely. We'll learn more from Han. He's in with Dryx and Schneider. Tough luck. One of them is not going to make it, unless they all run damn good times."

"It will be interesting to see what Han does," Sean said. "I wonder if now that they're used to the blood, they'll drop that strategy of trying to run at the same speed throughout the race." He had almost forgotten "our little remedy" as Bob called it.

Sean turned eagerly to the women's list. Susie's heat had a little more balance. The other good runner was Klara Heinz whom Susie had beaten for her indoor record in London. Susie would be the clear favorite, in fact, she would be the favorite throughout. But there were others in the heat with a chance of placing, and Klara's best strategy, Sean felt, would be to ignore Susie and concentrate on beating them. *We're going to learn some things from this race too,* Sean thought, *including what Susie's really made of.*

Thursday morning was a runner's dream, temperature still in the sixties at race time with low humidity. "My official advice is not to watch Susie's heat," Bob Higgum told Sean. "But I know you will. Don't get too excited and don't worry about her. Jim gets paid to do that. You know he'll do a good job."

"I know."

Joan Danner was definitely prepared to watch Susie. The race was in the early evening Grenville time. Sean's race would be late at night. Joan had bought "goodies" from the local delicatessen and a bottle of wine with a price tag she would have considered obscene eight months earlier. For a small premium she had a TV cable service that would provide every single track and field event, preliminaries and finals, and she had a video tape recorder. She checked and rechecked everything. "I can run anything in a laboratory," she said to the set, "but I can never program one of these damn tape recorders. Anyway, this one just needs to be turned on."

Since there was still almost an hour before Susie's race, she decided to go for a walk. The campus was almost deserted. The undergraduates had not yet returned, and the summer school had been over for several weeks. As she strolled under the tall trees in the courtyards surrounded by old Gothic buildings, she thought of how much she loved the school. Somehow its being deserted seemed to intensify the relationship. The transient occupants, the students, were fickle suitors. At times like this it seemed to belong to her alone. It was her whole life, almost. How could she ever leave it? What would she be willing to do to stay? And where did Sean fit into her plans?

The weather was comfortably warm and dry. Sydney should be the same. The thought of Sean running the hills in Colorado reassured her, but then maybe the competition was all doing that. Maybe they were running bigger hills, and maybe no one was there to distract them. "That's crap," she said to herself. She wandered farther away from the apartment. Was she tempting fate? Did she not want to make it back in time? It was Susie's race she would miss. There wasn't any question about getting back for Sean. Finally, she turned around. *I wonder what he's going to do. Can he just let her win and not say anything, and if he does, will he regret it forever*?

Joan sprinted up the stairs to her apartment and switched on the television. The runners were warming up for the second heat. *Just in time*, she thought. It was easy to spot Susie in the silver uniform with USA across the front. She was as tall as most of the other women, and while some were thin, she was certainly the thinnest of all. For the first time Joan noticed how young she looked, like a young girl among the women. She just didn't know how to feel about Susie. "I wouldn't have known how to feel even if she hadn't used the hemoglobin," she said to herself. "I guess I would have thought she was a hero, regardless of her relationship with Sean. Now I should despise her for cheating." But it was difficult to do while watching her warm up on the track.

It would be twelve laps plus a little, the announcer was explaining. Then he was talking about Susie. "She was a promising runner at Grenville in Connecticut, and then went off to train with the great Paul Hopwell in England. Under his tutelage she suddenly *blossomed.* There's no other word for it," he emphasized, "into America's finest middle distance runner in years." Joan could hardly stand it. "She set the world record in the Olympic trials and is a heavy favorite for the gold medal."

God, thought Joan, *wait until Jim McBride hears that, and the Rhodes Committee. If this is how accurate the press is in everything, you wonder why we even bother to listen to them.* The announcer said a few words about a German runner, who seemed to be the co-favorite. Not really the co-favorite, but first and second places were the same. They both went on to the finals.

The runners were in position. The gun went off. Someone, an Italian Joan thought the announcer had said, sprinted into the lead. Susie followed a few yards behind, and together the two of them began slowly to open a lead over the remaining pack. *They seemed much too bunched up,* Joan thought. *Why don't they spread out where they'll have lots of room?* But they didn't seem to listen to her.

The announcer spoke with great authority, although based on what he had said before Joan wondered whether there was any truth to what he was saying. The Italian, he said, couldn't stay with the others and certainly wouldn't make it to the finals. The pack didn't want to chase Susie because they had no hope of catching her, they were all staying with the German, Heinz, whom they were hoping to beat for second place. And Heinz, for her part, was showing great discipline in not going after Susie. According to the announcer, Heinz had confidence in her kick, although what kicking had to do with running Joan was not sure. It seemed that she would be satisfied to finish second with a slow time, which would save her strength for the finals.

It all sounds reasonable, Joan admitted, *but how do I know it isn't just a lot of bull*? Slowly Susie began to draw even with the Italian. The announcer described it in painstaking detail and in self-congratulatory tones. "We can all see it!" Joan shouted at the television set. "Do you think we're blind? This is television, not radio."

Joan knew the race took only about fifteen minutes, but it seemed to go on forever. *Certainly nothing like those ten-second and twenty-second dashes*. She was trying not to cheer, not knowing whether she wanted Susie to win or not. *If she just lost right now, that would probably solve this whole problem*. But did she want the whole problem solved like that?

The leaders had gone more than two miles. The pack had stayed the same distance behind Susie. She certainly wasn't pulling away from the rest of them. "She's saving herself," assured the announcer. "It's a comfortable lead. There's no reason at all why she should wear herself out while Heinz cruises to second."

But to Joan's eye the pack was drawing a little closer. *It must be an optical illusion*, she thought. There were now three laps to go, the announcer informed them. Joan was sure that the pack was getting closer.

"She's maintaining her comfortable lead," the announcer insisted, "running smoothly and easily. Such a great champion."

The pack was beginning to break up. Joan wished she had paid attention earlier so that she could identify this Heinz woman they kept talking about. What were Germany's colors anyway? There were two laps to go, and the announcer was identifying Klara Heinz. By then, Joan had already figured out who she was, clearly in the front of what remained of the pack, while many straggled out behind. There were at least two who were right behind Heinz.

"Now they're gaining on Fredricks," the announcer informed his audience as if he had just discovered it.

"We knew that two laps ago, you idiot!" Joan shouted at the television set. In fact, they were gaining more rapidly.

"When she sees them, she'll just have to open it up a little," the announcer reassured.

It seemed to Joan that if Susie didn't see them they were all going to pass her. They entered the last lap. The announcer was able to explain for the ignorant audience that the two other runners, whose names or countries apparently were not worth knowing, were pushing Klara Heinz harder than she had expected, thus forcing her to run faster. The wily Fredricks, no doubt, was pleased by this because Heinz would have to expend almost as much energy as she had.

"The wily Fredricks may lose," Joan said to the set.

The announcer spoke with growing excitement. "Heinz is in her kick. She's in her kick."

Joan stared at the screen. Heinz just seemed to be running a little faster. She certainly was beginning to pull away from one of the pursuers, but the other was making a game try. Susie had picked up the pace but not as much as the others. It was getting really close.

"Where the hell is that damn finish line?" Joan cried, crouching in front of the television set. Now she could see it. The lead runners formed almost a single group. Everyone was kicking, if that was the right word. Susie was not ahead. Joan stared in disbelief. Heinz clearly had won, but who was second?

The announcer assured everyone that it was Fredricks, and that it was just bad luck, but of no significance whatever, that she had not won. Joan was not so sanguine. Heinz's name was first on the scoreboard, but the other names had not yet appeared. Finally, after what seemed an eternity, Susie's name appeared second. She and the third-place finisher, who turned out to be a woman from Czechoslovakia, had almost identical times. Just hundredths of a second separated them. Joan found that she was perspiring as if she had run the race herself.

"Jesus Christ, Susie," she said, again to the television set, "that's too close. That's just too damn close. We'll all have heart attacks." She stood up. Did she want to watch any more of the women's heats? She turned back to the television set. "Damn it, Sean. Don't you do anything like that."

Sean had watched the race on a closed circuit TV without the benefit of the irritating announcer. He smiled thinking of Bob's advice not to get too excited. He knew at once that Susie was second, and he recognized the significance of the times. Third place, the Czech woman, would probably not get a wild card into the finals. *Klara Heinz's strategy was for a slow race, but that's cutting it a lit-*

tle too close, thought Sean. But he could not have been happier with the result. "Okay, Alvila," he said to himself, "ready when you are. Let's go put on our little show." But he still had some time. He lay down for a nap on one of the mats in the training room and surprisingly fell sound asleep.

Bob Higgum shook him. "I was kidding when I told you not to get over excited during that race, but you're too relaxed."

"Ah," Sean said, stretching, "it's the result of a clear conscience and all those runs up Silver Mine peak." He smiled at Bob, who smiled back.

"You don't need any advice for this one. Don't try to set any world records. This is just a heat."

Joan sat in front of the television set. "I guess there are some things you can learn from this announcer," she had to admit. He was talking about the men's 10K, and as the favorite, Sean was frequently mentioned. The data were more accurate this time: Sean was the reigning world champion, and under most unlikely conditions, he had broken the world record just two months before. His coach, the famous Bob Higgum, expected to retire shortly, had carefully groomed him since his undergraduate days at St. Vincent. The only uncertainties were his decision to enter the marathon as well—how could Higgum have let him do it—and the sudden emergence of two Chinese runners, one of whom had set a wind-aided world record. The announcer went on to describe some of the other highly ranked runners. Difficult as it was for him to admit, the Americans were not strong candidates for medals in this event.

Joan had bought French bread, pate with real truffles, a slice of Brie and raspberries. She had opened her wine a proper one hour in advance and began to eat during the first 10K heat. It too contained two co-favorites, Matsu, the younger Kenyan, and Sandri, a Moroccan who apparently was returning after a series of injuries and, to the announcer's considerable pleasure, had demonstrated his old form. The two of them ran almost side by side from start to finish and won by a comfortable margin. But to Joan's surprise they completely ignored each other after the race, going off in opposite directions to retrieve their gear without even bothering to shake hands. *I guess there's no rule that they have to like each other, but at least they could be polite. Maybe they don't feel this was even a race. Maybe it was just like practice.*

The announcer assured his audience that this was the way favorites should perform. Runners of their quality should not be playing games in the heats. He predicted the same for the upcoming race.

The pay channel guaranteed complete coverage without advertisements. Joan began to realize what a pleasure that was, for she could even see the runners warming up on the track. There was Sean jogging and stretching, then suddenly running out half a lap. Then he was chatting with a slight, dark-haired runner. It had to be Alvila. He was solemn faced, almost expressionless. "You're supposed to be a fiery, hot-tempered Hispanic," she said to the television set, laughing. Sean was smiling. He shook hands with some of the others.

Finally the group gathered at the starting line. To Joan it resembled nothing so much as a mob waiting to rush into a theater for the unreserved seats. The gun sounded and the mass moved forward, many punching the buttons on their runners' watches. "It's to record their own splits," Sean had explained when she asked him whether they didn't believe the official timer. Two runners surged to the front, but Alvila and Sean were both back in the pack. No one seemed concerned with the leaders. Joan was beginning to feel more comfortable with the various strategies. She no longer worried that they could never be caught and would somehow sneak away unnoticed to win.

Sean had laughed when she had told him of her concerns. "I start slowly," he said, "and try to win it in the middle. Too many runners ignore the middle of the race. It's all a matter of concentration, of always doing exactly what you want."

Joan noticed that Sean was running slightly to the outside of the pack. *He's smart. It's too crowded inside. All that jostling and the missteps must cancel out the slightly shorter distance.*

Alvila obviously was also content with his position until well into the third mile. Then he too worked his way to the outside and came up on Sean's shoulder. They both set off after the leaders. Joan's resolve not to worry had long since disappeared. "Watch him, watch him!" she shouted at the screen as the Mexican drew near. But she allowed herself to be reassured by the announcer as the two of them, running almost as one, reeled in the others. By the fifth mile they were comfortably ahead and effortlessly increasing the lead.

"Beautiful, just beautiful," intoned the voice. Joan was inclined to agree. "They'll pull up now and just jog it out," the voice predicted. But they both kept going with Sean finally pulling ahead in the last two hundred yards.

Joan was out of her chair cheering, "Thank God not another one like Susie's."

"Was good, was good," Alvila gasped as he and Sean embraced.

"I just wanted to win," Sean said almost apologetically.

"I would let you today," Alvila said laughing, "but this good way . . . get ready . . . good way."

"And now our moment has come," Schultz proclaimed to the room in a boisterous voice. But Jurgen seemed more pensive. The "honored guest" dining room at the training center in the Wuyi mountains had been turned into a beer garden, festooned with German flags and gold and black bunting. The beer had been flowing freely for several hours. The technicians had managed to pirate the Japanese satellite feed of the trials. They stared at a silent television set. The excited announcer was more than they could stand, even after several years of practice in blotting out foreign gibberish.

"It is Han we will see first," Jurgen announced.

"And look, there is Rourke in the infield to observe. His enjoyment is about to end!" Schultz added.

On the screen Joan saw the next mob gather. The announcer had become much more enthusiastic. "At last a race that means something," he proclaimed.

"Some of us thought the last race meant something too," she answered back.

He explained yet again the significance of the results. It was a rerun of the Stuttgart race of the preceding October when two unknown Chinese runners had suddenly emerged on the international scene. Since then, Han had a wind-assisted world record to his credit. But Dryx had apparently recovered from a series of nagging minor injuries, and Schneider, embarrassed at home, was running better than ever. This would be Han's first important race without his teammates. Would he be comfortable with the more sophisticated strategy of the seasoned international veterans?

How he goes on, she thought, *and he just doesn't know. But how could he?*

There was only one Asian in the field, and Joan stared at him intently. Was he full of fish hemoglobin? What was that funny thing Sean used to see? Could she recognize it on the screen? But hadn't Sean said you couldn't tell anymore, not even Higgum, now that the runners were used to it?

Han stood by himself ignored by the other runners.

"If this were science fiction, I would have some magic spectrometer ray to see the hemoglobin in you," she told him through the screen. "Oh, I can't stand it." She got up and began to pace about the room.

Finally the gun sounded. Then came the usual confusion which finally after several laps settled into a pattern. Schneider was near the front with two others. Han was in the middle of the first pack. Dryx as usual, even in this otherwise weak field, had managed to be near the back. Joan caught occasional glimpses of Sean intently studying Han. *He's not leading*, she thought hopefully, *but maybe he's just doing what Sean always does.*

Dryx began to pass the backmarkers. "It's turning into a strategic race," the commentator advised his audience. At four miles the leaders began to widen the gap. That was too much for Han, who must have realized he was playing a dangerous game. He rather clumsily began to edge past runners who were bunched ahead of him. No one felt inclined to get out of his way, although eventually they had to yield.

Finally Han had clear running room, but by then Dryx had edged up along the outside and settled in about three yards behind. Did Han even know he was there? The two of them gained steadily on the lead runners. Joan stared at Dryx in disbelief. She had seen him earlier in the closeups and he had seemed to almost stumble along. Suddenly he had been transformed into a gazelle. So graceful. "He's hitting his stride," the announcer said. Joan noted that he didn't seem surprised.

The pack couldn't take this for long and began to accelerate en mass, leaving the usual stragglers behind. Two had already dropped out, Joan noticed. Schneider went for the lead. There was one mile to go.

Han was straining, but he and Dryx were gaining. With two laps to go they trailed Schneider by twenty yards. The others had been left behind.

"Third place could advance on the basis of time." The announcer was enjoying himself. "But who can be sure? Who can take the chance?"

Schneider was beginning to fade. Han was in a full kick. Dryx was still on his shoulder, looking much more relaxed. They swept past the German and finished in that order.

Joan stared at the set in stunned silence. She had failed. It hadn't worked. But the announcer was more reassuring. He was saying the things she wanted to hear. Yes, Han was first, but Dryx had looked the strongest. Had Han used too much to gain his victory? And Schneider and Dryx weren't exactly of the quality of Alvila and Rourke, not to mention Rossi, who had Dak in the next heat. The others would be delighted that it had been such a hard race.

"Why does Tse insist on these simple strategies?" Jurgen asked the room, his arms thrown up in resignation and disgust. "I have given him explicit instructions. He knows these are no ordinary runners. Must I coach them myself?"

"But they never listen to us, only to Tse," Schultz answered.

"Han might have lost! He should simply run from the front. Of course Tse could not permit that. Then the whole world would know that we don't need him," Jurgen went on bitterly.

Joan looked at the clock. "Ten minutes 'til the next heat. I've got to get out of here. I can't stand waiting, and I can't stand not knowing whether the Ganciclovir worked. There's time to go once around the block."

She returned just in time for the last heat. Again there was only one Asian runner, and by now she recognized the uniform. *That must be Dak. And the short one with the curly black hair must be Rossi. Those are the Italian colors. He's cute.*

For the announcer, there were only two men in the race. "The biggest mismatch of the trials," he called it. He was correct.

"You're not much of a salesman," Joan told him. "No wonder you're not on the regular network. You need 'hyperbole' lessons."

Rossi and Dak started comfortably but soon found themselves in the lead. That they would be first and second had been decided long before the four-mile mark when Rossi began a series of spurts, edging ahead and then falling behind.

"He's baiting him," the announcer pointed out. Sure enough, Dak would respond each time. Still, the pace was slow. Finally Rossi seemed to tire of the game and fell in behind. Another Chinese victory. Joan was beside herself.

"I wish I trusted you more," she told the announcer, as he explained that the order was not important. He seemed to like Rossi, and he obviously didn't like the Chinese. "I hope that isn't influencing your conclusions."

Nothing was ever mentioned of the possibility that the Chinese might be cheating. *I guess that just isn't done in public. Probably be sued*, she thought.

The beer garden was noticeably more relaxed.

"Now please tell me why Han could not just do it the same way?" Jurgen asked no one in particular.

"Dak was always smarter," one of the technicians answered.

"Huh. Who could notice? And why do they have to be smart just to follow orders?"

Chapter 50

It was early Friday evening, and Sean was sitting in front of the television set in his rented house eating pasta and watching the Games. The telephone rang. It was Susie.

"I have to see you right now." She sounded anxious and upset. He could hardly hear her.

"But your race is tomorrow."

"I'm not going to run," she said. "I have to see you right now. It can't wait."

"Do you want me to come over, or shall we meet somewhere?"

"I'll come over there. I just wanted to be sure you were in," she said. "I'll be there right away."

Sean hung up the phone and sat thinking. He had known there had to be a confrontation, be he had kept putting it off. He felt like a coward, but perhaps his patience had been the best strategy. A half hour later Susie appeared at the door looking awful. She had obviously been crying. He put his arms around her to comfort her. It was very hard not to when he saw her.

"No, no," she said, "you won't want to do that. I'm going to sit over here." She collapsed into an easy chair. "You sit over there." She pointed to a couch on the opposite side of the room.

"What's this about not running?" Sean asked. He had to say something.

"I'll get to that," she said. "I have something to tell you. It's going to make you hate me, but I have to tell you anyway." She looked totally crestfallen and was having trouble speaking. "The Grimes thing. The blood. I don't know how far you've gotten with it." Sean had stopped giving her progress reports. He nodded. "I know what it is, and I'm using it." He couldn't pretend to be surprised, but she assumed that his was a stunned silence. "I've known about it, and I've been cheating." She covered her face with her hands.

"But how could you?" he asked.

"Because I'm weak," she said, "and because I'm dishonest." She pulled a large pile of tissues from her pocket, chose one, and began wiping her eyes.

"I mean, how could you even know about it?"

"I found out. I've known for months, and I never told you, even though I knew how hard you were working on it. Even when you were telling me what you were doing. Even though I knew someone might use it to beat you, to ruin all your dreams."

"But how could you have figured it out when I couldn't? I mean, not that I should have been able to, but all those scientists." She was shaking her head, unable to answer. He just waited.

"I have a friend," she said at last, "Ted Whitfield, from Grenville, but before that. He's a family friend. I've known him forever." She paused and sniffled. "He worked in Grimes's lab, a volunteer, an undergraduate. Now he's in medical school, Stanford. He knew all about it. More than he was supposed to, I guess. He seemed to know everything."

"But when did you find this out?"

"By chance. It was just dumb luck. Dumb bad luck," she said and started to cry again. He waited. "When I went to Maine, before I went to England, he was there. He had a month before starting a clerkship, and I remembered that he had worked with Grimes, and I asked him. I thought I was doing something that might help you."

"And he just told you?"

"At first he didn't," she said, "but I finally managed to get the whole story." Sean decided he didn't want to know how. "He told me about the fish and the blood and the genes and even a virus."

"And you've known this for more than a year, since that June?" Now Sean was surprised.

"Yes, I did, and I never told you. I never told anyone." She was crying again.

Sean was still puzzled. "But even then, how could you have . . . how could you have made those things yourself? You don't know how to do that. Did you hire someone?" he asked, thinking of Joan's comment.

She shook her head. "It was right there. Right there."

"Where?" Sean asked. Every sentence was interrupted by sobbing.

"He had it, the blood and the virus."

"What!" Sean was amazed.

"He had stolen some of it."

Sean must have looked even more amazed.

"Not like that, not from Grimes. I mean, not while Grimes was alive." Sean was still staring at her. "When Grimes was killed, Ted was going back there anyway, on break. He really liked Grimes, and he went to the memorial service. It was strange. The whole lab had disappeared. There was an Australian who had left, and the woman who had taught him the most, Ann Somebody, was gone too. The only person still there was a Chinese woman, and he had never trusted her. He still had the key, so he just let himself into the laboratory one night. There were bags of the hemoglobin solution all ready to use, and he took a few of them. And the virus. It was in vials. It had been made by some company in California. He took some of that too."

"But why? What on earth was he going to do with it?"

"Oh, don't think, I mean, he would never steal it. I mean, he did steal it, but not to steal." She could see Sean's disbelief. "Ted's the nicest person in the world and totally honest. He was afraid that the Chinese woman would steal it."

"So he did it himself?"

"He had this vague feeling that if he preserved some of the samples he could always prove that it was Grimes's idea. You know, if that woman ever claimed to have invented it herself." Sean was shaking his head in amazement. He felt like laughing, but he didn't know why. "Look, he never did anything with it," she continued, anxious to exonerate her friend.

"Where did he put them? Don't they have to be stored properly?"

"Ted put them on ice and then took them to Maine. They were there when I was there. He wouldn't tell me where, but they weren't hard to find later. His grandfather, old Whit, still owned the estate. He was getting a little senile and never trusted the rest of the world anyway. We always used to laugh at him when we were children. He had bomb shelters, enough food stored to last for a decade, generators, and a huge freezer. It was a perfect place to hide them. No one would ever have looked. No one would have known about it except me, of course. I remembered it all from when we were children."

"So you took it from him?" Sean asked. "Didn't he ever find out?"

"I went back after they closed the compound. The freezers run all year. I didn't have any trouble finding the stuff. I had arranged to keep it cold and to take it back with me to England. Then I just turned off the freezer. I knew that when the help came to open the compound the next summer, they'd discover it and just throw everything out." She stopped, then almost smiled. "God, I hate to think what that freezer must have smelled like. Anyway, Ted would have assumed that it was thrown out with all the rotten food. He must know by now, but he's never mentioned it. He wouldn't have any reason to be suspicious. It never even occurred to me that he might figure it out, since he wouldn't have known that this thing had anything to do with running."

Now Sean really was amazed. "But why would you do it? You didn't even care about running. And this stuff. How did you know it was even safe? How do you know *now* that it's safe?"

"Well, I'm still here," she said. "I don't know why I did it. I've asked myself over and over again. There are so many reasons. Who knows which one? All of them, I guess. I was going to stop competing, it just didn't seem to matter that much to me. But that last race, for Grenville, when I lost, I felt I'd let everyone down, Jim, and the team, and you. I could never tell you that. But after the race in Central Park, I guess I just wanted to impress you. That was really silly. You're so much better than I am."

Sean shook his head.

"Then that last race for Grenville. I'd never trained right. I just wanted to publish that article. It was my choice. I know it. I thought it was more important to me than running. I thought I could make those choices. And the woman who beat me, she caught me from behind, you know. I must have beaten her three times before. When she went by, she said something racial and about my being rich. 'A rich . . .' Well, I won't repeat it. I thought about that every minute for two weeks. I don't know why. I'll never see her again. She could never even hope to compete at this level. But I guess in some sense every race is important. If winning is important, you want to win everything. I never thought it meant that much to me. Well, maybe I did, but I thought I had it under control, but I didn't. It was the idea of winning that mattered. Not just winning, but beating everyone." Her whole affect had changed. For an instant she looked almost triumphant. Sean was staring at her. He knew exactly how she felt.

"It's hard to get over it when you've been bitten," he said softly.

"I tried to justify it by remembering what you said to me. How I would be so much more effective in arguing for my environmental causes if I were a well-known sports figure, and there's some truth in that. It had some appeal. But it really wasn't the main reason." She had crashed again.

"Even when you had the stuff, the blood and the virus, how did you know how to use it. How were you able to do it?" Sean asked.

"Well, I knew what Ted had told me, and in England I found a laboratory technician from a blood bank. He was willing to do it, no questions asked, for enough money." Sean shook his head. So Joan had been right, he thought.

"The hemoglobin was packaged in units," she continued. "We just assumed one unit couldn't hurt, so that's what we used."

"You could have been killed."

"It was supposed to be safe." She shrugged. "They'd given it to animals, and I knew from you that Grimes had taken it. I was going to do it only once, like Grimes, I guess. But it worked." She smiled ruefully. "It worked unbelievably well."

"What was it like?" Sean asked eagerly. He had spent a great deal of time over the preceding months imagining how it would feel.

"It was like, well, like you could never get out of breath. Like you didn't have to breathe hard. You could just run until your muscles got so tired you finally had to stop." It was just as Sean had expected, and it explained the pattern of running that he had learned to recognize.

"I know. I know," he said.

"What do you mean, you know?" she asked, frowning.

"Oh, I'll tell you later."

"Well, once I'd done it, I just had to do it again. But, of course, eventually it ran out. We used all the hemoglobin. Each dose lasted only for a day, for a single race. Then it came out in my urine. It would be red for a day and a half. You could just barely see it on the third day. I guess that's one thing that made me feel safe. It seemed to go away with no lasting effects. I used it in London," she said. "I planned it in advance. I didn't know that you were going to be there, and then I didn't want you to come to the race in case something went wrong."

"Aside from the risk of taking the stuff," Sean told her, "you and your friend could have been in danger just by knowing about it."

"What kind of danger?"

"We know now that Grimes was killed by the people who stole the secret." She gasped. "And probably one of his co-workers was too. Your friend escaped only because they couldn't find him, or they didn't know about him, or it never occurred to them that he really knew what the project was about."

She seemed visibly shaken. "I was a fool," she said simply.

"And the virus?" Sean continued. "You really gave yourself the virus?" She nodded. "You really were willing to change your genes? How could you do that to yourself?"

"I don't know," she said, bursting into tears again. "I don't know. I couldn't not have it. It's like, like all those football players who can't stop taking steroids, even though they know it will give them liver cancer. Even though they see themselves changing. They have to have it. Just one more time, for just one more race."

"And you knew how to use it too?"

"It was easy," she said. Did he detect a note of pride in her voice? "You put it in these cells called bone marrow stem cells. I won't try to explain to you what they do, I'm sure you've never even heard of them, but you can get them right out of your blood. They do it for the chemotherapy patients. This technician, he knew how to do it. He took blood from me, and he got the cells out. All you have to do is put the virus with them for a while and then give them back to yourself. Just inject them into your bloodstream, into a vein. It's like, like nothing. You'd never even know you'd done anything. And then gradually, over about a month or two in the spring, I got better and better. It was just like when I took the blood."

She paused and took a deep breath. "But now I can't go through with it. This is just too much. I stood there Friday night, in the opening ceremony, watching the flame, taking the oath, and I knew I didn't deserve to be there. I could hardly bring myself to run in the preliminary heats. It would have been better if I'd lost. I finally decided today that I'm not going to run."

"But you're in the finals."

"I'll just make up some excuse. I'll tell them I'm sick. That's the least I can do. The world record, well I'm just going to have to admit I cheated. I don't know how I can face up to it, but I have to."

"No," Sean said vehemently. She looked up, startled. "You can never do that. They'd blame Jim, or Paul Hopwell."

"But they didn't have anything to do with it."

"I know, but no one would ever believe it."

"I could tell them," she pleaded.

"They still wouldn't believe it. They'd never believe that you could have done this yourself. No matter what any official investigation showed, there would always be a cloud over their heads. You can't do that to them."

"What can I do, then?" she asked.

"The only thing that you could ever do would be to break that record yourself, honestly."

"But I can't do that," she protested.

"Yes, you can. You're five years away from your prime. Middle distance runners aren't created in one year. Everyone who knows you thinks you're the greatest natural runner they've ever seen. You can do it. It's just going to take all the same hard work it took all the rest of us, and it's the only way you can clear your conscience without incriminating anyone else."

"But, Sean," she tried to explain, "I have these genes in me forever. I'll never be able to run fairly again, and when I think of that, all of a sudden the running becomes that much more important, now that I know I can never do it again."

"You're wrong about that."

"What do you mean, I'm wrong?"

"Now it's my turn to confess," he said. She stared at him.

"You don't have the virus in you anymore. It was there when you set the record. I know that. But it's not there now."

"How do you know that? You can't know that."

"Yes, I can. I got rid of it."

"What?" she said, squirming in her chair.

"Now it's your chance to hate me," he said. "But if you could deceive me all that time, I guess I could deceive you."

"What are you talking about?"

"We were slow," he said, "but we got there. Actually, you helped us to get there. I had seen the red urine from Grimes, and I knew there were Chinese runners with red urine, and then I saw your red urine."

"How?" she started.

"Never mind," he said. "But I could also tell just by watching you run. Remember, I was the first one to see Grimes run. I could pick out every one of you who was using it."

"But how?"

"Because it was just like you said. You didn't breathe hard enough. None of you did." She just looked dumbfounded. "Before that, we didn't even know it was blood. But then we, or actually someone else who was convinced that you were cheating, thought of it. It all came together." She was staring at him, wide-eyed. "But then you all, all of you, stopped having red urine."

"How did you know?"

"We had people monitoring your urine," he answered.

Suddenly she was furious. "Behind my back?"

"What were you doing behind *my* back?" he reminded her. "When the red urine stopped, we figured out about the gene transplants." Now she was just staring at the floor with a look of total defeat on her face. "Then this same person figured out what to do about it. Grimes or one of his co-workers, a woman named Ann Grossman, whom we think was probably killed too, had included a little surprise in their virus." She looked up at Sean again. "They made it susceptible to a poison, a drug, that would be totally harmless but would kill the virus and all the cells it had infected."

"You mean I can get rid of it," she said almost hopefully.

"It's already gone. I gave you the medicine."

"But when? How?"

"At dinner, in New York, on my way to Colorado."

"You—you poisoned me. And then you went to bed with me." She said it quietly but forcefully. "You knew all this, and you went to bed with me."

Sean felt sorry for her, but it didn't prevent him from wanting to hurt her. "Well, I gave it to you in an '82 Margaux." He couldn't help himself. He had to laugh. "I wanted to be sure that you'd finish it all. Of course, I took half of it myself, and besides, it made sure that we wouldn't give each other Herpes."

"What?"

"It isn't really poison. It's a standard medicine that people use to treat the Herpes virus. Grimes put a small piece of that virus, which makes it sensitive to the drug, into his own virus."

She stared at him in disbelief. "You could do that," she said finally.

"I could do that, and I did do that." He saw so many emotions on her face. Anger. Disbelief. Shame. "All right," Sean said. "Enough of everybody feeling sorry and stupid and deceived. Let's get to what we're going to do about it. There isn't any more of that virus in you. If you want to be sure, I'll give you more of the medicine. You can take it for a week. But the truth of the matter is that you qualified yesterday without any help from your fish hemoglobin. You didn't do it easily, and the time wasn't real fast, but you earned your place in an Olympic final. It's not worth speculating about whether you would have been here without the hemoglobin, but if you could do that well yesterday, I have to assume you would have been. That means you can do your best tomorrow and get what you fairly deserve. I'm not sure that you'll be able to win. In fact, I doubt it. But if you do I'll be cheering for you. If you don't, well remember, I was sixth last time. You can still be the best if you want it badly enough."

She sat there for a long time without speaking. Finally she said, "I can't believe this. I can't believe this has all happened to me. It's like a one-year-long nightmare."

"But it's over," Sean reassured her. "There's no pressure on you. Oh, some people will wonder why you didn't win. Tell them you had a cold. Just do your best. This is when you're supposed to enjoy the results of all that hard work. No matter where you finish, just enjoy it. Anything you do at this level is an achievement, and you didn't get here just because you had fish blood in you. I know how hard you work. You just haven't done it for quite as many years as some of the others. Don't spoil it. This is your year to be the young phenom. Next time you'll have all the pressure on you."

"As you do," she said to Sean.

"For four years I had it, to win that gold medal for my country, for Bob, for all the others who helped me, my family . . . But, you know, on opening night I turned it off. It's too late to change anything now. We have the ability we earned, let's see what we can do with it. I can't wait for that race."

He loves it. He just loves it. She looked into his eyes. It was the same person who had run down Bahel in Central Park. *And I'm just like he is.* Admitting it made her feel proud.

He stood up, she followed. They looked at each other. He put out his hand. "Good luck," he said.

"Good luck to you." She turned to go. But then she turned back, put her arms around his neck, and kissed him on the cheek. "Remember, I don't like you at all, and you're a damn lousy runner." She smiled and walked toward the door.

"Remember, you owe me a real world record, and I plan to be there to see it," he called after her.

Chapter 51

"Hi," Sean said into the phone. "Did I wake you?"

"Mmm," Joan responded. "Yes. It's, it's seven."

"It's eleven here, at night. Where have you been? I tried all day yesterday to get you."

"I've been hiding."

"I think it's time for you to come down here."

"But, Sean, we went over that."

"There's nothing left for me to do except to run."

"Oh."

"And I want you to be here."

"Oh."

"I've bought an open ticket for you on Quantas. There are still seats for the weekend flights. Saturday morning from New York will get you here in time for my race with an hour to spare, if everything goes perfectly."

"You must have been sure that I'd say yes."

"I was," he said. "I'm on a roll."

"Well, this time you happen to be right," she said. "Oh, and congratulations."

"You saw it."

"Every minute. I recorded it. I've played it back, not more than maybe ten or twenty times."

"Twenty times would take almost ten hours."

"Yes, that's about right."

"Just a couple more of those."

"You were terrific. The announcer said you were the best in the world."

"I hope he's right." Sean laughed.

"He doesn't think the Chinese are as good as you and Rossi and the Mexican . . ."

"Alvila. He's good."

"But both of the Chinese won."

"Rossi was just playing, trying to find out if Dak could respond late in the race. He's like that, always probing. Smart."

"And Han?"

"Who knows? I think Francois had more left. We'll see."

"You don't seem as worried as I am. I just keep thinking it didn't work, or that they didn't get it soon enough."

"Well, we have three more days. If it goes away three percent a day, maybe that will be the extra step I need."

"Don't you joke like that. And don't you win by just one step. I won't be able to stand it."

He laughed.

"You can win any way you want. I'll just close my eyes."

"Okay. I'll try for at least two steps."

"They mustn't win. Every time I look at them I think of how they killed Grimes."

"They didn't kill Grimes. They probably don't know anything about it. Neither strikes me as too bright."

"But their henchmen did it," Joan insisted. "Why don't you all just elbow them or trip them?"

Sean laughed

"Sometimes those fouls are called."

"Well, they deserve it."

"You didn't attack the television set, try to hold them back?"

"No," she said. "I did talk to the TV a little, though." Sean could easily imagine it. "I watched some of the other heats too," she said. "In fact, I taped them all. There are some good runners out there, you know." She laughed. "I thought I'd tell you, in case you hadn't noticed."

"I know almost all of them," he said, "only too well. Bob and I have been over the tapes many times. Anyway, let me give you the plane reservation number. It may be close. I won't be able to come and meet you, but there'll be a ticket waiting at the main courtesy booth by the stadium. You won't have any trouble finding it."

By now she was so anxious to go that she couldn't stand the

thought of having to wait a whole day.

"I love you," Sean said.

"That sounds like serious talk."

"Yes, but the ban on serious talk has been lifted."

For Sean Saturday was like most days, he had little to do. His training took only several hours, and he had resolved to do no sight-seeing on the days immediately before the races. It was early afternoon and he was sitting in the living room of his rented house wondering what he could do to pass the time. He had finished lunch, and there were still three hours to go before his second workout session of the day.

Joan must be packing, he thought, wishing that she were with him. His glance settled on the telephone book lying on the hall table where he had left it the night before.

"It would never work," he said aloud. "What would the chances be? Still he has to be somewhere, and Sydney is as likely as any place."

Sean sat down next to the phone and opened the book. There were sixteen Nevilles, two Johns and a J. He tried them first, without success. *Might as well try the others, they could be relatives*, he thought. In an hour he had managed to reach all but four, but with no luck. He got up to stretch. *Of course if he just got back here*, Sean thought, as he walked toward the kitchen for some water, *he might not be in the book yet*. He went back to the phone, called the operator, and asked for the recent listings. Yes, there was a J. Neville in Northbridge. He dialed, and the phone was answered almost at once. He heard a baby crying in the background before he heard the voice, and his heart sank. Somehow he couldn't picture Jack Neville as a father.

"Hello," a woman answered after a moment. It was an American voice.

"I'm sorry to disturb you," Sean began, using his now practiced opening, "but I'm visiting for the Games, and I'm trying to find a Jack Neville who used to be at Grenville University in the States."

"Jack, it's for you," she shouted away from the phone. It was a New York voice, precise, businesslike.

Sean heard the distant, muffled reply, "Whoos it, Annie, luv?"

The receiver slipped from his hand, but he caught it in midair.

The women's 5K final was held early Saturday evening. Sean watched it on television in his rented house. Joan watched it in her apartment in Grenville. It was four in the morning and she had finished packing. The limo would arrive in about an hour, plenty of time to reach JFK for the 8:40 flight to Los Angeles. She had been up almost the entire night watching the track and field channel. "Thank God the Olympics are only every four years," she said to herself. "I'm just sitting here doing nothing constructive, eating and drinking with my eyes glued to the stupid tube."

But to her surprise she enjoyed it, or at least found it interesting, especially the women's heptathlon. She had seen the long jump, and then the javelin throw, and then the 800-meter run, about half a mile the announcer had said. It was particularly fascinating because she remembered that Sean had told the search committee at Grenville that a woman heptathlete would be the perfect choice to be the head track coach. *Did he have one of these women in mind?* She wondered. She marveled at their skills. It didn't occur to her to envy them, since she had never considered for a minute that she might do the same things.

There is something to this, she thought. *It's not so simple. It's like anything else. The more you learn about it, the more you get out of it.*

Finally there was the women's 5K. It was the first real final that she had watched. They would be giving out the medals at the end of this race. The runners were out on the track warming up, and the announcer was introducing them, spending more time on the favorites. "Susie Fredricks is the world record holder and has to be considered a favorite, but she was not impressive in the heats. Greta Myerling, who beat Fredricks earlier in the year in Amsterdam but lost to her in London, is certainly looking forward to the 'rubber match.' Klara Heinz, who also lost in London, where incidentally Fredricks had set the indoor world record, had her revenge in their heat. The Canadian, Francine LaPointe, who failed to win medals in two previous Olympic finals, is healthy again after years of nagging injuries and is running better than ever. It's probably her last chance."

Joan tried to keep them straight in her mind as he continued. "Others to watch are the Kenyan, Christine Kinbu—the women from Kenya are just beginning to follow in the footsteps of the men, Jessie Fowler, a Jamaican, the Empire Games Champion, always a threat, up and down, as good as anyone when she's up, and Chenkova, the Russian. She raced too much during the winter season, but finally took some time off in the spring and now seems back to her peak form."

Susie felt totally relaxed. "I'm still the world record holder," she said to herself. "Will they all be keying off me, or will they think after the heat that I've lost it? No, if I were in their position, I'd just think that I had a bad race, or that I didn't feel well, or that I just miscalculated. After all, I set two world records this year. They have to look at me. Time for a little psyching."

She went over and chatted with several of the runners whom she recognized, something she had never done before. Then she surprised everyone by doing a complete circle of the track in the warmups. She glided along in her smoothest and most effortless stride. It was part of her aura. Other competitors stopped to watch.

Finally the runners were in position. The gun went off, and Jessie Fowler and Christine Kinbu went for the lead. The others stayed back. Susie had chosen her strategy. *My legs are better than my lungs*, she thought. *I'm going to try to slow them all down and outsprint them at the end. None of them have ever seen me do that. Now maybe I'll get something out of those quarter miles and half miles that Hopwell made me run until I couldn't stand them.*

Could she do it again without the fish blood? She thought of it with disgust. She thought of what it meant to deceive and to be deceived. The conversation with Sean, well, it certainly had not been what she expected. Somehow it had been easier than she had anticipated. She had been worrying about it for days, rehearsing it in her mind, and now her greatest sense was one of relief, of having been cleansed. For the first time in a year she felt that she was herself again and not someone else. She settled in on Klara Heinz's shoulder.

The young Kenyan, Kinbu, was falling back a bit and looking around. *She's wondering where the rest of us are and realizing how crazy it was to follow Fowler,* Susie thought. *She's done for.*

"They're reaching the first mile," the announcer intoned. "Fowler's time is fast, but the rest of the pack is slow. They refuse to be dragged along."

The pack swept along like some wonderful, many-legged creature. Their limbs had fallen into a synchronization. The same frequency is never right for everyone, Susie knew. You have to be the one whom the others are copying. She cleared her mind of the other runners. It was a practiced talent. She was running at precisely the pace she wished, and by her presence, she was controlling the others. When Chenkova began to pull ahead, she seemed to become almost self-conscious and deliberately came back. She reminded Susie of a bull. She ran like one, and she was having difficulty controlling herself. Susie smiled.

"Two miles," the announcer said. "It's remarkable, but the pack is still holding firm. You can see they're beginning to close the gap on Fowler and Kinbu."

Susie pretended it was a practice session. She kept telling herself to relax. "Run easily, run easily. Four laps to go and anything is possible." She could feel the anxiety building in the pack. Runners glanced around, trying to mark the rivals they feared most. Everyone, it seemed, stole a glance at her. She still had the smile on her face. She couldn't remember when she had enjoyed a race so much. Certainly not recently. The smile must be really disconcerting to the others, she thought.

With three laps to go, the pack passed Kinbu. They almost bumped her off the track. She was a traffic hazard. Fowler was fifteen yards ahead.

She's losing it, Susie thought, *how can I use her to bump someone?*

The pack was about to come apart. Everyone in it seemed to have something in reserve. The back markers were beginning to swing wide, feeling the panic that they might not make it through. A lap and a half, still too early, Susie felt. Chenkova went. She passed Fowler. Francine LaPointe came up on the outside. Susie didn't know her, but she saw the figure go by on her right side. Greta Myerling held steady. Klara Heinz was still on her left.

One lap to go. The pack was sweeping past Fowler who was drifting out. Greta Myerling passed her on the inside and went. Susie went on the outside. Klara Heinz was picked. She had to slow and pass on the inside, losing valuable time. Myerling was gaining on Chenkova. LaPointe was third. Susie was fourth.

"Hurry, hurry, hurry." Joan was out of her seat. "Kick, kick, or whatever you're supposed to do."

Greta Myerling passed Chenkova. LaPointe was running by herself, away from the others. She was closing on Chenkova unseen. Susie ran as hard as she could but with discipline, no break in her stride. She knew Klara Heinz was coming, and she expected Chenkova to fade. Chenkova finally noticed LaPointe, too late, but it caused her to renew her effort and charge after her. Greta Myerling was opening a lead. She won going away. LaPointe was second. Susie closed on Chenkova but not in time. Klara Heinz was on the inside, fifth.

"Oh, that's so terrible," Joan almost cried.

"Yes, yes," Sean exalted in front of his television set.

Susie doubled over gasping for breath. She felt an enormous sense of relief and pride. She had honestly run the best race she could. This was the perfect finish. She congratulated the winners. As the leading American finisher, the only American in the finals, she would be subjected to endless questioning. She already knew what her answer would be, "I was very pleased with my first attempt, and I'll be back when I'm older, and wiser, and better."

Chapter 52

Sean emerged from the darkness of the tunnel into the blazing light of the stadium. It was filled to capacity for the last event of the day. Attendants were moving the hurdles from the women's 400m into the infield. He stopped and turned, slowly letting his eyes sweep over the stands. No hope of finding Joan. She would have a good seat if she made it, if there had been no delays in the flight.

He regarded the track as a stage on which he was about to perform. Somehow it didn't seem like a competition. *Sunday will be a competition*, he thought. *This is a performance.* His feeling came in part from the strategy decided upon earlier in the day with Bob Higgum. It didn't rely on the tactics of any of the other runners. It didn't even rely on their presence. Bob ran the session like a quiz, as if it were his final examination.

"What will be your strategy?" he asked.

"Well, when you're the favorite, when you're the best in the field, no gimmicks, just play it straight. For me, that means my usual slow start."

"A little faster would be nice," Bob interrupted.

"Completely relaxed, fast middle. Move at four and a half or five. Have the lead by five and a half and kick on home."

Bob was nodding his agreement. "You can win like that tonight," he said. "Funny business and gimmicks are for people who are hoping for an upset. What do you suppose the others think you'll do?"

"They won't know what to think." Sean laughed. "During the last two years I've won major races using almost every possible strategy. Probably they'll pay most attention to the heats. That means they'll expect me to stay back with the pack and let the Kenyans set the pace and then make my move at about four and a half miles. They don't know about the Chinese, and after the trials the best probably aren't too worried about them. Rossi and Dryx certainly think they could have won if they wanted."

"Maybe they should be more worried. Suppose the Chinese were holding back too."

"I don't think so."

"I know you don't, and I know why." Bob winked. "So tell me what you're really planning to do."

"That's the question worth most of the points," Sean answered. "I have to ask, what's my biggest advantage? There's no one out there who's trained to run a marathon." Bob was grinning from ear to ear. "I can do more total work than any of the others. I just have to squeeze it into the allotted time."

"That's a very interesting way to put it," Bob said. "I never taught you that."

"I have to make them suffer. I have to punish them. I'll be there at the end, and they won't be. There shouldn't be another person on that track whose last mile is his fastest."

Bob was so pleased he couldn't sit still. He got up from his chair and began to pace. "Not too fast," he said. "Not too fast." He quoted a figure. "That will win it. No one there can do it faster." He quoted another figure. "You can do that, and they won't be in sight. You could break the record again, but it might cost you next Sunday. Think about it."

"I passed," Sean said to himself.

The strategy session was over. Bob shook Sean's hand and put his arm around his shoulder. "I don't know whether you're the best runner I've ever seen," he said, "but you're the best one I ever coached, and I've coached some good ones. And you're the smartest runner I've ever known."

Sean was trying to fight back his emotions. "I hang around in good company," he said.

"A lot of people hang around and don't learn a damn thing." Bob said, trying to sound gruff. "This is our race. Just go take it. We'll do our funny thing Sunday night."

Sean was stretching against one of the hurdles. He had never felt so well prepared, better than for the World Championship, better than for his World record. He had set it just eleven weeks earlier and followed that with the two best training months he had ever had. "What's this little flat oval compared to Silver Mine Peak?"

He knew all of the finalists and had gone over every one of them with Bob. The Kenyans, Kipu and Matsu. Sandri, looking better than ever. Alvila, so serious, a purist. Sean had always liked him. Paolo Rossi, the ebullient Italian, another of Sean's favorites, a professional who could rise to the occasion. And there were Dak and Han, ignored by the other runners, standing by themselves.

"Feeling a little out of place, I'll bet," Sean said to himself as he began to jog on the track. He wanted to be warm and loose right from the beginning.

"There, there they are, Schultz, and there is the Irishman Rourke."

"He cannot avoid us now as he did in Stuttgart. Now he will lose again for the second time to a Mr. Root, to Han Root and to Dak Root." Schultz laughed.

This time the beer garden had a direct TV feed, the event was being shown all over China. But the language might as well still have been Japanese as far as this select audience was concerned. They chose to watch without benefit of the sound.

"It is so satisfying to watch them develop, to watch them improve. So much work. They are almost like your own children." Jurgen was showing a side that Schultz had not seen before.

"We have no yellow children," he said with scorn. "Too bad they are not German. Think what Schneider could do with this blood. And now we must beat him."

"We would all prefer to work for our own, for the fatherland, as we have always done. But now we are forced to serve whoever will have us," Jurgen said with resignation in his voice.

"It is their fault. They discarded us. But we will show them."

The runners were being individually introduced. There was polite applause when the Chinese were named, more for Alvila, still more for Rossi. Finally, Sean was introduced last, as the World record-holder. The applause was substantially greater. There could be no doubt about who was the crowd favorite. There were no

Australians in the final.

The runners formed.

When the gun sounded, both Kenyans, who had lined up side by side, surged forward, intent on opening a large lead over the pack. Sean followed them. The others stayed back.

"Don't let them get away!" Joan shouted. She had just barely made it to her seat and already was on her feet.

"Sit down, lady," someone yelled behind her.

"I've got to stay calm," she rebuked herself.

Sean had an exact pace in mind. The Kenyans saw him and increased their speed. They wanted a lead. Sean smiled. *If they keep this up, they won't be running at the finish.* They began to circle the track with monotonous regularity, he and the Kenyans, gradually increasing their lead over the pack. The Chinese were well behind.

"There must be a lot of anxiety back there," Sean said to himself. "How I would love to listen to their thoughts."

He considered dropping back a little to see if he could tow them along, but decided not to, wisely as it turned out because the nervous pack began to increase its speed without his help. Sean wanted them to work. He ran comfortably behind the Kenyans, careful not to be influenced by their pace. By the ninth lap, stragglers were already falling behind. He decided to wait a little longer. On the eleventh lap Sean went by on the outside, staying wide long enough to avoid any possible confrontation, then cutting back to the inside of the track. The Kenyans were unable to respond, in fact they slowed.

As his lead grew, Sean concentrated on his favorite racing image, one that he often held in his mind in the middle sections of long runs. He could see it as clearly as if he were standing by the rail on the back stretch at Belmont Park: the big reddish horse with the huge stride slowly drawing farther and farther ahead, ten lengths, twenty lengths, thirty lengths, all by himself and seemingly oblivious to everything around him. He had picked his own pace. It was a performance far beyond the urging of the jockey, beyond the influence of his trainer, beyond the need to win, bred into him over generations. It was running for the pure joy of running. If horses could smile, Secretariat would have been grinning from ear to ear. Sean knew the feeling so well. He had it now. It was one of those days when everything is perfect, when your feet don't touch the ground and you can run forever.

Gloom had settled over the beer garden. The early cheers had turned to stunned silence. It was mission control with a malfunctioning satellite, but in this case there was nothing to be done except hope.

"They aren't going to do it."

"At least Dak is trying."

"Something has gone wrong," Jurgen was the first to proclaim.

"But what? We did everything correctly."

The four-mile split was announced. It was incredibly fast and had a dramatic effect on the runners. Some surged ahead. Others clearly gave up. The two Kenyans added to the confusion by slowing even more just when the leaders of the pack were about to swallow them. Sean's plan had worked to perfection. The only remaining hope was that this crazy Irishman would run himself into the ground, but there was little possibility of that. He was the World record-holder, and he was marathon trained.

For the others, the strategy now shifted to winning the silver. Everyone was suffering. Few runners would voluntarily drop out of an Olympic final, but at least one had pulled off into the infield. The pack no longer existed. Alvila was in second. Rossi, who looked awful, was in third, and Sandri, running smoothly, was in fourth. Han was far back. Dryx and Joan had taken care of him. Dak had tried to follow Rossi, but he was soon to learn the difference between the heats and the finals.

Joan was trying to control herself. She managed not to cheer when Sean passed the Kenyans. And the other runners, what was happening to them? Then she remembered the Chinese. *How could I forget? I wouldn't be here without them.* There they were in the middle of the pack, going nowhere. *I should have used something lethal, they deserve it. Well no, I guess the runners don't. And what we used obviously worked well enough.* Finally it came to her. Susie! He had given Susie the Ganciclovir! That was why he was so sure it would work.

Sean hurt, but he knew everyone else hurt more. He still had something in reserve. He wanted to run faster but thought better of it. No one was gaining; his race was over. *And I have the record. Of course I don't have the Olympic record. This would be the year to set it. The conditions are perfect.* Then he thought of the upcoming marathon and held steady.

Just beyond five miles Sandri made his move. He was on the outside, and he went to second, but Alvila was not about to let him get away. They ran almost side by side, Alvila slightly behind but having the advantage of the inside. Rossi trailed them, perhaps five yards back.

On a sudden impulse Sean glanced at the scoreboard. Sure enough there they were, displayed right next to the running time: the Olympic record and *his* World record. *It's mine, but only because of the wind. Of course I know Han cheated. And there he is, the son of a bitch. Damn it. To hell with cheating and with fish blood and viruses and the wind and to hell with the marathon. This is my distance. I'm sick of hearing that someone ran faster. I want the best time ever.* He increased his pace.

The race behind him was exciting, but it was being fought out at gradually decreasing speed. Sean could see them. He was picking his way through the back markers. Most were too tired to swing outside as he approached, as they would have done at this point in a race if they were not so completely exhausted. He lapped Han.

"Hardly worth an elbow," he said to himself, "but Joan will be so disappointed."

"He lapped Han," Jurgen was almost in tears.

"The Australians did this," Schultz proclaimed. "Han and Dak both. They're sick. They were poisoned."

"Don't be foolish. How could they? Why would they? There are no Australians in the race."

"Tse didn't protect them. It's his fault."

Two laps to go. What image should he use now? Colorado? Climbing Silver Mine Peak? He rejected them immediately. "That would slow me down," he said to himself. The new red Porsche secretly waiting in Grenville for Joan? "I sure could use it now." Then finally he made the connection, it was the same kind of car that Grimes had driven to Bradsford when he ran as Root. "This one's for you, Andy Grimes," he said out loud and increased his pace again.

With a lap to go, he passed Dak. Sean would have ignored the others except that they were in front of him, stretched across the track, right in his line of vision. Alvila, Rossi and Sandri. No strategy. It was a matter of who dropped first. He suddenly wanted to see their finish. *Worry about your own,* he admonished himself. They disappeared around the corner ahead of him.

Half a lap to go. The crowd was on its feet cheering wildly. They sensed a record. The workers in the infield were frantically urging him on. Finally he called upon the image that seemed never to fail him, the image that he had learned to reserve for times like this: running home, alone, up the tree-lined hill. The air felt damp and cool, and he could see the lights in the house at the end of the lane. He sprinted down the last straight. "Lift, lift, lift," he told his knees. At every one of the countless 10K's he had run with Bob watching, no matter what the pace, no matter how far ahead, no matter how exhausted, he had sprinted at the end. Paying the dues, like the mile races, like Colorado, like the mountain.

Joan would not even have noticed what was happening, she was just hoping that nothing would go wrong, but the others around her had begun shouting. "He's going to get it, go, go, kick, he's going to break it." She finally realized what they meant, and she was screaming along with them. Bob Higgum sat fixed in his seat. He didn't have to stand. He was in the first row. There were tears in his eyes, but he could still see. The others were fans. He was a connoisseur.

Sean dove through the tape. He would have fallen, but two of the assistants reached out and grabbed him, dragged him off the track away from the runners who were beginning their last lap. The roar was deafening.

He turned to the one on the left. "How much?"

The aide had to look back to the scoreboard. The "OR" and "WR" signs were both flashing. He paused to subtract. "Eighteen off the World," he said. They started to lead Sean into the infield.

"No, no," he said. "No, I want to see the end."

They knew what he meant. The three of them turned around to face the finish line. With his practiced eye, Sean sized up the race in an instant. Sandri still looked best, and Rossi looked like he would die on the track. "He can't be conscious," thought Sean. Rossi wouldn't let him go. They drew nearer and nearer. Still Rossi would not fall back. Alvila fell back. Then Sandri's stride began to break.

Rossi's had broken a mile back, but he wouldn't be denied. Sandri had the bronze. Sean broke away from the aides, who were no longer trying to steady him, and was the first to reach Rossi, who had turned completely around and was falling to the track. Sean caught him, and together with the aides supported him upright. Sean shouted for water, and they poured it over Rossi's head. They were surrounded by photographers, but other aides kept them at bay. They walked Rossi across the infield.

He really is unconscious, Sean thought, becoming anxious. But finally, Rossi was able to stand. He took some water, and he looked at Sean, recognizing him. He winked, and his first words were, "So you are still here. I thought we would never see you again." Sean laughed out loud, partly because of the joke, but mainly with relief. He put his hands on Rossi's shoulders. "Silver," he said. "You got silver." He didn't know whether Rossi knew. "That took more guts than anything I've ever seen."

Susie stared at Sean on the television set. She had never relaxed, even when he had his huge lead. She had thought about the record from the beginning and of all the work that went into it. Suddenly she wanted to go out to run. "Training starts tomorrow," she said to the television set.

Bob Higgum rose to leave. He never watched awards ceremonies. Then he turned around and went back to his seat. He had trained gold medal winners before, but this would probably be his last. Maybe he should watch this one.

Sean was still standing with Rossi. Alvila came over and then Sandri. The crowd was chanting. There had been no victory lap. Sean wanted to wait and take it with the others, but he wasn't sure about Rossi. He delayed. Finally, he took Rossi by the arm.

"Let's go," he said to the other two, "they're waiting for us." Rossi hesitated. "We'll walk," Sean said. "It's a nice night for a stroll."

Together, the four old friends ambled once around the track. It had been the last event of the evening, and the medals were to be presented almost immediately. On the platform, Sean felt joy and relief, satisfaction, and pride, and humility, and power. The ceremony was as grand as he had expected, but even in the midst of it he recalled as best he could Jesse Owens's simple but elegant description. "You stand on a platform. They put a wreath on your head. They raise your country's flag, and they play the national anthem."

Everything else, he thought, *can be left to the imagination.*

The Chinese station did not cover the award ceremony. It had already switched to the late evening rerun of "Dynasty," in English but with Chinese subtitles.

Chapter 53

Jim McBride's official pass got him into the dressing room. He pumped Sean's hand and pounded him on the back. "The best," he said to him. "You're the best. Absolutely the best."

"Thanks to you, and to Bob, and to a lot of others," Sean said graciously.

"A very small part, a very small part," Jim insisted. "Just relax. I have everything organized. You're going to have to fight your way out through a horde of reporters, but I have everything under control. I have all the others."

Sean had a flash of anxiety. "All the others?" he asked.

"Everyone except Susie," Jim said. "She made an excuse. I think she's just so down from her race. But I told her we all understood." Sean wondered if his relief were visible. "Bob and Joan and Helen have gone to the restaurant. Take your time, and when you're ready I'll get you over there."

By the time Jim and Sean finally reached the restaurant, the others were well into the champagne. Joan was there, and the way she and Sean greeted each other left no room for uncertainty about the nature of their relationship. "I look a mess," she whispered to him. "I came right from the plane." It was the least characteristic thing he had ever heard her say.

"I have the biggest surprise for you, you won't believe it," he told them all after they had taken their seats. He paused for effect.

"What? What is it?" Joan asked.

"Jack Neville is living here in Sydney with his lovely wife, Ann . . . Grossman, and their son, Andrew." There was a stunned silence. Joan stared at him in disbelief.

Finally Jim broke the spell. "You've seen him?"

"Just talked to him on the phone. He seems very nice." Sean smiled at Joan. She was still staring. "They're both at the university."

"But what did you say to them?" Joan finally managed to speak.

"Nothing," Sean answered. "Neville seemed a little nervous at first, but I guess that's easy to understand. I told him I was a friend of yours, here for the Games, and that you had told me to say 'hello' if I could find him. I pretended not to know anything about Ann."

"And had they heard what's been going on?" Jim asked.

"I didn't ask directly, and he never brought it up. I don't think they have a clue. He said they had just arrived here for the new semester and that they had traveled around the world for about a year waiting for their new positions to open."

"You know she must have changed her name and closed her accounts," Helen said. "That's why no one could trace her. The same thing happened to me when I got married." She looked at Jim and then at Joan. "Don't you do that."

Joan was regaining her composure. She even managed a small smile. "She must talk science better than I do."

"Maybe you just use the proper precautions better than she does," Sean suggested. "Thank goodness."

"I like that interpretation." Joan's smile grew larger.

"I didn't tell them you were coming," Sean said. "I thought I would leave it up to you if you want to see them, alone or together, as you like."

Joan thought for a moment. "Neither."

The party went on for several hours. As they were leaving, Helen nudged Sean. "This one's the one," she said.

"Do you think so?" Sean teased. He recovered Joan's luggage from the coatroom, and they gave the cab driver directions back to the rented house.

"You're not the Irish runner who just broke that record?" the driver asked.

"It's started," Sean whispered to Joan. "How did you know? Did you see it?"

"No, I've been driving all night. The doorman told me he was in there. You seemed the most likely chap."

When they reached the house, the driver unloaded the bags and actually carried them up the front steps. Sean started to pay him.

"No mate, not tonight, not in my cab. This one's on me. Wait til I tell my boy who I drove." He started back down the steps.

"Wait a minute." Sean stopped him. He zipped open his bag, rummaged inside, and pulled out a heavy white piece of paper with the large block number 661 on the front. He turned it over and took out his pen. "What's your son's name?" he asked.

"Jason," the driver answered.

Sean wrote a note. He put the date, 10K, Olympic Final, World Record, Gold, and signed his name. "Here," he handed it to the driver. "You Aussies are great. I really like this country. Jason can see this on television tonight." Then he laughed. "Actually, he'll probably see it ten thousand times in television ads and get sick of it."

"No, he'll never get sick of this. Thanks, Irishman. I hope to visit your country someday too. Good luck to you and the missus."

Sean turned to Joan. "Shall I carry you across the threshold?"

"This is getting serious, and we haven't even started to talk."

"Well, you could carry *me* if you'd feel more comfortable that way."

They went directly to bed.

"Funny, you don't feel any different now that you have a gold medal," she said after a while, "and you obviously didn't use all your energy."

"Remember, I'm trained to go another twenty miles. But you must be exhausted," Sean said.

"No. I slept all the way from L.A. First class, what a luxury."

"Well, I had my reasons for wanting you well rested."

"Oh, you! Of course now I'm wide awake. It's just time to get up in Grenville," she said.

Sean went to the kitchen and brought back a bottle of wine and two glasses. "A little of that champagne goes a long way with me," he said. "I guess it's the thing for celebrating, but I much prefer a good wine."

"And what would you pick on a Gold Medal night?" she asked, sitting up and rearranging the pillows.

"A '71 La Tache." He opened the bottle and showed her the label.

"You're kidding."

"I've never had one, but then I've never had most of them, so I just go by the book."

"And this is in the book under super all time world's best?" she asked.

"Somewhere in that part of the book."

"So, Bob is actually letting you drink tonight?"

"Bob doesn't care about drinking. It's interesting, all the times I've spent with him that's one of the few things he's never said a word about."

"Well, I'm not sure you should do it," she said. "Especially on your own like that without getting permission. I think that I should just drink this by myself, and perhaps you should have a nice sports drink." She laughed. "You may need it later tonight anyway."

"No," he said. "I'm rewarding myself with one night off. I don't have to do anything until Sunday. Marathoners always take the week off before their races."

"Oh," she said. "And what did Higgum mean when he kept saying Sunday was just going to be fun and games."

"I think I know, but we haven't talked about it yet. It's going to be fun and games because I don't have to win, and I probably won't. But I think we have something else to do." He poured the wine and handed her a glass.

"What?"

"We have to pay back some favors."

"What kinds of favors?" she asked.

"Well, we owe a debt. You know, I've been with Bob so long I not only think like him, but I have the same set of values."

"That doesn't sound too bad," she said. "Cheers!"

"Oh, I wasn't complaining."

"But you don't want to tell me what it is?"

"Oh," he said, "I have all those stock answers for situations like this, which I learned from you. Like, 'I'm sure you could understand it, but we don't have enough time right now.'"

"Ha, ha," she said. "Well, you know I won't throw this wine at you. It's wonderful."

"Maybe that's a reason for always buying good wine."

"Why wouldn't we have enough time right now?" she asked.

"Well, maybe something will come up that will make us want to stop talking." They both drank.

"I did something yesterday." She paused, then went on. "I took Kerr's job."

"You did! Yesterday?"

"Whatever day, Friday, who knows on this side of the dateline, right after you called."

"Didn't you want time to negotiate?"

"I didn't want my accepting it to be because of . . . to be because of you."

"Because of me?"

"That was important to me, Sean. It was my compromise. If I'm sorry about it later, I don't ever want to blame you for it. Maybe I'm fooling myself, because you might have had just a tiny little bit to do with it, but it's the way I chose to fool myself. It's the way I structured it."

"But what made you do it at all? You had so many reservations, being in a clinical department, the kind of research project . . ."

"I still have them. It's hard to explain. I think I made up my mind after watching Susie set that world record."

Sean leaned forward and turned to look directly at Joan. "Oh."

"It was actually seeing what Grimes's discovery was able to do. His hemoglobin turned a good runner into the world's best. I know, I know, she was a promising runner, but he made it possible for her to run faster than any other woman had ever run. It was seeing for myself what came from his research. I never get that feeling from mine."

"But we've talked so much about the differences between basic research and applied research," Sean reminded her.

"I know we have. My projects are fun and very satisfying. And it's true that you need basic discoveries to build on later. But this was a whole different experience, so powerful and so immediate. And I wanted to be part of it. You know, my role this time was to turn off the Root-effect hemoglobin. But next time it will be to turn it on, to treat some disease."

"And you did all that before the flight?" he asked.

"It took about five minutes of negotiating," she said. "Then I listened while he dictated the whole thing to Beth Markham. I told him everything had to be in writing, in case someday he wasn't there. I learned that from you. It didn't bother him at all. In fact, he said it's the only way to do business. Then he muttered something about the damn little plane he takes to Washington, like it's fifty-fifty they'll all be killed." She laughed.

"Was he delighted? I'm sure he was."

"He seemed very pleased."

"It sounds to me like it's okay to carry on serious discussions now," he said.

"I guess so. It seems to be a day for serious discussions."

"Well, then," he said, "would you consider marrying me?"

"Is that a question, or a proposal?"

"I always thought that someday I would propose to someone, but with you, well, I've been watching Kerr pretty carefully. His strategy seems to have worked. There's a lot to be learned from these medical types, especially these wise old chairmen." He was grinning from ear to ear.

Joan wasn't surprised, but she hadn't expected to be asked just like that. She couldn't help it. She was terrified. She had been terrified that he never would ask, that he would go away with Susie. Now she was terrified that he had asked. *Oh why couldn't it always be the day before he asked,* she thought. *Of course I'd have to know he was going to, so I wouldn't worry about it.* She had to say something. None of the rehearsed answers seemed to fit.

"Yes, I would certainly consider doing that," she said. "If you're as good a negotiator as Kerr. He made a very attractive initial offer and then was quite flexible in terms of improving it."

"I'm prepared to negotiate. I can offer all kinds of inducements, but what was it Kerr said, I'll need to have a list of what you want."

She hadn't expected that either, but it sounded like a good opportunity. "I guess this is the best time to get what I want," she said, "before I surrender my . . . well I guess I can't say that. Let's just say, before we make our final agreement."

"What did you have in mind?" he asked.

"First of all, you'll have to live nearby, so I guess you'll have to move to Grenville. No, that's really not fair. I just told you that I didn't want to think that you had influenced what job I took, so I can't do that to you. Of course, you can be anywhere. You don't have to take the job in Grenville. What a nice life. Nothing but a little fresh air and exercise. Isn't that what it's like?"

Sean laughed. "I think I remember doing it in the winter and in the rain, too. But anyway, I'm going to take the Grenville position. It'll be fun, and it's not going to interfere with my training."

"Okay, well that's settled," she said. "See how easy this is going to be. Now, let's see. Opera. Regular subscriptions."

"Done."

"This is too easy. Maybe I should specify the seats and, of course, the wine," she said. "It'll have to be La Tache every night, of course."

"I think Kerr said he could meet any reasonable demands. Anyway, you'd get sick of burgundies. Surely, you'd be willing to have a Lafite occasionally just to break up the monotony."

"Well," she said, "I guess we could work out the details of that, but I think we've established a ground rule for the expectations. Now what else? Oh, yes. I liked Colorado, and I didn't find it too hard to drive that Jeep up the mountain while you were running. And even throwing the water bottles at you, that's actually kind of fun. Of course, I think I might like skiing there even more."

"It seems to me that I started to suggest that once, but you interrupted me before I could finish."

"That was then," Joan said. "There were different rules then. Now you should feel perfectly free to suggest it. In fact, I accept. I accept that, I mean. I'm not done negotiating."

"You still haven't come to the one I thought would be first." He gave her a knowing smile.

"The one that would be first?" she said, wrinkling her brow. "The one that would be first? Something about counting in bed?"

"No, no," he said. "I figured that didn't need to be negotiated."

"Something that would be first? I need a hint. If I miss this, can I ask for it later?"

"You can ask, but I can't guarantee it, once we've come to an agreement. I mean, would Kerr go back and give you an extra electron centrifuge or something?"

"There is no such thing," she said.

"Whatever. One of those fancy gadgets. I doubt if he'd do that."

"Huh," she said. "Well, we'll just have to have a pause in the negotiation because I certainly can't end . . . Ha, I've got it, a car. A car, of course. You must get rid of the wreck."

"You *are* slow tonight. I thought you'd get it right away."

"I've had other things on my mind. But there's no way I wasn't going to think of that. In fact that was so obvious, I would have considered that it was implied, even if I hadn't actually said it."

"Ho, ho, ho," he said. "That doesn't count."

"Well, now I have said it. Yes, we'll certainly get rid of the wreck. What would I want?"

"It's got to be practical," Sean insisted. "It has to have four-wheel drive if we're going to live in Grenville with all that snow. And to be safe it shouldn't just blend into the background like the wreck does, so nobody can see it. You don't want to get run over by a truck or something. It should stand out."

"Get a red one," she said.

"We could, although that might be a little too bright."

"We don't have to be conservative," she said.

"How about one like this?" He reached under the bed for a large box and handed it to her. It had a white bow and a card which said, "For Joan Danner, Molecular Detective."

"What's this?" she asked looking down at the box in her lap.

"Open it and find out."

"It's a trick," she said pulling off the bow and opening the lid. "Another box! This had better be good."

Sean smiled smugly. "Keep going."

Joan had to open three more boxes before finally arriving at a matchbox containing a model of a red Porsche convertible.

"Oh!" She looked at him, disbelieving, then threw her arms around his neck. "You don't mean this."

"It's already waiting for you in Grenville. And it does have four wheel drive. I thought of buying one down here so we could explore the country after the Games, but they all have right hand drive."

"But when did you get it?"

"About four weeks ago," he said. "But I didn't want to give it to you earlier in the evening. You might have suspected that I was buying sexual favors."

"Well, I don't know. Maybe there's a charge account system for those things. You know, make love now, pay later."

"Hmm," he said. "I was counting on it being a pay in advance system."

"Well, that too," she said. "That could be arranged."

"But first you'd like to wait until you can test drive it?" He laughed.

"No," she said. "First I'd like to pay for it. I have a feeling it's going to be satisfactory."

"What is?" he asked.

"Everything," she said.

Chapter 54

They were eating breakfast in bed the following morning when Joan said, "If it's true that you just relax the week before the marathon, I can think of some interesting things to do." She gave him a sexy look. "Hmm."

Sean laughed. "I didn't say I wasn't going to run at all. My schedule has been so crazy because of the 10K, that I'm going out this morning to do a very slow twelve miles."

"That's relaxing?" She couldn't imagine even walking twelve miles.

"Listen, this isn't an easy marathon course. There are so many hills, and most of them in the second half. At least the weather has been good. By six thirty in the evening it will have cooled off nicely. That time was picked so that the race ends right before the closing ceremonies. It's a tradition. But in Atlanta it was so hot that the race was moved to the morning. Here we should be okay."

Joan took a sip of coffee. "I thought that poor fellow last night, the Italian, was just going to die."

"You mean Rossi. That was all guts," Sean said with emotion. "He's a *real* competitor."

"Now, I get to be at the closing, right? We do have tickets?" she asked.

"Bob arranged the whole thing. He wouldn't let me do anything about it. I think he's in one of his mother-hen phases." They both laughed. "Oh, and I also heard from Bob that Lin Pao wants to meet with me. I thought you'd enjoy going along. I scheduled it for lunch today. On principle I thought we should do it in public."

"That's going to be fun," Joan said.

They met in the restaurant adjacent to the lobby of the Regent

Hotel.

"We seem to carry out most of our important business in restaurants," Joan said to Lin Pao as they were being seated. She had been introduced as the scientist who had solved the mystery of the fish blood.

"In my country, also, that is true."

"What do you think of the Chinese restaurants here?" Joan asked. "Have you been to any?"

Lin Pao smiled. "Every day, almost. This will be nice change."

"But they tell us that what we get in our Chinese restaurants isn't really what Chinese people eat," Joan continued.

"Most Chinese people cannot afford," Lin Pao said. "Eat very simple food. In Hong Kong, very many wealthy Chinese, best restaurants, serve food just like in Chinese restaurant in this country or in Germany. Probably America is same."

"Really!" Joan exclaimed. "So if we came to China . . ."

"We'd probably be murdered," Sean said under his breath.

". . . would we find Chinese food we would recognize?"

Lin Pao laughed. "If come to China as tourist, will have worst possible Chinese food. Every meal will be banquet to impress visitor. Food we never think to eat. Bear paw, snake, blah." He made a face. "Considered traditional. Only crazy man eat paw of bear, crazy man and tourist." They all laughed.

Over lunch, Sean described how Joan had solved the puzzle. He didn't tell Lin Pao all the details, but enough so that he understood that Sean had been telling the truth when he said that Root had been murdered.

Lin Pao in turn described how he had fed the Ganciclovir to the runners. ". . . and to half of training center. We must trust you. Yan Tse do anything for Mr. Higgum. Drug really named Ganciclovir? We not know if that was cover. Were afraid to have analyzed. Very good, very smart." He turned to Sean. "You tell me in Stuttgart, police know who killed Dr. Root." Sean told him about the hit man, conveniently leaving out the fact that he had not *yet* been discovered that previous October.

"And police arrest him?"

Sean shook his head no. "It was, ah, it was taken care of in a different way."

"Maybe I understand," Lin Pao said. Sean didn't know whether it was a statement or a question.

"Well, it was taken care of."

"He is in jail?"

"No, he is dining with the fishes." Joan laughed. Lin Pao was confused.

Sean explained the Mafia expression. "Cement boots. Dining with the fishes."

Finally Lin Pao shook his head and smiled. "And fishes is pun. Pun, you say."

"Yes," Joan assured him. "In this case it's a good pun."

"He was killed by other gangsters, but not before they made him answer some questions. The person who hired this man was in the Chinese embassy," Sean told him.

Lin Pao's face darkened. "What happen him?"

"I don't know," Sean said. "It would be harder to do something about him."

"You find out," said Lin Pao. "You know name? It is big favor you tell Lin Pao. You tell me, please."

"The name is George Zeng. He was in the New York embassy at least from about eighteen months ago to six months ago," Sean said.

"Is important I should know."

"Sean, do you want to tell Mr. Pao about Nancy Li?" Joan asked.

"You say name in Stuttgart. Friend of Root. Don't know."

"At that time, I only knew what people called her in America. I still can't pronounce her real name," Sean said. "It's spelled X I A O J I A N."

"Xiaojian Li? *Xiaojian Li!*" Lin Pao exclaimed. "Mickey?"

"Do you know her?" Joan asked.

"Doctor at training center. For year maybe last spring." He looked shyly at her. "Very few women. Know when come."

"That's the right time. She must be the one who worked with Grimes," Joan interjected. "The one who stole the blood and the virus."

"Oh." Lin Pao was visibly upset.

"You called her 'Mickey'?" Sean asked.

"Has Mickey Mouse shirt."

"You do know her." Sean pressed him. "What does she do?"

"Works in clinic. Cannot leave center."

Joan and Sean looked at each other in amazement.

"She say not allowed," Lin Pao explained. "Invite to visit town, invite to disco music, not go." He turned to Joan again with the same shy look. "Think maybe doesn't like, but never goes."

"Is she a prisoner?" Joan asked.

Lin Pao shrugged. He was deep in thought. "Is important I should know. Is important."

Sean could see how upset Lin Pao had become and decided to change the subject. "Now I need a favor from you," he said as he finished his meal and wiped his mouth with a napkin.

Lin Pao was still eating ice cream. "Very good. Have many colors."

"Flavors," Joan corrected.

"Yes, flavors," Lin Pao agreed.

"I need you to teach me some Chinese words," Sean said.

"You want know Chinese words?"

"Yes, I have a list here, twelve, that's enough to try to remember. I want you to pronounce each word for me, and I'll write it down in a way that will let me say it." Lin Pao looked puzzled, but he started in on the task. Joan said nothing. She too was puzzled initially, but then she thought she knew. It wasn't something to talk about right then.

"Go."

"Don't go."

"Follow."

"Drink."

They worked through the list.

Later Joan and Sean bid goodbye to Lin Pao outside the restaurant.

"You will come to China."

Again, Sean couldn't tell if this were a question or a statement.

"Mr. Higgum says you are great coach. Perhaps you will come and help us like Mr. Higgum do many years ago."

"Would we be welcome?" Sean asked.

"Of course. You be very welcome. I welcome you."

"There might be some who would not be glad to see us."

Lin Pao thought for a moment. Then he shook his head vigorously.

"No, no. No people like that there."

Joan and Sean both had the same thought. "Sometimes it's an advantage not to be able to tell the tenses of the verbs."

"We have Olympics. You come run."

"You'll have to do it soon," Sean joked, "or I'll be too old."

"Plan for '96 not successful. Plan for 2000 not successful. 2004, hope successful. Not too old then."

"Pick a cool place," Sean advised.

"Beijing is cool. Air very bad."

"I'll bring a gas mask."

Lin Pao waved and hurried to catch the shuttle bus back to the Olympic village.

Joan and Sean ambled off, hand in hand, in the opposite direction toward the cross-harbor ferry that would take them to the zoo.

"What do you make of this Li—I still can't say her name—Nancy Li?" Joan asked, turning toward him.

"I don't know. Sounds like he tried to take her out. I suppose she could have been forced to be involved. They must have ways."

"Like through her family?"

"I guess." He shrugged. "It's so strange how this turned out. I was sure that Pao had a hand in murdering Grimes and Ann Grossman and that Li was involved too."

"I hope he can help her, if she's in trouble."

He squeezed her hand. "Somehow I get the feeling that he has more power than he lets on."

Chapter 55

"Do you know what I don't understand," Sean said to Joan, "why Ann Grossman would give up the Grimes project?"

They were in Sean's rented car driving toward Hunter Valley where they planned to spend the day sightseeing and visiting wineries.

"Because she wants to do basic research. The Root hemoglobin thing was never hers, she was hired to do it," Joan answered with a grin. "Have you ever heard that argument before? Maybe she doesn't compromise as easily as I do," she paused, "in some things."

"But if she was doing it for money, wouldn't she have gotten a lot, if it worked?"

"Oh, not that much." Joan dismissed the suggestion with the wave of a hand. "The university takes half, and most of the other half would go to Grimes himself, or now to his heirs. It was certainly his original idea. Then all the other lab people split the small amount that's left. So it would be maybe a couple percent of something that might not work anyway."

"She could steal it," Sean persisted.

"Never get away with it. If it went commercial, everyone would know where it came from. Then she'd be in real trouble."

"I guess you're right. Now it will all become public when Grenville files for the patent. And since Susie is clean now, and there's no threat to Jim or Paul Hopwell, we can tell Ralph Hooker all about Grimes and the Chinese. And everyone will know that hemoglobin needs to be included in the routine screening. It will never be possible to use it after that. It's value for cheating will be gone." He hesitated. "You're sure you don't want to see Jack and Ann?"

"No. I wish them well. I hope they got good positions down

here. They deserve them. Now to change the subject, are you ever going to tell me what you and Bob are planning for Sunday? Not that I would pry."

"Sounds like you *are* prying." Sean laughed.

"No. You don't have to answer if you don't want to."

"Okay." Sean stared straight ahead at the road.

"Course, I'll be mad as hell if you don't," she said just loud enough for him to hear.

"It's just running strategy."

"It's more than that."

"No, it isn't. It's just that the strategy has to be different for this race."

"Why is that? Just because it's longer?"

"And I'm not the favorite. I'm not the best person in this race. For the 10K, I just had to go and do it. It was more a matter of not blowing it. But now that I'm a long shot, I get to use the funny strategies."

"But the way you ran the other night, you were so much fresher than the others at the end."

"The marathon is a totally different race," Sean said. "That's why it's so hard to train for both of them."

"But all the running you did. It's all the same thing. You ran miles and miles."

"No, it's different," Sean insisted. "For people like us, I mean at our level, the marathon is almost a pure test of endurance. All of us can run one mile in less than five minutes. Hell, I used to be able to run the mile in less than four minutes, so that's not the issue. The important thing is whether you can keep it up after about twenty miles."

"Why do you say 'after about twenty miles' as if it were something special?"

"It is. It's a physiological thing. You probably know more about it than I do. It was just dumb luck that the marathon was made to be a little more than twenty-six miles long."

"But I thought that's because some Greek ran from the battle of Marathon?"

"No, no. He ran something close to that, but the exact distance comes from the 1908 Olympics in London. It was either the third or the fourth of the modern Olympics. The stadiums were all in central London, but they decided to start the race in front of Windsor Castle, so the Queen's children could watch. It's way out to the west, beyond where Heathrow Airport is now. They ran from there into the Olympic stadium." Joan had never heard this story before. "At the next Olympics they decided to standardize the distance, so they went back and measured that course. It was a little more than twenty six miles, and that's been the official distance ever since."

"That's amazing. They should call it the Windsor-a-Thon or something."

"Right." Sean laughed. "It turns out that it was a good distance. It accomplished what it should have. Maybe if it hadn't, they would have picked some other distance as the standard."

"What do you mean, it was a good distance?"

"Physiologically it demands something that a shorter distance, like even say eighteen miles, doesn't demand."

"Oh."

"When you're running a mile or two or more, the muscles burn glycogen, you know, the carbohydrate that's stored right in the muscle itself. But the muscles can hold only a certain amount. All the endurance training you do is to teach the muscles to store more and more glycogen. That's why I can run fifteen miles and you can't."

"I don't think I could run a mile," Joan interrupted.

"Anyway, as I said, there's a limit. In the old days people used to talk about 'hitting the wall' where all of a sudden they just couldn't go on. There was nothing left. They couldn't move their muscles."

"I've heard of hitting the wall," Joan said.

"Well, we don't see that anymore because we know how to train through it, but the physiological thing still happens. At about twenty miles, give or take a couple depending on the runner, the glycogen is gone."

"What happens then? No, let me guess. I'm the scientist here. You make more glycogen from other things. 'Gluco neo genesis' it's called," Joan said it slowly. "You make new sugar from something else, mostly from fat, and a little from protein."

"Right," Sean said. "That's led to this romantic notion that you burn the body itself. It always reminds me of this movie, set in China actually. John Wayne and Lauren Bacall are on a steamboat trying to outrun the communists. Of course they start running out of fuel. So then they burn the deck chairs, they burn everything they can pry off and begin to burn the deck. They're actually burning the ship, using it up to make it go faster."

"And that's what you're doing?"

"Yes, but it's over emphasized," Sean said. "Most of what we're burning is fat, which most people would like to get rid of anyway. Even these really thin runners, have a lot of calories stored in fat."

"Sure," Joan agreed. "You'd use much more of the fat than the protein. And how fast you could use your fat would depend on how much lipase you have, and the other enzymes involved in fat metabolism, of course. I'll bet there are ways to train to make more lipase."

"It's all the hot topic this year, running when you're starving. I guess what you're doing is first lowering the glycogen stores. You run hard one day, don't eat much of anything or maybe eat some fat, then go out the next day and do a long run until you're exhausted. See, that will send a message to the body, to make some more lipase."

"Hmm." Joan was rubbing her chin. "It would be easier to do it through genetic engineering. If only we knew something about the regulation of the lipase gene, its promoters and enhancers, we could make a super marathoner."

"Oh, no," Sean exclaimed. "Didn't we just go through this? Then some Chinese scientist would have to figure out what we did and poison us." They both laughed.

"All right, all right," she said. "I know I'll think about it now that you've raised it as a problem, but I promise no more genetic engineering of the runners."

"Anyway in the marathon the energy sources are most important. You don't see us out there panting and puffing and getting out of breath. It's not the oxygen delivery system that counts. That's why Grimes's invention wouldn't have done much good for the marathoners, it's the total amount of fuel that counts. And this year I just haven't done enough of that kind of training. But don't count me out. I'm plenty fast enough, and I've run this distance before in not bad time. But for now, there's nothing I can do except hope the lipase kicks in when the going gets tough and stuff the old glycogen storage sites."

"And, of course, take moderate amounts of exercise," Joan suggested. "We could do a controlled experiment, but then, who wants to be in the control group."

"What does it mean to be in the control group?"

"They're the ones who don't do it before the race," she said.

Chapter 56

"I will not tolerate this insult from some minor functionary. It is outrageous," Jurgen said, as Schultz maneuvered the Mercedes down the narrow, winding mountain road from the training center. "And this petty slight, we are to drive ourselves to give our report. Chan cannot take us."

"I do not care. The car reminds me of home. At least something here works right," Schultz answered.

"Yes, the things we brought with us. You will not enjoy it so much, Schultz, when we have left the mountains, and you must drive in that awful city. The Chinese are incompetent in everything."

"But what could have gone wrong? We gave them the perfect weapon, two perfect weapons. Ha, even with a spare, they still manage to fail."

"Tse is a fool, an imbecile. He is too old. What do they expect from someone like that? He should be retired—permanently." Suddenly Schultz paused. Fortunately the implication of the remark had gone unnoticed. Jurgen was certainly older than Tse.

"It was my mistake to let them dictate these conditions," Jurgen pronounced with regret. "I will issue an ultimatum to them. We must have complete control, or we will not be here for the next games."

"So unfortunate. Such a lost opportunity. We will never have such a chance again. Someone will surely learn of it," Schultz added.

"Don't be so discouraged. We have kept other secrets through many Olympics. We can do it again. It was an unusual idea. We were lucky to find it, just because the American wished to show off. Perhaps no one else will think of it."

"But we should not keep it secret for so long. It could do good for many people."

"It can do more good for us. That is enough. Was ist's? Zu schnell, Schultz. Brake."

"Nicht, nicht. Keine brakes. Machts nichts."

"Gottes Himmels . . . Schultz . . ."

The great car crashed through the wooden barrier and for a moment seemed to take flight, following a graceful arc out into space. Then it plummeted into the valley below.

Chapter 57

The marathon started at the North Sydney Oval and, after passing through some of the most scenic and historic parts of Sydney, ended in the Olympic stadium in the western suburb of Homebush. At six on Sunday evening it was still in the low seventies, warmer than expected. "I hope he's trained for this heat," Sean said to himself as he searched in vain for Chao Lee among the gathering runners. It was a large group, but there was enough room inside the cricket grounds so that there was no sense of crowding. Sean did some stretching and a little jogging.

At last the call came to assemble just outside on Miller Street. Nervous runners silently edged forward to be nearer to the starting line. *So silly. These races aren't won in the first ten yards. Hell they're not won in the first ten miles,* Sean thought. He tried to stay calm, but the tension was contagious. Nothing else is like a marathon. So much preparation, so few chances in a lifetime. Sean stared over the heads of the others, seeing nothing. *Oh, where's that gun*? Finally it sounded.

The group surged forward. The first hill came almost at once, the climb up the approach to Harbour Bridge. It and the ensuing decline on the south side of the bridge leading into the center of the city did little to sort out the favorites from the hopefuls. Not until they had passed the Rocks, the old section built with the forced labor of the original Crown prisoners, and turned south on Macquarie, leaving behind the spectacular Sydney Opera House and the Botanic Gardens, did the potential medalists emerge near the front.

In this fashionable section the crowds of spectators were truly immense. For the millions who could not attend the closing ceremonies, this was the place to be. They would watch this last event and then party long into the night.

As they started down Anzac Parade, Sean found himself well positioned in the middle of the second pack. The runners gave one another plenty of room. There was no difficulty in finding a comfortable pace. Several smaller groups were ahead of Sean, and already runners lagged behind, but the favorites were all nearby. Pedro Rodriguez, Higgum's choice, and Jose San Martin ran side by side. Close friends, they trained together throughout the year. Kitana was the best of the Kenyans, but they were all good. The Japanese, it was so hard to know what they'd do. Sato, their leader, was in the first group setting the early pace. One thing was certain, they would never give up. *They may be carried off, but they won't quit*, thought Sean. Sung, the Korean, had had a big victory in the early spring, but perhaps that was too close. It took time to recover from a marathon.

There were too many runners to study carefully, but realistically, the victor would probably come from a group of about twenty. "Although surprises have happened before," as Bob had warned. "In the Olympics people rise to the occasion." Sean and Bob had played their usual game.

"What will the opponents think of me? Will they even know I exist?" Sean wondered aloud. The marathoners were their own tight little group.

"Oh, they'll know very well," Bob had said. "Most of them have run the 10K at some time. You know they watched it. None of them will want you around at the finish. That may scare some of them into doing something foolish."

The scenic thoroughfare passed parks, a golf course and a race track on its way south to the suburb of Kingsford, where the runners made a U-turn and retraced their steps back to the central city. Although it was more convenient for the spectators, Sean usually preferred a course that did not double back on itself. It disturbed him to be passing so near to others going in the opposite direction. However, it was near the hairpin that he was finally able to spot Chao Lee. He eased his way toward him and after the next water station managed to be alongside.

"Hi," Sean greeted him. Chao looked over surprised, but then he recognized Sean. He had run the 10K in the last Olympics but had failed to reach the finals. He nodded. His English was very limited, but he knew how to say congratulations.

"Thanks," Sean replied. They ran along together silently. Chao Lee made some noises. He was clearly warming up to say something but was finding it difficult.

Finally, "Lin Pao." Sean looked over. "Lin Pao say . . ." Another pause. Sean swung wide to avoid a runner they were passing. They came back together. He wondered if it would be easier to understand if he were looking at him, but he didn't really want to turn his head. "Lin Pao say Xiaojian Li okay. Others are with fishes." Sean almost stopped and stared. He regained his stride. Chao Lee clearly thought he had not said it right. "Others eat fishes . . . Others eat with fishes," he repeated.

"I understand," Sean wanted to say, but that wasn't on his list of Chinese words. "You" and "thank you" were.

"You, thank you Lin Pao," he said.

A grin spread over the face of the usually serious-looking Lee. "You Chinese?" Both chuckled.

They ran along together. Others passed them and then fell back. The lead groups formed and dissolved and reformed with new members. Some runners were skipping water stops, but not Sean and Chao, even if Sean had to practically shove him off the course.

Finally the route swung west toward Darling Harbour, the renovated dock and warehouse district now replete with modern office buildings and chic shopping centers. Even though there were still many miles to go, Sean felt the psychological boost of the turn toward home. Now at last they were headed directly toward the Olympic Complex. Whenever the runners drew near the shore or passed over a bridge the multitude of boats in the harbor blew their horns. The noise excited the runners and made discipline that much more important.

When the 25K, approximately fifteen miles, time was announced, and to Sean's delight it was very slow, it had an electrifying effect on the group. The pace quickened in general, and some runners from his pack hurried up to the pack in front. Chao Lee wanted to follow.

"No. Don't go," Sean said in his best Chinese. Perhaps it was the surprise of hearing the admonition in his own language, but Chao Lee settled back. They were running comfortably except for the heat. Their singlets were drenched with perspiration, and they poured water over themselves when they reached the stops.

Sato left the lead group and begun to open a gap. Sean realized that he was hoping to use the hill at the Glebe Island Bridge to build a lead and then try to hold off the others. Sean and Chao Lee both saw him go and looked at each other. Sean gave the universal sign for crazy. "No Chinese," he said. It hadn't been on his list. Chao spoke the word in Chinese, first slowly and then more rapidly and emphatically. They both laughed. Chao was starting to relax. Sean was enjoying himself. It had been a long time since he'd been in a race that he wasn't expected to win. Chao Lee looked strong.

Soon they were back on the waterfront along the Dobroyd Parade. The flags on the boathouse of Harborfield Rowing Club showed the direction of the breeze. Sean cut in front of Chao Lee. It was only a slight head wind, but there would be a positive effect. Tucking in right behind someone always made it seem easier. Now they were passing other runners. Still, they ran within themselves. Even on the slight downhills, Sean refused to be hurried. He watched the others with the eye of the coach. "Lots of them are losing it," he said to himself. "This is the varsity, they all know about pacing. When they get tired, they stop thinking. That isn't the way to survive."

As they turned onto Ramsay Street, Sean watched for the intersection with Connecticut Avenue. He and Joan had joked about it meaning he was home. It did mean that about six miles remained. "My distance," he said to himself, "but the gas tank is a little low, and there are three, really four, hills still to go."

By twenty-two miles, they were among the leaders, a group of about fifteen. As the hills took their toll, the favorites emerged at the front. Sean recognized more and more of them. The Mexicans, no sign of weakness, no sign of anything. Kitana was there and Sung. Sato was still with them, but you could tell from his stride that he was done. He had the guts of Paolo Rossi, but Sean doubted whether he would manage to finish. His was the wrong strategy for today.

Sean glanced at a tall blond runner. *At least six feet four*, he thought. *He shouldn't be up here. Tall runners do worse in the heat. Well, maybe he didn't read the right articles.* Sean laughed to himself. The blond actually looked good. *The right training and enough water and you don't have to complain about the way you're built.*

Now they were on the motorway, from here on it would be fairly flat. The Olympic Park was ahead of them with its beautiful skyline of new and interesting modern buildings. Sean was beginning to tire. He tried to think of other things. Chao Lee and he were running side by side again. He reached for a drink for the last time, choosing one with sugar.

Everyone was struggling except Pedro Rodriguez. *He's staying there to keep San Martin company, but he's ready to go*, Sean felt sure. He was always the keen observer, but could he do anything with the information? Kitana kept looking at Rodriguez. Obviously he thought he could do something. You could see the whites completely around his eyes. *He looks like he has that thyroid disease*, Sean thought. *And he's so thin, maybe he does.*

Less than two miles to go. There were seven of them now. The blond was still there. And so was Sung. He was short and very muscular, like a lightweight wrestler. Probably most of the runners recognized each other. Sean didn't know the blond. Some wouldn't know Chao Lee. Sean wondered if they were all thinking about his closing speed. "Too bad I don't have anything left," he said to himself.

Rodriguez finally had to break up his partnership. He went. Kitana went after him. San Martin fell back rapidly; it was as if he had let go of a tow rope. The blond passed them, and Sung was even. They were all passing San Martin. Their group was maintaining a distance about fifteen yards behind Rodriguez and Kitana, who were now playing games with each other. First one, then the other, would sprint ahead and slow down. *One of the sprints will be for real,* Sean predicted, *and then we'll see what the other can do.* He was still thinking of how he could make the best of it. Chao Lee was tiring too. They all were. He wanted to surge ahead. He looked over at Sean, his new-found friend. Sean shook his head but then shrugged. His list of Chinese words didn't include enough to say, "Do what you want, but I still think it's a little too early." And why should Lee trust him? After all, they were both in the same race.

The stadium was in sight. There was a little more than a mile to go. Rodriguez spurted. Was this for real? It lasted a little longer than the previous ones, but Kitana closed up. The runners in the second group were ignoring them. *Wisely*, Sean felt. *That's not our game.*

Now there was less than a mile. The final lap, of course, would be inside the stadium. He looked at the blond. He could be taken. Sung, he couldn't tell. He looked at Chao Lee and smiled. He could manage only a tiny smile.

"Go. Go, Chao Lee, go."

Chao Lee increased his speed and began to pull away. Sung went after him. The blond, who was a step ahead of Sean, didn't respond. Suddenly Rodriguez took off. Kitana tried to stay with him. Sean was delighted. *That race is over. If Kitana were smart, he never would have gone.* Sean could see Rodriguez entering the stadium. The cheers had started even earlier, because inside the capacity crowd was watching on huge television screens. Kitana went into the stadium. Chao Lee was after him. He was opening a gap on Sung. Sung entered, and finally Sean and the blond.

The lights were dazzling. Sean could hardly see. Of course, he knew which way to run, but there were aides everywhere pointing in the right direction. His mind flashed back over so many Olympic marathon finishes that he had seen on television, runners staggering, falling, running in the wrong direction, stopping too soon. But, in fact, the runners in his group looked good. They had run smart races. When he felt the track, he took off. "Pavlovian conditioning," he said to himself. "Just ring a bell and point me in the right direction." Rodriguez was about to cross the finish line. Sean could see Chao Lee running down Kitana. He wanted to stand at the finish and watch it, but by his calculation, he was going to miss the moment, for he would be facing in the wrong direction.

Sean had left the blond. Sung was slowing. "I can get him too," he said to himself. "But what will it mean? But, this is what I do. Racehorses race. They don't like to be beaten by anyone." He was laughing at himself. "I've already used the image of home just seven days ago. I need something cool." Another huge roar. Silver and bronze had obviously been determined, but Sean didn't know the outcome. He thought of his ads. None of the images fit. Then he thought of the mile races that Bob had forced him to do the season before, and he thought of all the closing sprints. Marathoners don't train that way. Sung was in his sights. He was gaining on him with every step. Around the last turn, he waited until he touched the apex and then swung wide. He pulled alongside and outsprinted Sung for fourth.

Rodriguez was on his victory lap, right next to the grandstand to stay out of the way of the other runners who were straggling into the stadium. He looked totally fresh and was still running faster than some of the others who had not yet finished. Aides were helping Sean, one on each arm and another pouring water over him. He turned to the scoreboard. Chao Lee had second. "Yes!" Sean exclaimed, raising a fist into the air. Finally he found Chao Lee. If he had known how, he would have said, "You look worse than I feel." Chao Lee had obviously used it all. Still, he managed a big grin. They threw their arms around each other. They were too tired to dance.

Chapter 58

Sean marched in directly behind the flag bearer. "I'm not sure I can carry it through the whole thing," he had said.

"I think you deserve a little rest," one of his teammates had joked.

Another added, "I couldn't have run a mile tonight."

"This is the warmest night, and for the hardest event."

"Good show."

The closing ceremonies would be less formal. It would be harder to keep any form of discipline, and why bother. Some of the athletes had already left. *Their mistake*, thought Sean who loved the closing ceremony as much as the opening. In fact, he found it more moving, more bittersweet. Something he loved was ending, but there was the promise to meet again in four years. It occurred to him that this was just the right interval. *If we did this every year, it would never be as special. For many, this will happen only once. For the best, two, three,* he thought of himself, *four times maybe.*

There was the usual roar as each team entered. How was he going to find Joan? Bob, he was sure, would have a front row seat somewhere, but he couldn't even find him. There had been no chance to talk to him since the race. Sean had barely had time to recover and to shower and dress. He carried two containers of sport drink with him, still trying to rehydrate. The Irish team marched into their position in the infield. Searchlights played back and forth. The faithful flame still burned, but not for much longer, Sean knew. There was a carnival atmosphere with music and noise. It would hush for the ceremonies and then rise again and last far into the night.

Toward the end of the procession came the massive American team. As they were parading past, one of the women athletes suddenly broke ranks and began running directly toward Sean. No one seemed concerned. Many romances developed between the athletes of different nations during the games. Some were short lived, others lasted. Some couples married and went on to compete in subsequent Olympics for the same team, Connolly, the great American hammer thrower and his wife, Olga, a gold medal winner in the discus who fled from Czechoslovakia.

The figure drew nearer. Blue blazer, official competitor's pass, that silly hat. "Sean, Sean," she called, rushing up and throwing her arms around his neck. A cheer went up from the Irish. It was answered by the Italians, who had seen it all. As captain, even though he was not carrying the flag, he was standing in front of his group. "Bravo, Brava, Bravi," came from the Italians. Suddenly Paolo Rossi emerged from the group and ran over to where they were standing.

"So," he said in his broken English, "this is your secret, Sean. Next time I will do the same and beat you." He gave Joan a kiss. He gave Sean a kiss.

Joan looked at him. "You're . . . you're the one who has so much heart. Sean says you're the greatest competitor in his field."

Rossi was clearly moved. He shrugged. "I try hard. I have fun. You will come to visit. To Tuscany. I will show you how we eat." He laughed and hugged them both simultaneously. Then he turned and ran back to his team.

"How did you get here?" Sean asked, putting one arm around her shoulders. "Nobody's allowed down here except . . ."

"How do you think?" Joan said. "Your friend Bob forged a pass and stole this jacket."

"Didn't anybody notice?"

"The team is so large. Most of them don't know each other. A couple asked me what I did. I told them I was sneaking in to meet someone on another team. They all thought it was a terrific idea. They just offered me champagne. Half of them are drunk already, or maybe, all of them are half drunk already."

"I must be with the wrong team. I'm standing here drinking sports ade."

"Well, you've probably started training for next time," she said.

"I'm glad you found me."

"Bob said not to wait for a minute, just to run right over here, that you would never be able to find me in that mob, but that I could find you. He said all the groups would break up before the ceremony was even finished, probably before it had even started."

"That always happens," Sean said, "and I think everybody likes it. It's part of the symbolism of the thing."

Finally, to the appreciative roar of more than one hundred and ten thousand fans, the Australian team entered. It had been a magnificent two weeks, and as usual the home team had outdone itself. The incentive of wealth and lasting fame for the host country's athletes always brought out their best, and unexpected medals had been won in many sports. Few were as surprising as cycling, not traditionally an Australian strength, which this year produced the home team's only double Gold Medal winner. The team was huge and noisy and raucous.

"How long will they stay in formation," Sean wondered, "through the invocation, through the call to return?" It would be a long night.

In the confusion one athlete climbed unnoticed into the stands to find his wife. He took the two Gold Medals from around his neck and slipped them over her head. "They're yours, Annie luv," he said, kissing her on the cheek. "But it's going to be damn hard to take that Ganciclovir."

"You have to, Jack, or eventually someone will certainly find out about it. From now on, you have to be squeaky clean. And I think I've been paid in full for all the work I did for Grimes." She laughed. "Don't ever let me get involved in one of those applied projects again."

"One is enough, Annie, if it's the right one." He put his arms around her and hugged her.

The ceremony had begun. Joan and Sean stood arm in arm. It was finally beginning to cool. He knew he would cry when the torch went out.

"You haven't answered me yet," he said.

She lowered her eyes. "I know. I'm terrified. I'm just terrified."

"You don't have to be."

"Yes, I do," she said. "I can't help it."

"You can always chuck me if you decide you made a mistake,"

he said.

"That won't happen. It's just so hard to do. It's not like me. Maybe, maybe we should just extend our term to say, six months, a year."

"Okay, one year. Renewable."

"Of course."

"How many times?"

"Suppose I give you fifty coupons," she said and smiled.

"But what happens when they run out?"

She laughed. "Well, we'll have to renegotiate."

"What about children?"

"Well, two of the coupons will have stars on them," she said.

"Two?"

"Well, maybe three."

"All right, it's a deal," he said. "Do I get to cash one of the star coupons right away?"

"Um, maybe next year."

They stopped talking to listen to the pledge. The torch began to grow dimmer and finally it went out. The stadium was in complete darkness. Joan and Sean were hugging each other. Sean was crying as promised. She was too; he could feel it. Then the sky was filled with fireworks. Colored searchlights played over the athletes. There was no semblance of order. People from all nations hugged and kissed and congratulated one another.

"It's the most wonderful thing I've ever experienced," Joan shouted above the noise. Sean nodded. He could hardly speak.

"How can we arrange for me to sneak in next time?" she asked.

THE END